REVEALING HANNAH

The Myth of Cassandra

Laura Fedolfi

Illuminated Myth Publishing

REVEALING HANNAH

This is a work of fiction. Names, characters, businesses, places, events and incidents are either the products of the author's imagination or used in a fictitious manner. Any resemblance to actual persons, living or dead, or actual events is purely coincidental.

Illuminated Myth Publishing
www.illuminatedmyth.com

© 2015 Laura Fedolfi

All rights reserved. This book or any portion thereof may not be reproduced or used in any manner whatsoever without the express written permission of the publisher.

Printed in the United States of America

First Printing 2015

ISBN: 978-0-9909793-2-6

www.revealinghannah.com

Cover art, *Portrait of Hannah*, © Amy Flannery, 2015
Book cover design by Ricky Puorro, 2015

For Steve

REVEALING HANNAH

"Cassandra cried, and curs'd th' unhappy hour; Foretold our fate; but, by the god's decree, All heard, and none believ'd the prophecy."
Virgil, *The Aeneid, Book II*

PROLOGUE

Yada yada yada

◆◆◆

Cassandra

Troy, 1184 BCE

She'd always wondered why the mad were laughing, but it was clear to her now. *Life was hilarious.*She heard a strange high-pitched giggle, and realized it was coming from her. She pressed her lips together, and shook her head. She would not go mad. As she felt her sanity sliding sideways out of her mind, she traced the path that had brought her to this point, desperate to find an escape.

She was *Cassandra*, daughter of King Priam and Queen Hecuba of Troy. Her life had been her own design; her father had agreed to postpone an arranged marriage to allow her to devote herself to Athena, at least for awhile. Her father's concession had been a major triumph for her over her mother's protests, and had, in no small part, been due to the cleverness with which she had argued, pleasing her father with the elegance of her words.

Words. Words which now not only failed her, but doomed her to a life of absurd irony. It had been her carelessness with words that had started the unraveling of her life. She'd been tending to Athena's temple, when Apollo, the god of the Sun, had swept her up, taking her to his castle in the clouds. Attempting to bed her, he had placed his hands on her head, announcing his gift of prophecy. She could actually feel the edges of her mind opening.

If only she'd paused long enough to see her own future. But no, she was Cassandra, daughter of kings, devotee of Athena, not some farm girl content to be the plaything of Apollo. Pushing him away, she had suggested he try his seduction on simpler females. Sheep perhaps. His shock had been comical, and she had laughed. His response was swift. Cursing her name, he had thrown her from his castle.

She awoke to find herself back in the temple, relieved to have avoided Apollo's lechery. But that was before she'd realized the power of his gift and the bitterness of his curse. Her prophetic visions had begun almost immediately. In her mind she saw the ships filled with Greek warriors landing on her father's shores. She had tried in vain to warn them of the coming violence, the shocking deaths, the betrayals. But Apollo's curse ensured no one listened. Not even her father who had once been so moved by her speech.

In the final act of irony, her mother had ordered the guards to lock her in this cell, not wanting the celebrations to be marred by her daughter's ravings. Cassandra could see that it was only because she was here in this cell that she would be spared the brutal killing to come.

There was no escape. Not from the cell, nor from the fact that it was her own words which had brought her to this end. Maybe she *would* go mad. As the sounds of the Greek soldiers emerging from their wooden horse and slaughtering her countrymen filled the night air, she let loose her thin grasp on sanity, preferring the echoes of her own demented laughter to the screams of the dying.

The Myth of Cassandra

CHAPTER ONE

One Small Step for Womankind

❈❈❈

Hannah

Monday afternoon

Ducking behind the campus kiosk outside her dorm, Hannah did a quick scan to ensure no one was watching before using both hands to yank up the nylons that had already started migrating south after only a dozen steps. *Nylons. Tights. Stockings.* She refused to even think the word "pantyhose." Any word with "panty" in it was impossible to say without cringing. As she tried to return the offensive undergarment to its original position, she realized that she hadn't worn anything like this since her middle school days of ballet, and had forgotten how restrictive they felt. Like she was walking in pants that were two sizes too small. Shimmying them up was made more complicated by the tight dress she was wearing; which despite its restrictive fit, was the inverse of sexy. That probably had something to do with its length and material. It was a sleeveless navy wool sheath hitting below the knee; the epitome of conservative. And on this first day in June it was effectively functioning as a sweat chamber, adding to the slipping of the torturous tights. As she tugged and itched and struggled to right her clothes she was brought up short by the low wolf whistle coming from a passerby.

"Yo, Harriet! Great costume! You look like my mom, but *hot*. Is that for the Omegas' party? I didn't know it was dress up..."

She bit back on her irritation. His mistake was understandable. All put together, she did look like a Doris Day wannabe. She never wore clothes like this. She preferred clothes made out of cotton with useful pockets. But she had voluntarily put herself into this state of discomfort for her boyfriend, Carl. Not that he was in the habit of dressing her. In their three years together he had never expressed an opinion about her clothes, except to tell her she looked nice. So when he showed up with a garment bag and white pumps with a matching clutch purse, she'd been surprised. He had thought of everything. Jewelry, makeup. It was all in the purse, including a photo of a high chignon for her hair.

Much like her perpetually stoned, wolf-whistling classmate, she had also jumped to the conclusion that it was a costume, some sort of practical joke, but Carl was completely serious and seriously anxious. They were having dinner with his parents tonight. A dinner at which she felt certain he would be proposing marriage. Something she hadn't planned for, but had come to terms with. After making a pro/con list, of course. So she had agreed to wear the outfit, while inside she prayed fervently that he wasn't working off a dated photo of his mother. Being a classics major, she was sensitive to signs of Oedipal inclinations. Her concerns about Carl's relationship with his mother were interrupted by the continued commentary of her newly arrived audience.

"I *like* it. Are you going for Slutty Hillary Clinton? Sexy Barbara Bush? 'Cause you nailed it, Harriet. Totally radical critique of the hegemony of the oligarchy. Like totally radical..."and his voice trailed off as his eyes traveled down her body.

Following his stare, she saw that she had pulled her dress up with her stockings so that the hem was barely covering her backside. Yanking it back down below her knees, she shook her head, her smile slightly forced as she felt the crotch of the tights slide south again, "No. Not a costume. But thanks, Cam, I guess. See you later." And she took off down the path with a backward wave, not waiting for his reply.

Harriet. She had long since stopped correcting people who got her name wrong. It really didn't matter. The wolf-whistler, Cameron Sutter, was actually the originator of the Harriet misnomer. He was one of those forever students. By her count he had been at Whitfield for at least the last six years; slowly working his way through his classes *and* every campus party. She had taken a Western Civ class with him her freshman year. It was one of the few large lecture classes at Whitfield and the seating had been alphabetical. Cam had repeatedly called her Harriet— *Do you have a pencil, Harriet? Do you have the answers to the homework, Harriet? Do you have any snacks, Harriet?*. When she had corrected him, he had argued with her, insisting she *looked* like a Harriet. She had decided it was a battle not worth fighting. Besides, she'd gambled that he wouldn't remember her, real name or not, based on the ever present aroma of marijuana that permeated his clothes. In the end, she had lost the bet and his name for her had stuck. There was more than one place on campus where she answered to Harriet. It didn't matter, because none of those people were important to her. It was easier to let it slide.

Sliding was definitely the verb of the moment, as she stared down Foss Hill. She started to consider that she might not have added enough time to compensate for crossing it in high heels, not to mention a dress that restricted her normal stride to some kind of geisha-like mince. On the map she had drawn to plan this adventure, she had assumed her normal path across campus. But since that normal path had her walking down a grassy hill, impossible in the tread-less shoes, she would just take an alternate route. She always had a contingency plan.

Planning was one of her strong suits. She could compile a mental list of pros and cons for any given situation in under a minute. She had found, as she worked her way through college, that lists made her life simpler. She had worked hard to achieve calm and simplicity in her life. Take today. She had awoken this morning to three emails; one from the Honors College telling her that her senior thesis had been rejected for "mismanagement of margins." This was enough to send her into a panic spiral. It didn't help that Cynthia Dixon, The Honors College Administrator, felt it had been necessary to include a link in the email to the fall course scheduling, stating that seniors with formatting problems might need to retake English 101. Dixon was known on campus as the Margins Nazi for obvious reasons. The email ended with a reminder that any thesis submitted after five pm would not qualify for graduation on Sunday.

Before she could fully panic, she opened the second email. It was from the University Copy Center with the subject line, "Having Margin Issues?" The email was informing all students that the Copy Center had experienced a software problem that had resulted in printing irregularities which might have affected senior thesis manuscripts. Free reprints were being offered on a first come first serve basis. She had immediately resent her thesis file and received a confirmation of a pick-up time from them. She felt the panic recede slightly.

Still on edge, she'd opened the third email, braced for whatever might come next. It was from her advisor, asking if he could publish her thesis précis on his website and congratulating her on her impending graduation and employment as the Classics Curator at the Whitfield Library. While his email was lovely, Professor Tetley had always been so kind and supportive of her, it still drove home the tension of the morning. The job he was congratulating her on was a job she needed to graduate to keep, a graduation that depended entirely on her picking up her reprinted thesis from the Copy Center and turning it into the Honors College; all before five, no exceptions made— each step depending on the next for success.

And then there was dinner with Carl's parents, a dinner at which she anticipated a marriage proposal. Despite asking her to wear the outfit she was currently sweating in, Carl had been the best of boyfriends; nice, dependable, kind, and good-looking, in a kind of mid-western, preppy way. He was a big talker, an external processor. That had been tricky at first, as she had struggled to keep up with his conversation, but once she had learned that she only needed to zone in as he was wrapping up, it was easy enough to be agreeable. And Carl seemed to really appreciate that. She far preferred the predictable happiness of agreeing with Carl to the contentious passion of her parents' marriage, and when Carl had given her the promise ring she now wore on her hand, she knew that they were on the same page about this. So, with the pros far outweighing the cons, she decided she would say yes when he asked her to marry him at dinner tonight.

All of this would have been manageable, the copy center, the thesis, the job, the dinner, if she hadn't decided to lie back down after the stress of the morning and inexplicably fallen back to sleep. She had slept through two alarm clocks and lost seven hours. She now had only two and a half hours to get it all done. How she had fallen back to sleep, she still didn't know, but she had awoken to a moment of panic. Correction. She had awoken to the sound of her mother's voice on the answering machine and then she panicked.

"Hannah! Hannah! This is your mother. Pick up the phone...I know you are there...come on...pick up the phone... Hannah Marie you need to answer me... Pick up, honey... I can talk until your tape runs out... and then I will call you on your cell and leave messages until you pick up..."

Her mother. She had a mantra for dealing with her mother. *Agree, Avoid, Ignore.* But she was so disoriented waking up in the bright sunlight of her dorm room, that she answered the phone, still somewhat asleep. Which had been a mistake. Elise Summers was not a woman to waste an opening.

"Hannah? Is that really you? Why didn't you pick up when you saw it was me? I know you have caller ID. Are you screening my calls?"

Avoid! "Of course not, Mom, I didn't hear the phone ring. I'm glad you left a message; it woke me up. Oh, no, Mom, it can't be two o'clock, can it?"

"Yes, Hannah. It is two. You know, claiming to be sleeping in the middle of the day is a ridiculous lie, honey. *Ladies' Home and Hearth* says that when looking to make an excuse, stick as close to the truth as you can. You don't need to concoct a story for my sake; I am a grown woman. If you are screening your calls and avoiding your mother you need only tell me. It's not as if I am anyone you need to talk to. You can let me leave messages and return my calls when it's convenient for you..."

Ignore! With the effortless grace of an expert fly-fisherman, her mother could cast guilt into any conversation. From an early age, Hannah had learned to slip back under the rock and let the bait hang. But she was disoriented from her Sleeping Beauty episode, off her game, and so rose to the lure, "But Mom, your message said I had to pick up or you wouldn't stop talking. You do know that answering machines are digital now. There is no tape to run out."

The silence from her mother's end of the call stretched out and Hannah realized she'd chosen the wrong time to go on the offensive. Her mother was doubling down. Damn it. *Agree!* "Not that that matters, tapes and all, it's just that I wasn't screening the call, I really was asleep, which wasn't a lie, by the way, so please, can you just tell me what you need?" Hannah cringed at the pleading tone she heard emitting from her traitorous mouth.

"I fail to see why a healthy young woman would take a nap in the middle of the day. Do you have a fever? Could it be Lyme disease? Or mono?" There was a slight pause in her mother's speech, and her tone became carefully solicitous, "Did you go out drinking last night, Hannah? Because I read in *Ladies' Home and Hearth* that unscrupulous men can slip drugs into a woman's drink and then take advantage of her. Do you have soreness? You know, soreness? Oh honey, don't worry, we will come out early to help you with this. We'll take you to the hospital first and then talk to the police..."

Avoid! Avoid! Hannah crossed her legs tightly and used both hands to hold the phone while she tried not to yell, "MOM. I was not drugged and assaulted. Please do not come out early. I just fell asleep, and my alarms didn't work and I overslept which is actually pretty strange but I don't have time to worry about it now..."

"Oh my poor, poor Hannah. *Ladies' Home and Hearth* said that denial is the first stage. How do you know you weren't drugged? Was Carl with you?"

Ladies' Home and Hearth was the Bible to Elise— the Bible with fashion tips, advice, recipes, and a serialized romance. Elise could quote verse, line and volume number. Beauty advice? July 1999, "Make the Best of Your Best (And Hide the Rest!)" Fashion survival tips? October 2003, "What Fruit Are You? 5 Shapes and How to Dress Them." Relationship advice? June, 1989, "Letting your Man feel Like a Man: Three Simple Answers to All His Questions." She had gifted Hannah with her own subscription when she left for Whitfield, and would often use the articles to not so subtly interfere with her life in the weekly phone call from home. Had she seen the photo shoot about the unfortunate girl who didn't know her best features? Elise confided to Hannah that with her unfortunately nice but unremarkable profile that she inherited from her father, she should make the most of her hair. It was a thick, honey blonde that fell in a curtain down her back. Not only is it pretty, honey, but you can use it to disguise your ears. Had she read the article about choosing the right hemline for your body shape? "Honey, you are between a pear and an upside down triangle and you really should consider shortening your skirts if you have any hope of keeping your man. Because you know, the odds of meeting someone after college get really low, and I don't think you are ready for that type of competition. *Ladies' Home and Hearth* says that after college there is only one good man for every ten women." Then Hannah's father, Tom, would get on the line to ask if she had enough money for the week. It might have been easier if Hannah had had a sister to commiserate with, or even a brother to diffuse their attention, but she was an only child.

Hannah scrambled for the words that would get her mother to call off the dogs, "No Mom, I wasn't with Carl last night. I..."

"*Ladies' Home and Hearth* says that the first twenty-four hours after an assault are the most critical for getting medical attention. What is the name of the hospital in Centreville? Maybe your father knows someone there."

Though her inner warning system was yelling "Avoid! Avoid!" she found herself asking, "How would dad know someone at the hospital? He's a financial planner, not a doctor." Oh, no. Mistake. Her mother's next words were all reprimand.

"Your father knows a lot of important people, Hannah. Don't underestimate him."

Hannah closed her eyes, and tried to find a way out of the call. In her calmest voice, she stuck to definitive statements, "I am not underestimating Dad. I don't need to go to the Emergency Room because I was not out drinking and did not have someone drug and assault me and I am not in denial, but I am in trouble. My senior thesis was rejected and I can't graduate without it..."

"Hannah, now don't be dramatic. Your thesis being rejected is no excuse to become hysterical. *Ladies' Home and Hearth* says that a mother sometimes has to help her children by taking away their blinders. I failed you. If I had been honest, this might not have happened. The Horticultural Metaphors in Ancient Greek Mythology, really? I read your thesis, well, at least the title. It was not a very exciting title, honey. Did you consider sexing it up a little? I thought you could have used a title that was a question, like, Who Shot Zeus? Was It All A Dream? You know, like they do on TV. Or maybe a list title, Top 10 Secrets You Need To Know About The Ancient Greeks And Their Plant Metaphors. Now those would have been dynamic titles. As for the content, well, surely there were more compelling topics. You spent four years studying the Classics and you decided to write an index of references to laurel leaves? Darling, you need to take more risks. If you had only consulted me, I might have helped save your thesis from rejection."

She could not agree, avoid or ignore. It was all she could do not to yell, "The content wasn't rejected, Mom, just the formatting. I need to resubmit it before five or I can't graduate."

She had to graduate. Everything depended on it. Her mother launched into lecture mode, hitting all the highlights like, "classics is not a very practical degree" and "we expect you to make use of those clever computer classes," and "we want you to come home for the summer so we can plan your future together." *Ignore!* She waited for a break in the conversation and made a non-committal noise, promising to call her mother back later and ended the call.

Her mother probably thought she had bullied her into not taking the job at the university. But she would take the job she wanted. She would live in her own apartment with visits from her boyfriend, soon to be fiancé, Carl. She would make no casseroles, no matter how convenient and practical they might be and she would give a fake forwarding address for her *Ladies' Home and Hearth* subscription. She would do all this without a word to her parents until she invited them to her place after the graduation on Sunday for brunch. A fait accompli. She'd always wanted one of those. So she had made a list.

Pulling it out of her purse, she scanned it again.

Things to Do Today or Spend Your Summer Sleeping in Your Childhood Bedroom.

1.Pick up Thesis from Copy Center. Allow ten minutes to walk to copy center at the Southern end of campus, and plan on at least sixty minute wait time to get to front of line, along with a fifteen minute check to confirm that all formatting measurements are correct, and the three copies are bound properly, and in number eleven manila envelopes. *Plan for chaos.*

2.Turn in thesis at Honors College prior to five o'clock. Allow at least fifteen minutes to walk from Copy Center to the Western edge of Campus. Allow at least ten minutes to wait in line with all the other seniors dropping off their reprinted theses. Allow a five-minute cushion for the Margins Nazi's possible nit-picking. *Plan for high levels of controlling bitchiness from said nazi.*

3.Dress for Dinner. Allow fifteen minutes to walk back to dorm on Northern edge of campus. Allow at least twenty minutes to pull on nylons, get a run, put on back-up nylons, use hairspray, and put on lipstick. *Plan for discomfort.*

4.Meet Carl and his parents at Turlington's for dinner at five o'clock sharp. Allow twenty-five minutes to walk to restaurant with five minutes added for having to walk in pumps. Allow fifteen minutes to go to restaurant bar and down a shot of vodka— odorless —*Important as Helene disapproves of women drinking spirits.*

It added up to three hours and ten minutes. Taking into account her bizarre nap, she'd had to strategize to shorten the time. She was not going to cut out the drink before dinner unless she had no other choice. She was an infrequent drinker, but she'd spent last Christmas with Carl's family in Akron, Ohio, and knew that the shot of vodka was not an optional element in the plan. She needed to find a place to save time. There were four locations on her list; her dorm, the Copy Center, the Honors College and the restaurant. So she drew a map. The first three were all on campus but at disparate edges— her room was to the North, the Copy Center due South and the Honors College to the West. The restaurant was actually just southeast of the Honors College in the downtown area.

Scanning her drawing, she'd noticed that her dorm was the furthest from the restaurant, while the Honors College was the closest to the restaurant. If she dressed for dinner before going out, she could easily save enough time for a drink, maybe two, in the restaurant bar. Even taking into account a slower walking speed due to the pumps she'd be wearing, she could clear forty minutes if she didn't have to go back to her dorm before dinner. Pleased with the outcome of carefully applied planning and visual mapping, she knew not only what she needed to do, but that everything would get done in time, which meant there was no reason to rush. She had edited her list to reflect the new order and proceeded to get dressed in Carl's parent-pleasing outfit.

"Excuse me ma'am, are you lost?"

Hannah looked up from her papers into the eyes of Ashley Green, an eager-to-please undergraduate who lived in her dorm. She was wearing a red Whitfield t-shirt stating in large letters, "ASK ME. I CAN HELP." She was part of the campus commencement team. For a moment Hannah felt dizzy. Her last class had only been three days ago. She knew she looked weird in clothes atypical for the average student, but did she really look unfamiliar to her dorm-mate? Lost at her school? She felt like time had pushed her out and folded back in around her.

"Oh, Hannah! I almost didn't recognize you! You look so fancy! Are you returning to Sweden today?"

It was such a relief that Ashley, who had lived with her for the last two years, had finally recognized her, it didn't matter that she still thought Hannah was a foreign exchange student. She had no idea how Ashley had gotten that impression when they first met, and she had tried to correct it, but Ashley wasn't the best listener. It must have been the emotional nature of her impending graduation, because she took a stab at answering Ashley's question directly and shook her head "Actually, I am staying after graduation. I have a job here. I'm going to work..."

Ashley squealed and hugged her, "I can't believe you're leaving! Fly safe and send us a postcard to hang in the dorm when you get to Stockholm! Adios!"

"Um, that's Spanish..." But Ashley was already gone, having spotted an older couple turning a campus map around in their hands, clearly in need of help. Shrugging, Hannah folded her list and map back into her purse, and continued down the path to the right of Foss Hill. The day was gorgeous. The leaves on the trees were open but still that bright new green color and the annual flowers that the Buildings and Grounds crew had shoved into every ugly patch of dirt had started to really produce, softening the edges of the buildings.

She smiled. For a moment she forgot the stress of the morning and appreciated Whitfield. She had a secret love for her school's campus— it had the charm of the traditional ivy-covered New England campus with the slightly ungainly edge of the dirty business of modern education. With graduation approaching, the administration was cleaning up the exteriors, all the better to reassure the parents that it really was worth the money. Which might make them seem like the jaded capitalists they surely were. But despite the campus makeover, the Administration also left untouched the somewhat divisive and angry student flyers on the campus kiosks. Passing the University Library, she was exhorted to divest from big oil, separate her recyclables and fuck the patriarchy. She felt a warm glow for her university's leaders' clear pride in their controversial student body. Fuck the patriarchy indeed!

Thinking of the patriarchy, she was certain that high-heeled shoes had been an invention of the aforementioned patriarchs. They seemed designed to keep a woman off balance and slow. As she crossed the quad, however, she started to make up for some lost time. She had discovered that if she swung her hips enough she could rotate her legs faster and land reliably on the ball of her foot, keeping her balance and increasing her speed, despite the restrictive cut of the sheath dress. It did create a swing to her hips that she normally lacked. She could hear a voice in her head admonishing her, "That is what a woman's walk is supposed to look like, Hannah." Silence, mother!

She was almost at the Copy Center, which was downhill from the main campus and technically part of the town. She reached into the clutch purse, compliments of Carl, to get her phone to check the time. Two thirty five. Pulling out the list as she slipped the phone back into her bag, she scanned it and smiled. Perfect. Everything was falling into place. Looking back up from her list she took a second to let the satisfaction of a well-executed plan fill her chest, and somehow missed seeing the gaping pothole in the sidewalk. And instead of her plan falling into place, it was her high-heeled foot that fell into the hole. As her body twisted, she flung her arms out and the contents of her purse went flying into the street. While her phone and various toiletries landed in the road, her carefully constructed list and map sped away, caught on the windshield of a passing car.

✺✺✺✺✺✺✺✺✺✺✺✺

Hera

Martha's Vineyard, Massachusetts.

Hera loaded the groceries into the trunk and took her time starting the car. Pulling out of the Safeway parking lot onto Beach Road, she drove slowly towards her seaside home just south of the East Chop Lighthouse. Her speed was not motivated by safety, but by dread. She hated to admit, even to herself, that she'd fled her home three hours ago, and that even now, she was trying to delay returning. She rounded the bend and felt her spirits sink. It wasn't the sight of her grey-shingled Victorian manse surrounded by a graceful wrap-around porch angled out over the cliffs that made her stomach churn. No, it was the rental car sitting in the driveway. Despite the cheer of the afternoon sun, she felt certain that something dark and fetid was inside her beloved home. The darkness was the publicist Apollo had convinced her to hire, Archer Adams, and the fetidness was his assistant, Lee something or other, she

The Myth of Cassandra

could never remember his name. Or her name? She couldn't tell and it didn't matter.

What did matter was that they had set up shop in her living room and she couldn't avoid them, regardless of how many grocery stores she visited. The publicist and his minion were all part of Apollo's latest scheme. Apollo had waltzed through her front door last week singing in a loud baritone, "Here comes the Sun, da na na na, here comes the Sun and I say, it's all right, get it? Here comes the SUN, you know, me. Clever, right?"

Hera's true pleasure in Apollo's company was tempered by his habit of always showing up working an angle. He was full of stories of almost-successes and his appearance meant that he either needed a place to hide or he had another ridiculous scheme and was here to borrow money. Hera wondered, not for the first time, how their lives might have been different if creation of wealth had been one of their powers. Though not worshipped as gods, the Olympians still had many of their original powers, but one thing they could not seem to master was the creation of money. They actually had to earn it.

Unless they stole it. She was certain that Hermes, another one of Zeus' bastard sons, supplemented his income with thievery. Apollo was different. He didn't have his brother's temperament for stealing. Apollo was a compulsive taker. He wrapped his requests in shinning optimism and a naïve lack of perspective. It didn't hurt that he was beautiful. It was hard to say no to him. He'd rolled in and swept her up in a hug that lifted her off the floor, "Dear Step-Mom, if you aren't the picture of domestic terror! Where would I find the big guy? I have the best news for him— really great!" Putting her feet back down, Apollo tried his most blinding smile, definitely kicking in extra wattage.

"The proper expression is domestic bliss, Apollo, domestic bliss."

Zeus had emerged from his basement dark room to greet his son, scowling at her, convinced by some paranoid notion that she was trying to keep him from Apollo. Apollo loved an audience, and with Zeus' and her full attention, he proceeded to sell them on the idea of a comeback for the Greek gods, worshipped again with all the glory and power that entailed. He had a plan; and a publicist. The publicist said they needed Zeus' involvement to make it work. You can't bring back the Olympians without the king. And then, as if it were an afterthought, Apollo asked for her money. Comebacks aren't cheap, Auntie Hera. There's the market research and the advertising budget, not to mention the staff needed to pull this off. It had been on her lips to refuse but then she had glanced at Zeus, and she had been touched by the excitement she had seen in his face, and so she had agreed to bankroll this absurd plan.

Post-Olympus had been rough for Zeus. There'd been no build up of battles leading to the ultimate confrontation, like when they'd overthrown the Titans. There'd been no battle at all; just a lot of complacency on the part of the Olympians that'd led them to rationalize away all the signs of their own decline: the dwindling numbers of humans making sacrifice, the decline of the Oracles, major festivals going uncelebrated. In the end, it was the slow and inexorable rise of Human Rationalism that relegated them from Gods and Goddesses to metaphors and "personifications" until one day, Mt. Olympus was only one hill among many and they were left immortals without followers. And Zeus had been left a ruler of nothing.

In the time that'd followed they'd all found their way in this modern world of humans. Hades and Persephone still had control of the Underworld, and with 85% occupancy at the time of the Fall, they were content to reign over the afterlife of the souls in their sphere. Athena ran a political think tank in Washington DC. Artemis was a National Parks Ranger, Demeter, a radical environmentalist, and Aphrodite had slipped off her radar, no one had seen her in years. But not so Hera's brother, Poseidon. Poseidon made a big show of wasting his time drinking in the Florida Keys and going to Jimmy Buffett shows. When he needed money, he ran a fishing charter. No one ever knew when he'd go out, but he always had a full boat that would pay for another four months of rum and Buffett. Grinding her teeth, Hera reminded herself of the futility of trying to reform the God of the Sea. Her last attempt had led to her backside being pinched as he laughed, "You have to learn how to relax, sister, it's five o'clock somewhere in the world!" and then he'd knocked back another drink.

The Myth of Cassandra

Five o'clock indeed. She often worked well past that, as did her staff. You worked until the job was done. Period. She smiled, thinking how her leadership had brought her company into preeminence. The fall had not been bad for everyone. She was even happier with her influence on women now and felt she lived more truly her title of Goddess of Hearth and Home. She had found her true calling. But Zeus had been at a loss. Immediately after the fall, he'd slept a lot. Then he'd eaten a lot. Then he'd tried to distract himself by attempting to seduce women; a lot of women. But he should have thought of that before he had spent a hundred years over-eating. On the plus side, the rejection of countless women did prod him into returning to his marriage.

He'd come to the home she'd made on Martha's Vineyard, an island off the coast of Massachusetts. Unfortunately, he'd just moped around, channel surfing and eating pan after pan of brownies. Not exactly the husband she'd been waiting for. She'd tried to get him interested in hobbies; pottery, flower pressing, even breeding purebred hairless cats. Humans were willing to pay a fortune for these freaks of nature. But all she was left with was a depressed god and some very unattractive pets. She disposed of them as Christmas "presents" to her staff. All they could do was smile and say thank you. It'd been fun watching them try to express their gratitude. She gave a big bonus to the most convincing liar.

The only hobby Zeus had tried that seemed to stick was photography. He liked to roam the island capturing images both majestic and minute. He had a knack for lighting. A small art gallery on the Island displayed his photographs in their Spring Show. He had a steady following. And just when it had looked like Zeus had found his modern-world calling, he'd been seduced by Apollo's fantasy of being worshipped again, and her well-ordered life fell into disarray. She saw that now. If only he had never come up from the darkroom.

Instead of improving Zeus' mood, this plan of Apollo's made it significantly worse. Zeus had stopped spending time on his photography, and instead was always underfoot complaining about the diet Apollo's publicist had put him on. Whining about the lack of butter on his vegetables. Decrying the absence of bread in his meal. Accusing her of stealing his stash of microwaveable brownies. Her peaceful home had become unbearable. She placed the blame squarely on one set of blindingly white shoulders: Archer Adams, the publicist. Once he'd arrived from Los Angeles last Friday, it had taken her five minutes to come to a decision. She'd made a few calls, set up some meetings and worked from Boston all weekend, hoping that when she made it home on Monday Adams would be gone. But he wasn't. And the drama that unfolded this morning had made an extended grocery trip a necessity to keep her from poisoning him with her kitchen garden herbs.

The man, if he was a man, had this strangely plastic energy, as if he was made out of synthetic polymers strung together to look perfect, but completely lacking in anything real. His face and hair had an unnatural stiffness and his words seemed to come out of his perfectly white teeth without his lips moving. His clothes were exclusively white— white suit with a white tie and white shirt and white socks and even white shoes. Looking at him made her temples pound. His minion was almost worse— all rumpled brown and grey clothes piled on top of a body that could have been a man or a woman. It smelled of cheese and mumbled when it talked. It would find a corner of the room to nest down with its laptop and only looked up when called. It answered to the name of Lee. Hera found that after it moved from its nesting spot, she had to clean the walls, as they tended to be greasy. As she'd packed up her things to get off Island on Friday, she'd actually stepped on him, so little impression did he make on the world. It'd taken her assistant all day Saturday to find a cleanser to remove the stain from her linen heels.

Forget the intrusion into her home or Zeus's grumbling; the worst part was that the entire plan Adams had laid out for reclaiming Olympus was undignified. Adams claimed that humans' "belief" was a "commodity." That humans in this century would not be willing to" invest" their "faith capital" in a deity they felt had screwed them in the past. Adams had run several focus groups before coming, and it appeared that from the insultingly small pool of humans who even knew who the Olympians were, those humans associated the Greek gods with screwing over humanity. Just another sign of their appalling education. One would have hoped that the touchstones of the modern American would be the po-

The Myth of Cassandra

etry of Ovid or the paintings of The Masters— instead it appeared to be DC comic books and Hollywood B-flicks. Contrary to popular opinion, the Greek gods had not screwed humans over; they had meted out justice. Mostly. Those were the facts.

But Adams didn't care about facts. He claimed that perception was fact in today's society. He insisted that the best way to counter negative publicity was to "get ahead of it" with your own positive story. And with that absurd notion in place, he had proposed the idea to make "reparations" for Cassandra. Cassandra of Priam, a human Apollo had imagined he was madly in love with. Apollo was always falling in love; a serial monogamist. In the throes of passionate desire, he gave the girl the gift of prophecy as a sign of his devotion. But when she'd been daft enough to openly reject him, he'd been rightly insulted. In her opinion, humans would do well to learn the art of subservience to the gods. Apollo had cursed Cassandra to have the gift of prophecy but to have no one believe a word she said. While Hera had agreed with his instinct to punish the girl, he might have chosen a better way. There'd been a tedious confrontation with the Oracle from Delphi wanting Zeus to rescind Apollo's curse, saying that one ignored human prophet, could become many ignored prophecies, until humans turn away from the gods altogether, but Zeus had expressed pleasure at the creativity of his son's punishment, and had refused. Unfortunately the Oracle had actually succeeded in being prophetic, and the downfall of the gods reign had its beginnings in the debacle of the Trojan War, when no one listened to Cassandra's warnings.

Adams' so-called brilliant idea was to rebrand the Greek gods as "gifters" of humanity. He proposed giving a "gift" to one of Cassandra's descendants. He felt that if they could find a descendant of Cassandra's who was articulate and attractive and give her the "gift" of being listened to, then not only would the Olympians be making up for past wrongs, but they would be getting a built-in human spokes-model to promote their ascendancy. He called it a "two-for." What an imbecile. Even if Apollo might have gone slightly overboard with that woman, the Greek gods do not apologize. For anything.

Hera could see a dozen things wrong with this plan, not the least was how this "gift" was going to work. All the immortals were held to a Non-Interference Accord, where they could not unduly impact human events, enforced by a council of representative immortals. When she pointed this out, Adams claimed to have found a loophole in the Accord allowing for acts intended to compensate for past wrongs. That struck her as a weak precedent, one that the council could decimate, leaving them all liable to fines or worse. But no one was asking her thoughts on the matter, and so she sat back and watched. Careful observation was often overlooked as a viable way to assert oneself. She'd written that in her advice column. There would come a time when she would act. And then the time came. This morning. She only hoped it would work to put an end to this.

She'd taken the early ferry from Woods Hole and had walked into her home, her sanctuary, only to be assaulted by the sound of Archer Adam's voice, pitched one note higher than obnoxious.

"Talk to me, Lee— It's seven o'clock and I have been waiting a half an hour for your answer. I want the perfect answer. Give me the perfect answer. She needs to be in her early twenties; attractive, but not too attractive, more Sandra Bullock than Angelina, yes? Intelligent, but not too smart, not short, but not too tall, most importantly, she has to be sincere. You can't teach sincerity. We want her to be someone people will want to listen to. Perfection, Lee. Find it for me." Turning her way, Archer only barely concealed his disdain before addressing her, "Hera. You have returned. Any chance you can fix me up some breakfast? I'd love your famous eggs Florentine and make mine with extra Mornay sauce." Smirking as he stroked his torso, "Don't worry about my waistline, I have a fabulous metabolism. But it is strictly an egg white omelet for Zeus." And he turned back to his minion without waiting for her response.

She'd walked right through his "request" for eggs and let his words fall to the ground. As if she catered to anyone. He was forgetting who and what she was. She should fill his eggs with ground lobelia from her kitchen garden. A morning spent vomiting might teach him some manners. Yes. Although, it might be a little early to harvest; she could skip the herbal route and fill his Mornay sauce with laxatives. Butter covers up the taste of everything. Let's see how his metabolism keeps up with that. Every step she took toward the kitchen was another step up the ladder of her temper and further up the biological threat level for Adams. Control, Hera, control. She needed to keep her head. Think about Zeus and Apollo. How can you help them if you have no control?

And as if her thoughts had beckoned them, Zeus and Apollo had come up from the basement as she'd entered the kitchen. Zeus scowled at her, "It's about damn time you came back, woman. For the goddess of hearth and home you've been putting in a poor showing. I haven't had a decent meal in 48 hours. All this one feeds me is protein crap shake. I want a steak, rare. And potatoes. Au gratin." Then he leaned in close to her face and whispered in her ear, "Please."

The look in Zeus's eyes softened her, and she narrowed her gaze on Apollo, "I make this meal and you take them away. Anywhere but here. There are over fifty hotels, motels and B&Bs on this island, and I want them out of my house." Apollo had simply nodded and sat at the counter like a patient retriever waiting his treat. Hera wondered if anyone had bothered to make food while she was gone. Why didn't men cook when left to their own devices? Hmm... She made a note to think about that idea; there could be an article there.

Lee's voice warbled back towards them from the living room, "I found her! The perfect woman! I mean I think she might be perfect maybe...." Despite the lack of conviction in Lee's statement, they all converged on him, though the Olympians maintained a safe perimeter back from the odiferous computer minion. Hera sniffed. Bleu cheese. Definitely bleu cheese. And was that a hint of garlic? She made a mental note to give the housecleaners hazard pay.

Lee appeared unaware of their ring of avoidance and continued talking in his monotone, directing himself to the room at large while nervously cutting his eyes to Adams, who was pacing behind him. "We started with a list of 3,893 women who are probable descendants of Cassandra. I refined that list using limiters on age and geography. We are looking for someone in her twenties who speaks English. That left me with 876 possible candidates. I wrote a program to analyze their available biometrics: height and weight from driver's licenses, mostly to exclude any outliers— physically, that is. That excluded 273. I used face recognition software to measure the objective beauty of each of the 603 girls and only kept those who fell in the mid-range for symmetry. 201. A standard background check on arrest warrants left me with 149 potential candidates. Finally, I created a web net to catch any activity or posts by said candidates, and just now I caught the mighty white whale in my net. She's written a thesis about Greek mythology. She's perfect. I think...."

"Good lord, Lee, I told you she had to be attractive. I can't work with a whale of a girl!" Archer squeezed Lee's shoulder and Hera saw the minion wince, "I need Sandra-freaking-Bullock. I thought I was clear about that."

Archer's voice had risen to a pitch that made Hera mirror the minion's wince. Despite that, she laughed, "It was a literary reference," you moron, she finished in her head. "He didn't mean that she was large, just that she'd been elusive, but finally caught. Haven't you heard of Moby Dick? Captain Ahab hunting the great white whale? I am sure there was a movie about it."

Archer seemed impervious to Hera's mocking. Instead he looked to Lee, "So she's attractive, Lee? That was just a metaphor? Do you have a photo?" Lee hit a key on his computer and the screen filled with a serious-looking girl with thick blonde hair, grey eyes and even teeth. She was pretty, but Hera didn't like the look of her at all. How she managed to look serious when she was nominally smiling for the camera made her suspicious. What was she hiding? If the decision was based on this one picture, she was a definite "no" in Hera's opinion.

But Archer had a completely opposite reaction, "It's her. The one, Lee. How did you find her?" Archer reached out to trace the slight furrow between her brows on the computer screen.

"Well, remember, I started with 3,893 women who were probable..." but Lee's words were cut off as Archer placed his other hand on Lee's shoulder and squeezed again. This time Hera noticed the distinct odor of sulfur. And the minion seemed to be trying not to squirm.

The Myth of Cassandra

"I don't care how you did it, Lee."

"But you just asked..." and this time Lee's words ended with a yelp as Archer's grip tightened visibly. Despite the clear violence of his actions, Archer's voice took on a polished, publicist's veneer.

"Focus, Lee, we need her name and location. We have gifts to bestow and a campaign to launch to return the gods to their glory." At this he smiled his whitest smile at Zeus and Apollo, "Am I right, men?"

Conferring a gift on a human was no small act, and Hera decided that it was time to pull on the reins, "Oh Archer, didn't Zeus tell you? He had a wonderful idea. Before he'll allow Apollo to bestow any gifts, he wants his investigator to check her out and make sure that it's a good fit, wasn't that right dear? You men definitely know best. It might be good if you give Hermes a call, and he can look into this "perfect" candidate. I have to run to the store for some groceries." And without waiting for a reply, she left the living room, walked through the kitchen and out the back door, escaping in her car. She had spent hours traveling from one grocery store to another, looking for something to keep her away from Adams until she no longer felt like killing him. The urge was not gone completely, but she was back and she needed to get the food out of the trunk and into the kitchen where she could make something delicious while she waited for Hermes' report.

Her suggestion to use Hermes to investigate the girl was not idle. She'd used him for many jobs, and felt sure he wouldn't recommend the girl for the gift. Hermes may be a thief and a liar, but he had a history of being on the wrong end of power and he seemed to feel an affinity for the weak. She was sure the parameters of this "gift" would push him to discourage the use of this girl, whoever she was. With the girl nixed, the next step would be to convince Zeus to evict the publicist. She'd bought the ingredients for Zeus's favorite meal, coq au vin, and tucked the bottle of wine under one arm while she shouldered the grocery bags through the back door. Forget about food being the way to a man's heart, she hoped it would be the way to his common sense.

CHAPTER TWO

The Past is Never Gone

❋❋❋

Hannah

Falling into a pothole

Flinging her arms out to catch her balance as her ankle twisted, she watched as the contents of her purse flew through the air. Her phone had the misfortune of landing in the path of a swiftly moving Escalade, the behemoth of SUVs, and died a sudden crunchy death. Hannah herself avoided any major injury by grabbing onto the backpack of the student in front of her and hanging on for dear life.

Fortunately, the student she had grabbed was leaning over, so Hannah didn't pull him backward. Unfortunately, her momentum combined with his position caused them both to fall forward, though he did manage to break their fall on his hands and knees. As they fell forward Hannah's knees were trapped by the dress and she couldn't stop herself from landing directly on top of him. The good luck continued as he was still wearing his bike helmet because the force of Hannah landing on him caused his head to hit the ground, and she heard him exhale what sounded like a curse, but could have simply been the sound of pain.

Scrambling in the ridiculously confining clothes, she tried to get off him without increasing his injury. Getting her feet under her while apologizing non-stop, Hannah managed to push herself backward off of him and stand— though a little wobbly— as she had to favor her right

The Myth of Cassandra

ankle which was hot from the twist. Miraculously she had not gotten a single run in her pantyhose— what were the odds of that?

He seemed to be taking his time standing up— first rolling back on his heels and checking his hands— then pausing before standing up in one fluid motion. The entire move was so graceful it seemed like some advanced Yoga maneuver; "upward rising dog." With his back to her and his helmet on she had no idea who he was. Whoever he was, Hannah felt both grateful for his breaking her fall and terrible if she had hurt him.

"Are you okay? I'm so sorry I fell on you— did you hurt your hands and knees? I just looked away for a second, and I should've seen that hole, and I didn't even think, I just reached out and grabbed as I started to fall, and I'm so sorry that I knocked you over and then landed on you. Did you get hurt?" Dismayed by the uncharacteristic volume of words spewing out of her mouth, she clamped her jaw shut, smoothed her skirt down, and tried again, "Are you okay?"

He seemed to have frozen when he heard her voice and she couldn't tell why. Maybe he was a foreign exchange student and didn't understand English? Or maybe "he" was really a "she"— all she could see was a slim body in low slung jeans and a ratty t-shirt with the words "Wasted Youth" on a British Flag— damn, it could be a woman.-Had she said anything that had assumed a gender? This could be a problem at her school.

He/she was now taking off her/his helmet— and this didn't help either— as the shoulder length wavy brown hair could go either way. But at the first word from the mystery "person" she felt her face freeze in a comic parallel to his reaction to her: she knew that voice.

"I'm not the worse for wear," turning while putting his helmet on the back of his moped, he narrowed his eyes at her— taking in the navy wool dress and lingering on the white pumps— and a poorly repressed smile lurked around his mouth, "Which is more than I can say for you, Hannah— what's with the 1950's Stepford Wives get up? Did falling in that pothole cause a rift in the time/space continuum?"

Exhaling slowly through her teeth, she reminded herself that she had just used him as a human airbag and common decency dictated that she should be thanking him. Pasting a smile on, she drew on years of practiced politeness, "Thank you for breaking my fall, John. I'm glad that you didn't get hurt and I'd love to catch up, but I have a very busy schedule…" One last flash of smile as she performed a brilliant exit, stage left, and confidently walked past him.

At least that was how it was supposed to be. Except as her right foot came down, she was reminded of how she had twisted her ankle ten seconds ago, and she let out an involuntary yelp and tottered, certain this time that she was going to hit the ground— her exit completely ruined. But to her utter humiliation, he saved her again— this time catching her in his arms, the entire maneuver looking like the elaborate choreography in a ballroom dancing competition. If only it had been someone else, almost anyone else, it might have seemed romantic; she was suspended in the air, one leg lifted, her head dropping back and looking right into his deep blue eyes. Which were definitely not stunning, despite their blueness.

There was a frown between said eyes and his next words clarified the source of his concern, "Not a single hair on your head moved throughout your fall— did you break open your own personal hole in the ozone getting "dolled" up today?"

He seemed to have forgotten that he had her hanging in the air as he took pot shots at her. Still a jerk. The pretense of politeness dissolved in her mouth and she hissed, "Let go of me!"

John's gaze slide past her to the ground below her, and he raised an eyebrow speculatively. Clenching her jaw, she looked for the inner calm that had worked for her in the past, but all she found was irritation, "Put me upright. And then let go of me."

Holding her suspended, he seemed to be considering his options, and Hannah felt something in her snap, "I have a very tight schedule and I don't have time to deconstruct my hemline or analyze the shade of my lipstick and its implications for the communist movement. I used a non-CFC hairspray by the way— not that it's any of your business." Han-

The Myth of Cassandra

nah's voice had been rising with each word, and his continued look of calm appraisal only stoked her anger, but she made a Herculean effort to level out, "I am sure that if you would please return me to my upright position we can go our separate ways." Looking pointedly at her feet, she was gratified to see that her little speech had had the desired effect and he was levering her upright.

"You might want to get that ankle looked at, it's starting to swell…" he finished righting her, his hands sliding from her shoulders to her elbows, appearing to want to help her walk.

She stared at him in wonder—was he going to pretend they had anything other than a mutual loathing? She had already lost her temper with him once, so to put a stop to it, she subjected herself to a brutal internal flogging. Ignore the supposed concern in his eyes. He was no one to her, just an acquaintance, an arrogant man-child, a smug pseudo-intellectual, self-satisfied campus Lothario whom she had successfully avoided for the last three and a half years. And in the last three minutes, he had broken her fall. Twice. She had already thanked him. She would walk away. Politely. Except some dark instinct in her wanted to let him know both what she thought of him and that she didn't think of him at all.

There were very few people on campus who actually made her feel physically angry— most people were easy to pacify, ignore or to just get along with. But John MacCallister was in a class alone. Correction— the class he was in was small and included her mother and Carl's mother. But unlike the other members of that infamous class, he had no bearing on her life and she could simply walk away from him. Providing she didn't fall again.

She had known him since freshman year and had taken an instant dislike to him. She was the only one on campus who had. Try to imagine someone with the confidence and sex appeal of Mick Jagger, but with great bone structure and flawless skin, intense blue eyes, wavy brown hair and a long lean build. Clothes always looked like they had just been thrown on his body or were about to come off. Men and women alike seemed to stumble over themselves to get closer to him, and there had been a group of long-haired girls with flowing skirts who had proudly claimed to have formed a harem to serve him for their Intro to Sociology mid-term project.

She didn't hate him because he was popular. No, she hated his intellectual privilege. She had had the misfortune of sitting behind him in her Western Civ class— a requirement for every freshman and she had to spend her first semester listening to John MacCallister's thoughts on everything. It didn't help that the Professor teaching the class also seemed enthralled by the Mac Man, often encouraging John to come to the front of the class and use the blackboard to make his point, and joined in when the class applauded at the end of a particularly rousing speech. Hannah didn't clap. She simply endured.

It wasn't that he was stupid, or that all his ideas were lame. It was that he spoke with such unselfconscious entitlement. As if all his ideas were worthy of being expressed. The class's enthusiastic reaction to him only made her more annoyed. If she were willing to think it, she knew that part of why she hated him was that he existed effortlessly. Everything seemed so easy for him. But she wasn't willing to think that she was that petty, and so she focused on hating his ideas and denying him her approbation.

And that must be why he had always seemed to pick on her. There was one particular class that seemed to epitomize the antipathy between them. It was in the sixth week of Western Civ and the topic that had been assigned was to identify the Hellenistic influence on Roman society. She had come to class excited to discuss the rich and varied implications of Greek culture and its effects on Roman society. But instead of a class spent analyzing whether the spread was simply the natural process of cultural diffusion or an intentional policy of cultural co-option, the class was co-opted by the MacMan.

This particular day it was his campaign to change the university's use of the term "freshman" to the more gender neutral, and in Hannah's opinion, completely absurd, term "frosh." Before class had even started, Mac's Minions, Hannah's private name for the horde of sycophants who did his bidding, were passing out buttons; a combination of the male and female symbols with the words "I'M A FROSH" printed underneath. Mac himself was guiding a petition up and down the lecture hall rows.

Before long John was handing it to her, and without even glancing at it, she passed it to Cam, the stoned sophomore to the left of her. She'd found the contact high she got from sitting next to him helped her in her endurance of the MacMan, who was, at that moment, frowning at her in a way that seemed to say, "I'm charming even when I am disappointed in you." Cam had signed it with a flourish and sent it along.

"You won't even read it, Hannah?"

"No thank you."

"No thank you? Really? Did you throw the "thank you" in for politeness sake? If you hold politeness in such high esteem, it would have been truly polite to at least read the petition before making up your mind. Are you are too busy to read the one paragraph? Or do you assume that you already know what it says and you don't agree? Which is it Hannah?"

"I am waiting for class to start. Have you seen the Professor?"

"I saw him grabbing a coffee at the Student Center, I'm sure he'll be here soon. But you didn't answer my question. Do you disagree with altering the language to reflect our changing cultural values or are you simply above this kind of intellectual exchange? I notice that you don't say much in this class but I get the sense from your silences that you have a lot to say— so what is it? Are you apathetic or a traditionalist?"

"Are those my only choices?"

"Ah, so you do have an opinion. All right, what is it?"

"I want to talk about the Hellenistic influences on Roman Society and you want to talk about yourself."

At this point in the exchange, more than half the class was following their "conversation" like a tennis match. Hannah could feel her face flushing and she just wished he would shut up and sit down. One of his harem had put her hand on Mac's arm and was murmuring about how he shouldn't waste his time. Hannah looked away from the girl's disdainful stare and noticed that the Professor had entered the room. Mac was still focused on her though; he shook the girl off his arm and raised his voice a little louder,

"An ad homonym attack is the best you've got, Hannah? I'm disappointed; I thought still waters ran deep?"

For a minute, she had thought she would be able to pull back from this argument. She made it a policy never to argue with anyone. Arguments were the breeding ground for recriminations and regret. She followed a straightforward policy when confronted with other people's opinions: first, assess how important it is to you to tell them what you really think. Second, assess how important it is to that person to be right. Third, if the second is larger than the first— simply accommodate. On the occasions when the first was more important than the second, she would make a plan for helping them to come around to her point of view. There was no reason to argue. But at the moment, rational discourse had taken a back seat to burning rage. The frustrations of having to listen to John MacCallister prattle on every Monday and Wednesday afternoon for the last 6 weeks seemed to have found a vent.

"Just because your ad homonym attack is buried in a tired cliché doesn't make it "intellectual discourse," John. If you insist on knowing what I really think about your pompous petition, I'll tell you, but I don't think you are interested in real debate— you just want more people to fall at your feet." She batted her eyelashes at him, and in a high pitched voice, simpered, "Oh, Mac, please help me understand— you are an intellectual beacon to us all. Why do we celebrate the Founding Fathers and not the Founding Mothers? Why do we bother to study Western Civilization when we know that it is just propaganda disseminated by the Establishment to justify our rape of other cultures? What color should I paint my toenails if I want to avoid the trap of the patriarchy?" Seething, her voice lowered and became all accusation, "Let's assume for the moment that you have a real interest in what I think about your campaign to force the university to change the word "freshman" to "frosh". I agree with you that language reflects a culture's values— but real change in a culture's values are not reflected in artificial changes to the structure of a word, "her-story," "womyn," or "frosh"— those changes only create changes in the denotation of words. Real cultural change is reflected in the changing connotations to the existing language. The fact that College students are 60% female and we still use the word freshman means to me that we have changed the word "freshman" to include women— by its very definition in our society. To change it to a word as amorphous and second-class as "frosh" is condescending. Besides, "frosh" sounds like a something they might serve in a café in Paris that only the native Parisians would eat. Do you even know the etymology of the word "freshman"? It means "novice"— a term you should consider, given the simpleness of your argument."

The silence in the class was profound. Hannah realized that at some point in the middle of her rant, she had actually stood up and was inches from John MacCallister's face— which had an expression on it she couldn't read. Into the silence came the Professor's exuberant declaration,

"Excellent start to the class, Hannah and Mac! I can see that this topic is much more compelling than the assignment, so why don't we spend the rest of the period discussing whether the term "freshman" is phallocentric. Mac, do you have a response to Hannah's vigorous objections?"

She braced herself for his scathing response, but he just smiled and shook his head, "Not at this time, though I would like to reserve the right to re-call the witness," and taking his seat in front of her, he leaned back, resting his arm along the back of the chair next to him, much to the delight of its occupant, who seemed to be melting. Hannah couldn't believe it— he had played her. He had heckled and insulted her into a horribly embarrassing display of anger in front of 125 of her classmates. He had purposely exposed her. But why? For the crime of not being enthralled by him? She felt numb.

The professor continued the class, asking the others if they agreed with Hannah or Mac. It had seemed to Hannah that every person who spoke ripped into her— and each time, the professor asked if she wanted to respond— she shook her head every time. It was interminable. When the bell finally rang, she stood up, walked out, and knew she was not going back. She wrote to the professor to request that she be allowed to take the final early on the pre-text that she had to leave campus before the end of the semester to join a cross-country protest bus; an excuse she was certain would win him over. He seemed pleased, convinced that his class had inspired her. He didn't even ask what she was protesting.

She never spoke to John MacCallister about it, though he had cornered her at a campus party once sophomore year and tried to talk to her. She had pretended she couldn't hear him over the band, and smiling blandly, had turned to the guy standing next to him and asked him to dance. As for the discussion she had wanted to have about the Hellenistic influences on Roman society, she had gone to the Classics Department, and had found her intellectual home. So some good had come from it. She couldn't avoid John completely— it was not a big campus— but she had vowed to never let him get under her skin again. And here he was now— taunting her about her clothes while pretending concern for her ankle. He could dangle the reddest, juiciest, most perfect apple in her face and she was determined not to bite.

Ignoring his hands on her arms, she looked at him blandly and waited for him to let go. "I am sure that if I go slowly, I can walk— it's just a twist, not a sprain. Thank you again, John."

The expression on his face could only be described as oddly disappointed, but his voice was easy as he released her slowly. "No problem, I was happy to help. Wait." And then he bent over, sweeping up her scattered belongings into her forgotten purse. "I think you phone is DOA, but I can get it for you..."

"No, no, that's not ..." But he had already turned back to his bike, chaining it to the street sign. "Thanks." Feeling a little deflated, as there was now no one watching her triumphantly composed exit, she tucked her purse under her arm and hobbled down the sidewalk to the lower level of the bookstore to pick up her thesis. The time on the bank clock across the street read 2:38 p.m. She was right on schedule, despite her adventure with the pothole and the MacMan. Aside from her burning ankle and dead phone, everything was going perfectly— right? Riffling through her purse, she realized she had lost her list, but that was no problem. She could easily remember it. All she had to do was follow the plan and pick up her thesis, turn it in and get to dinner. She would end her time at Whitfield with the same calm grace and lack of drama that she had perfected in her four years as an undergraduate. She had this under control.

●●●●●●●●●●

Hermes

La Boca Restaurant, Centreville, CT

Sipping on the lukewarm beer, he contemplated his current job. While he was technically the messenger god, email and texting had really cut into his business. So he got some professional advice and checked the color of his parachute. His career counselor told him that he had the skills and temperament to make an excellent private eye: observant, well versed in human frailties and extremely comfortable with deception.

So he started his own PI firm, Fleet Footed Investigations. He specialized in background checks on humans, but drew the line at taking pictures of cheating spouses. Scorned and angry women were dangerous clients. Which made it somewhat ironic that Hera, goddess of scorned and angry women, was his biggest client. Hera. Talk about survival of the fittest. She had evolved herself into a major player with very deep pockets. So when he got the call from Zeus about this assignment, he knew who was really holding the purse strings and jumped at the chance to make some cash.

The waitress, who had been flirting with him since he had sat down, stopped by to deliver another beer. Hermes wasn't vain. He knew that he wasn't classically attractive, but he seemed to radiate trouble and there had been plenty of humans who had been drawn to him. She seemed on the verge of saying something, but he kept his eyes on the computer screen in front of him, and she faded out of sight. A shame, but it was for the best. He had no time for distractions. He needed the money, and

Zeus had made it clear he needed the job done fast. So he reviewed his notes on the investigation he'd conducted into Hannah Summers, the potential "gift" girl, and tried to decide what to say.

The address Zeus had given him for the girl was a college in southern Connecticut, Whitfield University. He'd made good time on his winged sandals, and had landed on campus a little before eight o'clock. She was a college student, so he had a fair shot of finding her still asleep even though it was Monday. Jimmying the lock, he'd slipped into her room. Yep. There she was, asleep and alone. Aces. He'd sidled up to the skinny bed and placed his hand lightly on her head. Murmuring to her in his native tongue, he'd slipped her deeper into sleep. Being a god had certain benefits for this type of work.

Her computer was open to her email and with a few keystrokes; he had scanned her recent activity. It was less than enlightening. A rejected thesis, a thesis reprint. That was all fairly straightforward. The third email was more interesting, more personal:

"My dear Hannah,

I hope that this e-mail finds you well. You are poised to begin a long and illustrious career in the study of the Classics and I anticipate that you are eager to begin your post-graduation employment. I have tremendous confidence in your abilities to care for our precious collection and know that our good mutual friend, Mr. Tobias Blean, holds you in similarly high regard. He is delighted that you will be taking over his position as curator.

It may have come to your attention that I have recently acquired a computer. I have found it to be a delightfully useful tool and have similarly discovered the myriad of options for advancing my knowledge on the World Wide Web. The Internet is a fascinating experiment in collaborative myth creation. I am sure that this is not news to you, but I find myself often sitting back in awe at the range of information available with the click of my mouse. I used that term correctly, yes? "Mouse"?

I must get to my point. In my exploration of the World Wide Web, I have discovered that I, too, may have a web page and have established myself at CoolProfTetley.com. I was uncertain about the site name, but have been reassured by our IT professional, Geoffrey, that CoolProfTetley.com was appropriate. He seemed very pleased with it and I was grateful for his assistance. You are invited to visit it at your leisure, but more than that, I would be honored if you would permit me to publish your thesis on my site. As your advisor I take great pride in your thoughtful and excellent work and would very much like to share it online. Would you be amenable to this? I certainly hope so.

If you are willing, please attach your thesis along with your précis in your reply e-mail. Geoffrey tells me that I should let you know that you may "zip" the file as he has taught me how to "unzip" it on my end. Isn't that clever of him? If that is difficult for you, please do not concern yourself. I will simply ask the most efficient Miss Guildersleeves to type your thesis directly onto the site from the hardcopy you gave me. I am sure that she would not mind.

I am looking forward to your graduation on Sunday and to the evolution of our relationship from Professor and student to one of highly valued colleagues. Mr. Blean and I would very much like to sit down with you and discuss some of the details of the job of curator, preferably over a pot of decent tea. My treat. Please let me know your availability.

Sincerest regards,

Prof. Tetley

Tetley...that name rang a bell for some reason. Maybe a past investigation? As Hermes read her reply, he noted that she seemed to have a nice relationship with the professor, a decent sense of humor, and more than a passing knowledge of his own twisted family tree:

Dear Prof. Tetley,

I am happy to let you post my thesis on your site, coolproftetley.com, though I am not sure that it will spark much intellectual discussion, as I doubt anyone beyond yourself and possibly Mr. Blean will be much interested in the Taxonomy of Horticultural Metaphors in Ancient Greek Mythology, but who am I to deny you this lesson firsthand? Enjoy posting it. I enjoyed writing it with your thoughtful and considerate guidance. Thank you again.

Though I am sure that Miss Guildersleeves would oblige your request to retype my 238-page thesis, I feel that this would be a punishment on par with Sisyphus's. Therefore I am attaching the file, "zipped" as requested, and hope that Geoffrey has indeed taught you how to "unzip." Let me know if you run into any trouble, as I would be happy to help.

Give my best to Mr. Blean at your cribbage game this Thursday and watch his pegging, he loves to hold onto aces just to grab that 31st point.

See you on Sunday at Commencement. I am available next Monday; would 4:00 pm at your office work?

All my best,

Hannah

Other than this one exchange, her email was remarkably uninformative. Actually, non-existent would be a more accurate description. She'd had only eight emails in her entire account, including her spam and trash folders. That was odd. Most humans he'd investigated had hundreds if not thousands of old emails, and they could be a useful source of information. Who was this girl?

Settling in at her desk he had started going through her files. The girl made a lot of lists. And outlines. Opening her thesis, Hermes only got through the first page before he started to yawn. Another really dead end. Not badly written, just bland. The literary equivalent of an overly wordy index. Checking her Internet activity revealed more nothingness. No inappropriately personal blog entries. No confessional videos in her underwear. Not even a single mildly dirty picture, which was a shame; she wasn't bad looking. He had a thing for blondes. But if her writing was merely boring, her photos showed a woman frozen in the land of nice, devoid of anything particular. Scanning the pictures she did have, he had started a mental list of known associates.

Glancing over at the girl sleeping in her bed, he'd considered lightening her sleep before leaving. But she looked so peaceful. She should only sleep for an hour or so at the most, and she looked like she needed the extra rest. He left her as is, locked the door behind him and went in search of real information on her.

The humans had an expression, "you are what you eat" but in the PI world, the expression was "you are who you piss off." And after spending all morning interviewing people, all Hermes had determined was that Hannah Summers pissed off no one. He couldn't find a single person with a grudge, big or small, against her. No "she stole my boyfriend." No "she cheated on the exam." Not even "she took the last parking space." There was one interesting story. A guy hanging out at the student center looked at Hermes' photo of the girl, and insisted her name was Harriet. He said she got into a yelling match with some "cool dude" in a freshman lecture class, but then he had hit him up for some righteous weed, and Hermes filed his story under the heading "questionable source."

The *Boyfriend*. He'd been an easy read. Hermes had chatted him up at the dining hall. He found him inhaling a mountain of cheese fries at 8:00 am. Carl Rogerson. The kid was in great shape, so unless he was a bulimic, he was clearly stress eating. He told Carl he was writing an article for the NY Times about recent college grads and their relationships. The boy looked askance at him when asked about Hannah, but when he offered to buy Carl a pizza he opened up like the preppy clam he was. In between bites the boyfriend said she was dependable, pretty, a good listener and super easy going. Not in any kind of hippy way, his words, but "easy going" as in willing to accommodate others. Then he started droning on about some important dinner and how she made life so much better. He proceeded to talk about himself and his plans for postgraduation. He would have kept on talking, but the food service called his name to let him know his pizza was ready to be picked up. Breakfast of champions. Hermes had no trouble slipping out the back door.

The *Advisor*. He found Professor Tetley holding office hours in the Classics department. That was kind of a trip, if he was honest. There on the wall behind the old man's desk was a painting of Hephaestus's workshop. The scene was of Apollo ratting out Aphrodite, Heph's wife. She and Ares had been knocking boots. What a drama that had been. Hermes approved of the artist's depiction of Apollo as a snitch, all whiny and accusing. The medium was definitely oils and if he wasn't wrong, it looked to be an original Titian, which would make it worth several million. An eccentric possession for a college professor to cavalierly hang on the wall. Though his palms itched looking at it, he never stole art. It was impossible to fence clean.

The artwork wasn't the only thing surprising about the professor. Despite looking ancient and completely harmless, he was clearly still very spry. Hermes laid his whole, "I'm doing an article" move on him and he did not fall for it. He was much more circumspect than the boyfriend, and would only say that Hannah was a lovely young woman and a gifted scholar. The only thing he offered up was his own website, CoolProfTetley.com, where he directed Hermes to Hannah's thesis. Then he clammed up.

The *Best-friend*. Okay, this was the hardest; as it did not appear that Hannah had any friends. No roommate— he already knew she lived in a single. So he asked around her dorm, and everyone thought she was nice but quiet. He did get a few stories about how she'd leant someone money for the laundry machine, or how she'd helped someone get to the Health Center when they were drunk. They all knew she had a boyfriend, but not one of them could name him. They called him "Rolph" after the kid in the Sound of Music. They didn't even seem to know where Hannah was from. Most guessed New England— not exactly that specific— and one girl even thought Hannah was a foreign exchange student.

Her classmates were only marginally better. Within her own department she was described as nice but aloof. When he asked one of the students to give him an example— had she blown you off for some party? Refused to pitch in for the class gift? She said, no, that Hannah was always happy to do either of those things. She found Hannah intellectually aloof. "She sits through class listening to others, but never volunteers her own ideas and you know she has them. It used to intrigue me, and then it frustrated me, and finally I just lost interest in what she might be thinking."

The *Mom*. Strapping on his winged sandals, he'd zipped over to Cambridge, MA, Hannah's actual hometown, and chatted up her mom in the grocery store. Hermes assumed the appearance of a middle-aged dad and told her he was heading to his son's graduation this weekend. At her "me too" he prompted, "Won't it be a relief to stop paying those bills, my son's a real drain on my wallet." The mom had just smiled at him and shook her head, "It's certainly true that college is expensive, but my daughter is a gift. I am so lucky. A true gift. I hope you have a nice weekend." And she turned her attention back to the tomatoes she was scrutinizing. Hermes left the store as underwhelmed as when he had entered.

No big revelations, just basic info. No one could be this vanilla. He decided that it was time to pull out the big guns, so he flew back to Connecticut to poke around in the girl's mind. She was only barely asleep, moments away from reaching the surface, when he dropped her down deeper, into a profound unconsciousness. All the evidence pointed to this girl being a sieve, a non-entity, but he needed to be sure. He was a professional, after all.

He'd been in a lot of human's minds before, a staple of his investigative services. Most humans say one thing and think another. Like, "I love your haircut/Because it distracts from that hideous dress." The unsaid thought was normally stored in a human's subconscious, resembling a rubbish bin filled with repression. Slipping into Hannah's subconscious, he had found the smoking gun to her apparent easy-going nature; her unspoken thoughts so numerous as to render her subconscious a virtual landfill.

So many words filled her head. Words heard and stored. Words thought but not said. Words edited and rephrased and carefully released. The writing on the wall of her mind indicated that the girl said one thing, thought another, edited that thought and only admitted to thinking a third thing. She seemed to say, "yes" to people because she told herself that it wasn't worth the effort to disagree, but underneath that there was some thought she pushed so far down he couldn't find it. It was impossible for him to determine what she thought was actually good advice. Which advice does she take? Why does she take it? From the large category of words she thinks, how many of them has she actually said? More to the point, with this gift, what might she say?

The waitress' voice brought him back to the present greasy restaurant and sticky table, "Would you like me to get you another?"

He looked down at his almost full glass of beer, and lifting a speculative eyebrow gave the waitress a more thorough examination. She was in her late twenties, early thirties, short brown hair, big eyes: attractive. The ease with which she carried her tray loaded with dishes promised strength. He liked strong women. Besides, struggling with morality made him edgy, and a little athletic sex might be just the thing to set him right. He downed the beer in his hand in one long drink. Handing her the empty he smiled, the slight gap in his front teeth making his smirk seem more charming than sleazy. At least her response seemed to bear this up.

Her half smile widened, "I have a break coming up..."

Later he would acknowledge to his therapist that there were a million possible questions he could have asked the waitress that would have led to mutually satisfactory sex, but instead his next words to her were, "Just out of curiosity, what do you know about the Greek Gods?"

Still smiling, she tilted her head towards his laptop, "Are you a professor from the college or something?"

"No, I'm a god." He had always gotten a good response with this answer. Though no one ever took him seriously, the honesty behind the answer always seemed to put the person in question at ease.

Shifting her tray to her hip, she laughed, "My kid reads these books that I think have Greek Gods, he talks a lot about Zeus, he's a Greek God, right?" Biting her lip, she scanned the room, then easing the tray onto the table, slid onto the seat next to him and lowered her voice, "Do you like to role play or something? I mean, you're definitely my type, but I am not into anything too...you know...I was just looking for a little fun ..."

Zeus. The goal of mood enhancing sex was eclipsed by the overwhelming shadow of his daddy issues. It would have been one thing if Zeus ignored all his bastards, he could have passed it off as impersonal— Zeus was a crappy dad. But Zeus didn't ignore all of his children. Hermes knew that he should change the subject to the weather or sports, but instead found himself lecturing, "Those Greek Gods, they are quite the characters. Did you know that Zeus's dad was a Titan named Kronos? Old Kronos ruled the world with his wife, Rhea. But he wasn't the best of dads. See, Kronos had taken seriously a prophecy that one day a child of his would overthrow him, so he did what any dad would do and ate all of his children as they were born. Demeter, Hera, Hades, Hestia, and Poseidon. Down the hatch." The waitress's widening eyes indicated her appalled interest and he leaned closer and lowered his voice.

"By the time Rhea gave birth to Zeus, she was fed up with her husband's antics, so she gave him a stone wrapped in a blanket instead of baby Zeus. Kronos swallowed the stone without a thought." Hermes shook his head, "Clearly he didn't chew his food well enough before swallowing."

"But what about Zeus? What happened next?" Elbows on the table, head tilted forward, she waited for him to continue.

Her obvious interest should have been a good thing, yet it irritated him, "Zeus, the hero of your son's novels? He heroically hid behind some fauns. He was raised in secret, and once adult, poisoned his dad, Kronos, causing him to vomit up whole each of his swallowed children. Now that's indigestion." He had started this conversation, so why was he acting like such a jerk? He attempted to shift the tone with humor, "Well, you'd know all about indigestion working here."

But she answered matter-of-factly, "I never eat here." She glanced over her shoulder at the sour face of an older woman at the Hostess station and raised her voice, "I'm on my break." Turning back to Hermes, she leaned closer, "But what happened? When he threw up his babies? That is seriously disgusting."

Her enthusiasm grated. It seemed humans couldn't get enough of dear old dad. His therapist would point out that it was he who had introduced the topic of Zeus; in fact he had forced the conversation to this very point. His internal analysis was interrupted by the overly minty breath of the waitress, as she leaned forward, hand on his thigh, and asked again, "How did Zeus save them?"

All the potential fun with the waitress was gone. He affected a tone of bored arrogance hoping it would put an end to her attention. "They weren't babies anymore. They had grown while inside Kronos, and emerged from his mouth as adults. Trust me, nothing breeds bitterness like spending your formative years in your father's intestinal track. Together the regurgitated offspring staged a coup to dethrone their dad and the other Titans. As the final act in the war Zeus, your heroic Zeus, cut his father up into tiny pieces and imprisoned him in Tartarus, a pit below the lowest level of Hades— thus fulfilling the very prophecy Old Kronos had tried so hard to avoid."

His tone had worked to remove her hand from his thigh, but she stayed seated, such was the allure of the King of the Gods, "Zeus killed his father?"

"Well, not technically. You can't actually kill immortals, but with Kronos shredded and locked away, he definitely caused Zeus fewer problems. Now, if you wouldn't mind..." and he looked pointedly at his laptop.

But she barreled ahead, "Well Kronos was evil. I mean, he ate his kids. Zeus was the good guy. A hero for defeating him, right? I mean he was protecting his brothers and sisters. Fighting for justice." She nodded her head and actually made that ridiculous fist lifting movement associated with her last statement.

The confident pronouncement filled him with an anger he hadn't anticipated, and he stared at her for a full second before answering, "Humans are so obsessed with good and evil. Good and evil are moot as they relate to the Greek Gods. Zeus and Kronos were neither good nor evil. One had power and the other took it. Period. Power. You want to know what your hero Zeus did with that power? He conned his brothers into drawing straws for the kingdoms. Would it surprise you that Zeus drew the longest straw and became ruler of Heaven and Earth, banishing his brother Poseidon to the Sea, and leaving the Underworld to poor old Hades? Power. Not good or evil. You know what Zeus did when he was unhappy in his first marriage? He ate his wife. Talk about the sins of the father. For his second try at marriage, Zeus married Hera, the most powerful of his sisters. Then he spent his time screwing half the female population because he could. A father killing, con artist, matricidal, sister marrying, serial sleaze. Zeus the Hero."

The waitress was slowly easing the tray off the table, holding it in front of her as if to defend herself as she stood up, "I'll be right back with that beer, sir." The glasses on the tray were wobbling and he realized that she was shaking. A quick scan of the other patrons' stares made him realize that in the midst of his speech he had started to yell. A little. Damn it, he didn't mean to scare her. Giving himself a mental shake, he slowly closed the laptop, slipping it into his messenger bag. He was done here. He would have to finish his work at the University Library.

Why should he care what people thought about Zeus? It was unlike him to lose his cool, he was Hermes, the life of the party, the easy going one. The god most likely to defuse a bar fight. But if he was honest with himself, he knew that he devolved into a dick whenever the topic was Zeus. Add in his half-brother Apollo, god of the sun, such a clear favorite of their father, and he tended toward colossal dick. And though Zeus hadn't said as much, he knew that this job he'd been working on with the college girl was all about Apollo.

When Zeus had described the job, he'd asked Hermes to determine if the girl was a good match for the "gift." As Zeus described what powers the "gift" entailed, Hermes knew that whatever Zeus had planned, it had to be connected to Cassandra of Priam, a crime against humanity with Apollo's golden fingerprints all over it. And in his humble opinion, this "gift" was idiotic, certain to end in disaster – which would mean a disaster for Zeus and Apollo and whatever absurd end game they were pursuing with Hera's money. Which was, if not a good thing, certainly entertaining. He should be focused on enjoying their failure.

But the knowledge that the "gift" was likely to be a disaster for the girl as well made him uncomfortable. And so he had sat here in this stanky Tex Mex joint struggling to swallow pissy beer, scaring waitresses out of sex with classics lectures delivered with a little too much vehemence, while he experienced the vague twinges of guilt; a human emotion he found particularly tedious. He should just give Zeus the big thumbs up, take Hera's money, and find a good vantage point to watch it all implode.

Looking up, he saw a large man with "manager" written all over him walking toward his table. It was fine. He was done anyway. Pulling money out of his wallet, he tossed it on the table and started to leave, plucking the bill out of the manager's hand. Hera was a stickler for receipts on an expense report, and he would be filing that with his assessment of the "gift girl" within the hour. The manager wordlessly pointed to the door, and he saw his waitress hovering by the kitchen, watching. He could have tried to explain his outburst, attempted to charm the manager and waitress into excusing his anger, but there was no point. He knew what he needed to put in the report. He wouldn't be back here again.

CHAPTER THREE

The Truth Will Set You Falling

●●●

Hannah

Navigating the Labyrinth

Entering the University Bookstore, Hannah skirted around the clusters of students and parents buying up University tchotchkes and hobbled right into the overenthusiastic display of graduation robes hanging from a wire strung across the store, with a sign proclaiming, "Pick up Your Robes this Week or go to Graduation Naked!" Pushing through the red slippery robes like so many sheets hung on the line to dry, Hannah considered how many students would seriously consider taking them up on that offer. When this day from hell was over, she would need to sit down, preferably with her leg elevated and an ice pack on her ankle, and add, "get graduation robe" to her to-do list. She would not go naked.

But for now, she needed to keep her eye on the prize: collect her reprinted thesis and turn it into the Honors College long before five o'clock. Then, on to the other items on her to-do list. Despite her fall and wasted time sparring with John, she was still on schedule. That seemed a slight miracle, but she wasn't going to question it now. Tomorrow, in the company of her ice pack, she would break from her normal habit of focusing on what happens to consider why things happened. Like why she had slept for seven hours in bright daylight. Or why, on a day where nothing should be going wrong, everything seemed to be going wrong. Tomorrow seemed like a day ripe with possibility and the leisure to speculate. Today she had no time to wonder.

Once she got past the crimson robes, she saw a line that was winding down the stairs and into the Copy Center, located in the basement of the Book Store. That's odd. Maybe that was the line to pick up Yearbooks? Leaning against the railing, she wondered if there could be a special pick-up-your-thesis line downstairs? She hoped so.

Favoring her twisted ankle, she hopped past the people waiting in the line. Some of them were oblivious to her passing, playing with their phones, ear buds plugged into devices, but others had clearly judged her as a scofflaw, intent on cutting. Telling herself she was just going down to check, she ignored the rolled-eyes of the judgmental and kept hopping, hanging on to the railing to move down the stairs one-footed. When she got to the bottom, she realized the line was much longer, as the Copy Center had broken out the velvet ropes of crowd control, and the line snaked back and forth like a Labyrinth.

Her unease growing, she hobbled past the packed-in hordes to the front desk. There were only two clerks working, and they both seemed intent on not seeing her. This was bad. Clearly there was no "special" pick-up line. She could feel the eyes of the other students on her back, drilling into her. Her head had started to throb in syncopation with her ankle. It did not take a genius to determine that if she went to the back of the line there would be no time for the self-medication in the form of a vodka shot prior to dinner with Helene and Roger. She would be lucky to make the Honors College deadline. She was faced with a choice; she could accept the line or make an attempt to finagle her thesis out of this. She heard her mother's voice in her head, "Hannah, *Ladies' Home and Hearth* says that a woman aware of her own power can make anything happen. " That might have sounded downright feministic if only it hadn't been the advice on how to get out of a speeding ticket by flirting. Flirting was not her strong suit, but desperate times call for desperate measures.

Hannah straightened her shoulders and assessed the field. There was a man and a woman working at the checkout. This being Whitfield, either could be a good target for attempting to use her questionable wiles to cut the line. The woman had dyed black hair, dyed black clothes, and was openly scowling at the hapless student digging in his backpack for his wallet. Remembering that she was dressed in a way that might alienate the sensibilities of the typical Whitfield woman, regardless of her sexual orientation, she opted to focus on the guy, a man with a thin goatee on an even thinner face.

Trying to channel her inner flirt, she used her most guileless expression, "Excuse me, I'm sorry to bother you, but I was wondering if you could tell me where the line is for confirmed reprinted theses? My pick-up time is 2:35...."

Goatee-boy handed the student in front of him her receipt, and then gave Hannah a kind smile and spoke slowly, so that she could understand, "The end of the line is at the top of the stairs, behind you.."

Returning the smile, Hannah swallowed down her discomfort and chose her most innocent tone. "Oh, I know that, I don't mean this line. See, I have a confirmed pick-up time, and I have to meet my boyfriend's parents for dinner." Leaning in to confide, she attempted to display some cleavage and failed miserably in her conservative dress. At his slow blink, she shifted gears from seduction to pity, "I can't be late. They already hate me." His face remained noncommittal. She scrambled for something that might move him, lowering her voice she confided, "They blame me for introducing their son to swinging. We are joining a swingers' commune after graduation. Free love, man...am I right?" Panicking, she begged, "Um, if you could just look in the back, I am sure it's there, I had a confirmed pick-up time...."

Something had worked, because he looked over his shoulder, and then bent forward and whispered, "Well, if you have a confirmed time to pick up...What's your name?"

She felt the rush of adrenaline as she opened her mouth to answer, but then the other clerk looked over, and without missing a beat on her cash register, barked," They all have confirmed pick-ups. To the back of the line, Miller, tell Marilyn Monroe there that she has to go to the back of the line." The triumphant look she shot Hannah sealed her fate. And like that, her attempt to circumvent the system was stopped in its tracks.

Giving her a sheepish grin, Miller took a second to jot a phone number on a slip of register tape and handed it back, murmuring "Sorry, I wanted to get it for you... Good luck... Call me about your commune... You know, free love," and turning to the line yelled out, "Next!"

Crap. That's what she gets for channeling her mother. Hannah headed back toward the stairs. Avoiding eye contact with the others in line who had clearly witnessed her botched attempt to circumvent the line, she could not avoid their sniggers as she hobbled past and started hopping up the stairs. Looking up, she saw that the line had actually grown since she had made her fruitless attempt at cutting, and she felt her desperation start to ramp up. Was the end of the line now wrapping around the Bookstore, somewhere behind the graduation gowns? Forget the drink before dinner; she might be looking at failing to make the 5pm deadline. She felt the cold snake of panic curl in her stomach. But as she hopped up the top step, an arm whipped out and pulled her into the line.

"Here honey, I saved your space while you used the bathroom," John stepped back, making room for Hannah in front of him and confided to the guy behind him in a stage whisper, "she has such a small bladder— you should see how much trouble she has finding bathrooms— they have an app for that, you know— finding bathrooms for people with tiny bladders. It's called "My Wee Pee.""

Already ramped up, Hannah failed to suppress her instincts and elbowed him with her free arm, complaining, "Are you insane?" She lowered her eyebrows discouragingly at the guy behind John, who was now looking speculatively at her, clearly wondering if a small bladder was something that could be detected externally.

John, feigning contriteness, said loudly, "Sorry Kitten." and then leaned back to the guy and continued, "She's sensitive about it, but I tell her that she shouldn't be embarrassed. She should stand up and fight for the rights of the bladder-impaired. Wouldn't she make a cute spokesmodel? And the rallies; hundreds of people chanting, "I need to pee" while standing in front of rows and rows of porta-potties. Now that would make a statement!"

The guy was nodding enthusiastically and despite herself she smiled. She hopped down the next step, shaking her head. Grabbing the banister, she ignored the fluttering in her midsection as John mock whispered in her ear, "So what did your recon mission uncover? Any weaknesses we can exploit?"

She hadn't asked for his help with the line, she hadn't asked him to whisper in her ear, she hadn't invited him to forget who they weren't to each other. They were not friends. Only barely acquaintances. She ruthlessly suppressed not only her instinct to joke back, but could not control the creeping blush spreading across her cheeks. It was completely ridiculous for her to find him remotely appealing. And he had talked about her bladder to a total stranger. Despite finding *Ladies' Home and Hearth* to be an anachronistic collection of banalities, *LH&H* had very strict guidelines about discussing bodily functions in public that she happened to agree with.

Slipping her iPod out of her purse, she looked to end the connection, "Thank you for the place in line, and for, well catching me, before, but I have to catch up on some work."

He raised an eyebrow at the shift in conversation, but merely replied, "No problem." Hannah turned and inserted her ear buds of solitude. She had spent the last four years not talking about anything with John MacCallister; this was not a time to change.

Just as she was getting into her favorite podcast, the Hellenist Hour with Herb, a must for the classics major, her peace was shattered by the high-pitched squealing of a woman throwing her arms and sundry around the MacMan. The woman rear-ended Hannah as she herself was pushed aside by her two friends, who also made maximum body contact with him— at one point all three women were hugging him. John seemed pleased with the configuration; he certainly didn't protest. Just leaned back against the railing and resting his arms along the backs of two of the women, the third pouting about her lack of physical contact. At least that was how it looked to her. Hannah pushed her ear buds tighter into her ears, but still could hear him answering their eager questions. Was his band really breaking up? Would he be at Sandra's tonight? Did he have time in the week to join them on a road trip to the beach? Would he be wearing a robe at graduation or going naked? Would he be interested in a private trial run of the naked graduation march? Okay, that last one she made up, but it was between the lines of what they were asking him.

In that moment Hannah became aware that John was aware that she was staring at them and clearly listening to everything they were saying, despite her ear buds. He smiled that goddamn charming smile directly into her eyes. Eyes she promptly rolled at him.

Scowling, she turned away and noticed that the line had moved quite a bit while she'd been watching John and his women. As she hopped down, she found that she was now at the bottom of the stairs and in view of the large clock hanging behind the counter, five past three. While the line in front of her was still very long, twisting and turning back on itself, it was moving at a steady pace and she felt her spirits rise at the realization that her budgeted sixty minutes of wait time might prove to be accurate.

She indulged in a private reverie of how the rest of the day would fall obediently into line. She imagined herself gracefully waltzing into the Honors College and coolly handing her thesis to the Margins Nazi, no worry on her brow. Then she strolled to the restaurant, a better restaurant than the one they had reservations at, this was her daydream after all, ordered a gin and tonic, a more potent drink than the vodka shot, and as she finished it, turned and welcomed Carl and his parents, not a hair out of place. Carl would propose, she would accept, and Helene would pretend to be happy for them.

Surfacing from her daydream, she stepped forward, tentatively putting weight on her twisted ankle only to get more good news. Though the ankle barked at her, it held her full weight! The line was moving in front of her and she stepped forward. Everything on her list would fall into place and her attention to detail would provide her with the outcome she deserved.

The Myth of Cassandra

But as she entered the mouth of the labyrinth, she suffered a setback. The goateed cashier, Miller, was leaving. She watched him slip his backpack over one shoulder and reach under the counter for his bike helmet. He was clearly not just taking a break. Then he looked directly at her and made the international sign for "call me." Hannah smiled weakly and gave him a half-hearted wave.

The line groaned as Miller left the room and the trio of women behind John seemed to whine in unison, the tall one wagging a finger in her face, "Man, it is totally un-cool of your boyfriend to leave us all here, waiting..." The people around her seemed to join in the complaint and a generalized griping filled the room.

John's voice cut through the complaining, "I wonder how Carl would feel about you picking up guys at the Copy Center. He never struck me as the "open relationship" type."

Her frustration at the public misperception created by Miller's sign language was eclipsed by her shock at the mocking accusation in John's words. How the hell did he know about Carl? The trio of sirens around John was now laughing, slyly speculating about Hannah's ability to be in a three-way, and the steam of her embarrassment filled her mind. She found clarity at being annoyed at John, and spun on her heel, ready to tell him where to get off. But before she could rip him into the shreds he deserved, she felt a dizzying pain shoot straight up her leg and her ankle buckled; for while it could hold her weight, her ankle apparently was not up to indignant spins. And for the fourth time in less than an hour, John MacCallister saved her. He reached out and caught her elbows, lifting her up and against him to keep her from falling.

Her hands landed on his chest and as she struggled to keep her entire body from pressing against him, her head landed just south of his collarbone. Her brain must have derailed because she momentarily forgot all of her righteous indignation and shooting ankle pain. The sole thought in her mind was, "He smells really good." That thought was interrupted by him ducking his head down to look in her eyes, and now the how-good-he-smelled thought was joined by the how-pretty-his-eyelashes-are thought and she almost didn't hear him ask, "Are you okay?"

Luckily, like a train finally catching the tracks, her brain kicked back into gear with a vengeance and she pushed him away, hopping backwards on one foot, arms pin-wheeling to remain upright, all the while berating him, "Why do you keep catching me? If I am destined to fall, all you are doing is interfering with my destiny, MacCallister." With years of ballet class coming through, she found her center on her good foot and followed up on her initial indignation, accusing finger punctuating her words, "And how do you know anything about my boyfriend and our relationship status?"

Tilting his head to the side, he appeared amused, and in a voice loud enough to carry, "Did you have enough ventilation when you emptied that can of hairspray on your head? Because I think I just heard Hannah Summers, the Mistress of Rational Thought, the Den Mother of Descartes, invoke the irrational concept of Destiny. What's next? Are you going to read our auras? Triangulate our star signs?" He ended with a flourish, arms wide, clearly playing to the now avidly attentive line.

Hannah's eyes narrowed. Some part of her brain registered that she had lost her grip on her most prized possession, her control, but the rest of her brain was seething and didn't care. Not only were all her carefully laid plans for surviving the dinner tonight dashed, but the odds on her getting her thesis in on time were getting worse and worse and she was standing in line being mocked by the one person she had never managed to manage. "Mistress of Rational Thought? Really John? Was that supposed to be clever? Who are you? The Sultan of Bull Shit? The Preening Purveyor of Pretentiousness?"

"Easy now..." He was holding his hands up as if she had a gun trained on him, "All I have done to you today is keep you from hitting the ground, repeatedly." There were more laughs and some applause at this pronouncement, and he bowed slightly, "And yet it wouldn't surprise me if the next words out of your mouth are to tell me to go to Hell."

Those very words were on the tip of her tongue, and her shock at his prescience must have looked comical to the eavesdropping students in the line, because there was a definite spate of tittering. The sound only added to the surreal feeling that her life had been rapidly unspooling since she fell into that pothole. Despite her rising anger she reminded herself that this was no time to devolve into some crazed woman yelling insults at someone who meant nothing to her. Taking a cleansing breath, she leaned in close, trying to keep it just between them, "Answer the question, John. How do you know my boyfriend?"

John closed the distance between himself and Hannah. Gone was his sparring smile and in a heated whisper, he was all accusation, "How is it that you have been in a relationship with Carl for three years and you don't know how I know him?"

Was he talking in riddles? Had she breathed in too much hairspray? Confusion was swamping her, the sudden intensity in his eyes unnerving, and she shook her head.

He closed his eyes and seemed to make a decision, for when he opened them his tone was even again, almost conversational, though his volume was pitched for her alone, "Carl and I were first year roommates. Clark Hall. We became really good friends. Best friends. I've been to his house for more than one Christmas and we spent the last two summers living together in Boothbay Harbor, Maine, while we worked at the Lobsterman's Co-Op."

Hannah opened her mouth to disagree, to deny, to reject this outrageous claim, but he held his hand up and she closed her jaw, still somehow swamped by the situation, and let him continue unchallenged.

"We are like brothers. Brothers. Over the last three years Carl has talked a lot about you, but the Hannah Carl talks about is all sweet and nice and accommodating. According to Carl, you never lose your temper." At this he just looked at her for a long beat.

The heated protest exploded out of her. "I don't lose my temper. Ask anyone!"

His look encompassed the crowded room, and she snarled, "It's your fault! You just provoke me..."

"I provoke you? I seem to remember that you were the first to draw blood. Western Civ was a total waste of time. Except for that argument with you. Now that was fun. You were this enigma in class—sitting there silently judging every word— yet never speaking. So freaking tightly wound. It was a relief to hear you finally say something. You were rude and snarky and smart. You were actually interesting."

Over the course of his confession, his casual demeanor had given way to something more intense, and he leaned in closer to her face, not leaving any time for her reply, "I never thought that one argument would derail you. When you disappeared from class I just assumed you'd found a loophole in the requirement and had something better to do with your Mondays and Wednesdays. It was only after Carl started dating you that I found out that I'd upset you." He actually seemed angry. It was more than she could process.

Pressing her hands over her eyes, she tried to sift through his words. This was so much information and all of it so startling, that Hannah had trouble breathing. In and out, Hannah, in and out. How was it that Carl was a friend with, no, apparently best friends with, her nemesis and she had no idea? She started to run through events in her mind, looking for clues to orient herself to this new information. She remembered telling Carl how much she detested John. Had he said anything in response? She had visited Carl in Maine; he had told her his roommate had gone out to sea lobstering. She had never met him. Was that John? She did remember Carl making a vague reference to having company home for Christmas. That would explain Carl's mother, Helene's, more cryptic comments about "Carl's special friend." Carl's special friend loved her pancakes. Hannah was lactose intolerant and couldn't eat them. Carl's special friend told the most entertaining stories. Helene openly yawned when Hannah was talking. Carl's special friend always gave the most thoughtful hostess gifts. Helene was allergic to the scented candle Hannah had brought. At the time, she thought Helene had made up a fictitious past girlfriend to torture her with. But now she realized that Carl's special friend was none other than John MacCallister. And the confusion of her feelings around everything John had just told her coalesced into one simple emotion: rage.

"You're the special friend Carl's mother loves so much?" Finally giving into the urge, she hit him in the chest and it felt good, "That is so typical of you. You just fly out to Ohio and ooze your MacMan charm, complimenting her dreadful cooking, telling your amusing stories and giving your embossed stationary and leaving me to try to live up to that. I can't tell you how many times I had to hear about how amazing Carl's "special friend" was."

And now she was hitting him in syncopation to her accusations. "Of course it was you. You have made my life hell all because you have a pathological need to be liked and admired. You didn't provoke me in class because you liked my intellect; you provoked me because I didn't like yours. You couldn't stand it that I didn't find you brilliant. And now after enduring the humiliation of literally falling all over you and finding out that my boyfriend never felt it was important to tell me that he was best friends with the one person on campus I can't stand, I have to go to this dinner and sit across from a woman who seems biologically incapable of being nice to me! I will have to endure an entire meal of hidden barbs and backhanded compliments. And Carl is all worried because he knows his mother hates me! Why else would he ask me to look like this? Because his mother hates me, but she loves you! So you win, John. All hail John MacCallister, loved by everyone!"

Hannah found that she was winded from her yelling and hitting, and she tried to catch her breath, breathing in and out, in and out. She was starting to see spots, and the floor seemed to be tilting. The impending humiliation of fainting and being caught again by John MacCallister made it even harder to hold onto consciousness. Everything went dark.

●●●●●●●●●●●●

Zeus

In the driver's seat...

Client Report: The Cassandra Gift

REVEALING HANNAH

Fleet Footed Investigations, LLC

24 Valentine Lane, Bennington, VT 05201 (802)-220-9080

The Client has requested a background check and investigation into the character of Hannah Marie Summers, hereafter referred to as H. Client requested the specific focus of the investigation was into forming an opinion of how well suited H might be to receive the "Gift"- the terms of which were stipulated by the client- and after receiving it, how amenable H would be to use it for the good of the Olympians.

To accommodate the client's schedule, I conducted the investigation at an accelerated pace. The investigation began at seven forty-five on Monday morning and the report was submitted to the client at two that afternoon The investigation included a period of first hand observations, interviews of H's known associates, a sub-conscious scan, and review of her memories and thoughts.

H is a twenty-one year old female in good health. She is of medium height, medium build; average. She has long blonde hair and grey eyes. She is generally considered pretty by all accounts, though she does not appear to put much effort in her appearance. She appears to have had one serious relationship during her college years and is making plans to marry.

She is graduating from Whitfield University at the end of the week after spending four years earning her bachelor's degree with a major in Classics. H's transcript reveals a 3.87 GPA and shows no administrative actions taken against her for the duration of her degree. H has worked for the University as the student assistant to the Curator of the Classics collection for the last three years and has been hired to assume the Curatorship at the completion of her degree.

H will be receiving Honors for the submittal of a Senior Thesis entitled, A Taxonomy of Horticultural References in Greek Mythology. A quick scan of the thesis reveals it to be simply an academic endeavor to classify and organize said references and offers up only a tentative analysis of the implications of the taxonomy. While the work demonstrates thoroughness to H's scholarship, the lack of any meaningful analysis is consistent with the character of H as confirmed by this investigation.

From both direct observation and interviews with H's known associates, H does not have a history of making statements of her beliefs or thoughts. More than one person indicated that they felt she had strong

The Myth of Cassandra

ideas and opinions (and this was confirmed by the subconscious/memory scan) but that for reasons that were not obvious, she does not share them.

What she does seem to share is a willingness to accommodate the needs of others and help when help is needed- she is described both as nice and quiet. While this investigation could not find anyone beside a long-term boyfriend and her advisor who seemed to have a personal relationship with H, there was a clear absence of any detractors. This seems to be the direct result of H's reticence.

H avoids all forms of conflict to the extent that I could find only one example of her arguing, and that story came from a questionable source. This would indicate that H might be suitable for the "gift"- her desire to accommodate stronger personalities along with her basic attractiveness, intelligence, and considerable knowledge about the Olympians would make her a perfect candidate for the gift as described by the client.

However, it is important to note that both the subconscious and memory scan indicate a much more complicated picture of H's character. The subconscious scan revealed strata of repressed thoughts and feelings set aside for the last 10 years. Taken in conjunction with her memories that indicate unresolved issues between H and her mother, it is this investigator's opinion that H may be heading for a cataclysmic event that will alter her very strategy for living. Humans, though creatures of habit, seem to be wired for major emotional upheavals approximately every decade, and H seems ripe for this. So though on paper she is the perfect candidate, it is not advisable to "gift" this human at this time.

Please see attached itemized expenses and remit at your earliest convenience, Thank you for your business.

Respectfully submitted,

Hermes

Head Investigator

Fleet Footed Investigations, LLC.

Hera finished reading the report aloud and handed it to Archer, shaking her head. "Well, I guess it's back to the drawing board. What a shame."

Zeus frowned. Hera's expression of disappointment was patently insincere. He'd always suspected that she'd never intended to follow through with his and Apollo's return to power. She'd just been waiting for the report to put an end to it. It wouldn't have been hard to convince the Messenger to spin the report against giving the gift. That boy had always had an axe to grind with his brother, Apollo. Watching Hera turn back calmly to her cooking, so self-satisfied, rankled. But the look of shock on her face at Adams' next words soothed his temper. It was entertaining to watch someone get the better of his wife.

"Don't fret, Hera. It says right here that she is a perfect candidate for the gift!" Archer turned his back to Hera and addressed Apollo and Zeus, "We're started on the path to the glorious reclamation of Olympus, men! Lee, do we have any inspirational music selected yet? Something between the Star Wars Theme and Pachelbel's Cannon. Catchy and classy. Get right on that. We'll want that in place at the start of the news cycle. Also, we need a powerful graphic. Something with thunderbolts. Zeus, can you do the honors right away and gift the girl?"

"Don't fret? Are you a moron? Or merely illiterate? What part of "not advisable" means "yes, do it" to you? Hermes' report clearly states that the girl is NOT a good candidate." Her volume had grown with each word, and by the end she was yelling, "I will not put up with your sleazy inanity anymore!" and she slammed the garlic in her hand down on the counter, the cloves scattering.

Zeus admired her form; Hera threatened made for great theater. She got less careful and more nasty. He leaned back in the kitchen stool to watch how Adams would respond.

In a deeply condescending tone the publicist uttered the three words Zeus knew his wife hated the most, "Calm down, Hera." From his vantage point, Zeus watched the small smile that played over Adams' face disappear as he pivoted slowly to face Hera. Adams had more balls than he'd given him credit for. "I can understand why you might be nervous about Zeus reclaiming his power. I'm sure that you've been very comfortable in the driver's seat since the Fall, but you will need to adjust your way of thinking to accommodate Zeus as the head of the household once again. I am sure that he will be fair with you. Right, Zeus?" The publicist turned his back on Hera, while handing the report to him,

"What I see when I read this report is that every fact and observation Hermes has reported confirms that she is the perfect candidate. It's only Hermes' opinion that she is unsuitable. You aren't suggesting that Zeus, The God of Lightening, should bend to the opinions of a lesser being? You do believe Zeus should be ruler again, don't you?" Turning back to face Hera, the publicist's eyes were wide in feigned disbelief, a single eyebrow raised in question. Damn. He was either the moron Hera accused him of being or he was a genius.

The sound of Hera's teeth grinding shouldn't have satisfied him so deeply, but it had been a long time since he'd seen her thwarted. His wife was no fool. The publicist had boxed her in, twisting her objections about the girl into a referendum on whether she was for or against her husband. Zeus stared at her waiting for her response. Hera cornered was unpredictable.

Gathering up the scattered cloves of garlic, she spoke slowly, eyes averted, "I would never suggest that Zeus should defer to Hermes, only that we paid for Hermes skills as an investigator, and it seems to me to be a waste of our money to ignore his full report. Nevertheless, if Zeus feels like this is indeed the best candidate for the "gift", then by all means get to it. I look forward to a future where Zeus has his rightful place."

Zeus smiled. Worth the price of admission. Hearing his bossy wife submit to his authority felt almost as good as eating a fresh, warm, brownie. His brownie analogy was interrupted by the plaintive cry of his son. He'd forgotten that Apollo was in the room.

"Wait, you meant to say Zeus and Apollo, right? That we both get to our rightful place being worshipped again? I mean, I was the dealmaker here. I found Archer and this was my idea and I say we give her the gift. I say we do it. Now!" Apollo turned to him, expectant, "It's reparations for my curse, I should be the one to give the gift, right Dad?"

Zeus surveyed his wife, son and the damn publicist. All three were staring at him, awaiting his decision. He grimaced. The last time he'd been in a position to weigh in on a plan of Apollo's had been back in his throne room before the fall, discussing the same case they were in essence discussing now. Cassandra. His boy had come up with a brilliant way to deal with a difficult woman. If you can't stop them from talking, you could at least insure that no one paid any attention to their carping criticisms. So he'd sided with Apollo and let the curse stand, despite the Oracle's dire warnings. But it was said that the woman's inability to warn her family about the Greeks hiding in the wooden horse had lead to the defeat of Troy. Like a Sunday morning quarterback, Hera had argued that it was in the aftermath of the Trojan War that humans had started to defect to other less meddlesome gods. His wife had the annoying habit of being right about a lot of things, and he knew that he should probably listen to her now. But Archer's comments had stung. It'd been damn emasculating to live under that woman's smug success. He was the goddam god of thunder and lightning, ruler of the Olympians. It was his call to make.

Except that, in the intervening years since the Fall, he'd found that making decisions was not as satisfying as it used to be. There was always someone to complain about the choice you made, always someone to second-guess you. Leadership was lonely, brutal and stressful. All he wanted to do was to look at some of the negatives he'd developed before this had all started. And maybe eat some brownies. But before he could do that, he needed to make a decision about this girl and the gift.

He looked into Apollo's defiant, needy, beautiful face and found again that he couldn't deny him. "Apollo will give her the gift. Now. Call Hermes, he still delivers for the gods. He can find the girl and get it done. Adams, you should do whatever it is that you do to make this work. I have to check on something in the basement." He avoided Hera's glare and Adams glee, both badly masked, as he escaped the room to the chorus of Apollo's thanks, accidentally stepping on the strange little computer man.

⚫⚫⚫⚫⚫⚫⚫⚫⚫⚫⚫⚫

The Myth of Cassandra

Hermes

Beware of Gods bearing gifts...

He'd been minding his own business, literally. Going through his mail, sitting at his desk, and eating Tums to counteract the results of greasy Mexican food mixed with cheap beer. He had been content. Sure there were a lot of bills, but there was also a letter from his realtor in Port Angeles, Washington. He really only worked to make enough to pay for his summers in the Pacific Northwest. The PN had it all: the Pacific Ocean, mountains, some trees of a decent age, and best of all, no mosquitoes. Interesting fact about life as a post-Olympus immortal; mosquitoes are attracted to you, but can't bite you. This caused the stupid bugs to swarm him, as if they were trying to break the code. So he liked to spend his August on a sweet houseboat that he'd been renting for the last decade and watch the sunset over the ocean completely unmolested by bugs. He'd been running a little short for his June deposit when he'd gotten the call from Zeus about this gift girl. The timing had been perfect. He'd checked her out, delivered the report, and when Hera paid his bill, he'd be set. Expecting a confirmation of his rental dates, he opened the letter.

Dear Mr. Hermes,

I am sorry to tell you that the houseboat you've been renting for the last ten years is not available this year. The owners are selling. They are willing to give some of their past renters first bids on the house prior to listing it. I know how fond you've been of this property. If you are interested in purchasing it, call me, I have enclosed my card. We will need to act quickly as it is in a highly desired location, and we only have until Friday to make a pre-market offer.

If a purchase is not in your plans, I would be happy to forward you listings for other rentals.

All the best,
Verna Springs
Pacific NW Realty, Port Angeles, WA 360- 452-2363

He read through the letter twice. His own houseboat. Available all the time. One of the envelopes he'd shoved in his desk drawer was the statement from his bank, and it didn't take an investigation for him to know that he didn't have enough money to buy the houseboat. Yet. But this was Monday and he had until Friday. That was a week to find the cash. Or make it. If only the new US bills weren't so complicated to counterfeit. He'd had a great time in the '80's making money.

His next thought had been that he needed to make a list of ways to get the cash. Catching himself mirroring H, he smiled genuinely, glad that he'd decided to advise against gifting the girl. However much of a nut job that girl was, she did not deserve to be saddled with that kind of power.

No sooner had he thought those words than he received a terse phone call from Hera, instructing him to appear at her home to retrieve the gift from Apollo and then find the girl and give it to her. Hera was clearly pissed off, and vented her irritation all over him, while he had to stand there silently and take it. She was the boss. So off he flew to Martha's Vineyard to pick up the gift. Apollo had made him kneel before him to take it. What a prick.

So here he was now, in the parking lot of the bank across from the Book Store, looking for the girl. He bent over to pick squashed bugs out of his clothes. Flying in the spring was messy. With each bug he flicked off he muttered to himself, "How typical for them to completely ignore what they don't want to see!" Flick. "I'm not being paid for my opinions." Flick. "This is a no-win situation for me, now. If everything goes well, they get to say, "I told you so." Flick. Flick. "And they won't hire me for another job because clearly I suck." Flick. Flick. Flick. "If things go badly," flick," even though I warned them," flick, "they will blame me," flick, "for letting them," flick, "do something I could have seen going wrong," flick. "What the hell is up with all the goddamn bugs!" A gaggle of students wandering past with graduation robes in hand looked over at his cursing; reminding him that he might want to internalize his rant if he wanted to get in and out with a minimum of fuss.

The Myth of Cassandra

He angled his head and bared his teeth in the car side mirror, checking for more bugs, and considered the irony of his current position. In his profession he'd found it helpful to have a working knowledge of human psychology. There was a name for his situation, when the person who warns people about a bad thing they think is going to happen is ignored, and then when the bad thing happens, that person is blamed—sociologists call it the "Cassandra Effect." Nice. He could win the prize for Most Ironic God.

Wending his way through the crowded store, he continued his monologue, being careful to keep it a mental monologue, "Whatever. I'll deliver the "gift" and then place a few ads on cable access, as there is no way the Queen of Clean will be sending me any business now. Forget the houseboat. Hey, maybe if Apollo's scheme works and the Olympians get some followers I can cash in. I am a god, after all."

Reaching the bottom of the stairs, he spotted the girl yelling and hitting some boy in the line. Perfect, the cracks he had noticed in her tightly bound life were already expanding. The young woman he had investigated would never have yelled at anyone, much less engaged in a public brawl. He had warned them she was heading toward some breaking point. And they had ignored him. So now he had a job to do. He stood watching her sway and fall towards the floor. The Line Boy caught her.

Clearly she'd fainted. That was convenient. It would help that she was unconscious. A gift like the one he had to give her, well it wasn't like a birthday present. Like one minute you don't have it, and then you unwrap the package and pow! You've got it. No, this gift would take some time to percolate. Like a pot of really good coffee. If she hadn't fainted he would have had to induce unconsciousness just to pass it to her. So with her lying prone in that boy's arms, the time to pass it was now. The consequences were none of his business.

It was so simple. He offered to help the Line Boy carry H to the back of the store and held her hand, passing the gift in a matter of seconds. A goateed boy lead the way to an office and Hermes slipped out the exit, up the stairs and into the alley. He kicked the dumpster, and then sank down onto the stack of cut up boxes. It was such a powerful gift. He'd tried to convince himself that he'd been wrong in his assessment. That she'd prove to be an excellent candidate for this kind of power. It wasn't his fault. He'd told them she was unsuitable for the gift.

Cursing, he stood up and accepted what he already knew he'd do. He'd stick around, just in case. Humans were such sticky creatures. He wasn't attached to H, just having a little trouble shaking her off. It wasn't like he really cared what happened to her; he was just looking out for himself. He'd be blamed if something went wrong, so it was in his interest to see how she held up under her "gift."

CHAPTER FOUR

In Full Effect

❋❋❋

Hannah

On the floor

When Hannah came to she was being cradled on the floor and she looked up into the worried, goateed face of Miller the clerk. She blinked and resisted the urge to look for John, who had probably listened when she told him to stop catching her. Except that someone must have caught her, because aside from feeling disoriented, she was not in any pain. Groaning she relived the moments before she had fainted. She had acted like such a freak; yelling and hitting another human being. A human being she would probably never see again. Which was probably for the best; if you took today's events and their one argument four years ago, it was a pretty grim history.

She looked up into Miller's wide eyes, but before she could speak he was hushing her. He leaned closer, much closer, and asked her how many fingers he was holding up. Fingers it was impossible to see since her field of vision was completely filled with his face. "Um, I'm Okay, Miller, I think. Can you tell me what happened?"

He released her and rocked back on his heels as he launched into his story, oblivious to Hannah's muffled cry as her elbows hit the floor, "What happened? I had forgotten my bike lock, I seem to be forgetting a lot of things recently— I hope I don't have early onset Alzheimer's— I read about it on WebMD and I think I have 8 out of the 10 top signs, but

I haven't seen a doctor yet because I keep forgetting to go...oh man... that's another sign..."

"Miller? Me? What happened to me?"

"Oh, yeah, that was pretty freaky. I had forgotten my bike lock and just happened to be walking by and saw you yelling at that guy. And then you stopped yelling and went all limp—like you just kind of melted. I thought you might have had a stroke, you know, from being so angry, but that guy you were hitting said that you had hyperventilated and fainted and a couple of us carried you back here. John, the guy you beat on, he said that we needed to get you to a cool room where you could lie down. So we carried you here; it took three of us. You're kind of heavier than you look, you know. Though you are still totally cute, even though you kind of look like pictures of my grandma— when my grandma was young, and you know, cute. John said that you'd be fine and that I should get you to drink some water when you wake up. So here, have some water," and he held his water bottle to her lips.

Hannah sipped. Looking around her, she figured they were in a staff break room. Even with the lights out she could make out the plastic chairs and the smell of burnt coffee. Slipping her feet under her (someone had removed her shoes) she knelt up and tested her head. She didn't see any stars, and she felt steady enough to stand up.

"Whoa, he said you would try to go too fast. Man, that dude is prophetic, you know. And super cool. He said to tell you to take it easy, you just woke up and you need to take it slow."

A new and alarming thought hit Hannah, "Woke up? How long was I out? What time is it now? I have to get back to the line— I can't lose my place in line— where are my shoes?" and she started crawling across the floor searching for her shoes in the dimly light room.

Miller actually started laughing, "Dude! He so knew you were going to say that— 'she's gonna wake up and want to go so you keep her here'— and man, he took your shoes and I thought— weird why take her shoes? And I must have said, weird, why are you taking her shoes? And he said— 'so she won't go rushing out before she's recovered.' And man, the first thing you did was look for your shoes— check it out— just like he said. Wow, does he have your number. Is he a member of your secret swinger's commune?"

John took her shoes? What is he up to? Hannah shook her head to clear it, felt the room shimmy and quickly put her head between her knees, "I'm sorry, Miller, but there is no secret swingers' commune. I made that up to try to "distract" you into helping me cut the line." At Miller's audible gasp, she barely even paused. She could indulge in shame after she turned in her thesis, "I need to know the time. Do you know it?"

Miller was shaking his head and Hannah felt tingling in her feet and fingertips. She had to find out what time it was and get back on schedule. "It's okay if you don't have the time, Miller, but could you at least help me get back to the main room— there is a clock on that wall..."

Miller reached into his backpack and pulled out a phone, "I have the time; it's four thirty-five. I just can't believe that there is no super secret swinger's commune. That totally sucks. I was really jazzed about that."

"Did you say four thirty-five? But that can't be right. It was only a little after three o'clock when I got to the bottom of the stairs. How can I have possibly lost so much time? I was unconscious for ninety minutes? That doesn't make sense. I have to get out of here, I have to get my thesis, and I have to get to the Honors College." Looking down at her feet trapped in the nude pantyhose, Hannah made a decision, "I have to take these nylons off." And she started wiggling and yanking at them. She climbed onto one of the plastic chairs to get a better angle on pulling them off.

Miller's eyebrows shot up appreciatively at the sight of Hannah pulling off the nylons. Swallowing convulsively, he choked out, "Whoa, easy now Hannah. You weren't unconscious for ninety minutes. Man, that would have been super serious. No, you were only unconscious for about two minutes and then you woke up and asked for John. He checked your pulse, and told you that you were going to be fine. Then you told him how tired you were and he told you to close your eyes and rest and he would take care of everything. You said "thanks" and then drifted off to sleep, so sweetly man, it was beautiful. John told me what to do when you woke up, took your shoes and left. And then you woke up, and now you are taking off your clothes and man, I guess I can figure it out as we go." He proceeded to remove his sneakers.

Hannah frowned at the sight of Miller unlacing his high-tops, and then it fell into place. "NO! Miller! Keep your shoes on! I am not taking off my clothes, just these tights so that I can move faster. I have to hurry! I don't know why I was so tired, and I don't know what John meant by "taking care of things," but I have to get my thesis now! There is still a chance I can turn it in on time. You have been so great to sit with me but I feel much better now. Can you please lead me back to the front desk?"

She couldn't see Miller's face as he was bent over retying his shoes, but she heard his answer nonetheless, "Yeah, sure I can take you back to the front desk, but are you sure you don't want to wait for John to bring your shoes back? He promised to take care of everything. I've only known him for ninety minutes and I trust him. I mean, he is really looking out for you, and he let you sleep because you were really tired. That's why you slept. You were tired. Fainting probably made you more tired. You know I read on WEB MD that if you don't get enough rest your body will simply take it. Oh man, you could be narcoleptic! Do you fall asleep driving? Have you ever fallen asleep in your soup?"

"John is coming back? Are you sure?" Hannah leaned back in the chair, balling up the nylons in one hand. Man, it felt so much better to have totally free legs. Oh no, now her internal voice sounded like Miller. Before Miller could answer her question or be the second person that day to theorize about what other ailments she might have that would cause her to sleep at odd times, the door opened and there stood John; her ugly, white pumps in one hand and in the other, six envelopes containing what had to be his and her theses. Three copies each, properly formatted and bound and in manila envelopes. He smiled at her and handed her the shoes. "You look better. How's your balance? If you need another minute or two to be steady— you should take it. But then we have to fly. I can make it to the Honors College in five minutes on my Vespa, but we can't do that if you're still feeling dizzy."

"How did you get the clerk to give you my thesis? She didn't strike me as the accommodating type?" She stretched out one hand to take the shoes, while she clung to the bottom of the chair with the other, her instability not physical but psychological, as she struggled to assimilate this new turn of events. He was being so nice, and she had been so, well, unfriendly.

John pulled a silent movie charmer smile, "I just tapped into my pathological need to be liked and convinced Eloise that bending the rules this once would be really great of her." He lifted one eyebrow. "How are you? Can you balance?"

He had waited in line and, after charming the formidable Eloise, he had picked up both of their theses. And now he was offering her a ride. She had so many questions, but she wasn't sure she wanted the answers. So she asked the only question she could handle, "Eloise?"

Miller piped in, "Eloise is rock solid, man. And she lives every day with a deviated septum. That takes courage."

John nodded, "I'm sure it does. You are rock solid as well, Miller." He clapped a hand on Miller's shoulder, "Thanks for keeping an eye on her." As Miller blushed, John turned back to her, "Do you think you can ride? We have to move if we are going to graduate, and Carl needs you to graduate. "

Why would Carl need her to graduate? Like, sure. Appreciate, maybe. Even want would make sense. But need? She knew that she needed to graduate, but she hadn't even told Carl about the job yet, so what was John talking about? It would have to wait. John was right about at least one thing; the clock was ticking. She slipped the shoes on her bare feet. Standing on her left foot, she pirouetted slowly without a single bobble. Excellent. She met John's questioning look, "Six years of ballet."

Turning to Miller, she hugged him. "Thanks Miller. Can you thank Eloise for me?"

Miller nodded absently while frowning, "Are you sure you're not a narcoleptic, Hannah? I don't think a motor bike is the safest...."

John held the door open, "I'll make sure she doesn't fall asleep, don't worry."

Miller grabbed John around the middle and hugged him enthusiastically, "You're the best, man, the best." John smiled and hugged him back.

With their goodbyes said, John and Hannah walked out together, having navigated the Copy Center Labyrinth victoriously. Energized by her second bizarre sleep and having forged a tentative, albeit baffling, alliance with a former nemesis, Hannah straightened her shoulders and set forth to do battle with the Margins Nazi. All according to plan, more or less.

❖❖❖❖❖❖❖❖❖❖❖❖

Hera

Dinnertime

"So how will this work? Will it affect everyone? It won't affect us, will it?" Archer's query of Apollo carried into the kitchen where Hera was working on dinner. So Archer finally had questions. She crushed the garlic with the side of her knife. Well it was about time. He'd taken over the living room as his office, barking orders at his minion since Zeus had made the decision to let Apollo gift the girl. Not once had he asked about how gifting humans worked or what it might mean for them all. It wasn't as if the girl was getting a box of chocolates. She was getting the power to influence large swathes of the population. She was getting the undivided attention of the average person. Hera felt like her brain was spinning on the possible catastrophes this gift might unleash. This anxiety was new for her. None of Apollo's other schemes had ever actually come to pass.

She turned on the faucet and rubbed her hands on her stainless steel egg, washing the garlic off. So much could go wrong. Moving the cold, smooth egg from one hand to the other she tried not to think about all the ways this "gift" could blow up. For the first time her worry was weighing heavier than her annoyance and it made her feel unsettled. She turned off the water and walked to the doorway between the kitchen and the living room where Archer and Apollo were talking.

Apollo was pacing and giving off small sparks as he made a circuit around the room, "If Hermes didn't screw it up, she got the gift about 30 minutes ago. At first, it'll knock her out, but then she'll just feel it building inside her, and when it is fully built, it will start to affect others. We won't be affected because we know about the gift. If anyone figures out about the gift, they won't be affected either. It will also be less effective on anyone who has reason to doubt her honesty or sincerity. But that is what's so beautiful about our girl!" Apollo turned and caught sight of Hera in the doorway and his smile became luminous, "I've been going over Hermes' report, Auntie, and I think the power is going to work on virtually everyone. I mean, if his investigation was any good. It seems like she has barely spoken to anyone in years and when she does talk, she says nothing anyone is bothered by. No one dislikes her because she's a nobody. Why would anyone doubt her?"

Hera couldn't just stand there. Drying her hands on her apron, she frowned at Apollo's glowing optimism, "But what about the rest of Hermes report? She isn't some simpleton who hasn't expressed herself because she has nothing to say. She chooses, for whatever twisted human reason, not to say things. What if the gift changes that? What if she isn't so easily led? What if she can't handle the attention and she melts down? Remember what happened to Cassandra?"

Apollo walked up to Hera, gently clasping her shoulders, "Don't worry. Everything's going to be fine. I just have a good feeling about this. Besides, she's going to love having the attention, what woman wouldn't? Especially the shy and retiring types. This will be her dream come true! She'll be so grateful she'll be like putty in our hands." Giving Hera one last squeeze, Apollo turned back to Archer, "Cassandra's pathetic history isn't relevant here. A curse is supposed to make your life miserable. A gift will make this girl's life magical."

Hera opened her mouth to argue, but Archer beat her to it, beaming while he clapped Apollo on the back, "You are so right, Apollo. Magical! Do you think she will have the power yet?"

"It should be soon now, any minute. So what's the plan? Have you worked out a script for her? I've been thinking about the things I want to do once I regain Mt. Olympus. Would you like to see my list? " Hera walked out of the room not wanting to hear Archer's answer, more worried by Apollo's manic optimism than she'd been by her own pessimism. But the die was cast and all she could do now was wait.

Cooking had always helped when she felt agitated. It was so concrete. She went back to working on dinner. She was making Zeus' favorite; coq au vin with grilled asparagus and roasted baby potatoes. He'd gone down to the dark room immediately after making his decision and had surfaced only once, and that had been to ask if they had anything made of chocolate in the house. She'd only been able to produce some baker's chocolate and before she could explain that it was unsweetened, he'd eaten it with a straight face and asked if there was anything else. At her head shake he'd slumped back down to his lair and hadn't resurfaced. Yet.

She wished she could talk to him. He had the power to end this, but he was doing a fantastic job of hiding. She hoped the smell of the cooking chicken would tempt him to the table where she could make her case to stop this train wreck. Archer's high-pitched voice cut through her thoughts and she tried not to listen and to focus on cutting up her mushrooms. But it was impossible to ignore.

"I have been working on the script for the girl non-stop. All my plans rely on her saying just the right things..."

"And your plans are for me and Zeus, right Archer? All we have to do is have her encourage people to worship us again. That's the plan, right?" Apollo sounded concerned for the first time, and Hera suspended the knife in mid-air straining to hear Archer's response.

"That's not just my primary goal but my reason for living, Apollo. I've been killing myself on this project, but if you aren't happy with my work..."Hera brought the knife down hard, gritting her teeth to keep from butting in. Apollo's reply was only too predictable.

The Myth of Cassandra

"No, no, no, of course I'm happy with it, I'm just worried about the script for her. I mean, does it just come down to her saying, "Hey, this is Apollo, worship him"...?"

"Apollo, buddy, I think this neurotic coast is affecting you. In all my life I have never heard you utter the phrase, "I'm just worried." Insecurity does not look good on you, my friend, and I need you looking good. The gift will go perfectly and within twenty-four hours we'll have our first press conference. You wait and see. Hey, I have a movie premier in LA this weekend. What do you say? Friday we hop a flight west and immerse ourselves in beautiful women? It's been too long, hasn't it? Because the god that convinced me he could rule again would never experience anything as banal and common as doubt. Leave that to the humans. And Hera."

At Apollo's enthusiastic rejoinder Hera threw up her hands in frustration, sending the knife she was using winging across the room to lodge firmly in the closed door to the basement. Though the target had been entirely accidental, Hera's anger found a focal point as she pulled the quivering blade from the door. Zeus' continued absence was intolerable. If he would only get up here and put that manipulative jackass Archer Adams in his place, she could stop this ridiculous hovering and get back to her own work.

It was just like Apollo to ignore the signs that he was being used. He'd always been a vain and silly boy. She needed Zeus. Turning her attention to the mangled mushrooms on the cutting board, she sighed. She would have to start again. Screw coq au vin. If Zeus could hide in the basement, leaving her alone to wait and see what would happen next, he could have his chicken from the Colonel. Pulling the cork on the wine, she decided that if she needed to wait alone, she could be Hera au vin.

CHAPTER FIVE

Inappropriate Attractions

❊❊❊

Hannah

Facing the Margins Nazi

Hannah led the way through the Bookstore, weaving in and out of the chattering clusters of customers and burst out onto the street feeling a new determination filling her. It must have been her impromptu "nap" in the Copy Center break room because she felt great. Like she could take on the world, let alone one puny college administrator. She held the door open for John who had his hands full with their theses.

She followed him to where she'd fallen into the hole in the sidewalk and rotated her right ankle, pleased that it seemed to have benefited from her time off her feet too. John bent over his moped, unlocking it and pulled something from the basket in the front of the bike, "Here's the spare helmet. I am not sure what it will do to your hair, but...." Hannah took the helmet from him and shoved it on without hesitation. She wanted to graduate this Sunday and a hairdo wasn't going to impede her. She heard a distinctly crunchy sound as she attached the strap under her chin. Hair couldn't actually break off, could it?

Noticing the smashed bits of her phone in the street, Hannah felt a kernel of relief. She'd hated being tethered by a phone, but Carl had given it to her on their three-month anniversary. He said it only made sense that she carry a cell phone— everyone did. He had also spent three months trying to reach her and not being able to. She wondered idly if

The Myth of Cassandra

Carl was, at this moment, trying to make contact with the mangled plastic carcass of what had been her phone. He'd been so pleased with the gift, she hadn't wanted to disappoint him by explaining that she had purposely never gotten a cell phone— it gave her mother way too much access. So she had smiled, thanked him, and had been carrying it with her for the last three years.

While she had never grown fond of the phone, she had begun to rely on it for telling time, and had stopped wearing a watch. She looked over at John. "How much time do we have?"

John strapped the theses into the front basket and looked at the watch on his wrist, "It's four forty-five— we're going to make it. We have to assume that there might be a line at that end as well, but as long as we are in the line prior to five, I will not take no for an answer. I can be unrelenting when I need to be, you know?" And he shot her one of his quirky, and yes dammit, charming smiles.

Hannah smiled back. "Well if sound argument fails, we could always unleash your Mac Man persona on her. I hear that the Margins Nazi likes younger men…"

John shuddered and climbed onto the powder blue Vespa, scootching as far forward as he could to make room for Hannah on the back. "It's going to be kind of a tight fit. I promise to think of you like a sister."

Hannah didn't comment as she had hit a bigger problem than having to wrap herself around the Mac Man to get to the Honors College on time. Her dress was so straight that she couldn't figure out how to straddle the bike. She couldn't even shimmy it up her thighs. Why would women ever wear clothes like this voluntarily? It made everyday movement so tight and small. Remembering that she had loaded the clutch purse Carl had given her with her emergency supplies, she dug in and emerged with her Swiss army knife. "This will just take a second." And flipping through the tools on the knife, she opened up the tiny scissors, "These will do." But before John could ask "do what?" Hannah had snipped up both side seams of the skirt an inch or two. It was just enough to let her legs move, but not so much that anyone would notice.

Dropping the Swiss Army knife back into her purse, she smiled at John, proud of her cleverness, and swung her right leg over onto the back of the bike and grabbed him from behind.

Before she could lock her hands around his chest, she simultaneously felt and heard the skirt rip up both sides so that now the slits were a good four inches above her knees. Crap. There was no way Helene and Carl wouldn't notice. Hell, even Roger, Carl's dad, would register her now daringly slit dress.

John looked down at Hannah's significantly exposed thighs straddling him. "Okay, now it's going to be a little harder to think of you as a sister. Hang on and lean with me when I lean."

And with that, he stepped on the gas and they shot out into the street. As they turned the first corner and drove past the Bookstore Cafe, Hannah smelled the distinct odor of French fries. When had the bookstore started selling fries? Turning left on High Street, she again smelled French Fries and tried to locate the source. But all she could see was the Religion Department and the Foreign Languages Lab. Why would they be making French fries? Taking a right onto Wilson Avenue, more fries. The smell was starting to make her hungry. When was the last time she had eaten? Yesterday? That might have had as much to do with her faint as the hyperventilating.

She would have to force down a couple of the stale rolls they served at Turlington's before she started drinking. It would be a bad idea to drink on an empty stomach. Because, along with the nylons she shed in the break room, gone also was the idea that she would drink before dinner. No, she was going to drink during dinner. As much as she needed to. Maybe if everything went smoothly at the Honors College they would have time to grab some French Fries before dinner.

John pulled into the driveway next to the stately Honors College House and put the bike in park. She hopped off and shed her helmet. Handing it over, she asked, "Do you know where they are selling French fries around here? I am starving! Maybe if we have a few minutes before dinner, we could grab some fries?"

The Myth of Cassandra

She couldn't see his face, as he had turned to exchange the helmets for the copies. Were his shoulders shaking? He was laughing! "What is so funny? I haven't had anything to eat today and I could smell fries the entire way here, so they must be making them somewhere."

With his back still to her, he explained, "I'm sorry, but there are no fries nearby. I converted my bike to bio-diesel. It has a somewhat distinctive emission. Some people like it more than others, and it is good that you are one of those people, because the smell has a tendency to cling to clothes, particularly wool. But I wouldn't worry..." John turned with theses in hand when his voice died off. He was staring at her, mouth agape. He managed a strangled, "What happened to you?" as the envelopes slipped from his fingers, spilling onto the drive.

Hannah had been trying to find a way to sniff at her dress, but this was harder than you might think, as she was now bending in half to smell the hem of her ripped skirt. At the sound of his shocked question she looked up to see John's eyes wide on her in a mimic of the horror movie stare. Well, that was melodramatic. "I know that my hair must be a mess, but I can fix it after we turn in our theses. Which are on the ground for some reason." She bent to pick them up and looked up into John's alarmed face, "I am sure it's salvageable, so you can stop looking at me like I am the creature from the Black Lagoon." She stood and turned toward the Honors College entrance.

John reached out and grabbed her arm, stopping her. "No, Hannah, it's not your hair, although that does look terrifying. It's this." Placing his hands on her shoulders, he led her to the rearview mirror on his bike, "It's these. Did you get attacked by angry bees on the ride over?"

Looking into the mirror she understood why John had thought that bees were responsible. Her neck and ears were covered with angry looking red welts that seemed to be growing even as she watched. She dropped her head, shaking it. Things had seemed to be going better. As her head hung down, she felt the unmistakable tingling in her lips that indicated the allergic reaction was spreading. When she looked up, John actually jumped back. "Hannah, your lips! What is happening to you?"

He looked sincerely worried, so she quickly explained as she handed him the theses and reached into her purse for the Benadryl, "Don't worry. It's just an allergic reaction to the necklace and earrings. I just have to drink some of this, and it should fade in 20-30 minutes." She tipped back the bottle and drank, not bothering to measure out the dose. She extended her hand for the envelopes, but he just looked at her, the worry on his face morphing into what looked like anger.

"Are you telling me that you planned on this possibility? That you knew it was likely that you would develop hives if you wore the jewelry Carl asked you to, and he made you wear it anyway. I mean, I know that Carl can get pretty keyed up around his parents, but he never struck me as such a self-centered ass. To ask you to wear something that could hurt you just to impress his mother is ridiculous. And why didn't you refuse, instead of just packing a bottle of Benadryl in your purse? What is wrong with you?" The accusation hung in the air between them, and she looked away, wanting to snatch her copies from his hands. Not wanting this conversation.

"Don't blame Carl. He doesn't know that I have allergies." At his continued glare, she kept talking, "I wore them because sometimes I don't have a reaction, and it meant a lot to him, and it was just for one afternoon. Besides, I was hoping that the antihistamines I have been taking so that I could wear this ring" and she flashed him the gaudy promise ring, "would protect me from the hives. In case it didn't, I brought the Benadryl. It's really no big deal. So now that we have that out of the way, shall we turn in our theses?" She took all six copies out of his hands and started walking towards the Honors College door, ignoring her tingling lips and the last look she had seen on his face, where anger seemed to have degenerated into disgust.

He caught up with her and held open the door. As she walked through she narrowly avoided bumping into Cynthia Dixon, Honors College Administrator, aka the Margins Nazi. Her apology stuck in her throat as she looked into the woman's eyes and saw only dispassionate emptiness. Ms. Dixon had her hand on the other side of the door, keys inserted into the lock. Her look took in both of them and her eyes nar-

The Myth of Cassandra

rowed, "You got in just as I was locking the door. I could refuse you, but I will be generous. You are the final two I will accept." And with that, she closed the door behind John and rotated the key in the lock. Not two seconds later the sound of some poor senior trying the door and then realizing his failure resulted in a howl of anguish, which made every senior inside the Honors College cringe. The Margins Nazi simply smiled and walked back to her desk, calling out with surprising volume, "Next!"

Hannah followed the line in front of her and stepped forward, avoiding looking back at the ominously silent MacMan. Who was he to judge? If she didn't tell Carl she was allergic to jewelry it was because she didn't think it was important that he know. It wasn't like she was lying to him. No matter what John's accusing look had implied. If she had told Carl, he would have had to change his plans and it might have lead to more stress, and she didn't think either of them needed more stress. Anyway, she had dealt with her allergies her whole life and could handle her choices just fine. She knew the potential risks and how to counteract them. It wasn't like she had a really serious, life-threatening allergy. It was simply an annoyance she could handle. It was nothing to feel guilty about. Why was John making such a big deal about it? How dare he try to make her feel like she was some kind of liar because she wanted to handle this small annoyance privately?

Anger at John seemed totally wrong, though, as she knew that the only reason she was standing on this side of the locked door was because he had decided somewhere in that hellish line at the Copy Center to help her. She would have to be the one to break the silence and make peace. She was holding both of their theses, and the title of his jumped out at her, "The Politics of Distraction: The Systemic Obfuscation of Critical Issues in American Elections." That surprised her, as she had always pictured John as a Master practitioner of distraction. Why would the MacMan write an honors thesis that, from the title, seemed to be critical of the very behavior he seemed to have perfected? Maybe it was a "how-to"? Hannah resisted the urge to open the manila envelope and read the synopsis page. That would be rude. She could ask him about his work. But that went against years of practiced avoidance of this particular person. She felt a stubborn resistance to accepting this new and improved John as real. It was more than she could absorb, right now. This day had already overwhelmed her, and she was only partially through her to-do list. So she opted for a compromise. She could offer basic gratitude. Turning back to hand him his copies, she smiled, "Thank you, John. I never would have made it here on time without your help."

John's reaction was immediate, gasping audibly when he saw her face, "Are you sure that medication is working? You are much worse. How can you see? Your eyes are barely visible under the swelling. This is serious, Summers. I think you should go to the hospital."

As he said that last sentence, Hannah saw conviction take hold of his features and braced herself for an argument. This would be the second time today she would have to convince an overbearing person that she did not need to go to the hospital. She tried to appeal to his sense of reason, "It's a local reaction. The swelling should start to go down in the next fifteen minutes." Turning her back on him, she moved forward with the line.

But he seemed to feel that reason was on his side, stepping in front of her, he pointed at her face, "If it's a local reaction to the jewelry, why would your lips and eyes be swelling? Isn't that a sign of a more serious allergic reaction?"

"Well yes, it would be, but my lips and eyes aren't swelling up from the jewelry, but from the makeup I put on for this dinner. So see, just more local reaction. Absolutely no need to go to the hospital." John's brow had lowered at the mention of wearing makeup she was allergic to and looked prepared to launch into another lecture of how stupid she was, when she was saved by the Margins Nazi's crisp, "Next!"

Sidestepping John, she placed her three copies, properly formatted, bound and in manila envelopes on the desk and looked directly into the Margins Nazi's cold, dark eyes, reminding herself she had nothing to fear. Thesis done and submitted. Check. She would graduate and never have to face this terrifying woman again. But Ms. Dixon looked down at the copies and then back up at Hannah and said something Hannah had never anticipated, not in all her detailed lists, "Rejected." She pushed it back towards Hannah and called out, "Next!"

Pushing them right back at her, Hannah protested, "What do you mean rejected? It's formatted, bound and in the proper envelopes. On what grounds are you rejecting it? You can't reject it!" Catching her voice spiraling up, she took a quick breath and tried again in a softer tone, "Please, Ms. Marg, Ms. Dixon, look again. What is wrong?"

The implacable woman behind the desk sighed elaborately, as if she were repeatedly asked to explain to students why their work is found insufficient and unacceptable, "I don't know who you are. But you can let Ms. Summers know that it states clearly in the Honors Thesis Submittal Guide that all senior theses must be submitted in person to the Honors College. I couldn't fathom what she thought was more important to do than to do this herself, but I will not accept it from a third party. She will have to re-submit it in the fall. If she doesn't believe you, you may have her call me at this number," and she handed the gaping Hannah a business card.

"But I AM Hannah Summers, look, here is my student ID," and digging in her purse, she pulled out her photo ID, "See, she is me and I am her. We are the thame." That last word she said sounded a little fuzzy from her progressively swelling lips, and she closed her tight eyelids and sighed herself. Surely the swelling wasn't so much that she was unrecognizable. "I thwear that I am Hannah Thummers." She pulled the Benadryl from her purse and drank more.

The Margins Nazi studied the ID and looked back and forth from it to Hannah several times. "While I can see some family resemblance, you are clearly not Hannah Summers. I had to answer Ms. Summers' exhaustive questions in my office several times this semester, and I can state categorically that she is not you. Next!"

Hannah felt the absurdity change swiftly to panic, and she turned to John for backup, "John, please tell her it's me. If I don't graduate, I'll lose my job! Please...."

He bent to whisper in her ear, "I'll tell her if you agree to go to the hospital. I'll pop you by the restaurant so that you can explain quickly to

Carl, and then he can take you to the hospital in his car. That's the only way, Hannah. Otherwise I have no idea who you are..."

She knew she was trapped; without her thesis there was no graduation and all her plans were just a list on a piece of paper. So she would have to agree, but she didn't have to like it. John MacCallister was not some surprisingly nice guy, but just your run of the mill control freak. She had grown up with one and knew all about them. Blackmailing her into going to the hospital? Classic. Fine. She would agree and it would be a lie. Lying to control freaks was the quintessential two wrongs making a right. Ducking her head as if she were compliant, she murmured, "You win. I'll go." She dragged him to the desk to vouch for her.

"Ms. Dixon, I know this might be hard to believe, but this is indeed Hannah Summers. She's just suffering from a bad case of stupidity. She wore jewelry and makeup she knew she was allergic to, just to make her boyfriend happy. Brilliant, huh? So her face is all swollen from the hives. The hair is just a tragic mistake. And the dress, well that actually works for me..." Like an involuntary reflex, Hannah hit him in the shoulder, "Oof. Manners, Hannah dear," He rubbed his arm lightly with one hand while casually trapping her wrist with the other to keep her from further attack, "If you don't believe me, quiz her about the topic of her thesis, I bet that no one but her can answer you." And then he turned his lovely, charming smile on Cynthia Dixon, and Hannah saw the Margins Nazi actually blush. Good grief. Then it got worse.

"If you vouch for her, John, then of course I'll accept her thesis. Although why a woman would try so hard to be someone else for a man is beyond me. A real woman knows how to please her partner by pleasure alone. How sad." Without breaking eye contact with John, she held out her hand in Hannah's general direction, "I will accept your thesis to be considered for University Honors." Hannah quickly shoved her three copies at the Margins Nazi.

"Here is your receipt." She scrawled on a piece of paper and handed it absently to Hannah, her attention firmly on the next in

The Myth of Cassandra

line, "John, I have been looking forward to reading your thesis. Ever since I read your expose on the Centreville Mayoral Elections I have been a big fan. I've followed your work. So insightful and exciting. I would love to hear about your next project. You seem to have incredible instincts." Good god, the Margins Nazi really did have a thing for younger men, at least this younger man. Was there anyone immune to his charms? As Ms. Dixon handed John his receipt, Hannah could clearly see that she had written her phone number on it with the message, "call me" underlined. John merely smiled again and pocketed the receipt.

John's litany of insults had reminded her that she needed to make some repairs to her appearance before she could show up at the restaurant. To do that, she needed Ms. Dixon's permission to use the Honors College's bathroom. Well, if John was going to blackmail her into going to the hospital, then she could use him right back, "Ms. Dixon, would you mind if I borrowed the upstairs bathroom to freshen up? John can stay and keep you company. I won't take but a minute?" John had stiffened perceptibly at Hannah's offer, but Hannah felt no guilt about sacrificing him to the cougar at the desk. She walked away without waiting for an answer and she heard the Margins Nazi purr, "Tell me John, what's your sign? If I had to bet, based purely on the power of your presence, I 'd bet you are a Leo, I love lions..."

The Honors College was housed in one of the old mansions that had been home to the Centreville elite, back in the day when Centreville had an elite. It was all columns and molding and large gracious windows. The downstairs rooms were used for poetry readings, guest lecturers and string quartets. Hannah had spent many evenings here during her four years at Whitfield and knew the layout of the house. As she ascended the main staircase she looked back down to see that Ms. Dixon had cornered John in the front portico and seemed to be describing the painting hanging there while slowly rubbing her hand up and down his back. Hmm... though she had happily sacrificed him she didn't actually want him to get molested. She had better be quick with her repairs.

●●●●●●●●●●●●

Lee

Eating alone on Martha's Vineyard

Lee lay on the wool carpet in Hera's living room face first, inhaling deeply where Hermes had stood less than an hour ago. Mmmm.... Tacos and beer. Rolling onto his back, he closed his eyes and pulled up the image of the first time he'd laid eyes on the Messenger God.

Hermes. Everything about him was the epitome of cool. His bad boy looks, his gap-toothed smirk, even his winged shoes exuded testosterone. Only a man's man could wear delicate golden fluttering sandals and come off as cool as Bogart. Lee ran his hands down his lumpy exterior and hoped that Hermes had not noticed him yet. His basic shape was human, but his skill at transforming was still rudimentary. He tended to land between genders, as he had never mastered the pituitary system. Proper glandular functioning had a bigger impact on attractiveness than most people knew. Sliding his fingers through the carpet, he made a mental note to put a little more effort into his online demon coursework. After he ate.

Everyone else was gone or incapacitated. Apollo and Archer had taken off to hit the bars, keen to celebrate their eminent success with the plan. Not that they had remembered to invite him. He had found the girl, after all. He didn't blame Apollo. His lack of defined gender made most people uncomfortable, and they almost unconsciously ignored him. Archer was another story. Lee knew that his oversight was deliberate. He used every chance he got to make Lee feel unnecessary. Archer had resented being teamed up with him, but this mission had required a level of technical skill Archer just didn't possess. So the boss assigned them both. It didn't stop Archer from torturing him. Whatever.

The Myth of Cassandra

Zeus was hiding in the basement and had only emerged to get his pizza when it was delivered. Hera had somehow forced an entire chicken down the kitchen disposal before stalking to her office in the front of the house and kicking the door closed as her hands had been full of wine bottles. Neither she nor Zeus had made a sound since. Rising from the carpet, oblivious to the slight grease ring he'd left on the floor, Lee wandered into the kitchen and rummaged through the frozen casserole selection Hera had in the freezer. She may be terrifying, but she was one hell of a cook. Lasagna looked tempting, but he was in the mood for comfort food, and so he selected a two quart container of rendered fat. He sprinkled some bleu cheese on the top, added some raisins for color, and heated it with his breath. He didn't trust the microwave, and there was no one around to observe this break from his human persona.

Settling in at his computer with dinner on his lap, he started his daily report for the Boss. He played back the most recent events. Archer had done a masterful job of pushing for this girl and manipulating the Olympians forward with the plan, despite Hera's clear resistance to this girl. Lee had worried that Archer's insistence on this girl would ruin everything, but it had all worked out. He was still unsure why this particular girl was the one, but Archer hadn't discussed it with him. It probably didn't matter, any human would do. The key was to have the Olympians proceed with the comeback plan and give the gift to a human, and Archer had gotten the job done. Once Hera conceded to Zeus's judgment, Zeus had caved to Apollo's whining and commanded Hera to call the messenger god to deliver the gift. A simmering Hera had called Hermes and summoned him to the house.

And he had come, almost instantly. Hermes, even on bended knee taking the gift from Apollo, had managed to make subservient look masterful. Lee stared at the spot in the room where less than an hour ago Hermes had stood. Was there ever a man more compelling? A god more beguiling? A smirk more alluring? Lee took a huge spoonful of "dinner" and swished it back and forth between his cheeks, to better appreciate the delicate flavors. He wondered if Hermes liked cheese. Or lard? Swallowing, he came to a decision. The next time he saw Hermes, Hermes would notice him. The report to the Boss could wait. The plan was on track. Opening a new window on his screen, he logged onto The University of Arizona, Specialties Department, and entered his student ID. He had some glandular systems to master and a demon certification to attain.

CHAPTER SIX

Click, click, click

●●●

Hannah

The Honors College parking lot

With the Honors College door slamming behind them, Hannah and John tumbled out into the parking lot. Hannah doubled over, gasping for breath. John rushed to her side, cupping her shoulders in his hands, "Oh God, Hannah, can you breath? Are you. ...oh great!" Standing up and releasing her, he leaned away, "That's just great. No, keep laughing. It's funny, really. I mean, if you'd taken a few more minutes in the bathroom I was going to be learning much more than I want to know about the Margin Nazi's formatting preferences." Ignoring her laughs, he stalked to the Vespa and focused on disengaging the bike lock.

She couldn't tell if he was really offended or not, so she tried an apology. "I am sorry, John, really." But her apology was, at the least, diluted by her continued laughter, "I'm glad that I came down when I did. I definitely didn't imagine she'd be so interested in your "font" size."

At his pointed glare, Hannah's apology morphed into something more incredulous and she stepped closer to him, "Come on! You like to pretend you're some easy going easy loving hippy but the reality is far from it. Blackmailing me into going to the ER? Classic control freak move. I should know; I was raised by a master. I bet you sort your t-shirts on some spectrum of color and sleeve length. " It was a shot in the dark.

John's jaw tightened so hard she could have sworn she heard it crack. Before she could think, she started to laugh. His responding smile suddenly filled the space between them, and they were both smiling. In that instant the animosity that had been building simply evaporated. His next question sounded completely sarcasm-free, "What was taking you so long up there anyway?"

Hannah's smile faded. Rubbing the place on her finger where the ring had been most recently, she tried to play it down. "Oh, I lost the promise ring Carl gave me. In the toilet. It was one of those auto flush things, and it was stuck on my hand, from the swelling, and when I tugged at it, it fell in and when I bent over to look at it, whoosh! The toilet flushed. It's no problem. I'll replace it tomorrow. It was only glass and Carl will be none the wiser...."

Was that disgust on his face? How did things keep changing so quickly between them? "Nice, Summers. Why don't you just come clean to Carl and try telling the truth?"

The edge came back to her tone too. "Why don't you back off? Oh, right, because you are the bully who tried to blackmail me into going to the hospital."

The look on his face became carefully blank, but her instincts were telling her he was angry. Really angry. He turned his back to her and walked toward the bike and she held her breath, waiting for him to do something; yell, scream, mock her, something. Instead he reached for the helmets, and in a completely pleasant if slightly detached tone, faced her, "Speaking of that, let's get to the restaurant, explain everything to Carl, and head over to Mercy Hospital."

The specter of an Emergency Room wait made all other considerations pale. In the face of his calm certainty, she switched from attack mode to appeasement. "Look, I know I agreed to your terms, but don't I look better? I feel a lot better, like I have this internal energy pumping through me. I know the swelling is still pretty significant, but I can feel the Benadryl working and it would just be a massive waste of time. Can you please just drop me off at the restaurant?" And she extended her hand for the helmet, hoping he would relent.

Resting both helmets on his hips, he looked her up and down, "A deal is a deal, but I guess you do look a little better. A very little. The problem is that in the course of this afternoon I have learned that you have a real personal relationship with denial, Hannah, and that's your business." His voice took on an urgent tone. "But if you get hurt tonight because of it, I'd feel responsible, because I knew and didn't do anything. Does that make sense?"

No. Yes. How had the conversation developed so many levels at once? The moment stretched out. Some part of her brain, probably the part formed from years of being forced to read *Ladies' Home and Hearth*, dispassionately registered all the facts of the situation. They were standing too close. They were arguing one minute and laughing the next, the rapid change of tones in their words confusing. She had a soon-to-be fiancé who was waiting for her at the restaurant. Now. The part of her brain that had enumerated these facts commanded her to step away. Thank him for his help, say goodbye and walk to the restaurant on your own. Or...or she could do something else.

"I won't waste time arguing about why I choose to keep some information private from Carl. Let's say I accept your basic concern. Can we please just go to the restaurant? It'd be great if you could help me explain things to them. And by "them" I'm referring to Helene, who will torture Carl with this dinner if it's just me explaining why I showed up late looking the way I look, but if you tell the story, she's bound to find it charming."

Now that she had thought of it, she really wanted him to stay for the dinner. It made her feel less nervous. "Come on, if we hurry Carl won't be too annoyed. My swelling will be mostly gone in twenty minutes, so even if you just stay for a drink, you'll be able to see for yourself that I'll be fine, and then you can be free of me and my bizarre day. In fact, I insist that you let me buy you a drink to thank you." Hannah awaited his decision, hoping that he would hand her the helmet.

Her hopes started rising as the helmet floated toward her, "If you don't look significantly less large in the face after drinks, Carl takes you to the hospital: no arguments." At her nod he passed her the helmet and started strapping on his own, "I guess we do have to celebrate beating the Margins Nazi's deadline."

Relief filled her up and she moved to give him a quick hug, but her helmet became trapped between them. She backed away awkwardly, smiling, "Thanks. That's a deal. Let's go, I'm starving."

John climbed on the bike and waited for her to get on. Balancing on the back, Hannah stretched her hands out as the bike turned out of the parking lot and zoomed down the street. The feeling of the air streaming through her fingers mirrored the feeling inside of her as the stress of the day blew away on the wind. At least she hoped it was stress- something was definitely blowing away. How much Benadryl had she drunk? Didn't Benadryl make you feel sleepy? She was not remotely sleepy. She felt alert, aware, and weirdly sensitive. Not to mention talkative. Why was she talking so much? She felt like she was slipping into some type of altered state, and she wondered idly if this was post-traumatic stress. It had been an eventful day. She made a mental note to search online for posts about "stress and Benadryl." Tomorrow. Tonight she would celebrate.

Gripping John's hips to lean with the bike as they turned off High Street, her face made contact with his back, and she breathed deeply. How could he smell better than French fries? She breathed in again and tried to isolate the scent. It wasn't the smell of cologne or any other manufactured scent. He smelled like sun-warmed t-shirt with a subtle undertone of soap and something else.... she bit her lips and closed her eyes.

Get a grip, Hannah. It was embarrassing. Forget searching online for information on "stress and Benadryl," she wondered how many hits she would get if she searched for "horny and Benadryl." She needed to refocus her addled mind. Her mother had told her that *Ladies' Home and Hearth* said that inappropriate thoughts were best countered with the mundane. It was one of Elise's theories that church services were designed to be boring to quell any inappropriate speculation about what was under the priests' robes. Hannah had always thought her mother was crazy, but now, she wasn't so sure. Heeding the internalized voice of

The Myth of Cassandra

her mother, she scrambled for a safe topic. At the stoplight, Hannah tapped John's shoulder. "What are you doing after graduation?" Small talk. Her mother and LHH would be proud. Nothing more mundane and unsexy as small talk.

As this was Hannah's first time riding a moped, she didn't know that conversation could be frustrating on the bike. While the person in the rear can be understood fairly clearly by the person in front of them, due to the position of mouth to ear, the person in the front has to keep looking forward for the most part, especially when driving forward, so their ability to be understood is much less. What Hannah got back from John were fragments tossed back on the wind.

"I have a job at the Hartford Currant working at their…I hope to travel…like the appearance of serious…near my mom who is afraid … circus performers. I hope I can catch them with their pants…next year in Peru." He turned his head at the next stoplight and smiled at her. She smiled back and hoped that he hadn't just told her he was traveling to Peru to catch pant-less circus performers who had been scaring his mother. "What about you? Has it been hard to find a job without speaking the language?" and he turned forward to drive.

What? Not speaking the language? She must have misheard him. What language would you be expected to speak to work in the classics collection? She could read Latin and Greek— but her own translations were nothing to be proud of. That hadn't bothered Mr. Blean when he'd hired her. She leaned forward, "Language hasn't been an issue. I have a dream job lined up to start the week after graduation." Stoplight.

Looking over his shoulder, John's brow was furrowed, "Will you be going over that soon? Carl told me…" green light, "the end of July…a goofy picture…thought you had trouble with…a small box, but cozy."

Another smiling look from John she had no idea how to respond to. Had she mentioned the job to him when she was out of it at the copy center? Could he be referring to her going "over" as going "over" to the employee side of the University? Maybe he thought the school shut down until July? Had he looked in her purse and seen her employee ID? She didn't think it was goofy; maybe it was a little awkward. She always hated smiling for the camera. And what did he think she had trouble with? That was a mystery. But clearly his last reference must be to the apartment she would be moving into, which would probably be small, but calling it a "box"? Was that slang for something?

Going with the most innocent translation, she leaned forward again and answered in his ear, "It may be small, but it is really just for me. Carl will room with some friends in the city and we will see each other on weekends." John didn't respond to this, but Hannah didn't notice as she had just spotted Carl in the parking lot, frowning at his watch. She put on as big a smile as she could with the hives stretching her face and waved enthusiastically at Carl. But Carl kept frowning.

Even after she'd removed her helmet, Carl still looked past her, scanning the sidewalk for her approach. "Carl! It's me! I had a little problem with some allergies, and my face swelled up a bit, but the Benadryl has kicked in and I should be back to normal in twenty minutes." Helmet in one hand, she ran over to hug him, but he caught her shoulders in his hands and stared. She kept talking, "The great news is that I got my thesis turned in on time, with a lot of help from John." Carl had dropped her shoulders and she swiveled back towards John, handed him the helmet and murmured, "Thanks again."

But still Carl said nothing, though now he was looking back and forth between Hannah and John as if he was witnessing an anomaly of nature; like a five-legged goat or a two-headed frog. Hannah, more flummoxed by the continuing silence from Carl, threw herself into the breach again, "It's a really long story. I woke up this morning and found out my thesis was rejected by the Margins Nazi, and then I fell asleep for a really long time, which was weird, and then I fell into a hole walking to the Copy Center, well, not really fell into, that sounds like Alice in Wonderland, and though this day has been unusual it hasn't been that unusual, but to get back on point, these shoes are brutal and I tripped and managed to land on John, and in the process of waiting in the line learned about your friendship, and long story short, we both got our thesis turned in on time, so now we can graduate this Sunday. Isn't that great? And I've gotten to know John, so, I mean, you don't have to avoid him with me, and I invited him to stay and have dinner with us and your parents, but he might just stay for a drink, your mom will love that, don't you think? And I know that I look a little off, but I started the day picture-perfect, didn't I, John?" In her anxiety she looked back to John, who nodded his support. "But then I fainted, and the dress ripped on the bike, and the helmet squashed my hair, so I tried to fix it in the sink and the swelling, well, that's allergies, and I'm sorry that we're late, but I thought, better late than never..."

"Stop. Stop talking and give me a second to think." Carl turned his back to Hannah and proceeded to talk to himself in indecipherable grunts. Hannah refused to look at anyone; Carl's rebuke vibrating in her bones. She didn't normally rant like that, but he'd been so silent, and she'd had such a hard day, and all she'd wanted was for him to tell her that everything was going to be okay, and that he understood. So maybe she had been rambling, but that was understandable, right?

She closed her eyes. She felt the gravitational pull of one of those moments in life when you see yourself saying and doing the exact thing you have witnessed your parent say and do and you said to yourself, "I won't do that." Hannah's mind flipped through the Rolodex of moments when her mother had talked her father into submission when he was angry about something she'd done, as if the sheer force of her words could bend him into forgiving her and seeing her as the victim. Wasn't that exactly what she had wanted from Carl? Hannah straightened her shoulders, and in a quiet, but steady voice, attempted to rebalance the situation. "Carl, I made some unfortunate choices in trying to do too many things at once, and so I ended up late and a wreck for this dinner, which I know you put a lot of effort in preparing me for. I'm sorry." She reached out, resting her hand lightly on his shoulder, "What would you like to do about it now?"

Carl turned back to face her, his brow furrowed. "I'm sorry too, I shouldn't have snapped, but you look awful. Unrecognizable. It's shocking. Aside from the hideous swelling in your face and your soaked hair, you have managed to take what was the epitome of the respectable dress and turn it into a dress that could be worn by a stripper— how high do those slits go?" He stared at her legs. Under his scrutiny she instinctively tried to hold the sides of her dress together.

John piped in, "Strippers tend to favor machine washable fabrics, actually, and that dress is clearly made of wool, which is dry clean only..." They both shot him a quelling look, but he finished his thought, "I think it improved the dress, actually, but that's just me..."

Carl talked over him, "I'm glad you approve, John, but my mom will have a field day with it. Damn it, I just can't add one more thing they might disapprove of to this dinner..." He held his head in both hands, shaking back and forth, "I'm sorry, Han, I just had this really specific image in my head of what you'd be looking like." He peered more closely at her face. "That looks painful, you shouldn't be here." Turning to John, he had clearly come to a decision, "Can you take Hannah back to her dorm for me? You both know that I have a very important announcement to make at dinner, and Hannah, looking like this," and he swept his hand up and down, from her swollen eyes to her bare legs. "She will simply destabilize the table. Luckily my folks are inside having a drink and they haven't seen her yet. I'll go in and tell them that you came down with the flu and have been put into isolation at the Health Center."

Carl was nodding his head at them as if it would make everyone simply agree to his plan. Hannah wasn't sure if it was the Benadryl blurring her mind, but she was starting to feel as if she was missing some rather important information about this dinner. She mentally groped for a question to ask that didn't reveal her ignorance but would get her more information. Before she could ask, Carl's eyes widened in horror at the high-pitched squeal emanating from behind him.

"John MacCallister! You march over here and give me a hug right now!" John moved quickly to Helene's outstretched arms, trying to shield Hannah from Helene's view, but if Helene had noticed Hannah's appearance, she didn't let on and continued talking a blue streak, "I didn't know you were joining us for dinner! What a relief! We're just waiting on Carl's perennially aloof girlfriend to grace us with her presence. You must know her? That is one blonde who does not have more fun. She looks at you with those serious eyes and you just start to feel like you are back in Catholic School and the nuns are shaming you. We call her Hannah Lisa; she's like the Mona Lisa, because her eyes follow you everywhere, but without the smile. Serious with a capital "S." She is one grim dish." Releasing John she responded to Carl's offended intake of breath, "Oh don't make that face, Carl. You like her, and that's fine with me, but I don't have to like her." Swinging back to John, "Please stay and entertain us. You'd be doing us a tremendous favor if you could, you and your girlfriend."

At this point Helene focused on Hannah and said in her nicest hostess tone, "Hello honey, I am Helene Rogerson, and any friend of John's is welcome to join us."

Hannah simply stared, rooted to the spot. A Catholic School Nun, a grim Mona Lisa, "we" call her these names? Mocking from Helene was no surprise, but Roger too?

"Mom! This is Hannah, she was late because she... she... she had to get her wisdom teeth out, and the dentist had told her she'd be fine for dinner, but as you can see she's pretty swollen, so I called John to ask him to drive her home..." Carl started manically nodding now, a slightly crazed look in his eyes.

John flung himself into the gulf, "And the swelling blocks her Eustachian tubes— she can't hear a thing anyone says," John tapped Hannah on the shoulder and mimicked "no hearing" and nodded at her.

Hannah swallowed her laughter, not sure if it was hysterical or not, and raised her eyebrows at John, who shrugged back. She turned a huge smile on Helene and confirmed John's story by covering her ears and shaking her head while saying, "Can't hear a thing!"

John smiled at Hannah while he whispered, "Good thing for you, huh Helene? You dodged a bullet there."

Helene's laugh was definitely hysterical as she nodded vigorously at Hannah, smiling while clearly saying between clenched teeth, "Good God, Carl. She looks like a completely different girl— you had better hope she doesn't gain weight— her face is not attractive at this size. And what in holy heaven is she wearing? Is that what passes for appropriate for dinner with the parents?" Then in a loud, slow voice Helene continued, "HANNAH DEAR, SO GOOD TO SEE YOU? TRAGIC NEWS ABOUT YOUR HEARING. WE WERE SO LOOKING FORWARD TO DINNER WITH YOU. WILL YOU BE EATING WITH US?"

Whether it was a physiological reaction to having eaten no food that day or the incredible insincerity of Carl's mother, at that exact moment Hannah's stomach let loose a loud rumble. She was so hungry she didn't care that she would have to sit down with Helene, and she shot a pleading look at Carl who was shaking his head violently. On top of her hunger, it was starting to dawn on her that the big announcement Carl was going to make at dinner was apparently something she didn't need to be present for. Which seemed to rule out a proposal of marriage, didn't it? This thought had opened up a hole of worry in her stomach, making her even hungrier. She pressed her hands into her stomach.

John, witnessing the exchange, jumped in again, "Hannah hasn't eaten all day, due to the surgery, and the dentist insisted that she eat as soon as possible. He said the swelling would go down within the hour. So let's all go in." And he nodded forcefully at Carl, who seemed to finally accept that this dinner was going to happen and offered both his arms to Hannah and his mother to lead them in.

And with that all four walked toward the door; one with annoyance at having been made a fool of, one with dread for what would be revealed, one with irritation at best laid plans gone awry and one with the unabashed curiosity of a journalist. Despite everyone's inner commitment to get through this meal, none were aware that before they could even choke down a stale roll, this dinner would be over.

The Myth of Cassandra

Hermes

Turlington's Parking Lot

Hermes leaned back against the ancient Honda Civic covered in left-wing bumper stickers and watched H enter the restaurant with Line Boy, Boyfriend and what must have been the Boyfriend's mother. The mother's voice really carried. And not just in volume.

He should leave town. Gift delivered; job done. He should head back to Martha's Vineyard and collect his cash from Hera. No matter what happens to H, he'd done his job and he deserved his money. He had a few other clients who hadn't paid up yet. He could head out to collect. He should be focusing on the houseboat down payment; mosquito-less living twelve months a year. And yet.

H's gift was almost at full potency. It should be interesting to see what happens, and he decided he wanted a front row seat. He pushed off from the car and headed toward the alley behind the restaurant. No one will notice an extra busboy. Besides, H might need a little help. Not that it mattered to him what happened to her one way or the other. The "trickster" god does not get attached to humans. It was merely professional curiosity.

CHAPTER SEVEN

An Object in Motion

✺✺✺

Hannah

Dinner with the Parents

Having dropped Carl's arm the minute they walked through the door, Hannah tottered unsteadily towards the table in her white pumps, nerves singing. She resisted the urge to push her hands through her hair, knowing that they could get stuck in the residual hairspray. Priorities. She needed her hands to eat. She couldn't remember ever having this many intense feelings at once. Top of the list was hunger; when the smells of food hit her as she entered the restaurant she'd had to swallow to keep from drooling. In a close second was embarrassment. She knew that her face was swollen beyond recognition, her hair was a wild, wet mess and that every step she took in her now daring dress brought her one stitch closer to "full disclosure." At least she hadn't gone commando. Second runner-up: anxiety. Actually, it would be more accurate to say she was feeling ANXIETY. Carl's big announcement at this dinner was clearly not a marriage proposal, so what the hell was he so wired about? And how would it affect her? To top it off, due to his mother not recognizing her and being all kinds of rude, she now had to pretend to be hard of hearing. Perfect.

And then there was this strange feeling of power coursing through her veins. Could that be adrenaline? Does your body release adrenaline when you are experiencing the emotional trifecta of hunger, shame and worry? Sort of like the neurotic's second wind? Because even though the faces at the table had a slightly shimmery look, which she associated with a pre-cursor to fainting, she felt like she could run a marathon. It was unnerving.

Roger exchanged some perfectly friendly greetings with Hannah and John with absolutely no reference to Hannah's bizarre appearance. Then Helene explained about Hannah's oral surgery and supposed lack of hearing, which caused Roger to say hello again, just much louder, and they all sat down in silence. The waitress materialized to take drink orders, and before Hannah could open her mouth, Carl asked the waitress to come back in a few minutes, as he had something he had to say.

"Mom and Dad, I want you to know how much I love you and how much you mean to me. I know you had your heart set on us moving to Akron after we are married..."

What? Had Carl just said, "After we are married"? Had she missed Carl asking her to marry him? She frantically replayed the moment he'd given her the promise ring. What had he said exactly? "Hannah, this ring is a symbol of the promise I make to spend the rest of our lives together. Will you accept it?" She had. Crap. Was that a proposal of marriage? The proposal? How could she have misunderstood her own marriage proposal as a suggestion that they might want to consider getting married sometime?

And living in Akron? When had she agreed to that? Sure, he had told her how much he liked living near family, how important it was to him. And she had agreed. But "near" in her mind had been "less than a two-day drive" not "down the street from." Besides, she had graduate school and then an academic job hunt. They could end up in Nebraska for all she knew. Nebraska was the state she used to prepare herself for the academic wilderness she might fall into. Hadn't she explained this to Carl? Oh god, he was still talking and she had zoned him out in her panic.

"....so, I applied and they offered me the job. It's a once in a lifetime opportunity. I know it's a long flight, but Hannah and I would love to have you come and stay with us. Especially when the baby comes..."

Was this some sort of joke? She turned in her chair, looking for some film school student with a camera filming her "shock" at being punked. She was apparently as good as married moving someplace far away, having Carl's parents stay with them and having a baby. She tried to inhale and found it impossible. Carl looked deadly serious and there was no one with a camera hiding in the restaurant ferns. She looked up to see John watching her closely, and the realization that none of this was news to him washed over her like nausea. Hannah felt a spinning feeling start in her stomach as she struggled to catch up. What had John said about a language barrier? Where the hell had she agreed to go? Carl was still talking, but she'd only been hearing the spastic beating of her own heart. She stood up.

"I'm sorry Carl, but can you go back for a minute? Where is this job you are taking?" She felt her hands shaking and she made them into fists at her side.

Helene whispered to Roger, 'I guess her ears are clearing,"

Carl looked nonplussed and stared at her, while John murmured, "Japan."

Hannah's head swiveled between the two. Japan. No curatorship. No apartment to herself. No life of her own.

"Hannah, sit down. You're making a scene. We've talked about all of this." Carl's voice had that gentle but patronizing tone that made her teeth ache.

"I will not sit down. How can you say we've talked about this? This is the first time I've heard any of this or at least the first time I've heard it as if it is a done deal." At his stony expression, she felt more defensive, "You talk about a lot of things, Carl. You talk all the time. Just last week you were talking about the need to visit Venice before it goes under water, and I agreed, but we aren't going to Venice anytime soon...." Hannah stopped mid sentence at the look on Carl's face. "We're going to Venice?" More a statement than a question.

"For our honeymoon. I bought the tickets this morning. Prices are rock bottom in Italy right now." Carl's tone of patience was shifting to incredulity, "You know about all of this. The job in Tokyo. The wedding in Akron. The honeymoon in Venice. The baby in the first year. Why are you acting like you don't know about all of this? Is this a side effect of the Benadryl? Have you been drinking? Is that why you were so late?" Incredulity morphed into recrimination, "You knew this was an important dinner for me to tell my parents about our plans. All I asked you to do was to look nice and show up on time and you did neither of those things." Carl's voice shifted to a lower key, becoming more reserved and apparently calm, but his words belied his tone, and he stood up to face Hannah. "You're acting as if you had no idea about the most important decisions in our life. What the hell, Hannah? If this is a practical joke, it's not funny."

Something in Hannah snapped. Or surged. But she held up her hands and everyone fell silent. In the entire restaurant. "This is all wrong, Carl. I've made a terrible mistake. I've been so caught up in my own work and my own life that I haven't been paying close enough attention to you. But you haven't paid enough attention either. I can't move to Japan. I have a job lined up here that I am taking. It's a job I want. I care about you, but I will not turn down my life to follow yours. I'm so sorry if I led you to believe that I'd do that. I have no excuse for this," and she waved her hand at the table, "I should have listened to you. I just assumed you were thinking out loud. I didn't think it was important to disagree with vague notions. How could I know you were booking flights and naming our first born?" At Carl's gasp, Hannah pulled back, looked down. "I'm sorry. It's my fault. I should never have let you think that I would be happy to follow someone else's dream. I love you, but I'm not willing to follow you to Japan." Pushing her chair back, she reached down for her purse. "I'm done following anything but my own dreams. My entire crazy day today was toward one end: keeping my dream alive. I won't put it aside for anyone. But you should go to Tokyo. If it's your dream job, you should go and follow your dreams. We all should."

Tucking her clutch under her arm, she took a shaky breath. "I thought I could see our future together, but I was only seeing what I wanted to see. And I wasn't showing you anything you didn't want to see. I should have been honest with you from the start of our relationship. We all deserve honesty. I'm so sorry Carl, but I have to give this back to you," and she reached down to pull off the ring, only to find a naked finger. The memory of how she lost the ring flooded back to her and she flapped her hands, at a loss.

Carl didn't seem to notice. He was nodding, a strange look in his eyes. Scanning the room, she realized that no one was moving, not the waiters or the other diners. They were all looking at her and nodding. Everyone except John; he seemed to be the only other person not in some bizarre trance. He was looking around frowning. He moved to stand, but Carl pushed him back into his seat.

"I want you to hear this too, John." Holding Hannah's shoulders with both hands, Carl smiled sadly, "You're so right, Hannah. I don't know how I didn't see it. Thank you. Everything you say makes perfect sense." He hugged her in and then held her out again at arm's length, "I thought I loved you, but maybe I only loved how much you seemed to agree with me. I feel like everyone else in my life argues with me. And you always seemed to think I was right. It was the best feeling in the world. But now I know that you didn't agree with me, you just didn't bother to disagree. Thank you for telling me. I appreciate your honesty, even if it makes me really sad." Looking at his parents, "Mom and Dad, I'm moving to Tokyo. It's my dream. Oh, and in the interest of honesty, I took grandma's ring out of the safe at home to give to Hannah, even though you told me that you didn't want "that girl" to have it." In a stage whisper to Hannah he clarified, "They don't like you much. Sorry."

It would have been reasonable for Carl to think that the obvious distress on Hannah's face was due to the revelation, which was no big surprise to her, that his parents disliked her, but Hannah was much more concerned about his prior statement regarding the ring. It left her speechless. Noticing her bare finger for the first time, Carl continued, "Did you lose the ring? I thought you might. You never were very good at taking care of nice things, but I gave it to you anyway because I wanted you to have it." Pausing for a moment, Carl's face was transformed by some inner revelation, and he turned to his mother, "And I wanted to get back at you for all the mean things you've said about Hannah."

Helene, also strangely serene, spoke as if she were in a trance, "Well that really ticks me off, Carl. That was a 200K ring that you threw away on a woman who won't even put aside her selfish needs to eat dairy in my house. I know they make those dairy pills and if she wanted me to like her she could have taken them. She may be selfish and boring but she is definitely right. You should follow your dreams, honey. Even if that makes me very unhappy, which it does. But don't worry; I won't be unhappy for long. I'm going to follow my dreams." Turning to her husband, she continued in the same placid tone, "Roger, the truth is I want a divorce. I'm moving to Las Vegas to become a professional poker player and you would just weigh me down."

What was happening? The restaurant was now buzzing, as everyone seemed to be talking at once. What had been an eerie silence was now a cacophony of hysterical declarations. Hannah could barely absorb Carl's acceptance of her own bizarre speech let alone Helene's psychotic non sequitur. At Helene's polite declaration of freedom from twenty-five years of marriage to pursue a life of gambling, Hannah felt like the right thing would be to sit down and try to sort out what was happening, but she had frozen when she had heard that the ring she had assumed was made of glass was really a family heirloom worth a fortune. A fortune that was currently hanging out in the plumbing of the Honors College. She had to get it back, "I didn't lose the ring, Carl. I left it in a very safe place." She stared into his eyes, hoping to see that he believed her, but she was uncomfortable with how completely he did.

"It's in a safe place." Carl echoed her words, nodding all the while.

John had joined them "Listen, this has been an emotional night. I'm going to go with Hannah to get the ring and I will bring it back to you, man, I promise." John clapped Carl on the back, and Hannah had no time to speak, as John dragged her out the front door, which was being held open for them by a smirking busboy.

❄❄❄❄❄❄❄❄❄❄❄❄

Lee

Watching YouTube on Martha's Vineyard.

Lee watched the video for the third time, hoping he was high on the cleaning fumes Hera used to wash down her countertops to explain what he was seeing. No one else had seen it yet. Hera was sitting on the deck dozing after her third bottle of wine, oblivious to the ferries' horns as they moved back and forth from the mainland. Archer and Apollo had come back to drag Zeus out to some party over on Chappaquiddick, so Lee had logged on to Netflix to catch up on Mad Men, when his email filled with alerts from the cyber nets he'd set.

Grateful that no one was around to freak out before he could figure out a plan to minimize the damage done by the girl he hit play and watched again. Yep. The entire video was a nightmare. Disregard the fact that she looked hideous, she seemed to have bathed with her clothes on, clothes that were oddly old-fashioned and revealing at the same time. No, her wardrobe was the least of their worries. She appeared to have had some disfiguring accident. Her face was so swollen as to be virtually unrecognizable as a face. Lee couldn't image what had happened to her, unless she wasn't human and had trouble taking form too?

No, he'd researched Hannah Summer's lineage extensively. Not only was she human she was descended from Cassandra's only daughter, Iliana, born in secret three years prior to the Trojan War, and given to the Priestess at Delphi to raise. Lee had not been able to definitively determine the father, though he suspected King Mygdon's son, Coroebus. Not many people knew about Cassandra's love child. Luckily for them, that one child had been quite prolific, and there were literally thousands of descendants to choose from. Lee had been proud of his detective work on that one. Convincing the Olympians to give someone the gift of being listened to only really worked from this "reparations" angle. He knew that his research on this topic was what had secured him the spot on this mission. But it might all be over now.

Sweating, Lee trolled through the multiple videos posted, hoping it had just been the angle of the shot that had made her appear so grotesque, but no, every angle was equally hideous. As he sat there contemplating how much work it would be to hack into all the videos and alter her face and change her words, dozens of more videos of her were posted. And then hundreds. Opening them at random, Lee felt his stomach clench. It was as if everyone who viewed it was reposting it with commentary, music, and or graphic embellishments. She was being translated into multiple languages before his stinging eyes. While he was not privy to all the details of their assignment, even he knew that giving the girl the gift was only the first part of the plan. Finding the girl had been his job— the rest was up to Archer.

When Hermes had left to deliver the gift, Lee had sent her a somewhat threatening email. The threats had been Archer's idea. The email explained the gift and ordered her to contact them ASAP. Everything in Hermes report seemed to indicate that she would call. The last thing he would have imagined she'd do would be to start giving speeches in public arenas. Let alone telling people to follow their dreams and tell the truth. Crap.

Opening another window, Lee started searching for a way off the island. If he couldn't fix his mistake, he could at least get as far away as he could before Archer found out about it. He could go back to working for Demon Tech. Composing spam might be boring, after all, how many ways can you spell penis, but at least it was safe. Groaning, he pressed his fingers into his eyes and his head slowly dropped to his keyboard. The last ferry had left an hour ago and even if he could swim, the crunching of the gravel in the drive sealed his fate. They were back.

Once Archer walked through the door, he wouldn't let up until this was fixed. Lee needed protection. He shuffled to the kitchen and slipped two oven mitts under his shirt on his shoulders. That would help with Archer's favorite form of expressing his displeasure. Sniffing, Lee looked around the kitchen. He would also need sustenance. Food was essential in times of stress. Following his nose, he opened the fridge. He pulled out a hunk of Stilton and stuck some in his pockets for later. Humans may be a sad little race, short-lived and pawns of the immortals, but they made some damn good cheese.

CHAPTER EIGHT

Two Steps Forward

❈❈❈

Hannah

Fast Food

"Here, put this on and let's move." Slipping the helmet on, Hannah climbed on behind him. Before he could turn the ignition on, her stomach let loose with a rumble that John not only heard, but felt against his back. "But first, some French fries."

As they zoomed down Main Street, Hannah focused on holding on to John and blocking out the look on Carl's face when she told him she wouldn't go to Japan with him. He'd looked so betrayed. And yet he'd been so oddly docile. She leaned forward to ask John what he thought about Carl's weird behavior as he reached back to hand her the food, and their helmets hit with a resounding thunk. The impact knocked them both back.

Cradling his head with one hand, he handed her the French fries with the other, and snapped, "Just eat the fries. We can talk about what you did in there later, after we get the ring back." She nodded, mouth already crammed with fries, and he took off up College Street. Instead of taking a right on High Street where the Honors College was, John veered left and took another left on Williams Street. Hannah pulled on his sleeve, but he ignored her as he turned into a driveway of a narrow, white, three-story Victorian tucked behind the Language Arts Building.

"Why are we here? I don't under…"

"This is my house. We're here because although stealing back a ring might be something you do every day, I need to take a minute to think this through." Seeming to talk more to himself than to her, he continued, "We should check the University schedule to see if there are any events planned at the Honors College. If so, we might be able to simply blend in and get upstairs. If not, we can cross that bridge when we get to it."

Despite his implication that theft was second nature to her, he didn't look too angry, and she needed his help, "Um, thanks, John, I'm really grateful..."Hannah's voice died off as she watched John enter the shadow of the house.

Instead of walking to the front door, he unlocked the fire escape ladder, pulled it down and started climbing. Not sure why they appeared to be breaking into his apartment, she followed him up to the second floor and watched him disappear through the open window. As the ladder snapped back into place below her, she stayed out on the fire escape for a moment, looking out across the rooftops of downtown Centreville. The sky was darkening with heavy black clouds.

A storm. Where had all this turbulence come from? She closed her eyes and tried to re-inhabit the Hannah of this morning. Lying in her bed, she'd still had her whole life planned out; graduation, job, apartment, boyfriend, eventual marriage. She'd been so sure she knew what would be happening. And she'd liked that feeling, hadn't she? Didn't she believe that a carefully planned life leads to happiness?

Now she was standing on the fire escape outside the apartment of a man she'd avoided for four years about to plan a break-in to a University building to retrieve a lost heirloom after torpedoing the one relationship in her life that had seemed inevitable. And instead of feeling lost, she felt oddly free. Like she was finally about to do something.

Leading with her left leg, she braced her hands on the sill of the window John had disappeared through. Entering the room unsteadily, she felt before she heard the final ripping protest of the much-abused suitable-for-dinner-with-the-parents dress, and she was left wearing a wool smock whose only points of attachment were at her shoulders.

The Myth of Cassandra

Hugging the sides of the dress to her, she blinked rapidly to adjust to the bright lighting in John's apartment. He was in the far corner of the room at his computer.

"Don't turn around! I'm having a...wardrobe malfunction. Would you, I mean do you, I mean could I...."

"The room at the end of the hall. Take anything you like— shirts are in the second drawer, sweats and shorts below. You might want to pick something dark. You know...break-in clothes. I'll get the info we need to get the ring back." His face was glued to his computer monitor.

Hannah started moving into the room, only to be pulled back by her hair caught in the blinds, "Ouch, dammit!" She yanked her hair free and the blinds fell off the window with a crash. She looked down at the carcass of the window treatment and let out a small, "Oh, no..."

John's shoulders hunched at the sound of the destruction of his apartment, but he stayed resolutely still, "Don't worry about it; we have bigger things to deal with. If you want to use the shower to get off the last of whatever you didn't wash off in the Honors College bathroom, go right ahead. Towels are in the bookcase." As Hannah walked past she could see that he had gone so far as to cover his eyes with his hands.

"Thanks. A shower sounds good— I'll be quick." Realizing she was not going to be embarrassed by any witness to her clothing failure she took her first look at his apartment. It was scrupulously clean and orderly. No tapestries hanging from the ceiling to duck under, no pizza boxes to trip over, no pile of oversized pillows for lounging on. A big brown couch dominated the far end of the room next to a doorway through which she could spy a small equally glistening kitchen, all buffed chrome and stainless steel. The phrase echoing in her head was "neat as a pin." It was not at all what she was expecting. She scooted down the hall into the room at the end. Feeling unaccountably shy about being in his bedroom, she focused on getting some clothes out of his dresser.

The drawers were tidy, the shirts all folded carefully and sorted by color, just as she had predicted. She grabbed the t-shirt on the top of the pile, a black crewneck that looked like it would fit. She opened the bottom drawer and found the stacks of sweatpants terrifying in their precision. Careful not to disturb the piles, she nabbed a pair of dark grey sweats and quickly closed the drawer.

The thought of a hot shower was deeply appealing; she was itchy and sticky. He'd said that the towels would be in the bookcase. The hall was lined with bookcases filled to the edges with books. The librarian inside her was impressed by his rigorous shelving of titles by subject and within that subject, alpha by author. But no towels. She was certain he had said that the towels were in the bookcase— and just as she was about to call out for more instructions, she spied more bookcases actually in the bathroom. Who had a bookcase in their bathroom? She couldn't resist the urge to check out some of the titles as she grabbed a big fluffy towel— Boswell's Life of Johnson, Lady Chatterley's Lover by DH Lawrence, and an entire section of self-help novels with slightly skewed titles, "The 268 Habits of Highly Thorough People" and "Everything I needed to Know I Learned at the DMV." The librarian inside her was now appalled; moisture was death to bindings.

With a mental shake, she reminded herself she had to be quick. She pulled off the last remnants of the dress with a move any stripper would have been proud of and took a moment to stomp on it for good measure. She'd always hated that dress. Something else she should have told Carl. Carl. Why had Carl been so agreeable after her awful speech? Catching her reflection in the mirror over the sink, she forced herself to face it. She'd destroyed her relationship. Carl was leaving for Japan and she was staying here. People's paths diverged sometimes. And maybe she had kept them together by pretending to be someone she wasn't. It wasn't the worst reason to end a relationship. But the post-mortem on their three years together would have to wait. She turned away from her own accusing stare and turned the water to hot.

After a utilitarian scrubbing, she stepped out onto the bathmat, dried off and pulled on the borrowed clothes. Whether it was the soap she'd borrowed in the shower, or his laundry detergent, she was now enveloped in the appealing, subtle scent of John MacCallister. She closed her eyes and breathed deeply, feeling herself drift. Shaking her head, she marshaled her thoughts and formed a mental list; Retrieve priceless ring from toilet and.... Nope. Nothing else was list-worthy for tonight. Tomorrow she would consider how the events of today would impact her life. For now, she had one thing to do. Walking barefoot into the living room, evincing the high heeled shoes, she saw John sitting in the same spot she'd left him, hands in his hair. "Any luck with your research? What did you find?"

"I didn't find much..." John's voice trailed off as he turned to look at her. His gaze seemed to encompass her and she felt her heart start to ratchet up a notch. Getting the full attention of John MacCallister was more than a little unnerving. She scrambled to force her brain to ignore the heat climbing up her face. The ring. Think about the ring. Do not think about why the notorious MacMan was staring at her like she was the very thing he wanted. He was so intent, as if he was about to say something, something.... something completely clinical.

"The swelling is gone from your face. I guess the Benadryl worked."

His assessment sounded so matter of fact Hannah felt slightly disembodied. What the hell was wrong with her? Getting her bearings, Hannah tried to stabilize her reaction to him with humor, "Are you admitting I was right? Because I'll need to sit if that's the case..."

"You should sit anyway, the news about the Honors College is not promising. I checked the University schedule and there are no events at that location tonight. Which means blending in and slipping upstairs is out." He turned back to the screen, shaking his head, "The good news is that without an event there, the likelihood that someone else has flushed the toilet since we were there is low. The bad news, our friend Cynthia Dixon lives in an apartment on the ground floor. We could go to her and explain the situation..."

Hannah leaned over his shoulder, scanning the computer screen. She reached around him to hit a few keys to see where he'd been. Giving him a hip check, she bumped him out of the chair and started typing at a speed that made his eyes widen. "Hmm, we could, but she isn't top on my list of ethical people.... if we wait for tomorrow and go to Public Safety, the ring could be flushed further and lost forever.... We're going to have to break in to get it...Look," she swiveled in the chair to face him, "Here is the floor plan for the Honors College. There's an entrance near the kitchen in the back that's as far from the Margins Nazi's apartment as we can manage and, see, the servants staircase will get us to the second floor. There are security alarms," and she clicked on the mouse causing a security schematic to overlay the floor plan, "here and here. Give me a second and I will see if I can pull up the codes. If not, we can over-ride them with a master code." Her fingers flew across the keyboard. "Bingo!" and she hit print.

Hannah looked over to see John frowning at her, "Where are you getting this information? I spent the last 15 minutes checking every University site and there were no floor plans or security schematics." His voice was equal parts suspicion and admiration.

She shrugged. "Oh, right. Um. I know a few things about computer security protocols. This information is not, strictly speaking, publicly accessible. But if you know where to look you can find it." She looked back at the computer and pulled up a new window, "Look here. This is the assignment roster from the Public Safety office. They assign two guards to patrol that block and their 3 hour shift starts at 6pm which is 5 minutes from now." Tracing her finger along the map of the university on the screen, she continued, "The Honors College is on the Western corner of their patrol area. If we assume that they patrol together, we can hide in the bushes in the back of the Honors College and wait for them to do their check and then we'll have plenty of time to get the ring."

"Have you done this before? Because you are both impressing me and freaking me out a little, right now. Carl never mentioned that you were some computer genius..."

She pulled the pages out of the printer and scanned them, "I think we've already established that there are a few things I never told Carl. And "genius" is an overstatement. When my dad heard that I wanted to major in Classics, he insisted that I take some computer science classes for my electives, in case I couldn't find a job in my field. Finding this information was simple. I just need three things; I need to know where in the university system to look, what credentials are necessary to get in, and once there, how to find it. The University's computer systems are structured in a predictable org chart, so it was easy to find the location. Getting in can be harder, but I know a little bit about the guy who runs IT here, and that gives me some insights. All of his security passwords are in Klingon. Although Klingonese is fairly complex, his knowledge of it is limited to pick-up lines, which make his passwords easy to guess. After that it was a simple subject search." Hannah stood up, slipped on the dreaded pumps and handed John the paper with the security codes. "I don't have pockets. Thanks. Do you have a wrench? And a small flashlight? Because we should probably go…"

✦✦✦✦✦✦✦✦✦✦✦✦

Hera

Being right on Martha's Vineyard

"She said what? And how many people have heard her say this?" Peering over Lee's shoulder at the laptop, Adams recoiled as Hannah's misshapen head filled the screen," Who the hell is that? Is that our girl? What happened to her? Is this some side effect of the gift? This is an unmitigated disaster!" Archer's voice hit a note that caused the wineglass in Hera's hand to vibrate ominously.

Apollo was at the computer in Hera's office, playing the clip in a continuous loop. There were over 300 versions of it on YouTube by now. It had been translated into 157 different languages and counting. The one Apollo had chosen was labeled by some creative human, "Sermon on the Butter Roll" and had over 700,000 hits. It had a good view of the unusually swollen girl telling people to stop following others and to follow their dreams. There was also a lovely little bit about honesty. Hera's enjoyment of Archer's distress was tempered by her concern for Apollo. And Zeus. And humanity, for that matter.

She'd spent hundreds of years observing human society and she knew that while humans liked the myth of one day "following their dreams" the reality was that most people's dreams were stupid. Really stupid. They dreamed of being famous, or beautiful, or wealthy. They dreamed of traveling the world, or writing a best seller, or living on Mars. That was why they were dreams and not reality. Reality needed people to suck it up and do what was necessary. Why else would people work at tedious jobs for soulless corporations stuck in depressing cubicles? If even 10% of the population stopped doing these jobs and followed their dreams, the results would be catastrophic.

And honesty. While some humans prided themselves on their "honesty," she felt like they were the most deluded. Deluded and self-serving. When most people say they are "just being honest" it usually comes after they have said something completely, unnecessarily, mean. Not that she had any problem with cruelty; it was just that cruelty shouldn't be sullied by rationalizations. And anyone who claims that relationships are built on honesty is selling something. Relationships aren't built on honesty, but on effective lies. Face it; there's a reason that fantasy drives most couples' sex lives. They cannot handle a straight diet of unfiltered honesty.

She tried to catch Zeus's eye, but he was avoiding her. He could stop this with one word, but he seemed to be more interested in cradling his bucket of Kentucky Fried and sucking the last of the chicken fat off his fingers than he did in preventing the meltdown of human society. She should make him take charge, but the third bottle of wine she'd downed had left her strangely mute. She knew this was disastrous for human society, and the pleasure she felt in witnessing Archer's plans unraveling was not enough to compensate for the headache she'd feel in the morning when she'd not only have to face the effects of all the wine she'd drunk, but also of the girl's gift. A gift she'd known would be a disaster. But all she wanted to do now was to go to bed. She'd deal with what would come in the morning. Decision made. She walked out of the room keeping her righteous honesty to herself and wended up the stairs to her bed followed by the fading sound of Archer's anger.

CHAPTER NINE

Candy From a Baby

◊◊◊

Hannah

In the Rhododendrons

Hannah occupied herself trying to judge which part of her was most cold: her feet, her hands, or her ears. She and John had been crouching in the shrubs behind the Honors College for the better part of an hour while an unseasonably cold rain drizzled through the meager protection of the branches. The guards had arrived twenty minutes ago, but seemed to be making a thorough check of the place, and were still indoors. All they could do was wait for them to leave.

At first it had seemed exciting, even daring to be hiding in the bushes. The rain had only added to the dark cover and her feeling of adventure. When they realized that the guards were not there yet, they had talked a little, in whispers, which had made the waiting easier.

"John, why do you use the fire escape to go in and out of your apartment?"

"It's a long story."

"Tell me."

"No."

"Come on..."

"The landlady lives on the first floor and I want to avoid her."

"Why?"

"Because."

"Tell me. It's cold, and I need a distraction."

"I moved in last year and I stayed for the summer— I had an internship at the Hartford Currant. It was boring, but I met a lot of people."

"The story, John. The landlady. The Fire Escape."

"Right, well I came back from work late, and she was having drinks with some friends on the front porch, and they invited me to join them, and one thing led to another...and now I take the fire escape when a woman is with me. She's a little territorial."

"Ew. Really. How old is she?"

"I don't kiss and tell. At least not details."

"What does she do when you bring a woman home?"

"Nothing, at first, but she always seems to need to check the plumbing, or replace the screens or dust for ants. So I started using the fire escape when I want to be left alone. It's just easier."

"Why don't you ask her to come back another time, or better yet, move? There have to be other apartments?"

"I like my apartment. That, and I don't want to hurt her feelings. She's really nice and she claims that she understands that it was just a one-time thing, but then when I bring someone home.... So I found a solution. She doesn't bother the guys, or me when a group comes over, so I use the front door then. Besides, the rent is fantastic. Are you happy now?"

"Yes. But I have another question."

"Hannah, shouldn't a stake-out be quieter?"

"What? I am being quiet. I am quietly asking you questions. Why do you have a bookcase in the bathroom? Won't all that humidity ruin the books?"

"Yes it will."

"Oh."

"But John, I don't..."

"I read a lot of books. A lot. And most books have something to offer. But every so often there is a book I despise. Not because I disagree with the author, or hate the ending, but because there is something unsatisfying about its very structure. Or, it bores me. Lots of times I just donate those books to library fund raisers, but once in awhile there is a book that I think deserves a crueler fate. The bathroom bookcase is my version of book Tartarus."

"Though I am the kind of girl who loves a Hades reference, you are truly strange. Why don't you just recy...?"

"Shh. Look. Over there. It's them."

And that had been over twenty minutes ago and here they had crouched, in silence, being dripped on, waiting. John poked her in the ribs and then pointed to the side of the house. The Public Safety Officers were leaving. He motioned for her to follow him as he crept toward the kitchen door, the pillowcase with their tools in it slung over his shoulder. As she stepped out of the bushes to follow him she let out a gasp as her bare feet met the wet cold of the ground. Her white, open-toed pumps had sunk into the mud under the bush and had stayed behind when she stepped forward. She didn't have time to go back to pull them out, John was already at the door waiting. She would have to do without.

Her feet. That was definitely the coldest part of her body.

Not 10 minutes later....

It was done. Hannah gently closed the kitchen door behind her and reengaged the security alarm. It had been a little tricky getting the plumbing open, and she did not envy the next person who tried to flush the toilet, as she knew the pipes were not technically reconnected properly, but they had found the ring. She looked down at it on her finger and felt a huge weight lift off her shoulders. She still couldn't believe it was real; it was such a monstrosity. But all that mattered now was that she get it safely back to Carl.

John took her hand to pull her into the dark of the back lawn and they both froze as the light that shone in their faces blinded them momentarily.

"What have we here? Are you two lovebirds looking for a place to nest? What's the problem? Roommates cramping your style? You know that University property is off limits after hours, don't you? I am going to have to write you up." The disembodied voice sounded old and friendly, and though Hannah had frozen in terror, John stepped right up.

Slipping his arm around her shoulders, he hugged her to him, dropping the pillowcase discretely behind her and pleading with the voice, "You caught us, man. We're sorry. We didn't mean to break the rules. The door is locked anyway and we were just heading back to my place. You're right, dude, just looking for someplace to celebrate. It's not every day you ask a girl to marry you." Then, leaning forward as if he was confiding in the voice, "She said yes. But, dude, could you point the flashlight down, man, it's really harsh…"

The light slid down off their faces and onto Hannah's hand. The ring glittered and fractured the light, shining like a beacon. "Hmm…that's some ring you got there. How did a college student like you come up with the cash for that?"

Hannah was blinking rapidly, trying to adjust to the dark and could only make out the edges of a public safety uniform. Crap. How did she miss a third officer on the schedule? The two they had seen earlier had both been heavy set— but this guy was thin.

John kept up the charade, "Aw, man, why are you busting my chops?" Leaning forward with a stage whisper, "The ring isn't real. But my girl Brenda here, she like her some bling. It's genuine cubic zirconium. I know a guy. Hey, can you cut us a break about the write up, please. We've never done anything wrong before, and we won't do it again."

"Hmmm…well, you are asking a lot, you know. I could lose my job. I tell you what. I have a girlfriend with expensive tastes too. She might like one just like this. Can I see the ring?" And he put out his hand while he shined the flashlight back at their faces.

"Um, sure, I mean…it's just, she can't have this ring…." Hannah's voice cracked and she balled her hand into a fist, resisting the urge to hide it behind her back.

"Of course not Brenda. I wouldn't take your ring. I just want to see how it was made. My girlfriend is sophisticated," and at this his flashlight traveled up and down Hannah's t-shirt and sweats, ending on her muddy bare feet, "a stylish woman. I want to be sure it is up to her standards. But if you would rather show it to me while you wait for the police at the Public Safety Office...."

"No, no, that won't be necessary." John raised his hand to block the light and looked in her face, "Give him the ring, honey. He just wants to look." John took her hand and slipped the ring off while he whispered in her ear, "Cool it H, we're almost home free." He placed the ring in the hand and it disappeared into the dark.

There was a silence from the officer as he blinded them again and then a disembodied hand floated back out of the dark, handing the ring back. Hannah snatched the ring back and pushed it down her finger. The officer lowered the flashlight and she rubbed her eyes, trying to clear the spots left from the light.

"It's real sweet, but a little obvious. It's perfect for you, but my lady needs something more authentic. How about I escort you lovebirds back to your room? It's getting late and I wouldn't want you to run into anyone unscrupulous." As John and Hannah both started to protest, the officer put his hand on John's shoulder firmly, "I insist."

Damn. Hannah didn't like this. This would mean he would know where John lived and if something did go wrong with the plumbing, they might put two and two together. She could try to lead them to her place, and then at least she'd be able to keep John out of it, but John seemed to have read her thoughts, because he said out loud, "Brenda, the officer is right, babe. You should crash at my place. It's right around the corner." Then he turned to the officer and talked a blue streak the entire way back to his house. Hannah slid her thumb against the band of the ring and tried not to step on anything sharp.

By the time they got to the front door of John's house, her night vision was working, and she got a glimpse of the officer as he said good night. It must have been her nerves, but she could have sworn he looked just like the busboy that had held the door open at the restaurant. But that was impossible. It must just have been that they both seemed to be smirking.

Sagging against the closed door, Hannah and John shared a relieved smile. She extended her hand, ring sparkling in the faint light of the stairwell.

"We did it! I always thought we would but I have to admit that I froze when that third guard caught us. I can't believe I missed him on the schedule! Maybe they have a floating officer who just rambles around? And we left behind the pillowcase with all of our stuff in it. That's definitely going to raise questions in the..."

"Hannah, can we just be happy we got the ring back and save the post-game analysis for after we warm up and dry off." Without waiting for her reply John started sprinting up the stairs. "I call the first shower!"

Hannah followed after him at a slower pace, one step at a time. She couldn't take her eyes of Carl's grandma's ring. She'd been so focused on getting it back, she'd kept the other events of the evening at bay, but now they were flooding her. She'd ended everything with Carl, and he had simply smiled and thanked her. Thanked her as if she had just told him his car was ready to be picked up at the shop, or it was his turn at the dentist. She had stood up in a crowded restaurant and told him that she wouldn't marry him, or move to Japan with him, and that she hadn't really known him, and he hadn't really known her. By not listening well to Carl, and by not telling him the truth about what she thought, she had lost the thread of what had been real about her feelings.

She paused outside of John's apartment, dripping on the welcome mat. This was not how she had imagined this evening would turn out when she had sat in her dorm room plotting it out on graph paper. She'd pictured a future that didn't exist now. Staring at the many faceted ring, she forced herself to dissect her feelings. The shame that was swamping her was directly commensurate to the relief she felt. She dropped her head, stunned by the magnitude of the mistake she had almost made when she had been planning this evening back in her room. How could she have structured such an elaborate illusion of happiness?

The door opened and John jumped back, startled by Hannah's silent vigil on his doormat. His brow furrowed. "You weren't in the apartment, I thought maybe you.... um, the shower is free...."

It said something about the state of her distraction that she simply nodded and murmured, "Thanks," as she headed toward the bathroom, completely unaware that the man holding the door open for her was wearing only a towel.

For the second time that night Hannah stood under the hot spray and this time she did not rush. The ring was safely on her finger. She couldn't drag her eyes from it. It was as if the success of their caper and the failure of her relationship were captured together in the sparkle and garish light of the diamonds. In the privacy of the shower she allowed her tears to mix with the water running down her face and swallowed back any sobs that might be heard over the sound of the plumbing.

Stepping out and wrapping herself in a towel she heard a knock on the front door of the apartment. It was probably John's Mrs. Robinson-esque landlady come to stake her claim. That was fine with her; she needed to get dressed and find Carl. Standing in the bathroom she considered her next move. She could sprint to the bedroom and avoid the scene at the front door. She could hear John consoling someone. Someone who was crying. Sobbing really. Was it compassion or curiosity that caused her to head toward the front door? Turning the corner, she could see John hugging a distraught Carl. And at that moment Carl looked up and saw Hannah in his best friend's apartment, fresh from the shower and wrapped in a towel with the huge engagement ring on her finger fracturing the light.

●●●●●●●●●●●

Hermes

When opportunity presents itself

He'd run into the Former Boyfriend on the sidewalk as he was leaving Line Boy's place and couldn't resist the temptation to stay and watch the drama unfold. It'd been tedious waiting for H and Line Boy to steal the ring so he could relieve them of it, and a good betrayal scene was just the thing to enliven his evening. Come on; best friend, half-naked, ex-fiancé in a towel, engagement ring from crushed dream sparkling on her finger. This had all the makings of a great blow up. He'd hoped for some fireworks, or a fistfight, or maybe a threesome? But they had just talked. Correction; first they put clothes on and then they'd talked.

H came clean about the ring, handing it back to the Former Boyfriend with an apology. FB had stared at the ring, and then, while citing a summer working for his uncle on watch repair, put it under his heal and crushed it to dust. Hermes smirked, feeling a rush of adrenaline as he anticipated their plans to come after him once they realized he'd stolen the ring from them. Not as entertaining as a three-way, but still fun. But no, FB told her not to worry, that his mom, unbeknownst to him, had filed an insurance claim when she had found the ring missing a month ago. The claim was paid, and it was an ugly ring anyway, so they should just let it go. Nothing. No rash plan to go steal the ring back from the smirking stranger. Who knew insurance companies could suck the joy out of grand theft larceny?

But still, Hermes stayed and watched. It was like sitting on the couch watching TV after the show you liked ended. It was more interesting than sleep. Barely. Line Boy cooked everyone dinner, and then H and FB disappeared into Line Boy's room to talk. Line Boy crashed on the couch with the pillows piled over his ears, trying not to listen to their conversation. He had no such qualms; he disappeared and followed them into the bedroom to listen. For the first five minutes. But it was clear that there was not going to be any good dialogue, let alone any action. Only apologies, sadness, and acceptance of the end of their relationship. They had grown apart; they had different dreams, blah, blah, blah. Boring.

He really should apologize to whoever had coined the phrase "As easy as taking candy from a baby." He had thought it a stupid saying; what wasn't easy to take from a baby? Their chubby little arms had virtually no muscle mass to resist theft. But this heist had ended up being exactly like taking candy from a baby. He'd stolen a sweet ring from them and all H did about it was cry. He'd expected more from her. What

The Myth of Cassandra

had happened to the woman who had dumped her boyfriend in a spectacle of harshness and then broken in and stolen a ring like an expert? She was a woman to consider. Watching her finally stepping out and doing something had reminded him of the hatching chicks he'd seen at the science museum; he'd been tailing a mark. He had ducked behind the incubator for cover; when he had looked down to see the miracle of chicken birth. When the little chicks finally broke through and emerged, all wet and scraggly, some of them turned and ate their shells, standing taller and moving surer, while others tried to huddle in the broken shells, looking for the safety that they'd destroyed in emerging. He'd thought that H was finally ready to eat her shell, but she seemed to be huddling, and he was surprised at how disappointed that made him feel. Humans.

Stepping over the sleepless Line Boy, Hermes rolled his eyes. Human attraction. Line Boy hadn't come up once in his investigation of H and yet now he was helping her break into buildings, steal heirlooms and hosting a slumber party. He idly wondered how long it would take for Line Boy to make his move now that the Boyfriend was Former. Based on the side dish of repression that had been served with dinner, probably years, if ever. The three of them had been all polite and careful; he'd half expected them to start talking about the weather. Why mortals wasted so much time when it was such a measured commodity for them, he never understood.

He slipped back out the way he'd gotten in and sat there on the damp fire escape staring at the stars. He traced the W in the sky and landed on the second star from the right. The man he needed to find was most likely in a honkytonk in the Southern state just south of Cassiopeia. This could take awhile. Not getting there, that was a matter of seconds, but getting the deal done. His friend only liked to do business after a considerable amount of time spent drinking and talking and more drinking. He slipped the ring onto his own finger and admired its likeness to a houseboat. A very sparkly houseboat. Even given the social niceties, it shouldn't take too long; he'd easily be finished before Hera started looking for him. His gut was telling him that Hera would be calling him again, and soon, to clean up this mess. H's speech in the restaurant was going to cause all kinds of trouble. Honesty and dreams; a worse combination for human society was hard to fathom. Besides, when she did call, he already knew where H was staying, so it would be easy to bring her in.

He would follow H's advice and make his own dreams come true. Checking for rust on his pants, he stood up, found his bearings in the stars, and flew off into the night, the ring on his hand glowing in the moonlight.

CHAPTER TEN

The SOT

❀❀❀

Hannah

Cursed Woman Dreaming of Twain in Connecticut

She was floating on a raft down a wide lazy river— had she borrowed the raft from Huck and Jim? They weren't here, so maybe she'd stolen it? She'd never seen the Mississippi, had she? But this was definitely the Mississippi— wide and brown with birch trees clinging to the banks. Her feet hung off the end of the raft in the water and she lay back, eyes closed, feeling the sun on her face. Maybe the raft was motorized? She could hear the faint hum of an engine. She should feel peaceful, but the sun was so hot, and the water on her legs was so cold, she needed to change something. She sat up and looked down into the dark depths of the water, feeling the current pulling her legs out. She stared, looking for something. Some sign of what she should do. While she tried to make up her mind, she felt a shove from behind and fell face first....

Onto the floor. Oof. Her mind scrambled for bearings. She was on the floor of someone's bedroom. Sitting up, Hannah saw Carl sprawled out on the bed, his left foot inches from where she must have been sleeping. Well, that explained the ache in her lower back and trip to the floor. Carl had always been an active sleeper. And snorer. Carl's rhythmic snoring was muffled in the pillow. Ah... the distant motor in her dream...the dream. She fiercely wanted to return to her dream. If only because she knew that after waking from her dream she would have to face the now.

Sucking in a sharp breath, she remembered exactly where she was. John MacCallister's bedroom. After the ring debacle, Carl had explained that his roommate was in residence, and had asked John if he and Hannah could use his room to talk. They'd spent the entire night talking. Once they got through the basic facts of their breakup, they'd rambled down memory lane. They both must have drifted off at some point. Hence the dreaming and the snoring. And the being kicked out of the bed. Taking an inventory, she registered one very sore elbow that would certainly bruise. It was the least she deserved. She knew she should quietly run away before anyone else woke up, but she seemed to be lacking the will to move. It all seemed so sad and over, and she just wanted to stay in this cave of a room and go back to sleep. But the floor was hard and she would have to move to get back in the bed....

What would *Ladies' Home and Hearth* say to that? Hmm...something like, "Life is for living. Get in there and get it done." She was fairly certain that had been advice on how to tackle spring-cleaning, not dealing with the fallout of carpet-bombing your love life. Oh well, domestic chores/personal disasters, six of this, half dozen of the other. She could start with a list. Rolling onto her back, she visualized the writing on the ceiling. She was fairly certain that this was only Tuesday. First she'd get a graduation robe at the bookstore; she would not graduate naked. Then take Prof. Tetley and Mr. Blean out to lunch. Oh! And get a new phone....

"Hannah! Carl! You have to see this! You won't believe this! Wake up!" John's voice from down the hall penetrated Carl's sleep, and he sat bolt upright in the bed. Carl looked around in the same way she had, clearly trying to piece together what had happened. Hannah waved from the floor, "Hey Carl."

"Oh, crap. Did I do that? Are you okay?"

"I'm fine, don't worry. It's a futon; there's just not that far to go. We'd better go see what's up with John, he sounds like he's going to come bursting through the..."

"Hannah, did we? I mean, it all seems so fuzzy now. I remember talking, but then..."

"Then we both fell asleep." She climbed onto the bed and leaned over, kissing his forehead. "Let's go, okay?"

At that exact moment John did burst into the room, saw Hannah leaning over Carl in the bed, stared for a full five seconds, turned bright red, spun around and stammered, "Uh, I'm sorry to interrupt your reunion, but you guys have to come see this. I can't describe what's happening. You have to see it for yourselves; it's unbelievable. You have to come, NOW." And he beat a hasty retreat.

Hannah scrambled to follow John, wanting to counter his wrong impression of what had happened in that bedroom, but before she could, all thoughts of clarifying her evening activities were completely forgotten as she walked into the living room. John had a flat screen TV hung on the wall behind his computer and the images on it were beyond bizarre. The Channel 7 News logo was in the lower right hand corner with the date and time. A banner was running across the bottom of the screen, complete with swirling graphics. Hannah pinched herself hard on the arm, wincing. She was not still asleep. Carl stumbled into the room, eyes bugging out at the scene playing out in forty-two digitally enhanced inches. And then he said what they were all thinking.

"What the...?"

WHERE IS HANNAH— INQUIRING MINDS WANT TO KNOW?

DESPERATELY SEEKING HANNAH: THE STAKEOUT.

HANNAHGATE: THE SEARCH FOR THE SPEAKER OF TRUTH....

Hannah grabbed the remote out of John's hand and started flipping through the channels. Every single news station had a banner with a variation on the same theme: Where was Hannah Summers? There was a twenty-four hour camera feed of the parking lot of her dorm where it looked like hundreds of people were camping out. Some were sleeping in tents patch-worked across Foss Hill, but others were gathered around the front door of her dorm, quietly waiting. There were a few hand-lettered signs, "Follow your Dreams— so sayeth Hannah" and "I walk in the footsteps of the SOT." She wasn't sure what that meant, until she realized that the media was constantly referring to her as the Speaker of Truth. SOT.

An unfortunately unflattering acronym. The SOT. The only time she had heard the word "sot" used was in the phrase, "drunken sot." Her mother would not approve. Elise would find a way to lecture her about how best to engender flattering nicknames especially when the world turns upside down and the media becomes obsessed with you. Yes. A lecture about nicknames...acceptable nicknames; Cricket, Lovey, Scout, that imply that you are small and adorable, not hulking and inebriated.

Flipping through the channels, Hannah felt her mouth go dry. The stations that weren't actively looking for her were doing even stranger things. Entertainment Weekly had a special edition of the Fashion Police discussing her appearance on the now world famous video of her Restaurant Speech.

"It's brilliant how she took such a frumpy, staid dress and distressed it. Look at that detail on the hemline— she made it look like it had simply ripped— think of the work that went into that effect. Fabulous."

"I agree Jean Paul, her instincts are right on. Check out the ironic use of pearls on the neck and ears. So retro and bland— it is the new edge of fashion."

"I couldn't agree more, Ainsley, and if you needed any more evidence of her edgy, ironic, brilliant fashion sense— check out her hair and makeup. Badly applied lipstick and hair that looks like she survived a wet tornado. Perfection. Times a thousand. Pretty Ugly."

"I couldn't help noticing that you are sporting a Hannah-do this morning, Anne, and I must honestly say that you look just ugly in it. Not pretty ugly like Hannah. Just saying."

"Oh, Jean Paul, honesty forces me to tell you that your opinion means nothing to me. You talk but all I hear is blah, blah..." On and on.

There were even weirder shows. PBS had a round table discussion lead by Charlie Rose. Classical Scholars from the world over had gathered to dissect her thesis. Unfortunately, there wasn't that much to discuss. They all agreed that she was completely right and they had nothing to add, except how right she was. TV doctors were theorizing about her swollen face. Oprah's doctor was certain that the SOT had latent Proteus syndrome— the same diagnosis as John Merrick, the Elephant Man. He speculated that the onset of the disease was the root of Hannah's prophetic voice. Miller from the Copy Center was being interviewed on not one, but three morning talk shows. He looked ecstatic. He told everyone about the secret swingers commune, which the hosts loved. And that was just on TV.

Handing the remote back to the silent John, Hannah attacked his laptop. The Internet was worse. A Google search on her name produced 213,000,000 results— more hits than if you searched for "salt". She had become the top story on every online zine, news source and professional blog. People had set up countless web pages devoted to different aspects of her life: her past: fairly boring, middle class, suburban; her personal life, Carl; and her academics, CoolProfTetley.com. All were swamped with hits.

Other sites were simply attempts to honor her. Someone had started a comic book series about her titled, "The Incredible SOT." She was pictured wearing a bag over her deformed face, and a blue wool dress clinging to her significantly enhanced curves; so much for honesty. There was a lot of chatter about a secret society that had formed to decode her thesis. The rumor was that the Great SOT would not have written such a boring thesis; that it was actually a coded message and the Secret Society of SOT was close to breaking the code. Even on Twitter the buzz was all about the SOT: where you were when you heard the truth and what you had been doing with the truth. "This is so cool. I just told @ConsumerPRgod that he is a douche. The truth sets you free! I am following my dreams! #SOTisAce."

At the bottom of every website and TV broadcast was a clock counting the minutes since the last Proclamation of SOT, with a bulleted reminder of what SOT's last message was. The current bullets were;

• Follow your own dreams.

• We all deserve honesty.

It was all so much, so overwhelming, so completely incomprehensible. She put her head down on the desk and pleaded, "Turn it off." and with the small sound of the remote click, the silence in the room vibrated in her bones.

"I don't understand what's happening. Why is this happening?" Carl pushed her chair to the side and began furiously typing while John said something about getting them coffee and disappeared out the front door. Carl gasped and pointed at the screen, making inarticulate grunting noises, "What! How? Huh...?" He'd found a site dedicated to himself called, TheManSOTdumped.net Along with photos of him partying with his frat brothers, there was an active comments page where people were discussing how he must feel being dumped by the SOT, what he must have done to deserve it, and on and on. He turned away from the computer and faced her.

"You know, it's strange, but last night, at the restaurant, I remember how I felt when you were breaking up with me. It was odd. I felt hurt and sad, but more than that I felt like you were right. And not just any kind of right, but RIGHT right. You know? It was really kind of a peaceful feeling, like finally I was listening to someone who was unequivocally right. The kind of right you don't have to question. It was only later, when I was here that I started to feel really angry and hurt."

"But you don't feel that way anymore, right? I mean, when you first got here and I was in a towel, when you thought, you know, and you looked so angry but then I said no, that wasn't what was happening and asked you to wait and you..."

"I waited. I know. Just did what you said; relieved to have you tell me what to do. There is something else Hannah. I felt like I had to tell you exactly what I was thinking. It was just like in the restaurant. Like when I told you my parents didn't like you— I don't know why I said that exactly, except I felt like I should, which is totally messed up. And here, last night, I told you that I thought you were sleeping with John; it was the same, the compunction to tell you honestly what I had been thinking." Carl had stood up and begun pacing the room.

Hannah frowned and repositioned herself in front of the laptop, "Do you feel that way now? Think about it Carl, when we were talking last night about our breakup, did you have thoughts, honest reactions that you edited for my sake?"

"Well, yeah, of course, now that you mention it, I feel totally normal. Well, as normal as anyone can feel in this..."and his hand swept to encompass the computer, TV and Hannah, "situation. What did you do, Hannah? How did you do this?"

The door to the apartment swung open and John entered with three cups of coffee in a tray and the NY Times and the Hartford Currant in the other hand, "Forget how she did this, check out the paper. Yes, the first four sections are all devoted to Hannah, or more accurately, to the SOT. But look here in Section E— airports are shutting down. Apparently most air traffic controllers have left to follow their dreams, and there is no one to take their places. Public Schools are in chaos; at least half the teachers have left to pursue their dreams while the other half have gone rogue and stopped administering standardized tests, or are starting up "new" school communities. But it doesn't matter because all the students have left and are flooding into area amusement parks where there is rioting because there is no one to run the rides. You get the picture. And that's just here in Connecticut." He threw the Hartford paper on the floor. Hannah and Carl took their coffee wordlessly, waiting for John to drop the other shoe. He unfurled the NY Times and started to read, "Peace Talks Break Down as Fist Fight Breaks Out, Chinese Official Mocks American Secretary of State; American President Resigns to Become New Judge on American Idol: Vice President Thrilled; Germany's Chancellor to EU: You Are All Lazy." John's hands were shaking and he let the paper fall to the floor at his feet. He looked from Hannah to Carl and back again. "This could become very dangerous very quickly. Luckily everyone is so busy pursuing their dreams, no one seems to be launching any wars yet. Have you figured out why this is happening?"

Hannah turned back to the computer and typed in the query, "Why listen to SOT?" She got a massive number of hits, but as she started to scan them, it all came down to "because."

Carl was picking up the newspapers and straightening the sections, "We were just talking about that when you came in. I was telling Hannah that I had felt weirdly compelled to not only listen to her, but that she was RIGHT— even last night when I walked in on the two of you showering, well not showering exactly, but you know, and I don't feel that way anymore. Like right now, I am a little annoyed that Hannah took over the laptop, but I didn't say anything about it, but last night, when I was first here, I felt a compulsion to be HONEST with every thought. It was sort of awful."

John took the neatly folded newspapers from Carl and put them on top of a pile by the door. "Do you remember when that feeling changed? You were acting like you were under some kind of hypnotic spell. And then you weren't..."

"Guys, look! "The image on the screen was of Hannah's email in-box. She'd highlighted the email in question, hovering over the mouse, "should I open it? What if it is some kind of virus, or worm, or electronic bomb or something?" John and Carl both leaned over Hannah and stared at the screen.

"Do you only have two new emails? How is that possible?" John leaned closer, as if looking harder would make more appear.

"Hannah is totally crazy about SPAM. Obsessed, really." Carl confided, "She has like seven different filters on her account and set up a bunch of dummy folders and accounts she shuttles unwanted email to. She even made up some story about working for the government..."

"She has major control issues, you know that, right man? I mean in the last twenty-four hours, the stories I could tell..." John was shaking his head.

Carl rolled his eyes. "Stories you could tell? There was this one time in Ohio..."

"Excuse me, but wanting an inbox filled with only emails relevant to me doesn't make me a control freak. So if you wouldn't mind saving this fascinating exchange for later, I'd really appreciate it if you could turn your attention to the email that was sent to me this morning, from some party claiming to be the Greek Gods. Is that some secret campus society or acronym I don't know? How did they get through my filters?" This last was said under her breath as she enlarged her inbox to fill the screen.

Carl and John exchanged a look over Hannah's head but did as she asked and considered the highlighted subject line: Important Message from the Greek Gods. John was the first to speak, "I think you need to open it, Hannah. When you weigh the continuing disintegration of society against the possibility that the email has a virus, I think the choice is self-evident."

Carl squeezed her shoulder and whispered, "It's okay, Han. We've got your back. Open it."

Hannah looked at Carl for a moment and he nodded grimly. She swiveled to John, who also nodded. She faced the computer, took a deep breath and slid her pointer over the email and clicked. She read it aloud:

Hannah Summers:

As a descendant of Cassandra of Priam, you have been gifted a great power. Zeus and Apollo, immortal Gods, gave this gift to you from Mt. Olympus, to atone for the wrong done to your ancestor and to further the glorification of the Olympians. It is a wondrous gift.

But your use of it has been disastrous. You must cease and desist from any and all public statements until further notice, or you and your family will suffer dire consequences. DIRE consequences.

You have deeply displeased the God of Thunder and Lightning. We are offering you one chance, and once chance only, to redeem yourself. You must contact us at 617-433-3242, and we will collect you and bring you to face Zeus. Remember, you must act immediately and call us. Speak to no one. If you fail at any of these requests all measure of unpleasantness will shower down upon you and those you love.

The clock is ticking. Do what we say and no one will get hurt.

Sincerely,

Archer Adams

She exhaled swiftly, shut the laptop and spun away from the desktop, inadvertently knocking the cup of coffee out of John's hand. All three of them watched as the coffee flew across the room in a perfect arc, landing on the brown couch.

John was the first to break the silence, "Well, it could have been worse."

Hannah jumped up, looking for something to soak it up, "I'm so sorry, John, that will stain…"

"I think we can get the stain out." Carl was already moving toward the kitchen, looking for a towel, "Han, what did it say in *Ladies' Home and Hearth* about coffee stains?"

Pulling up the topic in her mind, Hannah recited, "LHH says you should never scrub a coffee stain. We need to gently blot the stain and then use vinegar and warm water to clean the edges." She walked to the couch to get a closer look at the stain. "John, do you have vinegar?"

John's voice was high pitched and got louder with each word, "Yes, I have vinegar. It's under the sink. But I don't give a damn about the coffee stain on the DARK BROWN COUCH. When I said, "it could have been worse," I was referring to the email from the GOD DAMN GREEK GODS WHO HAVE APPARENTLY GIFTED YOU WITH THE POWER TO HAVE EVERYONE LISTEN TO YOU. Or have you forgotten, SOT?" John's voice faded from the all out yell, and he stood staring at Hannah, arms at his sides. He exhaled slowly and this time spoke in a slow, measured tone, "Sure, the email was threatening and strange, but I mean, there are some pros to this situation that we should be focusing on. Not on stain removal techniques."

Carl emerged from the kitchen, vinegar and cloth in hand, and passed it to Hannah, "We can clean the spot and talk about the email at the same time."

It was as if Carl had read her mind. In the face of incontrovertible impossibilities, the concreteness of the stain kept her tethered to reality. Taking the cloth from Carl, she listened to his steady voice, "He's not wrong, Han. I know that email was a little intense, but there was some good information in it. I mean, there is no way they are Gods, right, they are probably some weird sect of role players, you know, like the Renaissance Faire people. But now we know what they want you to think is happening. Start with the blotting, I'm going to get a bowl of warm water to mix the vinegar in." And Carl disappeared back in the kitchen.

Hannah bent to the couch, pushing the towel into the stain, "Like what? This is the real world. The Greek Gods were simply personifications and projections of the Hellenist culture. Fiction. Myth. So whoever wrote that email must have been what? Making an analogy? Threatening me with classical references? Why? That email was obviously sent as some kind of sick joke. There are no such thing as immortals, Greek or otherwise." She turned to look at John who had sat back down at the computer.

John was rereading the email, "We have to look at this reasonably. Why is everyone reacting to your speech? Science can only account for three ways to affect perception: chemically, surgically or behaviorally. Let's rule surgical out from the start: this is clearly affecting a lot of people. Surgical would be completely impractical in a mass audience. If it is some chemical effect, some drug or additive, how would they have deployed it so quickly? Through water treatment plants? Flu vaccines? " He swiveled in the chair to look at them both, frowning, "But then how could they control for the overnight activation? Would they have had a two-stage process? Seed the chemical agent over a long period of time, and then induce a catalyst?"

Hannah had dropped her rag, and perching on the edge of the couch, started to sketch out the options on the back of a paper. "Behavioral might be a more reasonable explanation. Carl's reaction to whatever this is changed in a very short time period. If it were chemical I don't think it would have such a short effect-window. We need to list all the facts."

John nodded, "Good idea. We don't have any real facts yet, just observations. The only clue we have to what is happening is the email you got."

Carl chimed in from the kitchen, "Occam's razor!"

"Okay. Okay. Carl's got a point." John started pacing, "What if we imagine that, as crazy as it seems, the most obvious answer is the one in your inbox. They claim that a gift from the Greek gods is making everyone feel compelled to do what you say. " John had paused in front of her, frowning.

She looked down at the list she had been writing. "Not everyone feels compelled. You've never felt compelled to do what I say. I spent half of yesterday telling you to leave me alone, and the other half begging you to let me off the hook about the allergies. And you did neither. If this is some behavioral scam, why didn't it work on you?"

John cocked his head, staring at her, "That's a good point. Why didn't it affect me? Maybe because I'm a skeptical person? I am a reporter, after all..."

Carl re-entered with the bowl of vinegar water, "Maybe it's because you don't like her? Or that she doesn't like you?" As he looked back and forth between the two, Hannah went back to studying her list, avoiding Carl's gaze. He continued, "But that wouldn't really fit me, because I'm not affected anymore, and I still lov..."

"Here, let me work on this." Hannah grabbed the bowl from Carl and started to blot the coffee stain with vigor. For a minute the only sound was of Hannah muttering about *Ladies' Home and Hearth* as she worked on the cushion. Carl joined her with a second cloth.

"Can you two please stop it with the stain? We have to deal with this! I think we need to focus on figuring out a game plan for responding to whoever sent this email." John stood up abruptly. She and Carl perched on the couch and watched as John paced back forth in front of the couch, gesturing broadly as he talked, "Clearly you cannot call this number and wait to be collected. And that means that they will be coming for you at some point. We need a plan to figure out who they really are and how to stop this." His sweeping arm took in all of the media and Hannah, ending with a finger pointing at her, "Planning is your thing. You successfully planned our break-in last night. Here, let me finish the blotting. You plan." And he put his hand out for the towel. She looked at Carl.

"Go on, Han. Make your lists. We'll finish this. When you have the lists ready, we can all sit down and talk it out."

None of this felt real, and yet, something was definitely happening. Maybe a list would help. Surrendering her towel to John, she grabbed more paper from the bin, moved to the desk and started writing, chewing the rim of her coffee cup to help her stay calm as she forced herself to label the first list, "Reasons to consider The Greek Gods Theory."

The Myth of Cassandra

Thirty minutes later, they were all sitting around the coffee table, John and Carl on the slightly damp couch, Hannah facing them in the computer chair. She presented them with her lists. They ranged from "Facts we know about the "gift," to "Facts we know about Archer Adams and the so-called Greek Gods," and included sub-lists of "odd occurrences in the past 24 hours", and "out-of-character moments." Carl and John sifted through the lists as Hannah sipped her cold coffee out of the one portion of the rim she had not destroyed.

"That's all I have, right now. Can you guys think of anything else? Anything I might have missed?" Hannah prodded as they passed the papers back and forth.

John piped up, "Number three on "Facts We Know About Archer Adams and the so-called Greek Gods. " If someone hacked into your email to plant that message, can you trace the IP address to a server in Massachusetts? You said the cell phone number was activated in Boston. Can't we triangulate or something? Maybe if we can get the drop on them, we can case the joint."

Carl looked at John incredulously, "Are you high? This isn't CSI, man. What, shall we play some techno music while Hannah hits some keys on the computer and a digitalized picture of the assailant forms on the big screen? This is real life. Besides Hannah is a classics major, not some techie...and case the joint? Really?"

"Okay, okay, so maybe I do watch CSI and maybe there was a Bogart marathon on the other night, but Hannah is really good with computers. I watched her sit at that very computer and find things I couldn't, break passwords with freaking Klingon, and pull up security schematics..."

Carl interrupted, "You must have imagined it. Obsessively screening your email doesn't make you a computer whiz...Tell him Han."

Hannah had rolled back to the computer during their argument, and looked over her shoulder at Carl, "Well, I know a little bit more than you might think. But I would never describe myself as a "whiz." Both men looked up from the lists in their hands; Carl in confusion while John just rolled his eyes. She could almost hear him thinking "liar."

She turned back to the keyboard and continued, "And you weren't completely off track, John. I don't need to triangulate. While I can't find an exact origination of the email because it came over a burner phone, I can track the call to the cell tower it came in on, and that appears to be a fairly contained location." Hitting a string of keys, a map of Massachusetts loaded up slowly on the screen, with a red ring off the Southern coast. "Martha's Vineyard. It's not very big and it is fairly isolated. At least before the tourists hit. It's a start." The silence that met her announcement was only momentary, as it was broken by a loud siren blaring to life outside the window of the apartment. They all sprinted to look out and witnessed a parade of students being lead by the Campus Police heading to the dorms; many holding hand-made signs for the SOT.

John spoke first, "We have to get Hannah out of here. Now. If that sleazy fake Public Safety Officer who stole your ring is in any way connected to the email people, he knows Hannah is here. We need to move first and figure things out on the run. That's what laptops were made for."

Hannah turned away from the window wrapping her arms around herself, "I agree. We need to get on the road. I don't believe for a minute that this has anything to do with gods and gifts, but whatever this is, whoever is doing this, they seem to be using me, so someone has something planned, and I want to know as much about it as possible before we meet with them."

"So we all agree," John was nodding, "We'll go to Martha's Vineyard and learn as much as we can before we call them. Carl, where is your car? We can work out the details on the way. Every nerve ending I have is screaming at me that we need to leave this apartment NOW." John jammed his laptop into his messenger bag, wrapping the charger cord around his hand then shoving it on top.

Closing his mouth, Carl shook his head, "Actually, I've been thinking about this while Hannah was making her lists. The problem is, the media know who I am. I am the man the SOT dumped at the Sermon on the Dinner Roll. If I come with you, or you use my car, we won't make it past the campus border." He held up his hand to forestall their response,

"John, no one got a good look at you at the restaurant, and given your past history together, no one will figure that the two of you would be talking, let alone working together. You'll need a distraction, something to focus people's attention away from your escape. I have an idea. Hear me out."

Carl outlined his escape plan. In ten minutes they were out the door and the plan was in motion. It was a good thing, too, as John's nerves were right on target, and they had not a minute to lose.

✦✦✦✦✦✦✦✦✦✦✦✦

Hermes

Location, location, location

"You gonna answer that, Herms? Your phone's been buzzing like my mother-in-law after a fifth of Jim Beam."

"Just show me where to sign," Hermes shoved his phone deeper into his coat pocket and angled a slight smile at the woman in front of him. Charm, Hermes, remember to use a little charm. "Sorry, Verna, I don't mean to snap, it's just...."

"Don't worry, sweetie, I'm no mossy rosebud. Making an offer is stressful; it'd turn a nun into a bitch. Now you need to sign here, and here, and here and initial this here."

Hermes followed her somewhat chipped nail across the pages of the legal document, signing with a speed that didn't seem to faze his agent in the least.

"I'll just messenger this over to the owner's agent and we should have an answer by tonight." Slapping the document into a manila envelope, she narrowed her gaze on his face, "You have a place to grab a few hours of sleep? 'Cause my cousin runs an Inn up the road and you look like hell, and as for your smell, well I hope it was a good vintage."

Hermes grimaced. It was one of the quirks of his realtor, Verna Springs. She possessed a forthrightness that was particular to the Pacific

Northwest; it was saved from rudeness by the complete lack of pretension. Take the office he was currently standing in. To call it modest would be kind by anyone's standards; a battered metal desk, phone, fax and copy machine and two utilitarian chairs that appeared to have been mended with duct tape. One small window looked out over Puget Sound and the only thing on the walls was a framed copy of her realtor's license. Yet he knew for a fact that she was the top grossing realtor in the state and her net worth was well over 9 million. He considered himself lucky to have found her when he started renting in the Pacific NW and knew that her comments were a compliment of sorts. Verna didn't bother insulting you if she didn't like you.

Sniffing his sleeve his grimace deepened. There is only so much red wine a being should drink in a four-hour period. While Bacchus was a fabulous fence, he was a sloppy drunk. It wasn't only wine that had stained his clothing, but vomit as well. Maybe crashing at Verna's cousin's Inn was exactly what he needed before he listened to the dozens of voicemails Zeus had been leaving on his phone. "Sorry about the smell, Verna. That sounds nice, a shower and a real bed...."

"Consider it done. I'll give her a call to let her know that you're on the way. She'll like you, but try to remember that she's my cousin and this is a small town. She has a tendency to kiss and tell, that one. Oh, and stay close to your phone; if they counter I want to get in their face right away. I won't have that bastard playing you against some California couple wanting to spread their preppy bullshit in our fine islands. The place is yours. I promise. Now get out of here. The Bluenose Inn, three blocks south of here overlooking the sound. And whatever you do, do not eat her scones. They are god-awful."

And with that she waved him out of the room. Leaving, he heard her pick up the phone and a string of invectives followed him out the door. While Verna might not be the most refined individual, one of the benefits of her nature was that she was a ferocious negotiator and he felt confident that with the cash down payment he'd attached to his offer, the House Boat of his dreams was a sure thing. He turned left and lifted his face to morning mist that still hung over the Sound. Gods he loved this place: the sounds, the sights, the smells. Catching a whiff of his own person he amended that last one to be more specific: he loved the smell of the ocean.

Bacchus had gotten him a sweet deal on the ring and he had enough in the bank to take a break from the world of investigations and just enjoy his new home. Well, the home that would be his by tonight. Everything was right in the world, at least in his world, and that was all that mattered. Following the sidewalk, he sighted the sign for the Bluenose Inn and ordered himself not to think about H. It wasn't like it was his fault. He hadn't given H the gift, just delivered it. And he sure as hell hadn't told her to say all those things about following your dreams and everyone deserving some honesty. If he had happened to glance at the TV over the bar last night and seen disturbing images of chaos on a societal scale and overheard a few conversations about the Speaker of Truth while he and Bacchus had partied, well, it wasn't the end of the world. Yet.

He knew H was missing. When Bacchus had wandered off to empty his stomach to make room for another bottle, he'd caught a local Connecticut affiliate's report being rebroadcast on the TV above the bar. The reporter on the scene, Steve McKing, had been interviewing people who were camping outside of H's dorm, all eager to see the Speaker of Truth. No one knew where she was, but they'd decided to wait, eager to hear more from the SOT. After a few repetitive interviews, the anchor had repeated the "Lessons of the Great SOT" and urged viewers to follow their dreams and be more honest. Then he'd announced he was leaving the station to become an astronaut and proceeded to insult the station anchor, whom he had always thought of as an arrogant phony with a big butt. She insulted him back by outing his toupee and recent liposuction.

He'd been spared further displays of "honesty" by Bacchus' return and insistence that the next bottle should be drunk while dancing, changing the station to MTV and encouraging everyone in the bar to "Vogue."

Kicking a rock off the sidewalk, Hermes frowned. So no one knew where H was. It explained the unremitting string of phone calls he'd been ignoring from Zeus. He'd told them not to gift her. But no, Apollo wanted his gift girl, so Apollo got his gift girl. Well, let Zeus and Apollo find her and do whatever they needed to get her to say whatever it was they wanted her to say. He sure as hell wasn't going to answer the phone and be pulled into their mess.

Stepping up onto the front porch of the Blue Nose Inn Hermes felt it. The pulling. Oh crap. It was happening. He clenched his jaw and tried to think the word "no" in capital letters, but as he lifted the knocker to enter he felt the claim of a long past debt. A connection that could summon him whenever and wherever he might be, and against any conscious thought that clung to the idea that this was not his problem, he felt his shoes winging him across the country and onto the front porch of Hera's seaside home. Dammit. With the sun now high in the sky on this coast, he took one last breath of ocean air and walked into the bedlam he could see through the wide windows.

"You called, Hera?" Hermes walked past that publicist and his minion and through to the kitchen, taking in the scene. Empty wine bottles lined up on the counter, dirty dishes piled up in the sink, greasy cartons of Kentucky Fried balancing precariously on top of the garbage and Hera sitting statue-like amongst it all nursing her coffee. There was so much wrong with this picture, that Hermes felt the first edges of real anger at Zeus. Couldn't he see what was happening? That prick publicist had some seriously bad mojo about him for Hera to be this bad off. He hadn't seen her like this in thousands of years. Where the hell was the thunderbolt king?

Hera lifted a china cup so thin it was translucent and sipped before answering. She lowered it cautiously into the saucer and looked up, her voice quiet "I need you to find the girl and bring her to me. And me alone. Here. Will you do it?"

Hermes considered his choices. He didn't need this job. He had the money from the ring and the houseboat was calling. Sunsets on the water, cool breezes, peace and quiet, and mosquito free nights. But he could read between the lines. That prick publicist was using the Idiot Sun God to force some agenda on Hera and Zeus. What the goal of that agenda

The Myth of Cassandra

was remained unclear. He could feel the publicist's eyes boring into his back from the living room. He could go back to the Bluenose Inn and relax with Verna's cousin and forget this entire mess. But then there was the undeniable fact that Hera had asked him for help instead of ordering him. It wasn't like that mattered. Very much.

So he took the job. It was easy and eventually the ring money would run out and it wouldn't hurt to have Hera owe him one. But before he got started, he would get a meal and a shower from one of the Inns on this coast. It wasn't like he had to rush out and grab her immediately. He knew H was with the Former Boyfriend at the Line Boy's place, probably still weepy and afraid. It would be simple to collect her.

CHAPTER ELEVEN

The SOT on the Run

❋❋❋

Hannah

Slowly making her way up the coast

They had decided to take secondary roads up the coast to get to the ferry at Wood's Hole that would carry them to Martha's Vineyard. Well, "decided" wasn't particularly accurate, more like, "had no choice but to." When John had converted his Vespa to run on vegetable oil it had taken the engine power down a notch, add to that the extra weight of another passenger, and it struggled to get up to 45mph. It had seemed safer to stick to local roads. Carl had pointed out that this route had the benefit of avoiding the government cameras at the tollbooths. Hannah smiled at this Carl-ism. Regardless of that dubious advantage, it had taken what should have been a two-hour trip and stretched it out to at least twice that time.

Plenty of time to reflect on the events of the morning. Carl's plan had been simple; he would distract the media with a new message from the SOT. If they allowed themselves to believe that people were compelled to listen to her, then she wanted to send a message that would hopefully counter-act the chaotic effects of her first speech. The plan was to have Carl bring it to the media while she and John would get out of town undetected. John had helped her craft the new speech. It was harder than you might think, trying to anticipate the effect of your words when people have no choice but to hang on them. She wished they had more time to perfect it, but they had had to move quickly. It had been John's idea to add in the bit about not being Hannah Summers, and having a disfiguring disease. He had made the excellent point that when this was all over she would need to get back to being just Hannah Summers, so if these powers were real, which defied reason, why not use them to make her return to normal life easier.

So Carl would mesmerize the media, and she and John would investigate the people who had sent the email, providing they were still on Martha's Vineyard. While she could hope that the message Carl shared with the cameras would put society back on track, she felt shaky knowing that the people who had sent her that email would also now know that not only was she not going to be calling them to be collected, but she had disobeyed them by making another speech. That made her more than a little nervous for her mom and dad. Carl had promised that he would go to them after the press conference and make sure they understood what was going on.

She wished Carl all the luck with that task. Try as she might with list upon list, she had failed to understand what was happening. But a dispassionate analysis of the situation showed that understanding was not that important. As reasonable as it was to think that the Greek Gods were not real, it didn't help her formulate a response. If something doesn't exist, then you can't do anything about it. So, in the interest of doing something, she accepted it. The Greek Gods were real. At least in the context of what was happening to her. Once she got over that hurdle, all the pieces had fallen into place.

First known piece; she was, according to their publicist, a descendant of Cassandra of Priam. That was at least possible; her mother's family was Greek. Second piece; the gods, specifically Apollo and Zeus, had apparently hired a publicist, Archer Adams. A quick Google search had shown that he, Adams, did exist, at least online. Finally, the email said that the gods had given her a "gift" as reparations. While she couldn't deny that people were listening to her, and that this was indeed the opposite problem of her alleged-ancestor, Cassandra, who could get no one to listen to her, none of this made sense. Why would they bother to make reparations?

There was no way that the Greek Gods she had studied would be at all disposed to make "reparations." That would imply that they had accepted responsibility for committing a wrong against a human, and that just wasn't in keeping with their profile. This meant that there was something else behind all of this. So she and John were going to the Vineyard to get as much information as they could. Before whoever or whatever sent her that email decided to "collect" her forcibly.

The only one possibly connected to the strange events of the last twenty-four hours who might know where to find her was the thief who pretended to be a public safety officer from last night. If she theoretically accepted that the Greek Gods existed, then the stealing, lying, forging, smirking busboy/public safety officer might just be Hermes, the Messenger God. So she'd devised a trap, with the help of John's landlady, Candy, to keep him off their tails. At least until they figured out what was going on. Because if there was one thing she knew, theoretically, about the Greek Gods, is that humans must tread carefully. The Olympians tended to curse first and ask questions later. Her knowledge of which gods were involved and why, should help her avoid being cursed. She'd had no idea how practical her Classics Degree was going to be. She'd have to thank Prof. Tetley when this was all over.

So with the trap for Hermes, the diversion of media attention with a new SOT message, and the escape on the eco-friendly Vespa, she'd been filled with the optimism of having a plan. But she and John had been on the road for over an hour now and the optimism was yielding to second-guessing and physical discomfort. What if she should have called them, the unknown and threatening them? What if by not calling them, she had put her parents at risk? Or Carl? Or John? Or Candy? Or herself? She knew that "what ifs" were the first hills down which she would slide into panic, so she tried her own diversionary tactic and focused on her physical discomforts.

Top of the list, her wig. Her long, itchy, bright red wig. She couldn't reach her scalp to scratch it because the helmet was firmly in the way.

The Myth of Cassandra

Long strands of hair kept flying into her mouth, which made her gag. She tried to spit it out and wipe her mouth on her own shoulder with limited success. It would have been easier if she could have let go of John to use her hands to pull it back, but she was afraid to let go at this speed. Wishing she had chosen the short black bob wig instead, she replayed the scene in her head of getting this wig. That had been illuminating.

After taping the message, John was eager to hit the road, but Hannah pointed out that she had no shoes, and even though the media was looking for a Hannah Summers with a swollen face and her face was normal again, people on campus who knew she was Hannah Summers would recognize her, making it hard for them to slip out of town. She should probably try to disguise herself. Carl started to suggest he go back to the Frat house to look through the lost and found for some clothes to disguise her, but had John stopped him. "I know the perfect person to help us. Candy."

Hannah and Carl must have said it in unison, because it seemed to echo in the apartment, "Who's Candy?" John was already at the door, "She's my landlady. She's always willing to help out and I think you'll fit in her clothes. Mostly. Also, I happen to know that she has a lot of wigs, which I'm sure she'll let you borrow. Besides, if she isn't willing, you can just use your Jedi mind trick on her, and she'll fall in line, yes?" Hannah nodded slowly, wondering what he had meant by "mostly" and contemplating how she would look in an old lady wig.

As she followed John down the stairs, Carl leaned in from behind her and whispered, "Who has a landlady named Candy?"

Whispering back, she explained, "John does. She's some aging cougar John slept with one drunken night and now she stalks him. I knew she was old, but wig-wearing old? That's just wrong."

They heard John knock on the door and it opened. "Hey Candy. My friends and I, we need some help. Can we come in?" Hannah and Carl approached the door as it opened wider, and John's landlady smiled at them.

Her voice was low and melodic, with just a hint of rasp, "Well, sure, honey. I have an hour before my first class. Come in. I was just having some coffee..."

Carl stood frozen to the spot with a dumb vacant smile on his face. Hannah managed to get out a brief hello before she spun to face John. "This is your landlady?" And working purely on instinct, she punched him in the gut.

Laughing, Candy tossed back her silky red hair, putting her hand on her hourglass hip, "I'm not sure what he did, but I'm sure he deserved it. Most men do. Come on in and let me shut the door." Hannah stalked through the door, not sure exactly why she felt satisfied with the groan John had let out when her fist had made contact. She was certain it had something to do with how John had completely misled her about the reality of his landlady. Candy put her arm around Hannah and asked, "What kind of help do you need?" The men both managed to move before the door shut on them, Carl in a trance and John out of breath.

As Hannah launched into their story, it became clear that the "gift" didn't work on Candy, which was a tremendous relief to Hannah, as she had come to dread the vacant stare of people on whom the gift did work. Between the three of them they explained their problem and Candy did not hesitate to lend Hannah some clothes. They did fit, though they were a bit revealing in some places, and a little "loose" in others. Candy was built like a video game heroine and had curves that made Carl stammer every time he tried to talk to her. Candy seemed to think that was sweet and patted Carl on the cheek, which only made it worse. Hannah figured Candy had this affect on a lot of guys. On the other hand, John had seemed perfectly relaxed around her and spoke normally, after he got his breath back of course.

Hannah had liked her too. Sometimes really beautiful women only focused on men. But Candy had made her feel comfortable right away. John was right about the wigs. Though there was not one grey wig to be found, Candy had a closet full in every conceivable color. Blue, green, silver, etc. Hannah had decided on a shoulder length, curly, red one.

It became apparent that Hannah's long thick hair would have to be cut for the wig to stay on right. Candy had been worried that the cut might upset Hannah and offered to see if they could make do with a hat or scarf for the disguise, but the bike helmet made those options less viable. With time tight, Hannah asked Candy to cut her hair. She was a little surprised when it came down to it that she didn't mind. She had spent years growing it because it was supposedly the one thing that was attractive about her. But she saw now what a dumb idea that was. It was just hair. She was not Sampson, and would not lose whatever limited power she had if she cut her hair. So Candy pulled it into a ponytail and cut it off. Hannah remembered the feeling of running her fingers through her newly shorn head. She liked it. It made her feel bad ass, like a warrior.

Which was fitting, because at some point that morning— maybe when she was taping a speech with a bag over her head, or when she was riding out of town in a haze of French fried exhaust— she had decided that there was no way she was going to let these theoretical Greek Gods and their publicist push her around. She hadn't asked for their supremely stupid gift, and she refused to help them in whatever self-serving plan they must have. If she knew one thing about the Greek Gods, it was that they were not known for their altruism. She had to avoid getting caught until she knew in more detail what she was up against. When the time was right she would call their phone number and arrange to meet them on her own terms.

As they were heading out the door of Candy's apartment, she had asked if they was anything more she could do to help, and it occurred to Hannah that yes, there was one thing, if she was willing. Pushing the long red strands back from her face, she looked Candy in the eye, "How do you feel about removing a stranger's shoes?"

Hermes

Making his way back to Centreville

Hermes took his time getting to the Line Boy's place. There was no sense in waking H up before she had a chance to recover from yesterday. She'd spent half the night talking with the Boyfriend, correction, Former Boyfriend and was probably still asleep. And if she was awake, she was probably freaked out. Forget all the media attention, Hermes had seen a copy of the email that bastard Archer had sent her, and she was probably huddled in a corner waiting to be collected. Terrified by what was happening to her.

Hermes slipped up the fire escape and found the window unlocked. College students. A quick scan of the main apartment showed that it was empty, but he could hear the distinct sound of female sobs. Hannah must be crying in the bedroom. Figures. She'd been crying when he left— she probably never stopped. She was falling apart faster than even he had predicted. He shook his head, not sure which disgusted him more, her sad descent into helplessness or the fact that the boys left her alone in this state.

Dropping his invisibility, Hermes slipped down the hall and pried open the bedroom door. There she was, face down on the bed, crying into her pillow, long blond hair covering her face. She hadn't noticed him yet. But he noticed her a little more than normal. Had she always filled out sweatpants like this? Well, hello Hannah. Hermes tilted his head and considered his options. There was no real rush to get her to the Island; it would be heartless of him not to offer her a little comfort. She was clearly distressed. And "on the rebound" was his favorite time in a woman's life.

Not wanting to startle her, he sat on the edge of the bed and stroked her hair lightly, "Hannah, don't worry, everything is going to be okay. I'm here and I'll take care of you. You don't need to be worried about Zeus and Apollo; I'll protect you. I promise you won't have to do any-

The Myth of Cassandra

thing you don't want to..." That was good, she had stopped crying, and she hadn't freaked out, only gone still like, "I'd like to do more than protect you, Hannah, I'd like to make you feel better." And he slid his hand down to rest on the small of her back, "If you'll let me?" Oh let me, Hannah, let me.

He wasn't sure what happened next or how he ended up handcuffed to the futon frame, but that was definitely not Hannah Summers slithering down his body. Holding the long blonde wig in one locked hand and he spied a distinctly red head crouching at the foot of the bed. The mystery woman stood up and he tried to focus on the winged shoes she held triumphantly in her hands, but it was hard. If the rear view of this woman had been impressive, the frontal view was of a fantasy woman— all bodacious curves that couldn't possibly be real. Then she smiled and he liked her even more.

"Nice winged shoes! She thought you might be Hermes— she told me that you would come to get her. If you were real." She looked him up and down, which he didn't mind at all, "You are definitely real. She also told me you were a player, 'Let me make you feel better,' really, does that line work for you?"

Hermes merely shrugged and his captor dangled the shoes in front of her, "She told me that if I took your winged shoes you wouldn't be able to escape the handcuffs. She's one smart chick, that Hannah. Look at you, falling into her trap." And she let her gaze travel slowly up his body again, which was now at full attention. Hermes' smile deepened, certain that she was impressed with more than just his shoes.

He considered this new information about Hannah. She must have a plan and she seems to have an inkling of whom she is up against. Good for her. He was less concerned about escorting her back to Hera— H could clearly take care of herself. As for his situation, he could escape these insignificant handcuffs in less than three seconds, and while he did need his shoes to access his flying powers, he no longer cared about escaping. "Well, I like to be on a first name basis with my captors. You know my name, but I don't know yours, and that hardly seems fair."

"I'm the landlady." She turned and placed the fluttering sandals on the dresser, "I am also a yoga instructor and extremely flexible. You can call me Candy." She pulled her shirt up and over her head in one smooth move and climbed over him, "Candy. Remember that when you need to yell."

At that moment, Hermes again felt the unwelcome pull of a call from Hera. He ignored it, blocking it from his mind. Instead he focused on one word: Candy. He lifted his hips to help Candy remove his clothes. This was the second time in as many days that he had taken "candy" from H. He would have to thank her when next he saw her.

CHAPTER TWELVE

The 24 Hour News Cycle

●●●

Carl

Beware Frat Boys bearing iPhones

"This is Steve McKing for Channel 7 News with a SOT exclusive. I have with me Carl Rogerson, the man the most wondrous SOT broke up with in her first major address to the public. Carl, can you tell us, when will we see the SOT? Do you know when she will come home? When will we hear from her? What will she tell us?"

"Well, Steve, as a matter of fact, I have a message from her on my phone. I'd like to play it for you and the public, if you'll let me?" Carl nodded encouragingly at Steve, holding up his phone to show his sincerity.

"Let you? This is amazing! I can't believe that I'll have the exclusive interview with the man carrying the SOT's next message. I am one lucky bastard— in all honesty I am actually a fairly awful reporter— I usually just hang out and tail my competitor's van to get the news. My entire crew thinks I am an idiot. There is no way I deserve this kind of break. Will I let you play it? Of course I will. Play it. Wait, let me introduce it. Does my toupee look good?" The undeserving but very honest newsman leaned into the camera and turned his head from side to side.

"Um, sure, you look great, Steve." Carl frowned at the woman working the camera who was shaking her head, clearly about to unleash some unvarnished truth on good old Steve. Carl felt like he was Alice in Wonderland at the Mad Hatter's Party. Had this been what he had been like at dinner last night? Being under the spell of whatever was happening to Hannah was making idiots out of everyone. He hoped this second message fixed it.

"Okay. Ahem, this is Steve McKing with a worldwide exclusive. Prepare yourself for the second proclamation of the great SOT. " In an aside to Carl he whispered, "Okay, play it now."

Carl smiled at him, held his phone up to the camera and hit play on the message they had recorded in John's apartment. He was gratified to see every eye focus on the three-inch screen of his phone. None of them noticed the man with a leather messenger bag and woman with long red hair flying up Main Street on a light blue Vespa smelling of French fries. But he saw them. And as if she could feel his regard, the great SOT looked back and waved. Carl smiled and hit play:

"Hi. My name is not important, and I ask you to please stop using the name Hannah Summers. I am not her and she is not me. It's fine if you refer to me as the SOT. I'm sorry that I can't make this statement in person, but, as some of you have guessed, I'm suffering from a rare disease that has continued to disfigure me, and I'm simply more comfortable under this bag. I'd hate for my hideous appearance to distract you from my message.

I have three messages for you today. I respectfully ask you to please heed my words, as this message seeks to correct some past misunderstandings of my first message.

First: Although it is good to follow your dreams, it takes planning and work to achieve dreams, and in the meantime, it's important that everyone continue to fulfill their obligations while they consider how best to follow their dreams. Go back to work. Or school. Or whatever you were doing yesterday.

Second: Honesty is good, but so is kindness. When being honest, please consider how your honesty will affect others, and if it is hurtful, please try to find a way to be kinder. Also, you do not need to share every stray, honest thought. Think before you speak and above all, be kind.

Finally, I will speak to you again soon. Carl will be able to share my messages. He will let you know when I'm ready to talk, until then it would be good if you paid attention to all of the news in the world and not just wait for me to speak. Thank you."

Steve McKing looked momentarily dumbfounded, and then addressing the news anchor, he was all smiles, "Well, that was quite a speech. What did you think about it, Susan?"

"I agree with you, Steve, it was quite a speech. What do you think it means? You are the reporter who has been covering this story from the beginning, and you probably have the best perspective on the SOT's intent."

"That's so kind of you Susan, to defer to my experience. But I would really rather defer to you. You have a Master's Degree in Communications and I've always thought of you as a more intelligent person than me, so I would really like it if you would share your thoughts on the SOT's second speech. I'm sure the public would be interested too."

"Oh Steve, that's so kind of you to mention my degree. I've admired many things about you as well. You're very handsome, and your speaking voice is so pleasant to hear; like liquid honey. Maybe we should work together to share our thoughts about this speech, but after we finish covering all of the news in the world."

"That's a great idea, Susan. You have so many great ideas. And you have really clean fingernails. There are so many nice things about you, Susan; I think I'll make a list. Maybe after work. I'm leaving this campus, because I won't wait around for the most wise SOT anymore. You are totally right about the news of the word. I'm heading back to the station right now to start working on that. This is Steve McKing with Channel 7 News."

Hera

Tensions rising in Martha's Vineyard

"Shhh. It's starting." Hera waved Zeus out of the way of the TV. He had wandered in from the kitchen when the Special Report music had started. It seemed that a man identified as the gift girl's ex-boyfriend had come forward claiming to have a video message from her. They were calling her the Speaker of Truth, or the SOT for short. Humans were easily impressed and short on irony. Since when did power equal truth? Hera rolled her eyes as the news anchor reviewed the last speech given by the SOT and speculated on what she might say this time.

Apollo was sitting directly in front of the massive screen, neck craned back. Lee was furiously tapping at his computer, mumbling, "She opened the email….Clearly she has opened it….she should have called by now….why hasn't she called….I would have called…." Archer was standing in the furthest corner of the room, completely still, eyes trained on the TV and Hera had an instant impression of him as a bird of prey, watching the little rabbit from a distance, waiting to strike. It was not as if she cared what happened to this particular girl, she was more concerned with the bigger picture of human society, but still…. She thought rabbits deserved a chance. Where the hell was Hermes?

Zeus raised his eyebrows, and in a studiously casual voice noted, "That's odd, isn't it? Odd, that the girl is making another speech. Didn't you explicitly tell her to talk to no one, Archer? What was it you said in that email? Serious consequences? Hmm… clearly she's terrified." Archer's eyes narrowed infinitesimally, but other than that he had no response to Zeus' baiting.

Great. Hera rolled her eyes. The only thing worse than a depressed Zeus was a perverse Zeus. His needling was pushing this in one direction. She was certain Archer was something other than human with powers not usual to a publicist; she had not missed his smoking shirtsleeves the other night when he lost his temper. While she did not know precisely what he was, she recognized a soulless creature when she saw one. This would not go well for the girl.

The Myth of Cassandra

Why the hell hadn't Hermes returned with the girl yet? She straightened the pillows on the sofa, again. Hitting the pillows mercilessly into shape, her thoughts spun out. It wasn't something she liked to admit, but she'd grown fond of humans in general these last hundred years or so. They were short-lived and not very bright, but there was something endearing about how they cared for each other. And there was something in this young woman's defiance of Adam's threats that impressed her. She only hoped that the girl had more to her than stupid bravery. The room fell silent as the boy on the TV hit play on his phone and the video of a girl with a bag on her head filled the screen.

The entire message took less than a minute. Hera shook her head; the girl had no idea how to use power. What a mess. People should be kind above all else? That was brilliant. Because nothing gets things done like people being kind. Oh, and that little bit about going back to doing what you did yesterday; there were so many ways for that to go wrong. "Well, I guess that's it for the big plan to regain Olympus." She tried to sound disappointed.

"Where is your messenger boy, Hera? I thought he knew where she was? I thought he would be back with her ASAP? But instead she has made another FREAKING SPEECH! I WANT THAT GIRL BROUGHT TO ME NOW!" Archer's eyes glowed red.

"You forget yourself, Adams, or do you really think it's wise for you to yell at me?" Hera was completely still, face deceptively calm. "I abhor threats, unless I am the one doing the threatening, and if I perceived that someone as insignificant as say, you, was even remotely threatening me, I would see no alternative but to clean house. So, I must have misunderstood you? Yes?"

"You're right, you did misunderstand me. I wasn't threatening you. I was questioning you." Archer walked deliberately toward her, tilting his head to the side in mock wonder, "What kind of god can't make her messenger boy bring her what she wants? Which begs the question, what do you want, Hera?" Turning his back on her he looked at Zeus and continued with all the conviction of a prosecuting attorney making a closing argument, "Let's look at the facts. You've been against this project from the beginning and I wouldn't put it past you to be purposefully sabotaging it. It's very interesting that you brought up the idea of threats. You know what I think threatens you? Zeus becoming Zeus again. I think you like him as the over-weight, needy, basement dweller. What did you tell him to do, Hera? Get a hobby? That'd be real nice for you. Has it been good for you too, Zeus?" Lee and Apollo sat on the couch speechless. Apollo's head twisted back and forth between the three while Lee chewed nervously on a mozzarella stick he had stored in his sock.

Zeus filled the doorway, thunderbolt materializing in his hand, electricity sparking out the top. His face was positively stormy. Archer's became carefully blank, his red eyes the only sign he was excited. Hera looked with disdain on them both. The tension was palpable. The mozzarella stick slid out of Lee's sweaty hands while Apollo took up a defensive position behind the couch.

Hera looked only at Zeus when she spoke. "Are you really going to fall for this thing's obvious manipulations? I haven't thwarted you, I've supported you."

Archer's whisper filled the room as loudly as his previous screaming, "My point exactly, Zeus. Look how she takes every opportunity to remind you how she holds the purse strings. How she's in charge. How she has the power now. You know what that makes you, Zeus? A dependent. Zeus, King of the Olympians, supported by his wife. If she's so supportive, where is the messenger with the girl who could catapult you back into power? Why doesn't she summon him?"

Hera spun on her heel, startling Lee who was bent over retrieving his cheese, and pointed at Adams. Rage made her face austere, her voice icy, "You want the messenger? Fine— here he is!" She flicked her wrist and Hermes appeared in the room, completely naked. Lee dropped his rescued cheese stick from nerveless fingers, jaw hanging slack as he stared at the messenger god in all his glory.

Hermes appeared to take his sudden relocation in stride, his gaze taking in Zeus and his glowing thunderbolt, Hera frozen with rage from head to toe, and Archer's look of glee. Hands on his naked hips he deadpanned, "You called, Boss?"

CHAPTER THIRTEEN

A Three-Hour Tour

●●●

Hannah

The SOT hears a truth on the Ferry

Hannah watched the dock at Oak Bluffs come into sight. Leaning over the rail, she followed the flight of the seagulls swooping around the lower deck, catching the breeze off the ferry and floating up, only to drop back down again to ride it another time. Race to the front, catch the current, float up and over, drop down again. Sometimes they stopped to fight over the French fries tossed into the air by bored teens.

She and John had stowed the Vespa close to the ferry behind the garage of a summerhouse that was still shuttered up. The bike was too distinctive and they'd decided they might blend in better on foot. It was possible that Hermes had seen them leave the restaurant on it, and if Candy hadn't been able to trap him, he would be on their tail already.

She leaned back against the rail, pitching her face to the sun and enjoying the way she could see a pink swirl as the wind whipped her hair around. She had ditched the red wig when they'd stopped at the grocery store to pick up vegetable oil for the Vespa. The itch from the wig had been driving her crazy, and her complaints had motivated John to suggest that she pick up some hair dye while he refueled the bike with several gallons of safflower oil. She stuffed the wig into John's bag and left him in aisle six.

The Myth of Cassandra

It had been so easy to color her hair; she wondered why she'd never done it before. And then she heard her mother's voice in her head, "Your hair is your best feature, Hannah…" Okay, maybe she knew why she'd never done it before, but this was now. She stared at the myriad of choices, selected a product she could apply in the grocery store bathroom, and got it done. Bubble gum pink. If she'd imagined her choice would shock John, she was disappointed. He'd simply said, "That's nice." And then offered her half of the sub he was eating under the stunted tree in the grocery store parking lot.

For a moment she'd forgotten what was happening and she'd just been enjoying eating while John had shown her a WWSOTS shirt he had picked up as a souvenir — What Would the Speaker of Truth Say. But a woman overheard her joking about toothpaste, and started ranting about how true it was, that as the SOT says, all toothpaste should come in a pump. They had left before her yelling could draw a crowd.

The captain's announcement for drivers to return to their cars pulled her out of her reverie. Looking around to ensure that no one could overhear, Hannah poked John, "So, why did you let me believe that your landlady was some aging, chain smoking, crazy instead of a drop-dead gorgeous yoga instructor with a vast array of wigs?"

John was wearing sunglasses, so she couldn't quite read his face, but the length of his stare and his silence spoke volumes. Fine. She had sort of over-reacted when she had first met Candy. But that was only because she had been shocked by the discrepancy between the imagined landlady and the actual landlady. Not wanting to argue the point, she tried another topic. She pointed toward the looming shoreline, "Look, we're docking." Leaning her elbows on the railing, she kept talking, "I used to dream of living on an island. I had this vision of being on the porch of my cottage on the shore at night, alone, with the ocean all around, relaxed by the space of the sea and safe from the bigger world. But now, all I see are the restrictions. With the options limited, you and everyone else on the island would probably have to shop at the same grocery stores, the same pharmacy, and line up together to leave. Being careful not to flip off the car in front of you, because it could be the pharmacist's girlfriend, who could complain to him, and the next thing you know, there's arsenic in your antibiotic."

She could see his eyebrows rise above his glasses, "You take a dark turn fast, don't you Summers? Is your only exposure to island living Ten Little Indians by Agatha Christie? What about Gilligan and the Skipper— they had a perfectly nice island life that didn't involve murder."

"Then you apparently didn't pick up on the looks Lovey gave Mr. Howell when he was checking out Ginger."

"Touché." Taking Hannah's hand, he started towing her to the front of the boat. "We'll be sure to leave this god-forsaken island before we get knocked off by an avenging pharmacist, or the raging jealousy of another woman." He laced his fingers through hers, gently squeezing, "Or the Greek Gods and their homicidal publicist."

Hannah followed him slowly. The more time that had passed since Carl had played her speech, the more likely they would encounter the "serious consequences" promised in the threatening email. In the past four hours on the bike with only the back of John's helmet to look at, she had started to think through the ramifications of what it meant to have defied the Olympians. Greek Gods were not known for being reasonable. And she knew way too many stories, stories she had assumed were just myths, about how they reacted when humans defied them.

"Maybe this is a bad idea. Since we left Whitfield I've been feeling like a small fleeing rabbit, and I feel like, right now, we are walking into a rabbit trap. A rabbit snare? Maybe this isn't the best way to stop what's happening. What if I use the gift to stop this...?"

John turned and looked at her, "How?"

"What if I overwhelm them with minutiae, you know, flood people with mundane truths? I mean, in my first speech I inadvertently caused airports to shut down and world leaders to break treaties, and now, after trying to correct the effects of my first speech, I overheard the cashier when I was buying the hair dye offering to pay for his customers groceries out of an excess of kindness? Is that sustainable? Is that good? I don't know. How wrong can it go before we try to fix it again? It's like chasing a pendulum. So far people are listening to these big so-called "truths:" follow dreams, being honest, be kind. Maybe the trick is to overwhelm people with prophecies until they can't listen anymore? "The Speaker of Truth thinks mayo should be used sparingly" "The speaker of truth thinks bacon is yummy."

John removed the sunglasses and looked more closely at her face, "Are you hungry?"

"No. Well maybe a little. But, what do you think? About my idea?"

Bracing his hands on the railing as the ferry lurched into the dock, he shook his head, "Yeah, I'm not sure that it's such a good idea, Hannah. I mean you did see how that woman reacted to what you said in the parking lot about toothpaste in a pump...."

"But that's my point. That woman was prepared to defer her choice of toothpaste delivery system to an "entity" that supposedly "speaks the truth." If I generate a list of prophecies that is long and tedious enough, maybe everyone will stop listening? Don't people have standards for their prophets anymore? Shouldn't she be unwilling to let someone else's opinions matter so much to her?"

Hannah saw a glimpse of something on John's face, and felt the blush on her cheeks before she had even fully realized the obviousness of her hypocrisy. In the past twenty-four hours alone the outcome of her habit of deferring to other people's opinions had caused tremendous pain for Carl. And they both knew it. She could only imagine how he would choose to cut her down, and she mentally prepared to take it.

But John didn't bite, instead taking her hand again to join the flow of tourists heading off the boat, "I think we should stick to the plan. We can consider the "Overwhelm them with Minutiae" a back up plan. The cars have started to unload and since we're finally here, why don't we take a look around and see if we can't find your benefactors...."

"But, what if, right now, Carl is in danger, or Candy, or..."

John pushed through the crowd, talking over his shoulder at her, "Let's find a coffee shop with Wi-Fi and then we can fire up the laptop and search that phone number— can you do any of your fancy computer tricks to figure out where they live?" John was weaving through the crowd that was exiting the ferry, almost walking right into one of the cars that were starting to board the now outgoing ferry. Dodging a moving car, Hannah tried to keep up without getting run down.

"I could, but I don't think that's a great idea. If they have someone who can hack into my email to plant a message, then whoever it is has also probably set up a net to catch anyone who might search on the information they gave in the email. Including the phone number." Hannah stopped as the flow of pedestrians in front of her had suddenly halted. She tried to walk around, but found that she couldn't get through the now massing people. "Can you see what's happening?"

John stood up on his tiptoes trying to see over the heads in front of him. "I can't see anything but more heads. Wait, I have an idea," looking back over his shoulder at her, he lowered his voice, "Just stick close and don't say anything— we don't want any SOT attention right now."

John started tapping on shoulders and saying, "excuse me" to each person. Like magic, they stepped out of his way with a smile. Hannah slid through the crowd right behind him. In this way they parted the mob of departing ferry passengers and came upon another crowd of people heading to the ferry. The two crowds appeared to have met in the middle of the street and no one was moving. The people on both sides in the front of the crowd appeared at first to be singing some strange atonal song, but as they got closer, Hannah could make out what they were saying. Over and over again the people would go to step forward, then stop, say, "After you," and step back while the person opposite them would step forward with their arm stretched behind, "No, after you." Over and over. "After you, no after you, no I insist, you are too kind, you must go, no you...." Over and over.

A ferry worker had made it through the crowd, but seemed uncertain how to break the impasse. Hannah started to say something when John pulled on her arm, "Come on, Pinky, let's not get involved." And he dragged her through the rest of the crowd until they made it to the carousel at the bottom of the hill. Hannah pulled her arm back sharply.

"Hey, for starters, I'm not crazy about being pulled around like a naughty toddler in the grocery store. If you'd like me to come with you, use your words. Secondly, we have to go back and help those people.

The Myth of Cassandra

That was ridiculous. And thirdly, Pinky? Really?" Hannah started to walk away, throwing back at him, "I'm going back to help. You can wait here if you like."

John reached out and then dropped his arm stiffly to his side. 'Hannah, wait! You can't help them." As she stared at him, his tone softened, "Haven't you figured it out yet? Every time you tell people something it messes them up even more." She looked back and his next words came out strained, "I'm sorry— I shouldn't have pulled you— I was just a little freaked out. Those people were scary. It's disconcerting seeing people immobilized by kindness. I think Zombies would be less scary, at least we'd understand their motivation...."

Hannah found herself pleading with him, "Please, John, can't we do something? We could at least help them make lines or choose sides of the street. You could do the talking so that I don't screw them up...."

But John stood his ground, "Someone will figure it out. Eventually. Right now we need to keep a low profile and find you know who. If they were looking for us, just the fact that we walked out of that mess would draw attention. So let's focus on our part of the plan. Okay?" And he extended his hand and waited.

Hannah's brow furrowed and she looked back at the massed people, "But I didn't mean people should be kind above making sense. I mean if people are incapable of walking around each other because of what I said, what else is going wrong?" She sank down on the edge of the sidewalk and dropped her head into her hands, "I just want to go back to my dorm and go to sleep. Maybe if I go to sleep in the place before anything went wrong I can start it all over again and not have this. I can wake up and it'll be Monday and everything can happen the way it's supposed to."

John had come to stand in front of her, "Come on, Hannah. I can see a bar from here. If we're going to have this talk, let's do it with some reinforcements. My treat."

Hannah looked at him. He had not told her not to worry. He had not told her to look on the bright side. She could have handled that. Even if he had gotten angry with her for whining she could have held it together. But his simple offer to listen to her, talk with her, buy her a beer; it was more than she was prepared for. She dropped her head back into her hands and was sobbing before he could pull her to her feet. Together they walked not to the bar, but the public beach next to the ferry dock, where her tears could blend in with the ocean spray. They sat on a bench facing the ocean, his arm around her shoulders. She cried until she was done.

✪✪✪✪✪✪✪✪✪✪✪✪

Zeus

In charge on Martha's Vineyard

"No Carly, I do not think we should devote this month's issue to World Events. Yes, I am aware of the latest proclamation of the SOT, but....Yes, I'm sure that you did like it.....Oh, please stop it, you know I despise compliments....Oh, no, I didn't mean to snap at you....Listen, sit tight. Do NOT change the issue, I'll take the next ferry and we can all sit down together. Yes, please set up the meeting for three o'clock. Thank you Carly.... Yes, yes, you too...Okay... I am hanging up the phone now... Yes, now. Good bye." Hera snapped the phone shut and took a deep, cleansing breath. She addressed Zeus alone, "I need to head back to the city; my employees need settling. I'm sorry to leave, but I must go."

She narrowed her gaze on Hermes, "Get your sandals back and help Zeus. Those are my orders. Do everything you can to help Zeus."

Hermes nodded slightly, "It would be a bit quicker if you could send me back to the place from whence you pulled me— my shoes are there. Then I will be sure to do everything in my power to assist Zeus."

Zeus frowned, trying to figure out if the exchange was sincere. The fact that they kept saying his name made him feel like he was missing something significant.

Hera looked at him, "Does that meet with your approval?"

The Myth of Cassandra

All eyes turned to him: Archer, Apollo, Hermes, Hera, and even that lumpy thing looked up from his computer. Zeus tried to remember what it felt like to appreciate this degree of deference. Hadn't he loved it? Wasn't that at the root of this entire enterprise with the devious publicist? To be worshipped again? King of the Gods? At this moment all he could think was that their eyes reminded him of the brief period of time he had tried to keep fish in a tank for a hobby.

He'd liked picking out the brightly colored fish. Even enjoyed decorating the tank with plants and a treasure chest that blew open from the bubbler. What he hadn't liked was the way, every time he came to feed the fish, their eyes had followed his hand until he'd dropped in the flakes of food. They were so expectant. Waiting. It creeped him out. He'd tried feeding them with his eyes closed, but that was just messy. He tried to do it in the dark, but he could have sworn they watched him even more. In the end, he'd donated the tank to the local elementary school for its lobby just to get their fishy eyes out of his life.

Zeus came back from his reverie to find that they were all still waiting for him to answer. Just like the fish. Waiting, always waiting on him. Fine. "Go to work, Hera. Send Hermes back to his shoes first and you," pointing his thunderbolt at his smirking son, who looked for all the world like a small child, drowning under the excess fabric in a pair of sweatpants and t-shirt Hera had pulled from his closet, "get your own damn clothes. I want those back, Messenger. But clean them first." Feeling like his decisiveness was getting away from him as the list got longer, he shot a small bolt of lightning into the floor, "After you get the girl. Bring her back first. Then clean the clothes and return them to me." Hmm, he was not sounding as commanding as he would've liked to. He could see Archer's frown out of the corner of his eye. He slammed the thunderbolt down on the floor again, sparks shooting in all directions, causing Hermes to dance to avoid being burned, "NOW!" Ah, that was good, Archer and Apollo were smiling and Hera was frowning. She would lecture him later about the finish on the bamboo floors, but at least that thing named Lee was cowering and Hermes bowed respectfully.

"As you wish, Zeus."

With that, Hera flicked her wrist, Hermes disappeared, and she walked out, the front door slamming behind her. Good. He could still make things happen. Propping his thunderbolt against the counter, he turned to the fridge. Wielding power always made him hungry. He would just ignore the feeling that the power might have been wielding him and focus instead on the lobster risotto leftover from the other night. Mmmm, creamy...

✸✸✸✸✸✸✸✸✸✸✸✸

Hera

Waiting in line for the Ferry at Oak Bluffs

Hera unlocked the car door and nodded at Hermes to get in. She lowered her sunglasses to take in his fully clothed, winged shoe attire, "You work quickly. I don't suppose you've found the girl yet?"

"No, but I did ask my friend to wash Zeus' clothes, so I should be able to make good on that request." Closing the door behind him he turned in his seat to face her, "Do you really want me to find the girl? I was under the impression that you might have a different task in mind...."

"Yes, well, I do have slightly altered priorities. I want you to make them think you're very close to finding the girl. Keep them, Adams, Apollo, Zeus, on the hook. If it looks like they'll get motivated to bring her in themselves, get to her first and bring her to me. You do know where to find her, don't you?"

"I have a few ideas, but really, she's a wild card right now. The girl I investigated was not nearly open-minded enough to believe we are real. Yet she must believe enough to set a trap for me. My captor was clear on this. She told me Hannah figured out who I was and used that knowledge to catch me."

"So if she allows herself to believe in us, where would she go next? She couldn't know where we live now. She wouldn't head to Greece would she? Or do you think she's gone into hiding?" Getting to the girl first would give her the control she'd been missing since Archer Adams had insinuated himself into her life. She only hoped Hermes was up to the job.

"No. Her latest message said there would be more announcements, sounds more like she has a plan. I know the boyfriend headed out to H's parents in the Boston area...."

Hera lifted her sunglasses so that he could feel the full weight of her disdain, "But she humiliated him and she hates her mother. You said as much in your report. That would be the last place in the world she'd go. You're losing your touch, Hermes. Maybe I over-estimated your abilities...." She raised her right brow and looked down her long, thin, patrician nose.

Hermes stared out the passenger window in silence, his entire body tense. She could see him struggling not to argue, wanting to defend himself. But he knew his place. And sure enough, when he looked back, his tone was conciliatory, "You know best, Hera. I can find the girl. You just say the word. So what's the new "priority?"

Satisfied that her set down would motivate him sufficiently, Hera lowered her glasses, faced forward, and answered in a detached tone, "I want to know everything there is to know about Archer Adams. Dig deep. He's clearly not a human, but I want specifics. I want to know what he is, who he works for, and what their game plan is." She released her death-grip on the steering wheel, not wanting to betray the depth of her frustration with all of this.

Hermes smirked, "My pleasure, Boss. I'll get right on it. I'll get the dirt on Adams."

Hera didn't like his tone. Like he knew she was upset, and that entertained him. Except Hermes always sounded like that and she was getting paranoid. It would all be better when this was over. "And the girl...."

Hermes nodded, "I'll find the girl, boss, but wait to bring her in until you are ready. It shouldn't be hard to keep Adams and the Golden Idiot in the dark about her. Acting is one of my many talents. Hey, isn't your ferry running late? You haven't even loaded up yet."

Just then a young couple walked in front of the car lane. Hera scowled, "Tourists. They flock here in the thousands, mucking everything up. Look at that couple. The world is their tacky oyster— she probably thinks pink hair is edgy. No one over the age of 13 should wear their hair pink. Period." She revved her engine and watched with satisfaction as the couple jumped in reaction.

Hermes made an agreeing noise and exited the car, telling her he'd report to her soon. He seemed to stare at the retreating couple, and then crossed to her side of the car and knocked on her window. Obviously he needed her help. But the cars were finally loading and she had no time to hold his hand. He'd have to figure it out for himself. Ignoring him completely, she drove forward to the sounds of his pain as the car rolled over his winged foot. She could see him in her rearview window, standing on one leg, cradling his injured foot. His hatred of her was at war with his submissiveness as an employee, a battle clearly depicted in his face. She loved watching others struggle with these types of choices. Which would win out? And just like that he chose. Without an angry word or gesture he was gone. Submissiveness won. As she parked her car where the ferry attendant pointed she smiled. The day had just gotten a little bit better.

CHAPTER FOURTEEN

Between a Beer and a Harpy

000

Hannah

The East Chop Motor Inn

Hannah had rinsed her hair three times, and finally was not staining the towels pink. Wiping the steam off with her hand, she stared at her reflection in the bathroom mirror. Her blonde hair was still slightly red, but it should take the brown hair dye well. Hopefully it would make her look different enough. The plastic gloves stuck to her wet fingers, and she used her teeth to pull them down. Squeezing the bottle of color onto her scalp, she combed it through her hair with her fingertips. Checking her watch, she sat down on the toilet seat cover and waited to be Nice n Easy 116B Natural Light Caramel Brown.

It had all started in the bar, The Tipsy Seagull in Oak Bluffs. The bartender had asked if they wanted another, and she and John nodded simultaneously, laughing at their own agreement. She rarely had a second drink, but she felt like the circumstances called for it. She was engaged in a battle with the Greek Gods, who apparently lived on Martha's Vineyard of all places, and she'd spent the last hour bawling on the beach in the company of a man who two days ago she was certain was a complete jerk. She'd been seriously mistaken. About so many things. It made her wonder what else she'd been wrong about.

Swiveling away from the other patrons who were nursing drinks while staring at the TV, she leaned in to John, "Do you think I'm a liar?"

John's eyes narrowed slightly, but he must have decided against sharing, because he shrugged his shoulders and changed the topic, "Well, everyone lies sometimes. Do you want to order a burger or something? You didn't eat much at lunch. How do you take it, well done?"

"That's fine." As John turned to order, Hannah slapped her hand down on the bar, making him jump back, "No! I lied. The truth is I like my burgers just this south of mooing." At this point she started listing reasons on her fingers, "But since you presumed that I liked it well done, I just agreed. I thought to myself, just agree, you should like your burger well done. People are supposed to eat their meat well cooked to avoid food poisoning, right? *Ladies' Home and Hearth* says that a woman should never disagree with a man who is ordering her food. So I agreed. Even though I hate overcooked burgers and think *Ladies' Home and Hearth* is a misogynistic rag. Why would I do that? I am a liar." This last was said into her quickly emptying second beer.

John placed the order, his face carefully blank, "Two burgers please— one rare and one well done." The bartender nodded and John leaned back in his seat and looked toward the ceiling, avoiding all eye contact, "The truth as I see it is that you do a lot of processing before you speak, Hannah, which I guess makes you less a liar and more a control freak." He looked at her now, the force of his words growing, "Like the idea that anyone would judge you based on how you take your burger?" He lifted his second glass of beer and took a long swallow and looked away from her, "The times I like you best are when you just say something without so much...consideration...even if it's obnoxious at least it's interesting."

He went back to drinking while Hannah watched, mouth agape, wondering if it was beer he was drinking or some strange truth serum, "You prefer me to be obnoxious?"

John's voice lowered, all hints of playfulness absent, "Yes. Obnoxious is way better than your pre-packaged "niceness". You want the truth? Yes, I think you're a liar. You use other people's thoughts, matching your responses to the people who ask things of you, rather than giving anyone the power to know what you really think." Turning on his barstool, he looked directly at her, "And then you tell yourself that you do it for them."

Silence filled the space between them, broken suddenly by her own laughter, "Wow, what happens if I buy you a third beer? Will you tell me what you really think?" she smiled, oddly happy with his answer.

He blushed and looked away. "What can I say? I try to read people. When I first met you, you were like an Austen character, all politeness on the outside but sharp-edged and opinionated on the inside, but then, when I heard about you through Carl, you became more like a Dickens woman, written to be a foil to the man in the story, but now I think you are more like a Chekhov heroine; engrossing, flawed and surrounded by drama." At her continued stare, his blush spread and he took a long pull on his beer, almost emptying the glass. "What? I'm an English major. I read a lot."

And the truth of how much she liked him hit her in the gut, making her a little breathless. Liked him even though she was fairly certain there were some pretty unflattering truths in his soliloquy. Oh crap. She liked the MacMan. She found the next words coming out of her mouth before she had even thought of them, "Well if I am one of the Three Sisters, then you are Edmund from the Lion, the Witch and the Wardrobe— he starts out all self-absorbed but ends up coming through for everyone...of course that's only after cozying up to the Ice Queen...."

John shook his head, his smile now easy and direct and she found she had to concentrate to pay attention to what he was saying as opposed to how his mouth looked forming the words, "The Ice Queen is not all bad, she just gets a bad edit. It's not her fault C.S. Lewis was afraid of women...."

Ignoring her elevating pulse, Hannah decided that she needed a refill and swung back toward the bar at the same moment John was swiveling, and his knees striking hers sent her tilting on her stool. John reached out to steady her and his hand stayed on her shoulder. And now his head seemed to be moving towards her. Her brain started screaming, "No. No. No." She kept him at bay by patting him on the shoulder, straight-armed, and turning, so he had to release her shoulder. She blurted out, "You're right about good ole C.S.— look at the other females in his book...like Lucy." God, she felt like an idiot, but she kept talking and her voice hitched up into a whiny register, "Oh, Mr. Tumnus, here's my healing vial!" The hand she had dislodged was now on a newly filled beer glass and he seemed completely relaxed, no sign of reaction to her maniacal speech. She must have imagined his intention. Of course. She plowed on with the now safely uncharged conversation, "I could imagine being that other girl, you know, Lucy's sister, because at least she was a bad-ass with the bow and arrow...."

"Susan." John leaned forward, watching as someone entered the dim interior of the bar.

Hannah spun around, all subtlety having deserted her after her first beer, and stared at the man who took a stool one over from her. The man waved at her. Turning back to John, she whispered, "He doesn't look like a Susan...do you know him?"

"No, Susan was the oldest sister in the Wardrobe— you know, the bad-ass with the bow and arrows. And this might not be the best time to make new friends." He raised his eyebrows to indicate the man at the bar who had now moved to the stool next to Hannah. "We're in our own rather fantastical narrative at the moment, with some significant perils and it would probably be good if we focus on our goal."

John's reminder sobered her quickly. She ran her hands through her hair, which was a much faster nervous habit now that it was shorter, "I know. We can't just wander around the island hoping someone knows Zeus. We have to figure out how to find ...."

"I couldn't help but overhear...is it Zeus Montgomery you're looking for?" The gorgeous stranger was talking to her. He put his hand out, "I am Declan. Declan O'Quinn. I own the art gallery next door, and we're the exclusive gallery for Zeus's photographs. Are you interested in them? I just closed for the night, but I'd be more than happy to open the gallery for you. You and your brother there. When you're done with your dinner of course." Hannah shook his hand, eyes wide, nodding, just now registering the plates of burgers and fries that sat in front of them.

Declan O'Quinn looked to be in his late twenties, red hair, freckles and eyes so green that she could make them out in the dim light of the bar. Add to that his light Irish brogue and he was as easy to take as the beer, which had disappeared from her glass. Could this man lead them to Zeus? Was Zeus, the God of Thunder and Lightning, also the taker of arty photographs? She ignored John's palpable dislike of the man that she could actually feel through her back and tried for a flirty smile, "That would be so kind of you, my brother and I would love to see them, but not if it would trouble you…" She caught John's disgusted expression for the corner of her eye, but tried to focus on remembering what LH&H had said about how to capture a man's interest. Didn't it have something to do with exposing your pupils? She tried to open her eyes as wide as they could go while still looking casual. It was hard. But it seemed to work. He leaned closer to her, and she felt a small moment of triumph.

"No trouble at all, it would be my pleasure. Besides, doesn't the SOT want us to be kind to each other?" He nodded at the bartender, "I'll have a Guinness, mate, and pull my new friends another for their dinners on me. Thanks." This time he looked at both John and Hannah, "I've shared my name, so how does your mother call you for dinner?"

Hannah laughed what she hoped was an encouraging laugh. If this man's Zeus was their Zeus, he would not only know where he lived, but he also might know who else lived there— and she had started to worry about how many Greek gods might be in residence. She was about to answer when John cut in, "I'm Ed and my sister is Susan. And we don't need another beer with dinner, thanks though. Two waters, please." That last was addressed to the bartender, who was not hiding his amusement at the mini-drama unfolding between the three.

Hannah kicked John's stool surreptitiously, "My brother's right. A little rude, but right; I've already had enough to drink." She turned in her stool to face the gallery owner, "I'd love to hear more about your gallery, I have a friend in NY who mentioned Zeus Montgomery as a new artist to watch, and she asked me to come to the Vineyard to see what I could find out, without drawing too much attention to myself." Leaning in closer, she confided, "You know how quickly artists can skyrocket if it becomes common knowledge that museums are interested. I'm sure she'd be very appreciative of your help. As would I." Spinning back she gave John a pointed look and mouthed "ZEUS", then continued, "Ed, why don't you watch the news while Declan and I chat. Would you like to share my fries, Declan?"

Without a word, John turned his back on them and she tried to remember what else *Ladies' Home and Hearth* had to say about classy flirtation in bars, when John grabbed her arm and swiveled her back to face the TV over the bar....

"This is Steve McKing, outside of the Stop and Shop in Killingly, Connecticut, where we have the exclusive interview with Amy Flannery, who claims that she received a personal message directly from the SOT...."

Hannah frantically tried to get the bartender's attention, needing to stop whatever might be coming next, but the bartender, like everyone else in the bar, was engrossed in the images on the screen. Out of the corner of her eye she saw John lunge for the remote, which was on the other side of the bar, knocking glasses over in the process, and hit the off button, but not before Amy confidently asserted that the SOT had the most beautiful pink hair....

The silence in the bar was almost comic, as every eye turned to look at Hannah's glowing pink hair. With more agility than she knew she had, Hannah leapt on top of the bar, outstretched her arms, and said in her most commanding voice, "I am not the pink haired SOT you are looking for." This seemed to work on all the people in the room, including Declan. They were all nodding in agreement, starting to repeat what she had said to each other.

Turning to John for help to get off the bar, she was surprised by the strong arms lifting her to the ground, and looked down into Declan's deep green gaze. "If you're done with dinner, would you like to come back to my place and see my art collection?" Even though a part of her brain balked at such a completely absurd line, she seemed unable to break eye contact, and she found herself nodding. She did need to check his gallery out. Zeus. She was looking for Zeus.

The Myth of Cassandra

So she had walked out of the bar with Declan, aware that John was following, because she could hear him mumbling something that sounded rude, though she couldn't quite make it out.

The sun was setting as they walked across the village square from the bar to the art studio, and Hannah closed her eyes while Declan unlocked the door, finding that she had to concentrate to remember why she was looking for Zeus. If Zeus Montgomery was Zeus, god of Lightening and Thunder, then they could get a home address, case the joint, and make a plan for giving back this awful "gift." Hopefully before society's fabric completely unraveled.

As the tumblers in the lock clicked into place, she followed Declan into the gallery with John at her heels and found herself lost in the images lining the walls. The photographs were a mixture of black and white and color and ranged in size from massive to incredibly small. There were depictions of the wildlife on the island— birds, fish, and rabbits— all shown as disproportionately huge and threatening. The images of the ocean were myriad and ran the gamut from sleepy to furious. People were in some of the photographs, but only the sides or back angles. When they were in pictures they appeared as corners, bounding the edges of the image, never the central focus. What was compelling in every photograph was the use of light. Light that illuminated, light that blinded, light that warped, light that obscured.

She looked more closely at the massive images lining the walls, and felt that challenge in the angles and perspectives— and the power of the artist vibrated through her bones. Given her knowledge of the God of Thunder and Lightning, this could definitely be their Zeus. It was aggressive enough.

Declan interrupted her perusal, "Zeus has a strong local following, and he prices his work in a two-tier system: islander and non-islander price. If your friend in New York is sincerely interested in his work, I suggest using a local dealer to acquire the pieces." He moved between her and John, effectively blocking John from view.

Hannah laughed, "Like yourself, maybe?" John was saying something, but she couldn't hear him. He must be mumbling, because Declan's voice was so clear it was like he was speaking to her alone.

"I can be very useful, Susan. To understand this artist, you need to understand the island. I could buy you some breakfast tomorrow and give you a tour? Where are you staying on the island? Let me give you a ride home...or we could tour it by moonlight?"

John spoke up before she could answer. But even though he was only a few feet away, he sounded as if he were behind a thick wall of cotton batting, "Susan and I are staying with some friends in Vineyard Haven. We'll have to take a rain check on that breakfast. Come on, Susan, that's an island bus at the corner; we should grab it. Now."

John disappeared through the door, but Hannah lingered, confused by John's rejection of Declan's help. He was familiar with Zeus and was the only lead they had. They still didn't know where Zeus lived. Besides, Declan was very charming, and she liked breakfast and moonlight...

Declan took her hand, tracing the lines on her palm, "I'd love to show you my favorite place on the island, if you aren't ready to go with your brother...."

Hannah felt lured by everything about this man, his lovely green eyes, and the lilting sounds of his voice and the feel of his strong hand holding hers and she felt herself slipping into agreeing with him, when she was jolted by the sound of the bus driver laying on the horn. It took a physical effort to break eye contact and look in the direction of the bus. The driver made a "hurry up" motion with her hand and then let loose with another long blast. She shook herself and retrieved her hand.

"Another time, then, Declan. That would be nice...."

"Can't I have your phone number? How will I find you? I don't even know your real name...."

She stopped her in her tracks, hand on the doorknob, and looked over her shoulder. "I guess I'll have to find you then." She ran for the bus just as the driver laid on the horn for the third and final time.

When she'd climbed into the bus after leaving the gallery, John introduced her to Doris, the driver, and explained to Hannah that they would be hopping off at the Stop & Shop in Vineyard Haven. Then he went back to chatting with Doris, showering his famous MacCallister charm all over her. Hannah had zoned them out, still feeling the loss of Declan's regard, and more than a little annoyed at the abrupt separation. She stared out the window into the darkness, watching the trees slip by, and sighed.

At this, Doris let loose with a guffaw, "It looks like your sister has been hit with the O'Quinn blues. That Declan, he breaks half a dozen hearts a week, if that ain't the truth. Local gals know better and give him a wide berth. You'd best keep your sister away from him for the rest of your stay. I've seen grown women follow him around for weeks, as if they can't leave him. There are some women who come back every year just to be near him again."

John shook his head, "I bet they all end up collecting "art"— what a sleaze…"

"Mmm, it does wonders for his sister's Bed and Breakfast too— she's always booked full all season long." Doris turned into the Stop &Shop parking lot.

Hannah paused and turned toward Doris, following John down the bus steps, "What's the name of his sister's B&B?"

Doris smiled at her kindly, "Well, that would be the Ogygia Inn, but it is sure to be full, hon. I'm taking you and your brother to my cousin's motel on East Chop after you get your groceries. You take your time and get what you need, dear. I have Turow loaded up on my e-reader and you're my last passengers, so I don't mind waiting."

Hannah lost sight of John entering the store as she slowly exited the bus. Ogygia Inn. She knew that name from somewhere, but her brain still felt so fuzzy. She couldn't seem to catch up with what John had in mind. Why was the bus driver working as their own private taxi? Why were they at a grocery store? How would they find Zeus? She sank onto the bench outside the store and took slow, cleansing breaths. Ogygia. That was clearly a Greek word. How did she know it? It was hard to think when you wanted to sleep. Maybe Declan could help them. She felt certain that Declan could help her. He might still be at the gallery. Maybe they had a phone in the store and she could call him....

John came bursting through the double doors of the grocery store with two canvas bags slung over his shoulders. "Hey, how're you doing? I bought you a Coke. I thought you might need the caffeine. Doris said that you should feel better in a few hours. Here." And he handed her a cold plastic bottle of soda, sitting next to her on the bench.

"I'm sorry, but what does Doris know? Who is she? Why do I feel so sad and tired? What are we doing here?" and she spread her arms out to encompass the nearly deserted parking lot and the idling bus.

"Do you want the long or the short version?" John opened his own soda and sipped.

"Can I get the most direct version?" Hannah mirrored John and sipped her Coke, already feeling less thick as the acrid bubbles fizzed in her head.

"Well, while you were chatting with Mr. Smooth, I found a business card for Zeus with his home address on it by the front door of the gallery and told you that we needed to leave. I thought you were right behind me as I jumped on the bus, but you weren't. I tried to ask the driver to wait, but she was set on her schedule. I was going to get off at the next stop and walk back, but it was an express route, and she didn't stop until she was in Vineyard Haven. On the ride back to Oak Bluffs I got to talk with Doris, and she explained about O'Quinn's reputation for "ensnaring" women. I was pretty nervous about what might have happened to you in the 40 minutes I was gone."

Hannah reached out to stop John from drinking. "You were gone for 40 minutes? That's impossible. You left. And I said goodbye to Declan, and he asked for something and then the bus horn sounded and I came right out..., and I never told him my real name..." Just saying Declan's name made her feel the longing again. She took a bracing gulp of the coke and tried to fit the pieces of the puzzle together.

"Hannah, you were still in the gallery in almost the same exact place when the bus came back after forty minutes. That was one long ride back. I was all set to run in and pull you out, but Doris explained that it would be better for you if you left under your own impetus. She had to hit the horn three times before you even moved." John's formerly pragmatic demeanor cracked, and Hannah could see the strain in his eyes. "Then you got on the bus and ignored us. I tried to talk to you, but you just sat there staring... Doris said you'd bounce back..."

Whether it was the caffeine in the Coke or the worry on John's face, Hannah felt her mind clear and a connection click into place. Ogygia. "John, do you remember how Doris told us that Declan's sister's place was called the Ogygia Inn— I couldn't place it before, but I knew I recognized that name. Ogygia was the island home of the nymph Calypso. According to Homer she trapped Odysseus there for seven years with her "loveliness." Did you happen to grab a business card for the gallery when you were taking Zeus' card?"

John nodded and pulled out a simple black and white card from his pants— The Ospylac Gallery: Fine Art to Ensnare the Senses. Hannah barked what could have been a laugh if her face weren't so maniacal. "Oh great, they didn't even bother to be clever about it— Ospylac is Calypso backward. Why should we be surprised? We have after all been running from Hermes looking for Zeus. Of course we ran into a nymph intent on trapping unsuspecting travelers. What's next? A Cyclops? How many eyes does Doris have?"

John was staring at the business card. "No, Doris's human, I think. She's just an islander with a soft spot for Red Sox fans. And she's probably being more helpful under the influence of the SOT. I knew there was something wrong with that jerk."

She exhaled suddenly and pulled John upright, tugging him toward the bus. "I suddenly don't feel so great out here in the open. What do you have in the bags?"

John popped them open for Hannah to see. "New disguises. We'll officially be tourists in the morning, Black Dog t-shirts, shorts and flip flops— complete with new hairdos. You-know-who lives next to the East Chop Lighthouse. Tomorrow morning we mingle in with the other tourists, get some photos of them in their luxurious waterfront home, and catch the 9:02 ferry back to Woods Hole. We should be at your folks in time for lunch. Then we can draw on your extensive knowledge of these jokers to beat them at their own game." At Hannah's swift nod, he threw the bags back over his shoulder and followed her onto the waiting bus.

The very kind Doris drove them to her cousin's motel, and she convinced him to rent the room to them for an off-season rate. The room was simple and clean; two double beds with worn but laundered chenille bedspreads and a nightstand with a built-in lamp. After Hannah cut John's hair, she'd taken a bottle of water and gone to sit on the porch overlooking the ocean while he'd used the shower. When he was done, they swapped places and he stared at the ocean while she took over the tiny bathroom. She'd gone to work removing the pink from her own hair and transforming into a brunette. She glanced back at her watch. It was time to rinse. She set the faucet to cold and rinsed out the dye. She let it run until the water going down the drain was clear.

Wrapping her head in a towel and she headed for bed. John was still out on the porch. They both seemed to need a little time alone, and so she left him to his ocean gazing. She slipped into the bed closest to the bathroom and turned off the light. She finally felt free from the confusion that had swamped her in Declan's gallery. She had also stopped resisting the reality she had found herself in and accepted that art gallery owners might be nymphs and bus drivers could be helpful Nereids—that was Hannah's best guess. The Nereids were, correction, maybe are, friendly sea nymphs. Maybe Doris was just a kind Islander, but maybe she was more. She definitely had Declan's number.

She rolled over and looked at the clock. 11:30pm. She had to consciously remind herself that it was Tuesday night and only one day had passed since she'd gotten the gift. Which she now fully believed was a gift from the Greek Gods. She was filled with gratitude that her parents hadn't dissuaded her from her classics degree. Who could have anticipated the advantage this would give her? She wanted to graduate in four days time and this was going to be one hell of a final exam. Burrowing into the pillow, she slept a deep, dreamless sleep.

❀❀❀❀❀❀❀❀❀❀❀

Lee

I spy with my little eye

"I've been reviewing the different videos posted online of that last speech, and I think I've found something significant." Pointing to the screen, Lee drew Archer's attention to the far right corner. "Don't look at the recording of the girl, look at the boyfriend's face... See right there. See how his smile got bigger. On this video you can't see what he's looking at. But I found that same spot in the speech on a video shot from a different angle and look, right there. On the bike. That woman with the long red hair— she turned and waved just prior to his big smile. I think that's her." Lee looked from his computer screen to Archer, wincing only slightly, like a much-abused dog, hoping for the pat but trying to anticipate the slap.

Archer leaned closer to the screen. "Can you make that bigger? If that's the boyfriend holding the recording, who's the guy on the bike with her? Hermes report didn't mention him. Can you get the license number off the back?"

Lee perked right up. "Sure. I can get the license. There are other videos where this is in closer focus. I could get his name from the registration. You know, they are headed East on that street— if they were heading out of town on that bike, I bet they stuck to local roads. I could hack into the police cameras for the surrounding towns, see if I can follow them."

"Do it. Good work, Lee." Archer smiled at him and patted the air above his shoulder. Lee let out a slow breath and felt the glow of both the compliment and the lack of pain fill him.

"Should I call Hermes and give him this information or wait until I have more?" Lee relished the thought of seeing the messenger god again. He had enjoyed his last appearance very much, and wouldn't mind having the opportunity to call him. Especially with information that might help the god. Maybe they could talk about the case over some fine cheese and crackers.

"No. Let him muddle along. He's an idiot. You get the information and report only to me." This time Archer did touch Lee, his grasp searing Lee's shoulder. "Report only to me. That's an order." Lee started to whimper, wanting to pull away from the pain, but holding still, knowing Archer would punish him for any movement. "I'm going to go stroke some Olympian egos now. This could still work, despite that slippery girl. When we have her, we'll use her, and everything will fall into place. Everything." Letting go of Lee's shoulder, Archer turned to the door, "That was good work, Lee. Find her and I'll be sure the boss knows what a good job you did."

That had been hours ago. Lee stood in front of the open fridge and sniffed, not feeling his normal rush to grab the first cheese he found. He could savor the moment before he picked a cheese. Maybe he would make up a sampler plate? Anything was possible. He was alone for the first time. Zeus had emerged from his basement darkroom around dinner time with several cameras slung about his neck, and had not returned since. Hera had called to say that she would not be back until the morning, and Archer and Apollo had driven to Edgartown to drink and hit on tourists. Which meant Lee could leisurely consider his cheese options. He wasn't sure where to start— the fresh goat cheese in the kitchen fridge was definitely calling his name, but there was that intriguing sharp cheddar stored in the basement.

Archer had told him not to stop working until he'd found the girl. He hadn't given any instructions after that. Lee had easily tracked down the guy the gift girl was riding with through his bike's license. John MacCallister. He was a graduating senior at the University, and though he didn't show up on Hermes' report, he must be a friend of the girl's. Lee had tracked their progress through the small towns in CT to a parking lot where the girl took off her wig and came back out of the store with pink hair. From there, it was easy to follow them to Woods Hole and the ferry.

Lee was pleased. The girl must have decided it would be best to cooperate, and was coming to find them and turn herself in. He considered calling Archer and telling him that the gift girl was on this very

The Myth of Cassandra

island, but he rather hoped to be able to share the information with Hermes first. Lee still felt all fluttery when he thought about the messenger god. Hermes was just so, so, special. Lee indulged in a short fantasy while he sliced the Gouda he'd found in the back of the fridge.

They would meet at a late night coffee shop, both wearing trench coats and fedoras. In one version, that was all they were wearing, the magnificent vision of the naked Hermes still fresh in his mind...anyway, he would slip Hermes the file with the info on the girl while they sipped coffee laced with bourbon and talked in code.

Lee: I hear the weather has been a little stormy out there.

Hermes: The clouds are everywhere. I hope that there will be a change in the weather. Do you have any indication on whether we can expect the weather to move off to the east?

Lee: Oh, have I got weather news for you....

Well, he was sure that Hermes knew really cool ways to talk in code. The point was that he had information that would help Hermes, and even though he knew it was a risk to defy Archer, Lee was determined to take this opportunity to get Hermes' attention. Besides, he was still sore from the burns Archer had inflicted this afternoon. He ate a handful of the cheese, while sliding the rest into his socks. He would tell Archer, just after he told Hermes. Until then, he would catch up on the second season of Battlestar Galactica online. Cheese and sci-fi were a failsafe combination.

With the Cylon marathon over, Lee washed down the last of the brie with a gulp of Orangina, his favorite human drink, and paced across the living room. Hera's home looked out over the East Chop waters. He stared out the glass door leading out onto the deck at the ocean as the moon light made a path across the water. No one had come home yet. No one. At first he'd enjoyed being alone in the house. He'd cranked up the ABBA and danced from room to room. But sometime around two in the morning Lee had started waiting for someone, anyone, to come home.

He cleaned up all signs of the cheese-fest, put the empty bottles of O in the recycling bins in the basement, and hunkered down in front of the computer to give every sign of having been working non-stop to the first person to walk in the room. But there was no one to fool. Eventually he got bored of looking intent, and started surfing around for any information about Hermes. He had already read the entry in Wikipedia (and thought the pictures did not do Hermes justice), and was now looking for any more recent entries about him. There were a lot of entries for a line of luxury purses and scarves. Did they belong to Hermes? But his surfing kept getting interrupted by imaginary car door slams or approaching voices that would cause him to flash back to the screen where all the info on the gift girl was compiled and try to resume the illusion of intent focus on his work. After the fifth or sixth false alarm, he was sufficiently spooked to give up trying to do anything but sit and wait.

That strategy lasted for a good twenty minutes. Then he thought it would be a good idea to print up files on both Hannah and John, complete with detailed photos of them and their last known location (a grocery store ATM in Vineyard Haven). The files were impressive, the pictures surprising. Whatever had marred the girl's looks in the restaurant was no more; her short pink hair was very flattering. The boy, John, with his long wavy hair, blue eyes and flawless bone structure looked like a movie star. They were both distinctive and should be easy to find.

The existence of the files made Lee feel more comfortable about welcoming Archer home. Until he realized that Archer would figure out that he would have had to have known about the information for a long time— long enough to make the files in all their impressive detail— and not have called Archer on his cell immediately. There were a few panicked minutes of shredding and disposing of the files, and then Lee was back to waiting, hoping that Hermes would be the first through the door.

He had just restarted a new hand of solitaire when he spied movement on the deck. He edged toward the sliding doors, uncertain if it had been a person or a seagull that he had seen out of the corner of his eye. Unaware of the greasy stains he was leaving on the silk/linen drapes, he clung to them as he peered into the dark and let loose a high pitched scream as he realized he was staring into a set of eyes staring into his.

Hermes slipped into the room all apologies and reassurance. "Oh, Lee, so sorry. Easy, man, easy. I didn't mean to startle you. It's just me." Scanning the room, he asked, "Are you alone? Man, an empty house this time of night would make me edgy too. Why don't I pour us some scotch and we can wait together for everyone to come home." He crossed to the bar in the far corner of the room and poured out two massive drinks. Walking with them in hand, he extended one out to Lee with a smile and waited for him to take it.

Lee took a minute to register that Hermes was waiting for his response. In the seconds after screaming, he'd been trying to reconcile his panic with his pleasure at the serendipity that had brought Hermes home first. He could tell Hermes about the girl and then call Archer on his cell and no one would know that he'd figured this all out hours ago. The silence in the room lengthened, and Lee realized that Hermes was still holding the glass of amber liquid and smiling encouragingly at him. He had never tried alcohol, preferring the sweet fuzzy sodas and rich creamy milks. But there was Hermes, calling him "man" and offering him a drink. All Lee needed for this to be perfect was a smoky bar and a profusion of ferns. He reached out and took the drink.

In his head, Lee replied with a studied coolness, "Is it aged single malt? Because I like my bourbon the way I like my women... old and single." In reality, he replied with a breathless excitement, "Thanks, I'd love a drink! I just made a major break in the case. I know where the girl is." Lee hoped he looked casual as he waited for Hermes to ask him about the girl, and took a long, deep swallow of the scotch. He just couldn't wait for Hermes' response and enthused, "You won't believe where she..." and then the fire that had hit his stomach flashed through his body with a ferocity that left him breathless and his eyes watering. Before Hermes could stop him, he downed the rest of the scotch, under the mistaken impression that the liquid would put out the fire, not knowing that it was the fire.

Hermes cursed a low stream of obscenities (something about idiotic so-and-sos, liquor, and best laid plans) as he helped the now gasping Lee to the couch, taking the empty scotch glass from his limp hand. "Damn it, Lee, you're supposed to sip scotch slowly, not inhale it." He saw Lee staring at the untouched glass of scotch Hermes had put down on the coffee table, "No more scotch, man. No."

"But there's a fire...I need to drink something....cold....something to put the fire out...." Lee's face was frozen in a mask of pain and his breath was coming out in ragged gasps.

"Stay here, Lee, and I'll get you a cold glass of milk; no more scotch." Hermes hurried to the kitchen continuing to curse. Lee moaned and grabbed his head with both hands, the fire in his throat nothing compared to the spinning of the room. He squeezed his eyes shut, wanting everything to stop. Feeling arms cradling him, he opened his eyes to find Hermes beautiful face floating in front of him, and he sighed. Had he died and gone to the afterlife? Was Hermes his guardian through the trip of night? Hermes seemed to be saying something to him, urging him to drink something. If Hermes wanted him to do it, he would. He opened his mouth and swallowed while Hermes tipped back the drink. Ahh...cool, sweet, milk. That felt so nice. Lee was about to thank his hero, when once again he felt a disruption in his stomach, and this time it was not caused by fire, but the force of his insides rushing out.

Hermes rubbed his back while he vomited into an ancient Grecian urn that was conveniently next to the couch. Hmm...Hera would not be pleased with that. But better in the urn than on the wool rug. Hera seemed to be even more aggravated by stains on her fabrics— at least the urn could be washed. Oh, the retching was awful, and though Hermes wasn't holding his hair back, he did think to bring some fresh water to give to him when he was done.

"Here, man, sip this, but don't swallow— just rinse and spit. There, that's it. Oh, dude, you should have told me you were allergic to alcohol... you were lucky you got sick...we could have lost you."

Completely ignoring the fact that it was Hermes who had served him the alcohol in the first place, he apologized, "I'm so sorry, I had no

The Myth of Cassandra

idea I was allergic to alcohol— I've never had any. I thought it would be fine, I've seen Archer down entire bottles of vodka and not even burp, so I thought I could too."

"Well, that's understandable, Lee. You don't need to apologize— I'm just glad you're okay." Hermes leaned forward, confiding, "You need to be careful with human things, you know, I have a terrible time with salsa— it gives me the hiccups. Just because Archer can drink or eat something, you still need to be careful. He's a bit more advanced in his human shape, yes? That's not your fault, man; you are clearly a computer genius. So what if your human form is a little...indistinct.... You just need to be careful about what you put in your mouth..."

"Well, genius isn't really true, but if you think I am, well...I have been working on computers since the Commodore 64 and the Boss knew that I would be able to deliver... Archer thinks he is so much better than me because he can look human... but I've been working on improving my shape through an online course.... He tried to talk the boss out of assigning me...well, he'll sing a different song now...." Still a little green in the face Lee couldn't wait any longer to confide in Hermes, "I found her. She and the longhaired boy are here, right now, I even have photos of what they look like; she changed her hair, but it's definitely her. I think she came here to turn herself in...to work with us. It's the only explanation that makes any sense, don't you think?"

"Mm, wow! That was great detective work, Lee. She's here on MV, right now? That's a relief. I think you might be right; she's probably scared by her new power and needs our help to feel safe, so that she'll help us, yeah? I mean, that was the plan, right. To make good on Apollo's screw up with Cassandra and in the process win over an enthusiastic fan of the Olympians, right? It's not like Archer would actually hurt her, right?"

"Yeah, I mean, no, Archer wouldn't hurt her....if she followed the script. You think she'll follow the script, right? I mean your report indicated that she was very accommodating..." Lee pushed the urn away and stood up, still a little unstable on his legs. "She has to follow the script."

Hermes smiled comfortably. "Don't worry, Lee, I'm sure that Archer is very persuasive, he always seems to get what he wants..." And he dropped back into the leather armchair, having retrieved his own drink, took a quick swallow, and looking as if he had not a care in the world, "It's not like he would torture her if she resisted, right? I mean, what's the worst a disappointed publicist would do? Screen her calls? Not look at her head shot?"

Lee's face contorted with worry. "Do you think she might resist?" The type of motivation Archer preferred would be very bad for the girl.

Hermes' brow furrowed. "Well, I would definitely say that, in my long experience as a PI, scared humans, especially docile females, tend to balk at first— so, yeah, I think she'll resist. But I'm sure that Archer can turn on the charm and gently convince her, right?" Hermes's face was relaxed, and yet his words turned the final screw into Lee's mounting guilt. "It's not like he's going to ask her to say anything objectionable, right? So why would she refuse him. What kind of homicidal maniac would follow through on those ludicrous threats in that email he had you send her? I've seen how Archer encourages you when he needs you to do something. Motivational speeches, that's his forte, isn't it?" And he took another swig of his drink.

Lee winced, the burns on his shoulders still stinging, and he thought about the young woman, Hannah, with her pink hair and fair skin. In the picture Lee had pulled off the traffic camera she was smiling— laughing actually, at something the longhaired boy must have said. She looked so young, so vulnerable in her innocence. She'd have no idea what to do to be safe around something like Archer. "No....no.... Hermes, you don't understand. Archer can be....more than just motivational. If he gets angry... I think she might be in trouble! We have to do something. To keep her safe, until we can convince her to follow the script."

Hermes stood up to face him. "I don't understand, Lee, how could Archer Adams, publicist to the Stars, hurt our Hannah?"

The Myth of Cassandra

Lee, putting his hands on Hermes shoulders, shook him a little as he tried to convince him of the danger Hannah was in. "Because he's not a human, Hermes, he is, we both are, not human."

"I don't understand, Lee, what are you trying to tell me?" and Hermes shook him back, his face a study in confusion.

"We, Archer and I, are minions of Apep. My name isn't really Lee, but Mot. And Archer is Sek. Sek has a very bad temper— he always has. And he could do something really terrible to that poor girl if we don't help her."

Hermes shook Lee again, his voice incredulous. "You and Archer are Egyptian gods?"

"Not gods, demons. We work for an Egyptian god. He's not the best god, actually he's the god of evil and darkness, but a job is a job, and in this economy, you can't be picky." Lee drew himself up to his full height of 5 feet and made a decision, "Hermes, it's essential that Archer not know what I've told you about the girl. I have an idea how to help our Hannah do what we want without her getting hurt, but I am going to need you to lie, will you be okay with that?" Lee stood up a little straighter, never in his wildest dreams had he pictured telling Hermes what to do, but it felt right, he would lead his friend, Hermes, in a plan to save the girl.

"Well, if you think it's important to lie, this one time, I can do it. For you. What's your plan?" Hermes sat, looking up at Lee, an expectant follower.

Lee blushed under his gaze and tried to focus on his new role as the leader, but it was difficult with the undivided attention of such sexiness. Add to that the anxiety of going against Archer, and his mind went blank. Wringing his hands, he heard his voice come out as a whisper, "I know how to get the girl to cooperate, but I don't know how to hide it from Archer...."

Hermes stood, wrapping an arm around his back, and smiling broadly, gave him a squeeze, "If what you've told me is true, and I trust you completely, then I have an idea to buy us some time. Have you heard of the concept of plausible deniability?"

Lee had no idea what that was, but he nodded anyway. Hermes and he were a team. It was just a matter of time before they would be hanging out in bars with ferns.

CHAPTER FIFTEEN

Everything Looks Different

❂❂❂

John

Wednesday morning at the East Chop Motor Inn

John gazed at the space between the ocean and the sky as the first lights of sunrise split and stained the edges, picking up intensity at the center, the first sign of the sun, and for a moment he wondered what it must have been like to fly the chariot that had pulled the sun across the sky. To be that god; the beginning of every day; people grateful for your gift, worshipping your presence. And then to find yourself replaced by something as human centered and pragmatic as the Copernican Revolution. The Sun stops moving, the Earth begins to revolve around the Sun, and the chariot becomes nothing more than a cart for the local farmer to find in his wheat field. What would you do for a millennia for your second act? If Zeus was an artist, what was Apollo now? What would they find today at the home of Zeus? How could they use that information to help Hannah?

Hannah, The Speaker of Truth. Once he'd accepted the mythological parameters of her situation, he'd tried to imagine what was behind the gift. The simplest answer was also the most likely: power. But to what end? And after that run-in last night with Declan, the Nymph, they needed to be extra cautious. Apparently it wasn't just gods from Greek Mythology running around. He wished he'd paid more attention during his "Touchstones of Western Civ" class. He wasn't even certain what could be out there.

Sipping the high-octane brew sold at Doris's cousin's diner, John grimaced and regretted adding only three creamers. It was strong and bitter, and he hated to admit it, but he liked his coffee a bit less like coffee. But after he'd emptied his third little container of creamer into his cup, he noticed the guys at the counter staring and he'd mumbled something about his girlfriend liking a little coffee in her milk. He made a point of sipping from the cup of black coffee and nodded in a manly fashion. The guys all grunted some agreement as they turned back to the TV on the wall, missing him gag as he choked it down.

The TV was on Channel 7 and the news was not good. More chaos in the world, as it appeared some particularly rule-adherent humans had continued this day, Wednesday, doing what they did on Monday, exactly. In all fairness, Hannah had said to "go back to doing what you did yesterday." This particular story was focusing on advice to listeners on how to attract the attention of their local sanitation worker. Garbage collectors were only running their Monday routes, causing garbage to back up and citizens to panic. The "kindness" factor of the SOT's message meant that garbage collectors were happy to help when asked. So the reporter was encouraging people with trash to find their nearest garbage truck and simply ask them to take it. They cut to an interview with a young man in a navy jumpsuit with the name "Eddie" stitched on his chest. John didn't need to hear anymore and paid for the coffee just as the reporter started in.

They had to fix this. Today. He juggled the two coffees as he opened the diner door and hoped Hannah liked it black and bitter, as he hadn't wanted to raise coffee counter eyebrows by asking for even more creamers. He smiled at his own vanity. It made him think of Hannah and her rare burger. Maybe he'd been a bit hard on her last night at the pub. He'd definitely said way more than he'd wanted to. Or planned to. All that stuff about why she was so accommodating. It was a bad habit, armchair analysis, picked up from being raised by a psychiatrist mom. His mother would say that his little speech last night to Hannah about why she lied revealed much more about him than it did about her. Rolling his eyes at the internalized voice of his mom, he set both coffees down on the railing outside of their room. While there were some benefits to having a shrink for a mom, she was slow to judge and easy to talk to, the downside was that she'd ingrained in him an analytic rigor when it came to his personal life that left him little room to hide.

Case in point: the haircut. That hadn't been a good idea from any angle and he didn't want to consider what his mother would say about it if he were to tell her. But it had happened. It had started out innocently enough. When they'd gotten in last night, he'd asked Hannah to cut his hair— all part of their efforts to disguise themselves for today. And she had. Just thinking about it made him feel slightly disembodied and he sucked down a swig of the untreated java hoping the bitter brew would shake him free of the spell that Hannah seemed to effortlessly spin around him.

The slow and careful way she'd lifted his hair off his neck as she contemplated cutting it. The way they'd looked in each other's eyes in the reflection of the mirror. Without a word she'd started to cut off the hair, slowly at first, but with increasing confidence, faster and faster snips. As the hair covered the floor, she'd started to slide her fingers through the hair left on his scalp. Up and over his head— lightly, barely touching him, then harder, fingernails tracing a labyrinth round and round.

When she pulled the clippers out of the grocery bag— it was amazing what you could buy in a well-stocked grocery store on Martha's Vineyard— their eyes met in the mirror again. This time her eyes seemed to hint at mischief brewing close to the surface. There was a surprising look of anticipation on her face as she held the clippers up in the air like some ancient knife and he'd half expected her to let loose with a battle cry as she lowered them to his head.

Shoulders lifting, he must have shown some of the apprehension that her expression in the mirror had caused him. With a low murmur, she'd slid her fingers up and down his neck, slipping up and down the tense muscles, over and over and John felt his body relax almost against his will. Then she'd angled the clippers over his head with the same slow care that she'd used at the start of the haircut and he closed his eyes while she moved the clippers over his scalp.

It was over much sooner than he'd expected, the silence following the cessation of the buzzing clippers was deep and resonant. She'd rubbed her palm over the short hair left on his head. Stealing a look at her in the mirror, he saw that her eyes were closed and she seemed lost in the tingling feeling he now felt as he ran his own hand over his head. She'd stopped abruptly, like she'd caught herself. And dusting hair from his shoulders with her hands and had asked matter-of-factly, "Do you want to shower?"

John had only stared at her, incapable of saying anything as images of showering with Hannah started to flood his mind, and managed only to say, "Um..."

But instead of walking toward the bathroom, she had walked toward the outside door, "You really should, hair is so itchy. The best way to get it off is in the shower. I'm going to check out the "Ocean View" Doris's cousin charged us extra for." She looked over her shoulder at him and pulled a water bottle out of the grocery bag, "It looks different John, but it looks good. Let me know when you're all done, I'll need the bathroom to change this." and she'd waved her hand at the pink halo floating around her face. He just stood staring at her, concentrating on breathing evenly. He'd realized she was waiting for something, so he nodded and she nodded back. Without another word she slipped out into the dark night, and he grabbed his freshly shorn head with both hands.

That was last night. And after a cold shower, he'd slept unevenly. But the morning had brought with it the immediacy of their plan to gather information on Zeus and company, and the night seemed far away and somehow unreal. He reached down for his bag, tucked under the white plastic chair on the porch. He'd thrown his digital camera into his satchel when they left Whitfield, and now he was glad that he always kept it fully charged— the zoom lens on it would be perfect for snooping into Zeus's house. As he slipped the camera strap over his head he ran his fingers through the buzz cut, and tried to imagine how he would explain the haircut to his mom.

He knew that she'd cut through his bullshit. There was no need to have let the intensity spool out the way it did. There were at least a dozen ways he could have cut the tension and lightened the mood. And while he hadn't consciously planned for the haircut to evolve into an experience, he could admit to himself that his plan to have her cut his hair had created a plausible enough excuse to have her touch him. He'd been torturing himself since Monday in the bookstore line— it had been slightly surreal to have her finally talk to him again. When Carl had started dating her sophomore year he'd been surprised. She hadn't struck him as Carl's type. Way too opinionated. Not that he had minded that. He had liked arguing with her, but Carl was definitely conflict averse. At the time, he'd figured it would never last, but instead it had never ended.

He had heard about her at every Wednesday lunch at La Boca for the last three years and listening to Carl wax rhapsodic over how accommodating and easy going Hannah was convinced him that she wasn't who he had thought she was. Until Monday. There had been nothing accommodating or easy going about his day with Hannah and he had enjoyed every second of it. Everything he had felt in that freshman year class came rushing back. That was confusing enough, keeping his attraction to his best friend's girlfriend in rein all day. He'd known that Carl and Hannah were getting married and moving to Japan. And if he'd felt her leaning against his back on the bike, well he'd ignored it. She was as good as married.

Except then she'd ended it. She had dumped Carl in an over the top, public display in front of Carl's parents. Which had not only taken him by surprise, but had thrown his sense of man-code into confusion. And since then they had spent way too much time breaking and entering, running from vengeful gods and sharing too many showers. It was only human that he would be thinking of her, like that. The sexual attraction he felt for Hannah was not a forever thing, whereas her status as his best friend's ex was.

What she'd been thinking or feeling during all this was unclear. It hadn't changed any of the immutable facts that made her off-limits. Which was fine. As it should be.

They would get the pictures this morning, get to Cambridge to make a plan, and by this time tomorrow, they would be done; either they would have managed to set Hannah free from this curse or they would all be shrubs lining Zeus's walkway or some such punishment for defying the gods. Assuming they succeeded, all would go back to normal and on Sunday they would graduate and move on. He and Carl would stay in touch, but Hannah would remain a memory of the past. And that would be success.

Who knows, if he ran into Hannah five years from now he probably wouldn't even remember what it was about her that he'd found so compelling. She would just be another nice person from his college years. They'd get a drink and reminisce about that week in June when they were being hunted by Greek Gods— something he'd already decided never to confide in anyone else. And she'd be married to some stockbroker and live in NY, no, Connecticut, and she'd be a librarian, but not a sexy librarian, just a regular librarian. They'd split the check and hug as they said good-bye. Just like anyone else from his past.

John looked through the camera lens and focused on the line where the ocean met the sky. It could be that he'd just spent the last five minutes lying to himself. It was the only story he could deal with. Hannah Summers, nice, but not for him. He lowered the camera and looked toward the motel room door. At that moment she emerged from the room, in her t-shirt and flip flops, her now brown hair pushed back by the sunglasses perched on her head, and smiled.

"Do I look like me?" She lowered the glasses and held her arms out, spinning slowly.

Staring at her, he swallowed back a dozen different answers. "Nope. You look completely different. Are you ready to go? Doris's cousin's friend, Opis, has a landscaping business and he offered to drop us off at the Lighthouse. He's finishing up his breakfast at the diner."

"Opis?" She tilted her head a moment, but then shrugged, "Okay. Let's do it. Is this one mine?"

At his nod, she picked up the coffee cup from the railing and led the way down the street to the diner. John slung his bag across his chest, adjusting it to the back with the camera in the front. He grabbed his own coffee and followed. He watched her approach the waving man in the cab of the flatbed truck and heard her voice lift as she thanked Opis and climbed up on the gate. Facing him, she smiled and waved for him to hurry up. There she sat amidst rakes and lawnmowers, waving, and he had to resist the urge to run. He nodded and sipped on his coffee as he walked to the truck. This attraction to her would fade as surely as his coffee was now cold, but he was honest enough with himself to admit, as he ran his hand over his hair one more time, that he'd never forget that particular haircut.

⚜⚜⚜⚜⚜⚜⚜⚜⚜⚜⚜⚜

Hera

Plausible deniability in East Chop

Hera walked through her house, assessing the damage. She'd returned from the city to find her driveway blocked by the volunteer fire department. Zeus was talking with the Fire Chief, the only paid member of the Oak Bluffs FD, and she'd hurried past them, ignoring Zeus's attempts to draw her into their conversation. Pushing through the other fire fighters blocking her kitchen, she froze on the threshold. Seaweed and brine everywhere, all over her beautiful kitchen! Feeling something scuttle across her foot, she screamed as she jumped back, giving the unfortunate offender a swift kick. The crab in question flew into the living room, drawing her eye, and she saw that it looked even worse than the kitchen.

Her scream had alerted the other occupants in the destroyed house of her arrival. Apollo, Archer, Hermes and that other thing (Tree? Brie?) were all visible through the living room sliders on the deck staring out at the sea. Apollo was the first to move, his words sounding rehearsed, "Oh, Auntie, it's so awful what happened to your beautiful house— ruined, everything ruined!"

She stiffened at his attempt to hug her, "What happened?"

Apollo, with his typical obliviousness, hugged her anyway, patting her head. "It was not our fault, Auntie. Archer and I opened the sliders on the front deck so that we could come in without disturbing anyone, you know how I considerate I am, always thinking of others. Anyway, we had quite the night, met some girls at the bar in Oak Bluffs who invited us out on their party boat, and one thing lead to another, and…"

"Apollo." Her tone was severe, "Get back to the explanation of the destruction of my home." Hera's face was ominous.

Apollo appeared unaware of the mounting danger, but the other three on the deck surreptitiously stepped back from them. "Yes, yes, of course. So sad. So much destroyed. Well…so Archer and I came in early this morning, exhausted but happy, if you know what I mean, and the moment we opened the doors we were hit from behind by a massive wave. It filled the house. We weren't hurt, so there's that for good news. But everything else, well…. So terrible. Really a mess." He leaned in closer to whisper in her ear, "The VFD is saying that it was a freak storm surge, but between you and me this has Poseidon's fingerprints all over it. I think he got wind of my plan to reclaim Olympus, and he tried to sabotage it. He's always been jealous of me and my successes."

Hera looked at Apollo and wondered if he'd hit his head when the wave surged in. Apollo had never been the brightest, but he'd never been a complete idiot either. Clearly Poseidon did this, but it wasn't because he was jealous of Apollo. Poseidon was one of the big three; he loved his lot in this world. She was certain he had no desire to do more than enjoy his rum and beach blanket bimbos, so why did he do this? She was about to set Apollo straight when she caught a look from Hermes and bit back her words. Hmm. Instead she simply nodded at Apollo. "You're probably right, Apollo."

The Myth of Cassandra

Tilting her head to the side she took in the other three, "I can see that everyone has survived the freak storm surge, but has anyone started to take an inventory of the damage?"

That thing (was its name Flea? Bea?) who worked for Archer, stepped out from behind a seaweed strewn deck chair and spoke, "The furniture and fabrics could probably be cleaned, but all of the electronics are completely destroyed. Even my computer and everything on it."

Hera fought to be polite as she repressed her repulsion at being addressed by this lesser being. "I think I need some air." And she walked away from the four stooges towards the lee side of the deck. Lee! That was its name. Hermes had obviously flipped Lee. But for what? From here she could see Zeus wave goodbye to the Chief and climb the side stairs to join them. She forgot about the others as she walked to meet Zeus. "What about the darkroom? Did it get flooded?"

Zeus smiled, "No, miraculously the wave washed in and out, with water damage only to the main floor. The Chief says it's the strangest thing he's ever seen. He claims water shouldn't work that way. Called it a freak of nature." Zeus looked out over the ocean, "Have you figured out what the hell our freak of nature was up to?"

Hera gave a slight shake to her head and feigned a hug so that she could whisper to Zeus, "No, but I think Hermes has a plan to get rid of that creep Adams, and I think Poseidon did this to help out. I'm inclined to see how this plays out, how about you?" She leaned back against the deck railing to smile at him, and felt Zeus's regard slide up and down her body, reminding her of their early days of ruling Olympus. He'd always enjoyed her games with lesser beings; it had lead to quite a satisfying time in their marriage. She caught his eye and he returned her smile.

"Sounds good to me, I haven't had any fun since this whole business started. I'd have stopped it, if it didn't seem to mean so much to Apollo." Turning his back on the ocean, he offered Hera his arm, "Hey, on another note, Declan told me that a NY museum was interested in my work, not bad, huh?"

"That sounds right. You're an amazing artist. When did you talk to Declan?" Hera looped her arm through Zeus' as they moved slowly toward the group at the end of the deck. But she fell silent as they approached, realizing that the others were arguing. Good. She was in the mood to watch. Archer appeared to be grilling Lee about what he'd found out about the girl.

"Everything on your computer has been lost? What's the last thing you found out? If we lose her, it'll be all on you, Lee. The Boss won't like that at all; I told him you were an idiot...."

Hermes jumped in, "Hey now, Lee isn't an idiot; he's a genius. And if anyone is to blame, it's you, Archer, you and Apollo. You're the ones who let the wave in."

The Boss? She expected Hermes knew who that was already. Hermes was clearly the architect of this scene. He had always excelled at finding the weak link. His defense of Lee had Lee blushing and Archer fuming. This just got more entertaining.

Apollo joined the fray, "The wave was not our fault. That was clearly Poseidon's fault. He's obviously consumed with envy. Being a lesser god yourself, you know all about that, don't you Hermes..."

Hermes raised his eyebrows, but did not comment on Apollo's outburst. "The question of blame is moot. What we need now is a plan." And he subtly poked Lee in the side. "A plan to get the girl, convince her to help us, and get Apollo and Zeus on the way to worship-town."

Lee cleared his throat, "I have an idea of where they were heading. Would that help, Archer?"

Archer narrowed his eyes on Lee, "Of course, you moron. Start talking."

Hera exchanged a knowing look with Zeus, and they both grinned. Wanting to be comfortable while enjoying the show, she looked behind her to find lounge chairs for herself and Zeus and noticed an annoying tourist at the lighthouse taking pictures of them. He probably hoped they were Kennedys and he could sell his photographs to some gossip rag. She tossed a curse on him. A little poison ivy should teach him to keep his zoom lens to himself. She dragged the chairs back to the conversation on the deck and she and Zeus settled back to watch Hermes at work. The only thing that would make this better was if she had a big bowl of popcorn.

CHAPTER FIFTEEN

The Steamship Authority

⚙⚙⚙

Hannah

What's worse than poison ivy?

Hannah wound up and down the stairs on the ferry, looking for a spot where they could be alone. Or as alone as you can get on a crowded public ferry. The ride took an hour, and she wanted to use that time to look through John's photos and figure out whom they were dealing with. While the East Chop lighthouse had been next door to Zeus' house, she had still been too far away to make out any details with the naked eye. And she and John hadn't spoken since they'd caught the bus, surrounded on all sides by other tourists.

It was a beautiful day and the outside decks of the ferry were packed, as were the seats at the tables. She took a left off the stairs and found a row of dank seats on the internal wall of the ferry, just down from the bathrooms. While the bathrooms would draw people, the seats themselves were gloomy and isolated and would be perfect. Sliding in and taking the inside seat she was surprised when John didn't immediately sit next to her. Looking back over her shoulder she saw him standing in the stairwell doorway, rubbing his back against the frame.

"John? Over here…" and she patted the seat next to her. It seemed to take him a minute to move, but he joined her, handing over the camera as he sat.

Wordlessly she started scanning the pictures, and as each image moved across the small screen at the back of John's camera, she felt a little lightheaded.

"That's Zeus.... And oh, that has to be Hera.... And oh my, that's Apollo; and he was Hermes..." She was whispering. And then her voice died out completely as picture after picture crossed the screen. She felt a chill run up her spine and knew it was not from the dampness of the seats. Strangely enough they'd looked exactly like their images in paintings and pottery— just in modern clothes. She recognized Zeus and Hera right away, and Apollo— who was beautiful. And of course, their old friend, Hermes, smirk and all. The other two must be the publicist and his computer hacker. She suspected the man in white was the publicist, because the other one had a kinder face, and well, the man in white had soulless eyes.

"They are real. I am looking at them and it all seems so real...I mean I know the things I've said, this whole gift and the SOT, I know they've really been happening, and I knew, theoretically that the gift was from the Greek Gods, but to see them like this.... I have to get rid of this gift. If I don't, I'll never be able to talk to anyone and know that it's me they are responding to. Which is ironic, if you think about it. I've spent my adult life not really talking to people, because agreeing was easier. But in the end it was meaner. Not "mean" like I was trying to hurt anyone, but "mean," like miserly. How can I sustain a relationship if I never share my real thoughts with anyone..."She turned to John expecting to see him agreeing with her, but his eyes were closed and he was rubbing his back up and down the seat, hands gripping the arms of the chair, his knuckles white.

She set the camera down, "Not to be picky here, but I'm having an epiphany and you aren't even listening. What's wrong with you? Why are you doing," she waved her hand at his movement in the chair, "that?"

John's words were sharp, the sarcasm palpable, "I'm sorry, I'm really impressed by your personal insights, and that was an excellent use of the word "mean," It's almost as if you were an English major." At her gasp,

The Myth of Cassandra

he opened his eyes, "I'm sorry but my back really itches and it's getting worse. Can you scratch it for me? I can't reach..." he leaned forward and twisted his arms behind him, pointing to the spot between his shoulder blades.

Hannah frowned, excellent use of the English language my ass. Choosing to ignore his blithe reaction to her "personal insights" she edited her reply, "Fine."

She scratched his back lightly with one hand, twisting in her seat to face him, but he pleaded, "Harder, and more to the right."

He sounded so urgent. Hannah frowned and lifted his shirt to see what was causing the itch. Her hand froze in mid-scratch at the sight before her. She pulled his shirt down and leaned away from him, "John, that isn't normal."

"What is it?" he cradled his head in his hands and was taking slow, shuddering breaths.

"You have really bad poison ivy down the center of your back."

Releasing a pent up breath, John turned sideways to look at her, "You need to work on your bedside manner, Summers. I thought there was something really wrong with me. Poison ivy is the definition of normal. It's all over the island. We'll grab some calamine lotion when we get to shore. Until then, can you keep scratching? Please. Scratch?" He tucked his hands in his armpits to keep them from shaking and angled his back towards her.

Taking pity on him, she returned to scratching, but her hand was shaking, "This poison ivy isn't normal. Think, when exactly did you start to feel this itch?" Hannah forced herself to lift the hem of his shirt, looking at his back.

"I guess I felt the first itch when I was taking the last photos of the gods. I remember I was thinking about taking one more group shot, when I felt my back itch, and I dropped my camera to try to scratch it. Then you said something about catching the bus to the ferry. Since then, it just seems to be getting itchier. What makes you think it isn't normal?"

"Because it spells something." Hannah slid her fingers lightly down his spine, and John arched his back. She thought about whom she'd seen in John's photos. "I don't think poison ivy naturally forms words. Let alone insulting words. This has all the earmarks of a curse from Hera. She must have noticed you taking pictures. Thank god for our disguises, if this is what she does to random strangers..."

John blew out a slow breath, "How do you know she didn't recognize us? What does it say?"

"Well, the t-shirts and flip-flops definitely hid us." She picked up John's camera, pulled his shirt over his head and focused the lens, taking a picture. "It says, TOUR-ASS." And she handed him the camera so he could see.

He pulled the shirt off over his head and took the camera, "Hera likes wordplay, huh? I am glad she's not into limericks or I'd be itchy in very inconvenient places." Closing his eyes, his face went white, "Oh crap, I think I'm going to pass out...."

Hannah reached for him, urging him to put his head between his knees, when she felt a strong hand on her shoulder, "Now miss, this is a family ferry. We've gotten some complaints that there was a couple engaging in inappropriate behavior near the second floor facilities. I'm going to need you to put your clothes back on, put away the camera and follow me."

Hannah took in the huge man in the blue polo with the Steamship Authority logo stitched onto the chest. The name tag pinned underneath the logo identified him as a security officer by the name of Dero. Doris, Opis, Dero. She stared at the name tag as John struggled to stay conscious while he put his shirt back on. The officer was waiting for them to comply with his requests, when something clicked.

Hannah stood up and leant toward the man, lowering her voice to a whisper, "Dero? Are you a cousin of Doris? And Opis? Because my friend here is having a problem you would understand. You and all of your cousins...."Encouraged by his raised eyebrows, she murmured to John, "Bend over. Don't worry." And then lifting his shirt, she pointed to the angry pustules on John's back, "Look. We need help. She did this

The Myth of Cassandra

to him." John's breathing was getting shallow and Hannah pleaded, "Please. Is there anyone on the ferry who can help us?"

The officer leaned in to read John's back and let out a short guffaw, "She always did like to combine bitchiness with wordplay." Folding his arms across his chest, he looked her up and down, "I know about you. We all do. Why should we help you?"

John was now moaning and shaking in his seat, "Please. He's my friend..." Hannah knelt in front of John and held his shoulders, "Please. I don't know what else to say, what to do."

Shaking his head, he relented, "Your friend needs help. I suppose it's not his fault that you are who you are. And if Doris helped you, well then, I can too. Come with me, you're in luck. Eunice is working this shift and she has a way with curses..." and he moved toward a locked door that was marked, "Personnel Only."

Hannah helped John to walk and they followed Dero down a dark corridor. John whispered in her ear, "Who are these people? How did you know he knew Doris?"

"Nereids. I'll tell you later." And she nodded as Dero offered to help her maneuver John into what must have been the break room for the crew. Seated on a plastic chair reading People magazine was a middle-aged woman wearing a turban, sipping on a Dr. Pepper. She looked up at Dero's entrance.

"Eunice, these kids need your help. They're friends of Doris." And he led John to one of the cracked chairs, gently easing him down. John's breath was coming in short, sharp gasps and Hannah knelt by his side, holding his hand.

Eunice stood up and examined John's back. "Oh, hon, that must itch something awful. What're you two doing messing with Hera? She's a vindictive bitch."

"Can you help him? Please?" As Hannah spoke Eunice's head swung sharply up and she narrowed her eyes at Hannah.

"You're the one, aren't you? The SOT. Why are you leaving the Island? Why aren't you with them?" Suspicion made her eyes dark.

"I never asked to be the SOT— I want to get rid of this 'gift'. We were trying to get information on them, so we took some pictures, but she must have seen him shooting. Please?" Hannah, spurred on by John's slacking grip, took a shot, "I demand that you heal my friend."

Eunice and Dero both stared at her, and then burst out laughing. "Oh hon, you're precious. Your little parlor tricks don't work on us. We know all about Apollo's silly plan, but don't you worry. I'll help your friend. Here." With that she handed her unfinished soda to Hannah, unwrapped her turban, and the room was filled with the smell of salt water, as a luscious cascade of seaweed tumbled to her shoulders. Leaning close to John, Eunice spread her seaweed hair on his back and within seconds John shuddered and passed out.

"Don't fret. He's just fainted. He'll be right as rain in a few minutes. Look." And she lifted her locks off his back to reveal healthy skin, no sign of the rash that had been there before. "Dero, sweetie, will you pick him up and lay him down on the table? Yes, right there." Sitting back down in her plastic chair, she motioned for Hannah to hand her back the soda, "I like you, dear. You're clearly not in league with them, so why don't you sit and tell me all about it. We might be able to help..."

Hannah handed the sweaty can back to the sea nymph named Eunice and sank slowly into the seat opposite. John was stirring now and Dero was helping him to drink some water. John looked over at her and tried a weak smile. He looked terrible. Hannah felt the same chill steal down her spine as when she had first looked on Hera's face in the photos. If this was a taste of the danger they were up against, she was going to need all the help she could get. She looked at Eunice, seaweed hair once again under a turban, and started talking.

The Myth of Cassandra

Hera

Getting close to the end of Hera's rope

Archer Adams was pacing back and forth behind his lumpy computer minion, looking over the his shoulder at every pass, as that thing pecked away at the spare laptop Hera had pulled out of her car. Watching the sweat seeping off of that thing's hands onto the keyboard, Hera made a mental note to get it professionally cleaned as soon as this debacle was over.

The first floor flood from the "freak" wave that had careened up a sheer cliff and into only her house was being cleaned up by a team of housecleaners Hera used regularly, though she'd had to pay them double to come out today. It was the summer season, and housecleaners on the island were booked solid keeping the vacation rentals turning over. The main damage from the flood appeared to be the electronics on the first floor, with the publicist's computer being completely destroyed. After having to listen to Adams' high-pitched raging at his assistant, Hera had intervened and offered the use of a laptop from her work. It wasn't her private computer, so she wasn't too concerned about the lumpy little man's glandular condition. And anything to shut up Adams was worth the extra cleaning.

Besides, she hadn't missed the looks between Hermes and the little lumpy man and hoped her instincts were on target about the meaning of those looks. She'd not had a chance to speak with Hermes privately, but she'd used him on past assignments enough to know that building subversive alliances was one of his trademark moves. If she wasn't mistaken, the lumpy computer worker was trying to mislead Adams about the girl's location. It was unclear why this was necessary, but it was fun to watch Adams get screwed with by his own man.

This "gift" was a complete disaster. She'd just spent the past evening convincing her staff that they did NOT need to go back to doing what they had been doing on Monday, that her magazine did NOT need to cover all the news in the world, a ridiculous notion anyway, and when that was accomplished, she had to spend the rest of the evening listening to everyone be sickeningly nice to each other. The only consolation was that it was clear that this was not what Adams had wanted when he had suggested the girl for the gift; he was frantic to get his hands on her. His real purpose for gifting this girl remained hidden.

Hera had often lectured her staff that sometimes the best plan of action was no action. If she'd opposed the Reparations plan directly, Zeus would have pursued it just to spite her. By letting him do this with Apollo, Zeus had lost interest in it all on his own. Zeus was not only done with the plan, he seemed even more committed to his photography than before and was working without any nudges from her. Now that was a positive outcome. If anything, by doing nothing and letting Apollo follow this pipe dream, it'd brought Zeus and her closer, as they shared a deep antipathy for Adams. A real marriage was nurtured not by shared love, but by shared hatreds. Hmm...maybe there was an issue in that? The Top Ten Things to Hate with your Mate? Or "Who Does Your Mate Hate? Why you should hate him too...." Evil publicists topped her list.

She was on the fence about Hermes. Her initial pleasure at watching him turn Adams minion against him had waned, as she had not gotten any details directly from Hermes. It was frustrating. Whoever Adams worked for, The Boss clearly had it out for them, and maybe all Olympians. But Hermes hadn't deigned to fill her in yet. Come to think of it, he'd been somewhat of a disappointment lately. First, he'd failed to adequately warn them that the girl was a bad match for the gift, letting them give an incredibly powerful gift to an unpredictable and willful young woman. Then there was his subsequent inability to find the girl and bring her in. Another mark against him. Hera normally allowed her employees' one mistake before firing them, but this situation had reached a critical point, and since Hermes was already familiar with the details, she'd forborne. Besides, he was one of Zeus' bastards. But nepotism only went so far. If he couldn't unmask the publicist and his plan before the girl or Adams did any more damage, she'd have to lay a large portion of the blame on his smirking shoulders.

She made her way back to the kitchen to oversee the cleaning— too often women forget to clean under their major appliances— most food poisoning occurs not from tainted food but dirty kitchens. They had done an entire issue on the Ten Places Women Forget to Clean. The three women scrubbing the kitchen confirmed that they'd already cleaned under the appliances, so Hera slid a white napkin under the refrigerator with a collapsible pointer she kept handy for just such inspections. Pulling out a spotless cloth, she raised her eyebrows in acknowledgment and ordered the women to carry on. They did, with unfailing politeness, and started to complement each other on their hard work.

They quieted down to listen to the TV that was set to the Channel 7 newsman who was traveling the world to report on neighborhood disturbances and pointless local affairs. Really, why did that girl tell people to "pay attention to all the news in the world?" Hera pinched the bridge of her nose. She was going to have to do something about that girl and her gift.

Only the gifting god could take back the girl's power without inflicting any damage to the human. And that was Apollo, who was still blindly following Adams. If Hermes couldn't convince Apollo to do that, and soon, Hera would have to take matters into her own hands. There was more than one way to stop the gift. The gift wouldn't do the girl much good if she couldn't speak. And there were countless ways to achieve that. She could turn her into anything without a mouth. Shrubs were fairly quiet, and nothing was more silent than a rock. Hera would wait for only so long. After all, she couldn't be expected to listen to all of this incessant kindness.

✸✸✸✸✸✸✸✸✸✸✸✸

Hermes

More with rabbits on Martha's Vineyard

"See here, Archer, I have a photograph of their motorbike driving on 93 N towards Logan Airport. It would stand to reason that they've decided to leave the country. She clearly has no idea we're here on Martha's Vineyard. So she wouldn't be on this island, right now or ever. She definitely never used an ATM in Vineyard Haven. No, she's probably heading for Greece, Mt. Olympus and all, don't you think?" Lee looked back over his shoulder in an attempt to "casually" make eye contact with Hermes. Hermes smiled lightly but inwardly groaned— Lee was as subtle as a sow at the trough. Before Hermes called Poseidon for the flood, they had agreed to have Lee lead Adams and Apollo on a wild goose chase at the airport to give Hermes time to find H. Lee was under the impression that Hermes would convince H to cooperate with Adams, but he had never said that in so many words. Hermes had other plans for the girl.

"You're not paid to think, you're paid to know. Push a few more bleeding buttons, Lee, and tell me where the hell she went." Adams' socks were smoking and his eyes had morphed from an icy blue to a fiery red. Frowning, Hermes considered what might happen if Adams transformed in front of the housecleaners, and edged back to slide the doors between the kitchen and the living room closed.

"Well, the problem is that with all of the increased airport security it's really hard to access flight manifests, though it also means that it'll be hard for them to travel under any kind of alias, because they'd need photo id, and she's dyed her hair, which might be suspicious, although she is the SOT so maybe she can make people do what she wants..."

"Shut the hell up, Lee. I don't give a damn what won't work to find them. Find her! Pin her down like a god damn bug and hold her there until I can convince her that her only option is to say exactly what I want...."

"Hey there," Hermes strolled to the center of the room, "That's all good and well, I like humans to be obedient too, but just exactly what do you intend to have her say? Because you seem awfully irritated, even for a publicist." Hermes was gratified to see Apollo perk up from the prone position he'd assumed on the couch. Good, he was listening.

Hermes affected the confused expression of a child, "What's in this script, anyway? Isn't the script merely suggestions for how to fawn over the Olympians? I mean why wouldn't she want to say "thank you" to the gods, Apollo in particular, for this fabulous gift. Wasn't that the entire point for giving this "gift" in the first place?"

The Myth of Cassandra

Swinging to look at Apollo, Hermes leant forward pretending to confide a secret to him, "She's really quite attractive, Apollo, a nine or a ten, definitely your type," and then back to Adams, "so wouldn't "pinning her down like a bug" serve only to scare the "gratitude" right out of her? I may be a lowly private eye, but that seems like a bad idea to me."

All cool and collected, Archer actually manufactured a reasonably authentic sounding laugh, "This is show business, Hermes, something I don't expect you to understand." Hermes had to give it to him; Adams could recover in the blink of an eye. Smiling, Adams clapped a hand on Apollo's back, "Break a leg", "Pin Down Like a Bug"— they're just expressions that creative people like me and Apollo use to express the drama of a situation. Right Apollo? I mean, I am so stoked to get this girl here and get her on tape worshiping this fantastic god...."

Apollo was looking confused, "Wait, I thought she was only a seven. Where is that picture of her?"

Hermes could only sit back and watch as Adams expertly wound Apollo around his little demon finger. Archer's voice was smooth, commanding, "Give him the photo, Lee. Of course I wouldn't scare her, Hermes, if anything, I think Apollo here will be rescuing her from the left-wing, long-haired, scooter riding communist who has kidnapped her and made her tell everyone to "be kind" to everyone. What's next? Universal health care?"

Apollo joined Archer in laughing at that, saying, "That would be hilarious. The universe does not need healthcare!" Preening in the reflection of the coffee table, Apollo ran his hands through his hair, "I will save her from the evil long haired man who has kidnapped her; how hard is it to destroy one measly human? If there is one thing I know, I know women, and women loved to be saved. Where is that photo?"

"Um, I have this picture from the traffic camera. I don't think it does her justice, it's a profile and she really has very nice eyes, but it..." Apollo pulled the page out of Lee's hands.

"Wow, look at her pink hair! I like that. Very Cali. Very now. She is hot. Let's find this girl and get on with the business of saving her, and her thanking me. If you think she might still be at the airport, well I can fly us all there in a heartbeat in my chariot. I have it stowed in the shed. I'll call the horses now and harness them up. Let's go!"

So the three of them followed Apollo to the back of the house, ducking their heads as the winged horses flew into the yard. Hermes needed to get to H now. Not only did he need to tell her what she was up against in the "person" of Archer Adams, but also to warn her of Apollo's new-found plan to "save" her, and his expectations of her appreciation level. Then there was the danger of Hera's waning patience with the effects of the "gift." He'd seen that look on Hera's face when they were leaving and knew it was just a matter of time before she ended this all her way. Hannah's problems were increasing at a rapid pace. At least Zeus was safely tucked away in the dark room.

So far, Hermes had been impressed with Hannah's resourcefulness— she was still at large and still alive. He suspected that she'd gone to rendezvous with her former boyfriend, Carl, who he felt certain had gone to Hannah's parents' house in Cambridge. It was something he had inadvertently picked out of Candy's mind. Candy. So aptly named, luscious and sweet. When this was over, he'd promised to show her his boathouse. Another reason to help H. Candy had seemed fond of H and would be very unhappy with him if H ended up as a rock outcropping on the Massachusetts' shore. No, Candy would be more fun to vacation with if all of her friends remained fully functioning humans.

Lee, Archer and Apollo were waiting for him by the Sun Chariot. Hermes stopped short of them, and pretended to answer his phone, "What? Right now? Well, I'm sort of in the middle of…. What? Okay, Okay, I'll be right there." He closed the phone and addressed the others, "Sorry, that was my bookie in Vegas, it seems I have to make good on a little wager I placed last week, so I'll have to catch up with you later." And with that, he flew away, before anyone could reply.

He tried not to think about the abject panic he saw in Lee's eyes. He hoped Lee could stick to the plan and keep them at the airport for a couple of hours. But he knew that he'd better not rely too heavily on that. Lee might be a genius with computers, but it was clear that his acting chops were sub-par. He would only be able to stall Apollo and Adams for so long. Hermes hoped that H had made it to Cambridge already. He had his own plan, and he needed her to make it work.

CHAPTER SIXTEEN

Neighborliness

❋❋❋

Hannah

Wednesday afternoon, Cambridge, MA

"Are you sure you know the way? Because we seem to take a right, another right and then right again! All these right hand turns, and yet we end up in a completely new place…which would only make sense if Cambridge had been built by rabbits. Dammit!" Grabbing his foot and rubbing, he leaned back against the sandwich shop window, "My seven year old cousin could have laid these bricks better, why they hell didn't they just pave the sidewalks? Would it look too pedestrian?"

"Impressive John, in pain and you're still able to come up with a pun." She hazarded a smile at him, hoping to distract him from his grievances, but his frown was not encouraging, "We're almost there. It's just down the hill and to the right and then on your r…" Her voice died out as his scowl deepened, "Well, I mean it's just ahead, on the right.…"

He'd been in a foul mood since they'd left the Vespa in a long-term parking lot at Logan Airport and entered the city on the T. She'd made the point that they'd be more anonymous on foot, and though John had agreed at the time, he'd been getting surlier as they wound their way through Cambridge. Standing there rubbing his toe he looked like he might mutiny. Instead, he lowered his foot and bowing slightly, indicated for her to lead. Maybe he'd decided that discretion was the better part of valor and was keeping his thoughts to himself. Whatever the reasons, she'd take it. She needed a little silence to get her own thoughts in order.

Turning, she led the way down Franklin Avenue. John wasn't wrong, the bricks in the sidewalk were far from even, some of them sticking up at an angle designed to trip the uninitiated. She was of the opinion that the crooked sidewalks were intentional, not some sloppy masonry. Hannah had a love-hate relationship with her hometown. She loved it, but she knew its underbelly. Cambridge was a city of insider knowledge— where to park, how to find the post office, how not to fall on your knees walking the sidewalks— all of these required prior experience in Cambridge. They were such a city of insiders they'd passed an ordinance to keep non-Cambridge dogs from defecating in their parks, Cambridge dog crap only.

Nevertheless, John's complaints were becoming excessive. She could only assume that after being cursed, he was feeling a little more vulnerable. She didn't blame him. The conversation she'd had with Eunice had left her feeling as skittish as the rabbits he'd claimed had engineered her hometown. Eunice had made all too clear the power and reach of Hera and company. The knowledge that danger could come from any direction or source was hard to think about. It was exhausting being simultaneously on edge and vulnerable. Like she was on the verge of doing something, but she was too keyed up to know what it might be. Every time a high-heeled pedestrian wobbled near them, a passing dog sniffed their feet or a pigeon flew too close, she felt her hands raise up to ward them off.

Not that raised arms would provide her with any defense against a curse, but it was an instinct that was impossible to suppress. Hadn't she read somewhere that a rabbit's best defense was their high level of paranoia that caused them to run in extremely erratic patterns, thus confusing their predators? She was fairly certain that she did not have the groundspeed of the average rabbit, which meant that relying on the rabbit defense was not likely to work for her. If she was going to resist the urge to run into the nearest shrub and hide, she needed to stop being the bunny.

Keeping her eyes cast down, she tried to sort through her priorities. She shivered, thinking about that email and all the threats it'd contained. After seeing them on Martha's Vineyard, she could no longer imagine that the email had come from some deranged spammer, or that she was stuck in the middle of some extended acid trip. She'd privately entertained her mother's previous theory for explaining her strange sleep and had wondered if she'd been slipped some drug by an unscrupulous man. This lone and somewhat incredulous thought had given her the thinnest hope of waking up from this. But that hope was now gone. This was not some fictional event cooked up in her subconscious.

She saw the future in a whole new light now. It'd been different when she, John and Carl had made their plans back in Centreville. Though at the time she'd had to accept that something very strange was happening, there'd been something almost novelistic about their plans to thwart the Olympic Gods. The three of them hatched a scheme to trap Hermes, slip out of town in outlandish disguises, spy on the other gods, and then trick them into taking back the gift; all they needed was a theme song, and it was as if they'd agreed to play the parts of the Mystery Gang minus Scooby Doo. But this was not going to end with the creepy caretaker pulling off a rubber mask and cursing them for meddling while the police put him in handcuffs.

Curses. That poison ivy on John's back had been real— and if Eunice hadn't healed him, it might've ended up putting him in the hospital. Hannah made a mental note to thank Herb, of Herb's Hellenistic Hour, for the four-part series he'd done on Nereids. The Nereids are sea nymphs, companions of Poseidon and friends of the sailor. There are fifty of them and Herb had published a list of their names on his website. For fun, Hannah had memorized it. It had been fun. Fun for Classics nerds. Like memorizing the capitals of the fifty states. And more useful than she could have known.

She had been sarcastic when she'd voiced her suspicions about Doris, the friendly bus driver, being a mythical creature. But then John told her the man giving them a ride to the lighthouse was named Opis, and something clicked. Opis and Doris were two of the names on the

The Myth of Cassandra

list. When she saw the name tag on the ferry security guard, Dero, another name from the list, she took a chance and it paid off. Eunice, the sea nymph with the healing hair, had saved John. And she had filled Hannah in on the mythological scuttlebutt while Dero helped John recover.

Rumor had it that Apollo was looking to make an Olympian-themed comeback, complete with adoring worshippers and sacrifices at the altar and that Hannah's gift was some part of that plan. A plan that most mythological folk were convinced would fail. Turned out Apollo had the reputation of being somewhat of a buffoon. Nevertheless, he was a favorite of Hera and Zeus, which meant that there was a chance it might pan out. This had raised eyebrows between the other two big guys, Poseidon and Hades, and Poseidon had agreed to play point on the plan. He'd asked the Nereids to keep an eye out for Hannah, and to do whatever they could to wreck Apollo's plan. When she learned that was what Hannah wanted too, she opened up.

Eunice could not emphasize enough the danger Hera posed. Hera had a reputation of casting blame when plans went awry, and she had a quick hand with curses. Eunice had offered Hannah the help of the Nereids to hide. Hannah thanked her, but the thought of hiding on small, uncharted islands in the Caribbean Sea for the rest of her life was untenable. So she'd retrieved a dazed John from Dero and had traveled here to Cambridge to meet up with Carl at her parent's house.

She'd decided, somewhere between the airport parking and Harvard Square, that it was time for John and Carl to go back to Centreville. John had already been hurt on her behalf, and the guilt she felt about it made her certain. If Hera were going to cast blame, best that it land on her and her alone. She'd been trying to come up with a foolproof plan to get the boys safely out of the way, and the only one she could come up with involved a lie. Okay, a series of lies. Pausing at the stop sign on the corner, she looked back for John, who was muttering as he slowly worked his way through the uneven bricks, "John..." He looked up, tripped and went flying forward on his hands and knees. "Oh, John, here, I'm sorry," and she reached down to help him stand.

"Thanks." Accepting her help, he stood up and looked at her expectantly, while absently rubbing his knees.

"Yeah, um...there was something Eunice told me while you were recovering. Something I haven't told you yet." Hannah looked away, down the street, her home still out of view. She needed to be convincing, "She said that Hera has taken a contract out on Carl. According to Eunice, she hired some unemployed fauns to beat him up."

"Fauns? Aren't they just flute playing goat boys?"

Dammit. He knew about fauns. She should have chosen a more obscure mythological creature. More lying would be needed, "Oh, well...you're thinking of woodland fauns. It's a common mistake. Not a lot of people know about the different races of fauns. Woodland fauns are small and playful, but mountain fauns are another story. They tend to average six two, three hundred pounds. According to Eunice the fauns Hera has hired are mountain dwellers and they are bad-ass. Completely ruthless. Carl is in real danger. I need your help to get Carl out of town."

John frowned, "But wouldn't that leave you alone? That doesn't seem like a great idea..."

She might as well lie big, "No, see, the Nereids, all fifty of them, have offered to help me face down Hera." Maybe he'd believe it. *Ladies' Home and Hearth* said that the best lies were the ones people wanted to be true. She certainly wished this were true..."I hadn't told you because Eunice swore me to secrecy— Nereids align with Poseidon, and if word got out that Poseidon was working against Zeus, well, all hell could break lose. Literally— Hades would go on the offensive. It's a very delicate power balance. The Nereids will have my back. I swear. But no one can know about them. Just you and me."

"Wait, the Nereids are going to help us, I mean you, give back the gift? That's great news, Summers! What a relief. Honestly, after that poison ivy curse, I wasn't feeling too optimistic about our odds for a happy ending." She felt the bite of guilt at the magnitude of her lie to John, but squashed it down, as she nodded agreement at him. A series of expressions flitted across his face, and then he grimly continued, "I'll lie to Carl. I'll tell him that there is some ogre or something we have to take care of..."

"A Cyclops?'

"Right. A Cyclops we have to protect you from. He'd do anything for you. But you should stay out of it— he'll get suspicious if you suggest the mission." Hannah nodded again, relief compensating for the guilt. Two birds with one lie.

"That's a good plan, John, come on, my house is this way..." she grabbed his hand and tugged him across the street, ready to face what had become of her home. With Carl and John safely out of the way, all she had to do now was figure out how to manage the most difficult woman in the world. Oh, yeah, and to deal with Hera too.

Home. Home meant facing her mother. Her relief at having a plan to get Carl and John safely out of the way had evaporated at the first sign of her childhood home. She should be rushing in to be sure everyone was okay, but instead felt her feet flagging. What would her mother say about the "gift"? Was there an issue of *Ladies' Home and Hearth* that dealt with cursed children? What had Carl told her mother about Hannah and him? Did she know they broke up? What would she say about Hannah's hair? Hannah frowned. She knew the answer to that one. She pushed her hand through her short brown hair and tried to tell herself it didn't matter. It doesn't matter. It's just hair, hair grows....

Stopping completely, she reached out and rubbed the iron sparrow that was welded to the fence along the sidewalk, her fingers lightly tracing the familiar shape. John let out a low, "Ooohh, " as he noticed the home and garden on their right. The iron sparrow was perched on the upper edge of the fence with its wings folded, head cocked to one side, seeming to be searching the enclosed gardens for a tasty worm. The gardens in question were visible through clever openings in the wooden slats that were woven into a wrought iron framework of the fence, the openings clearly invitations to spy in. The views were astounding; elegant blooms, flowering trees, bubbling fountains and graceful benches. The house behind the garden was built with the same whimsy— crooked peaks and surprising turns, seemingly haphazard yet all gracefully aligned.

Hannah could feel John's amazement in his tone, "Is this your home? It's not at all what I pictured. I guess I'd picture you growing up in the quintessential WASP house, all carefully landscaped. Predictable. But this is really cool. Unexpected."

She stared into the distance, enunciating each word carefully, "This isn't my house; this is our neighbor's house." Still tethered to the stone bird, she turned her head, nodding at the house next door, "That's where I grew up."

John blanched. The house she'd indicated was a saltbox colonial set back from the road, its front yard planted with rhododendrons and holly trees, all mercilessly shaped and pruned into submission. White with black shutters and a red door, there was not a blade of grass out of place. Hannah frowned. It could have been on the cover of New England WASP Today. The contrast between the two homes was striking— one house inviting outsiders to look in and imagine possibilities while the other showing an aggressively perfect exterior and questioning the worthiness of an outsiders' approach.

"Oh. Um. That's nice too." Clearly scrambling to backtrack, John waved his hands in the air and tried again, "It looks very clean. And it hasn't been destroyed by the gods, which is a plus..."

Her tone was acid, "Yes. House not destroyed by vengeful gods. That is good news. " Glancing in his direction, she softened, "Sorry." Staring back at the Whimsy House, her longing was palpable, "When I was little I wanted to live here. I used to imagine that I could turn into a bird, maybe this bird, and fly into the house to find a storybook grandma making me cookies. Or maybe they were a couple of good hearted cobblers, who'd always wanted a child..."

"Who'd they turn out to be? Stockbrokers? Accountants? The big bad wolf and family?"

Hannah shrugged, "I don't know. We never met the neighbors. Never even saw them."

The Myth of Cassandra

"You never met your neighbors? You never went over and borrowed a cup of sugar? Asked them to move their garbage cans?"

John's voice sounded carefully flat. She could sense him reining in his attitude after his inopportune WASP comments, but it was impossible not to hear his questions as the judgments they were, and she found herself wanting to explain, "My mother didn't approve of knocking on strangers' doors," she rolled her eyes, "You should've heard her lecturing the moms of the girl scouts who tried to sell us cookies, telling them they were teaching their daughters poor manners by encouraging them to knock on our door, "Good neighbors are like small children; better seen, not heard. Or bothered by." Classic *Ladies' Home and Hearth*. Eventually the word got around and the girl scouts skipped our house. My mother believed she'd successfully educated a whole generation of Cambridge scouting families on proper neighborly etiquette. The truth was they all avoided her, and me, to some extent. Girls weren't exactly begging to come over and play."

She could feel a blush spreading up her cheeks, and some part of her brain was aware that she was revealing too much, but there was apparently a different part of her brain in control at the moment, a part of her brain that needed someone, no, John in particular, to understand. "I spent a lot of afternoons staring into this yard. The only human being I ever saw was an elderly gardener singing to the plants in some foreign language. That just added to magic— he didn't do anything so commonplace as weed or prune— just sing." Her gaze narrowed on her parent's front door, "My mother was obsessed with the plants they grew, and not in a good way. She was convinced that the plants were imported exotic weeds primed to take over her own compulsively ordered garden. "It's the purple loosestrife all over again, Tom." She used to sneak into their yard to grab samples to take to the authorities— I was her lookout. My mother...."

She looked again at John and saw that his patient carefulness had been replaced by something more challenging. And so she defended.

"I know. I know. Everyone has issues with their moms. And it isn't like my mom is some monster, but she isn't easy, John. She's always so definitive, so certain. Like with the girl scouts and the garden. She's never ambivalent. About anything." Hannah turned to her parent's house, still anchored by the bird in her hand. "My mother is in there, with Carl, who has told her about this," and she waved her hand at herself and John, "And what if.... What if..."

He slid his hand under Hannah's, releasing the iron sparrow, and linked his fingers lightly with hers, turning her to face him, "Come on Summers, what's the worst that can happen?"

She looked him full in the eye, imagining all of the possibilities. It was the first time she'd really looked at him since he'd recovered from the poison ivy curse. It was a lot less awful than she thought it would be. The blame she worried she might see in his expression, the blame she felt she deserved, wasn't there. Just friendliness and encouragement, and maybe something more she didn't want to think about now, but might think about later, alone. She took a deep breath, embarrassed by her neurotic rant, "I guess I picked a bad time to regress; sorry. You're right, let's go."

Keeping her hand in his, John stepped over a wayward brick, "Don't apologize, its fine, really. Come on, she can't be all that bad. Besides, moms love me. Remember? "

⁂

Lee/Mott

Parking Lot C, Logan Airport...

Lee breathed through his mouth, trying to settle the waves of nausea that were pushing him to the edge of retching. He'd already vomited and thought you were supposed to feel better after getting sick. He made a mental note to never, ever fly in a chariot pulled by winged horses again. He'd thought the flight would be smooth, but they had swung up and down in rhythm to the horses' strides. Even though he'd been on solid ground for 15 minutes, he seemed to be stuck on some carousel of

The Myth of Cassandra

torture, floating up and down, over and over, He needed to feel better, or how would he be able to follow the plans that he and Hermes had come up with?

Hermes had said that he was certain the girl would go to her mother, and had tasked Lee with the job of leading Archer and Apollo on a "wild goose chase" at Logan Airport. Hermes had insisted it would be easy to spend several hours just going from one terminal to another. The only problem was that Hannah and the boy had actually come to the airport. Because that was definitely the bike they were on when they left Connecticut. He had a picture of it. Even Archer had recognized it in the long-term parking lot. So it would seem that Hannah did not go home and was actually here, now. It was not much of a goose chase if the geese were nearby. Well, maybe it was still a goose chase, but not a very good one. If in a good goose chase, you have purposefully misled someone, what would you call a goose chase where you inadvertently led someone? A goose find?

Holding back a dry heave, Lee doubled over. The only plus side to the motion sickness was that Archer was giving him some space, everyone was giving him space, and seemed pre-occupied with trying to charm the Airport Shuttle Bus driver into giving him information on who had ridden the shuttle in the last few hours. The horses had flown off and Apollo had hidden the chariot in the corner of the parking lot under a blue tarp with orange cones around it. Lee wondered why it was that the humans didn't seem to notice them landing in the parking lot, but when he had voiced his amazement, Apollo had laughed. "Humans are expert at seeing what they believe, and when they stopped believing in me, they stopped seeing me as a god in a golden chariot— they just see me as an incredibly handsome man. Every once in awhile I run across a human who can see, but no one believes them, so it doesn't really count."

Lee had to stop himself from staring at Apollo, who he was just now seeing as the incredibly handsome man he was, and pull himself together to figure out where best to misdirect the hunt for Hannah. He hoped she was not still in the airport and that she had used an alias and a disguise to get out of the country. He wondered where she flew off to, and whether Hermes had already figured out that she hadn't gone to Cambridge like he'd predicted. Was she trying to hide in some exotic location? How would they find her?

Hermes' plan had been to find the girl to explain to her the importance of agreeing to the script, so that Archer wouldn't hurt her. All Lee had to do was delay Archer from finding the girl so Hermes could get it done. But that would be impossible if Hermes was in Cambridge and Archer was here with the girl. It was crucial to get Archer and Apollo away from the airport as fast as possible, to protect the girl. He needed Hermes to come up with a Plan B, but how to get to Hermes? And then he knew what to do. Hermes had told him that the best lies were based on truth. It was time for him to tell a little truth, to make the bigger lie work.

"Hey Archer, I have something! Apollo, come here, come and see!" And he held his phone in the air, waving it above his head, but that made him feel woozy, so he sat on the curb and waited for Archer and Apollo to converge on him.

Apollo hung back, still a little squeamish about the stability of Lee's stomach, but Archer bent down and glared at him, "What do you have, Lee? It'd better be good."

Lee pointed at the screen of his phone, which showed a map with a blinking dot on it. "I got suspicious of Hermes loyalties, I think he's really jealous of Apollo, I mean, who wouldn't be, Apollo is so tall, and strong, and ..."

Apollo sagely nodded, "Everyone feels jealous of me at some time, and for Hermes, well sometimes is all the time...."

Archer shook Lee, hard. "The point, Lee. Get to the point. It goes without saying that your existence hinges on the success of this mission, so I hope you have something more than statements of the obvious."

Lee burped, and the smell of vomit pushed Archer back, giving him a little more room to bait the hook, "I suspected that Hermes might be behind the flood, because I had just told him that I was close to finding the girl, and then SPLASH, all my data lost. That seemed more than coincidental. And it was Hermes who suggested that the girl would be fleeing the country, that she was heading to the airport when I found an image of them on the highway. So where is Hermes now? Why isn't he here with us looking for the girl?"

Archer sputtered, impatience making his ears smoke, but Apollo hushed him, "Let him talk, Archer, I want to know why Hermes isn't here. Do you know?"

Lee blushed, Apollo really was very beautiful and it was intoxicating to have his undivided attention. "I don't know for sure what his motives are, but I can guess. I think he wants to be the one to find the girl and get the glory. He wants to rescue her from the longhaired communist, and she'll be grateful to him. And then she will use your gift to tell everyone how wonderful he is. Yes! That must be it!"

Apollo was nodding, and even touching him. His touch was so nice— strong but soothing. And he smelled of sunshine. And his eyes; he had such blue eyes! Were they bluer than the sky? Oh, yes. They were. While Hermes had a definite appeal, in a Humphrey Bogart kind of way, Apollo was like a young Robert Redford. The Redfords of the world never talked to him. Let alone looked at him as if he had all the answers in the world. It wasn't like he was betraying Hermes; he was just protecting the girl. Hermes wanted to protect the girl too, so he was really doing something to help Hermes. If he made Apollo think Hermes had double-crossed him, so that he could lead Apollo and Archer away from the girl, then he could and get to Hermes himself to figure out a Plan B. It was all for the greater good. So if Apollo happened to smile and look at him, well, there was no crime in enjoying that attention, was there?

"Lee is right! Archer, you've been tricked! Hermes is stealing my spotlight, my glory! We have to stop him before he saves the girl!" Apollo had turned his back to Archer, to once again shower his sunlight on Lee, and so didn't witness Archer's elaborate eye roll. Archer was glaring at him, but Lee could only feel the glow of Apollo, as Apollo actually took his shoulder in his hands, "I don't know why I didn't see this before, Lee. Hermes has always been jealous of me. We have to stop him before he saves the girl from the communist. Tell me that you know where we can find him."

Lee's blush got even deeper, but his voice was strong. Looking into Apollo's eyes made him feel strong, "When I started to suspect he was up to something, I attached a very discreet electronic tag to his phone." He held up his own phone again, the screen showing a blinking dot at the intersections of Franklin and Bay Streets in Cambridge, "He's here, in Cambridge. While time is of the essence, it might be wise, among so many humans, to avail ourselves of the public transport to get there. I hear the T is very efficient, and I believe that Shuttle Bus can take us to the station." Wow. Not only had he derived strength and conviction from Apollo's deep blue eyes, he had apparently tapped into a well of vocabulary he had not realized he knew. Lee's crush grew even stronger.

Apollo slapped Lee on the shoulder, not noticing that it knocked him off the curb, and turned back to Archer. "Sounds like a plan to follow, Archer. Come, we have no time to waste to stop that smirking scene stealer." And without pausing to see if the other two were following, Apollo strode onto the Airport Shuttle, exclaiming, "To the Train, good driver! I have a hot woman to rescue!" It was all executed for maximum dramatic effect.

Archer climbed onto the bus behind Apollo, with Lee following, clapping. Neither Lee nor Apollo seemed to notice Archer's ominous silence, his focused stillness.

CHAPTER SEVENTEEN

Vervain and Catmint

ooo

Hannah

Cambridge hospitality...

It became clear in the first few seconds after her mother answered the door that Elise would prove to be the exception in the face of John's charm. Something else that was apparent: Carl had shared a lot of information with her mother. As Hannah and John were hustled into the foyer, it was obvious that he'd included the part of the story where he'd found Hannah in a towel in John's apartment.

"Hannah! I am glad you made it here safely and fully clothed. Quite an accomplishment given your present company." Elise executed a quick one-armed hug that rotated Hannah away from John, and placed Elise's back firmly to John's face, "Oh dear, please tell me that is a wig you're wearing, honey. Fixing your hair color is a simple matter of chemistry, but you don't have the bone structure to pull off that length."

Hannah should have been prepared for this, but found herself oddly mute in the face of her mother's criticisms, both direct and indirect. But John threw himself into the fray, "I like it short. But then, I've developed a taste for short hair myself." He rubbed his own buzz cut and attempted his best charming, self-deprecating smile. Hannah appreciated his courage, but cringed, knowing he had no idea whom he was dealing with.

Elise turned a cool appraising look at John, "You must be Carl's friend. The friend of Hannah's fiancé."

Hannah tapped Elise's shoulder, "Mom, technically, I never really knew that we were engaged, I mean I thought he was going to ask me at dinner, I didn't realize he'd already asked me…." she petered out under her mother's scrutiny.

Elise rolled her eyes, "The friend of Hannah's not-quite-fiancé. I am so pleased you like her new hair." She let her gaze travel down him and stared at his feet. Then, without another glance in his direction, intoned like a bored tour guide, "Please remove your shoes before entering our home."

Slipping her arm through Hannah's, she propelled her out of the foyer, speaking in a stream that denied interruption, "Don't worry, hair grows, honey, and until then, there are always hats. We'll be eating in a few minutes. I was just about to feed Carl an early dinner. I made chicken casserole, his favorite, so there's plenty to eat. Honey, Carl can't wait to see you, he's working in your father's office…"

Hannah whispered reprovingly at her mother, "That was so rude, mom. Since when do we take off our shoes? We're Episcopalians. We'd wear our shoes to bed…" But Hannah's voice disappeared as she caught sight of Carl. He was sitting at her father's desk across the room, frowning at the computer screen, and in that moment his resemblance to her father was striking, even down to the absent tugging of the hair at the back of his neck. Good lord, what blind, Freudian path had she been traveling on for the last two years? Well, if there were an upside to this curse from the gods, it would have to be that she'd ended things with Carl before they'd made it legally binding. Her relief at not being engaged to the replica of her father was followed quickly by a stab of guilt for her disloyal thoughts.

Elise pushed her forward, "Look Carl, Hannah's here! Isn't that wonderful? I know she looks…different…but she made it here safely, isn't that amazing?"

Hannah had a strange moment of unease. Why was her mother trying so hard to convince Carl to be happy to see her? Why was Carl still sitting behind the desk scrutinizing her? Was he actually steepling his fingers? What was happening here?

"Hello Hannah, have a seat, you must be tired." Carl pointed to the chair facing her father's desk, and she lowered into it slowly.

"Hey Carl, it is great to see...."

"Elise, the rope, NOW!" And with that, Elise lowered a slipknot around Hannah's chest and arms, effectively tying her to the chair.

"What the...MOM! What're you doing?" As Hannah grappled with the ropes, twisting in her chair, she realized that John was not in the room with her, "John! Where are you? Mom! What have you done with John? Why did you tie me to this chair?"

Her mother patted her head, "Hannah dear, you need to calm down. John's in a safe place— your father's looking after him. Now, if you can sit still and listen, Carl has some very important questions for you, honey."

"Thank you, Elise." Carl cleared his throat, "I've had some time in the last few days to do a little research, "Hannah," and he made air quotes around her name, "and the Greek Gods have quite a few tricks up their sleeves when trying to mess with humans. Hera in particular liked to take mortal form and convince humans to trust her. We just need to ascertain if you and John are really who you say you are before we can trust you."

"What? Of course I am myself! If I were Hera, do you think a measly rope would hold me? Mom, untie these ropes right now!' Hannah started to pull at the end of the rope that she could reach, and that was when she realized the rope was wet and smelled. She frowned down at it, "What is on this rope?"

"Oh yes, dear, it's a concoction of vervain and honey— Carl is so clever. He did some research online and found that vervain was used to break spells and such. It just so happened I had some growing in my garden, isn't that a wonderful coincidence? Really, very lucky. *Ladies' Home and Hearth* says that a well-tended garden is the sign of a well-tended mind. I have to say that I agree completely. You really should try to grow something, Hannah. It'd be good for your mental health. Oh, I mean, if you are Hannah." Elise straightened up and walked to a small bowl and towel laid out on the credenza, and began washing the honey off her hands, "Carl reasoned that if we tied Hera up in a vervain soaked rope, she might not be able to escape. I added the honey to make it more viscous— and it smells nice, don't you think? Carl has spent so much time at that computer, and all to help you, honey, if you are Hannah, that is. It is surely a sign of his devotion; he wouldn't go to the trouble of tying up someone he didn't love..."

Hannah closed her eyes and tried to keep from yelling at them both. Regardless of the dubious herbal properties of the rope, her mother had tied it firmly around her and she realized that she was not getting free until she convinced the two insane people in the room that she was herself. Opening her eyes, she looked straight at Carl and vented her frustration, "So how do you intend to determine if I'm truly Hannah Summers? Ask me what our pet names for each other are, snuggle bear? Or whether I know about that birthmark in the shape of Vermont on your right butt cheek? Because from certain angles, one could argue it looks like New Hampshire..."

Carl's cheeks flared, "See, that's just the kind of thing the real Hannah would never say. She would never be so crass or sarcastic, and she never would have yelled at me or her mother. Maybe we don't need the questions, Elise, maybe I should just get her to tell us where Hannah is, I have my ways, Hera...."

Carl was standing now, doing his best to look threatening, though in reality he simply looked somewhat constipated as he glared at her, and for the first time Hannah noticed the deep shadows under his eyes, and some of her anger melted. He looked like hell. And it was all her fault. "I guess I never really thought about what you all were going through here while John and I searched for the gods. I'm not Hera, Carl, but if proving who I am is what you need to trust me, go ahead and ask away." Twisting to look over at her mother, "Dad isn't hurting John, right?"

"Of course not, Hannah. Your father isn't a barbarian. He simply tied him up with vervain soaked rope and locked him in the closet. Oh, and he gagged him with some duct tape, but the Internet said that was perfectly safe. He's in no danger until we decide what to do with him." Elise walked to Carl's side, placing her hand on his shoulder "Go ahead,

The Myth of Cassandra

Carl, dear, ask her the three questions we came up with. I'll know if she's telling the truth."

Carl cleared his throat and looked down at a list in his hand. "What is your birth date?"

Hannah looked from Carl to her mother, and then down to the floor. This was harder to answer than it might seem. She'd been born on April 1, 1990, but she'd only found that out by accident. She'd been sixteen and angry with her mother. Convinced that she had to have been adopted, she'd gone looking for proof, and being somewhat gifted at breaking into computer security systems, she'd hacked into the hospital records. She couldn't console herself with the notion of being adopted, but what she'd found instead was even more disorienting. Her mother had been lying to her about her birthday her entire life. Elise had baked a cake and sung Happy Birthday every year on April second. The lie had been on every school form, permission slip, bank account, and family calendar.

Hannah could only assume that her mother had been embarrassed to have a child born on April Fool's Day? There seemed to be no other explanation. Even in her birth, she'd let her mother down. Hannah had never said a word about her discovery to her mom, and in time, it had bothered her less. She'd decided it was funny, though it had never made her smile, let alone laugh. In all that time since finding out, she'd told no one. But now she had to answer Carl's question, and she found herself wanting to say it out loud. Maybe the vervain soaked rope really did have power, "I was born on April 1, 1990."

Carl actually jumped back from the desk, flinging the list of questions in the air as he grabbed the fireplace poker and brandished it in front of her, "It's Hera! Hannah's birthday is April 2, 1990! Go get help, Elise, I'll try to keep her here for as long as the rope will hold!" He started waving the poker wildly in Hannah's face while he danced back and forth, as if dodging an attack.

But instead of fleeing the room Elise came to his side, stilling his dance with a hand on his arm. She spoke gently to him, sliding the poker from his hands, "Actually, she's right, Carl, her birthday is April first."

Placing the poker carefully on the desk, she turned to Hannah, "I thought you'd found out, but wasn't certain until now." She smiled a little sadly, "Why didn't you ask me about it?"

Hannah surprised herself as she gave voice to another truth, "There seemed no point in talking to you about it." Why hadn't she lied and told her mother she just recently found out and hadn't had a chance to talk to her yet? No one would know that was a lie and it would have made her admission, well, less bitter, not to mention simpler.

Carl grabbed his head, "What?" His voice cracked but then he coughed, visibly shaking himself, and he lowered his voice, as if he could force the answers to be reasonable, "Why would you change Hannah's birthday? If you knew about it, Hannah, why wouldn't you demand to know why? Why would you keep celebrating it on the wrong day after knowing? Why wouldn't you have told me, your fiancé?" Carl's head had swiveled back and forth between the women, and he ended looking expectantly at Hannah. But Hannah's eyes were on her shoes.

"Ask the next question, Carl dear, go ahead." Elise pointed to the list that had floated down and landed in front of him on the desk.

Frowning, Carl looked at it. "I know I know the answer to this one, so don't think you can fool me." Crossing his arms across his chest, he raised one eyebrow, "What is your favorite color?"

Hannah closed her eyes. There was the answer she knew Carl expected and then there was the truth. She surprised herself again, and opted for the truth, even knowing that by doing so she was extending this farce, "My favorite color is green."

"Aha! This was a trick question— Hannah has no favorite color— she thinks all colors are equally nice! I know!" Poker in hand once again, Carl lowered it in front of Hannah's chest, "I don't care if you are a vengeful goddess— what have you done with my Hannah? You will tell me the truth— where is she? Don't make me use the Prismatic Storm Spell, I've been practicing it for days, and I will use it if I have to. Just tell me where she is and this will all be over."

"A spell from Dungeons and Dragons? Really? Have you lost your mind, Carl? That's a game, not real life. And why the hell is Hannah tied to a chair?" Hannah craned her neck to see John MacCallister, neither tied nor gagged, standing in the doorway holding what appeared to be a tumbler of scotch in his hand.

"Oh, like the Greek Gods are just myths and stories?" Were Carl's eyes actually bugging out of his head? He seemed more than just tired, closer to unhinged. He started gesturing wildly with the fire poker, "Who's to say what's real anymore? Besides, that's not Hannah tied to a chair, but Hera in Hannah's shape." Carl flung his arm at Hannah, and she tilted back in the chair, just missing the poker as it cut through the air in front of her face.

Elise moved quickly, "I'm sure your spell-thing is very impressive, Carl dear. But, it's completely unnecessary to use on Hannah," and she ripped the poker from Carl's clenched fingers and swinging it through the air, used it to knock the drink out of John's hands, pushing the point against his chest, "Though you might want to keep it handy for your friend here," Bearing down on John, Elise raised the poker to his throat, "Where is my husband and what have you done with him!"

"Elise? Why did you waste perfectly good scotch? And why are you threatening Hannah's friend with a poker— that isn't very kind..." Tom came out from behind John and positioned himself between the poker and John, "Let me have that, honey, and you can get back to interrogating our daughter."

Elise made use of the fireplace tool on her husband, punctuating each word with a poke. "You were supposed to tie him up, gag him, and lock him in the closet! Why are you pouring him drinks?"

Tom smiled at her, "Well, you know what the SOT said, "Above all, be kind." The more I thought about it, the more I felt like the gagging wasn't very kind, and when I decided not to gag him, well, locking him in the closet also seemed fairly unkind, and from there it was not a huge leap to realize that tying someone up was also unkind. So I offered him a drink. He's really quite good company— very charming and knows the difference between single and double malt. By the way, that was single malt that you spilled on the rug, really a waste, dear."

"Daddy, you follow the SOT?" Hannah found this idea depressing. It'd been clear to her that her mother was not affected by the gift or she wouldn't still be tied to this chair, so why was her father?

"Of course, Hannah Banana. She isn't the Speaker of Truth for nothing. Hey, you changed your hair, I like it, pumpkin."

"Have you all forgotten that we have a real problem here? This is NOT Hannah! She got the question wrong! We need to make her tell us where the real Hannah is, and I am not going to stand here doing nothing while the rest of you talk about malted milk balls and the freaking SOT," And Carl started to spin in a circle, muttering words under his breath.

Tom shook his head and whispered back to John, "Nice boy, Carl, but he knows nothing about scotch...."

Hannah found herself staring at Carl as he turned and chanted and she saw the air around him start to shimmer and felt minute vibrations begin at the tips of her fingers. "John! Mom! Stop him— whatever he's doing, it's doing something!"

Elise reacted first, spun and whacked Carl on the toe with the poker. "Stop this instant!" Carl howled and grabbed his foot, and the shimmering stopped, "You may not have known that Hannah's favorite color is green, but that's definitely Hannah, so it stands to reason that if she says her favorite color is green, then green it is." Elise looked once again to her daughter, tied to the chair, "Green is all very nice on plants, Hannah, but it's not a very flattering color to someone with your skin tone. *Ladies' Home and Hearth* says that the wrong color can add 15 years to your age, and we don't want that, do we?"

Hannah rolled her eyes, an exact copy of her mother. "Mom, the question was not which color do I think I look best in, but what was my favorite color." As her mother opened her mouth to argue with her, Hannah lost it. "Oh for crying out loud, it's my favorite color, not yours!"

In all the activity around Carl's incantation, John had moved to Hannah's side and knelt to untie her, "What's her favorite color? Where did you get these questions anyway? Have you been watching Monty

The Myth of Cassandra

Python? Are you going to ask her the flight time of a sparrow?" He pulled at the knot, finding it almost impossible to undo, "And why is this rope so sticky?"

"You can't take it off her, John, its Vervain Rope— it can only be removed by the person who tied it. And I didn't come up with the questions— Elise did. But maybe that would be a good question, since I know that Hannah agrees with me and can't stand Monty Python..." Carl had removed his shoe and was rubbing his foot.

Now it was John's turn to look disgusted. "Come on man, did she ever disagree with you? Didn't that ever strike you as odd? Unnatural? Or at the least unlikely?"

Carl's voice kicked up another notch. "No! It struck me as perfect! We are perfect for each other! You wouldn't understand, you've never been in a real relationship. I know Hannah." He looked pleadingly from Tom to Elise and then to John. "Even if the stress of the last few days could excuse the behavioral changes in her— the sarcasm and annoyance completely atypical of Hannah – there's the fact that so far she's not gotten a single question right. I asked Hannah for her favorite color in the first month we were together and she told me this whole story about why she didn't have any favorite colors— and that she liked to be surprised for her birthday on the second of April, by a sweater in any color I choose, because she had no favorite color." And he looked frantically back and forth between the other occupants of the room, wide-eyed and nodding.

John stood up from kneeling at Hannah's side and walked to Carl slowly, as if he were approaching a cornered dog, and placed his hands on Carl's shoulders. "Come on man, that doesn't even make any sense. Who doesn't have a favorite color? Doesn't it make more sense if she was just lying to make you feel good about your present? This" and he turned Carl to face Hannah, "is Hannah. I've been with her this whole time. We've been on the same bike, slept in the same room. We changed our look to trick Hera— see, Hannah dyed her hair brown and then she cut my hair, but it's still us. It's her. I swear." He leaned in closer and whispered, "You look totally exhausted, man. Have you even slept since we left Centreville?"

Carl's unraveling cut her to the quick and Hannah's voice shook. "Oh, Carl. I promise, I am me. You have to believe me."

At that, Tom jumped to attention. "You heard her, big guy. She is me. You have to believe her. So Sayeth the SOT."

Tom's reaction to her as the SOT had an instant effect on Carl. It seemed to cut through the fear and exhaustion which had tied him up in knots and he stared at her and whispered, "Oh, Hannah, it is you. Oh god, I tied you up, and I could have hurt..."

But Elise was done. "Everyone be quiet! Tom, whenever you mention the SOT I feel a headache coming on, so please keep it to yourself. Carl, honey, stop apologizing, you didn't do anything wrong." She completely ignored John and put her arm around Carl and led him to door, discretely removing the poker from his hands for the last time, "I think the boys should go back to the living room and all have a stiff drink. It's been a very trying afternoon. Carl dear, you just need some good food and a nap. Please go, all of you. I'll untie Hannah. We'll call you to dinner when it's ready." And she herded the men to the door, and closed it firmly behind them.

"Now, let's see about getting this rope off you, Hannah. I hope it wasn't too tight, but we really did need to take the precaution, you know. Dealing with the Greek Gods is no laughing matter. Here we go. Be careful not to let the rope touch your hair, it's very sticky." And with that she lifted the rope up and off of Hannah, who was staring at her mother as if she had an extra head.

Hannah rubbed her arms, but the honey made her hands goopy. She sat immobile as if she were still tied to the chair and took a deep breath. Nerves singing, she knew she needed answers, but questioning her mother was a dangerous activity. "I don't understand, Mom, how could you be so sure it was me? You were always so sure I was telling the truth. Why? I mean, every truth I told just revealed more lies I'd already told..."

The Myth of Cassandra

Elise rolled the rope and knotted the ends. "That's easy, honey. I always know when you tell the truth. I can see it in your eyes. Now, since going to Whitfield, you generally lie to me on the phone, so I only can guess at what your eyes look like, but in those instances, you always sound so, well, guarded. When you sound guarded, I know you're lying. Just now, answering those questions, you were telling the truth. " She placed the coil of Vervain Rope in a cloth sack that Hannah could have sworn was made out of an old sundress she used to wear— was there no circumstance in life when her mother did not respond to it with a thrifty and tasteful craft? Said woman was washing her hands again in the basin on the credenza. She crossed the room and gave the air around Hannah a hug, careful not to get any honey on her own clothes, and in doing so, began to scold, "Now Hannah, this is not the time to get emotional, but to get changed. It's not like I expect you to dress for dinner, but a t-shirt and shorts...,well, I think we can do a little better than that."

But Hannah stayed frozen in the chair. "I'm sorry Mom, but I am not going to go upstairs like a good little girl to get dressed for the next act in this bizarre play. You said that you could tell when I tell the truth— but how? How can you know?" Frowning, she stared at her mother. "Do you somehow think you know me better than I know myself? Because I can tell you right now that I don't believe that could be possible. I've spent my entire life making myself into whatever is easiest for other people to see, saying what they want to hear, so what is there that is real to know?" Hannah's head dropped, her short brown hair masking her face.

Elise knelt in front of her, lifting her chin to look her in the eye. "Hannah, when did you become so dramatic? Of course you are real. I will always know you. I'm your mother." She peered more closely at Hannah's face, "Pull yourself together, darling. *Ladies' Home and Hearth* says that sixty-five percent of all wrinkles are caused by self-doubt. Wrinkles, honey, wrinkles. Carl loves you, but that doesn't mean you should let yourself go."

Hannah wasn't sure which emotion was stronger, her wonder at how her mother could so blithely claim to know her, or her irritation at what was clearly her mother's campaign to reunite her with Carl. It turned out that the feelings gelled quite easily into anger, "Mom, I broke up with Carl! I broke up with him. I don't want to marry him, as nice and wonderful as he is. He and I agreed to be friends. So we're not getting married. Let it go." Hannah took a deep breath, but instead of calming her, it intensified her outrage, "And you know me? Really? On what do you base this knowledge of me? Did *Ladies' Home and Hearth* tell you?"

Elise rocked back on her heels and narrowed her eyes, "There is no need for you to disparage LH& H just because you feel upset. I suppose you're allowed a little latitude. This has been quite the week for you." She stood up and dusted her hands, as if finishing the conversation, "I know you because I love you. There. It's not more complicated than that. As for all of this angst over lies and the truth, what does that have to do with who you are? The answer is simple, Hannah. You are yourself. Now we should be getting on with fixing your little Olympic problem." Hands on hips, Elise was finished with the conversation. But Hannah wasn't done yet.

"That's ironic. My little Olympic problem. The Greek gods gave me this "gift," and it is supposed to be reparations for Cassandra, to make up for when she was cursed with having no one listen. She knew the future, so it mattered what she said. It was a tragedy that no one heeded her warnings. I have this so-called gift, and I say nothing right. It's a tragedy that people do listen to me! People have listened to me tell them to be truthful, and we were on the brink of societal disintegration with everyone insulting each other. I tried to tell them to be kind, and people are unable to merge their damn cars, I just can't...."

"Language, Hannah, watch your language please. Ladies Home...." but whatever *Ladies' Home and Hearth* had to say about the use of strong language went un-discussed as Hannah glared at her mother.

"It doesn't matter what language I use, Mom. I have nothing real to say. I've spent so long saying things for other people, telling them what they want to hear, just so they would leave me alone, I wouldn't know how to tell the truth if I wanted to. I am a shell of a person capable only of lies."

The Myth of Cassandra

And now there were two angry women in the room. "I have no idea where you get the expectation that you have to be perfectly one thing or another— you can be both honest and lying and it doesn't cancel each other out. They are two sides of the same coin— the yin and the yang— a dichotomy. I would hope that in your four years of study you have come across the concept of dichotomies?" Elise lacked only a podium to complete the picture of the lecturing professor, "You need to accept that every person has dichotomies. And the more interesting people have the sharper dichotomies. Take me, for instance. I believe that as your mother it is my job to push and mold you into the best person you can be, by any means necessary. My job is to improve you. " Elise turned her back to Hannah and picked up the much bandied fireplace poker and walked to the fireplace. Sliding it in with the other tools, she looked at Hannah. "But I also think you are perfect just the way you are. See, a dichotomy." And she lifted her chin as if posing for a Hellenic allegorical statue of incompatible realities.

Had her mother just told her that she was perfect just the way she was? Without any conditional, *Ladies' Home and Hearth* inspired improvements? But she also believed Hannah needed to be fixed. Hannah shook her head. "But what if all I am is lies that satisfy others? What if I am missing the other side of my dichotomy?" Hannah slid her fingers over her face and felt the lines furrowed in her forehead. Maybe LHH was right about self-doubt.

"Well, let's see about that Hannah. You answered the first two questions truthfully, let's try the third." Elise stood up and turned to the desk, where the paper with the questions on it lay.

"I only answered those truthfully because of the Vervain Rope— I couldn't lie."

"Don't be silly, Hannah. There's no such thing as Vervain Rope. Carl has been under a lot of stress, dear. He's really very worried for you. So I indulged him in this "vervain" idea— I don't have vervain in my garden, but Carl doesn't know that. I just cut him some catmint and told him it was vervain." She leaned back on the desk, paper in hand, "You told the truth because you wanted to. And you haven't spent the last ten years lying— you've spent them listening, learning to hear what people need. You can choose what you say, for whatever reasons you have. Period. But here, I'll ask you the third question and we will see what you say." Clearing her throat, Elise read from the page, "Name at least one time in your life when you were truly happy."

A silence filled the room between Hannah and her mother, and Hannah closed her eyes to feel it more deeply. The silence felt light, buoyant. Hannah let her mind sift through this question, let her answer come from inside. She considered all the possible answers in light of what her mother had shared, all the memories whose shape had shifted slightly with her new understanding. Her mother thought she was perfect, just as she was. Even if her mother also thought she needed to be corrected and prodded and pushed. Happiness. Dichotomies. Being known. And then she knew. And she chose to tell the truth.

She opened her eyes. "Right now, Mom. This will do." She hazarded a look at her mother through her hair. "Providing you don't tell me how I could have answered this question better or start to tell me how I could be happier if I was still engaged to Carl or..." but Hannah's words were cutoff as Elise hugged her daughter, sticky clothes and all.

Elise cupped Hannah's shoulders in her hands. "See, that wasn't so hard." And she hugged her again, longer this time. "Now, let's both go change and get food on the table.... That friend of Carl's, he isn't a vegetarian, is he? He looks like a vegetarian. Vegetarians are all so smug. And really, Hannah, is it wise to rebound with Carl's friend?"

"What do you mean, "rebound"? John and I are just friends, mom, and no, he's not a vegetarian, not that there is anything wrong with being a ..."

"I think you are more than friends, Hannah. First you are in a towel in his apartment and then you are cutting his hair. Please. At least tell me you used protection, *Ladies' Home and Hearth* says....."

"Mom! Shouldn't we be thinking about dinner? We wouldn't want your chicken casserole to get dry; you know what LHH says about dry casseroles...."

The Myth of Cassandra

"Fine, Hannah, I'll concede the field and we'll talk about your disastrous love life later. But for the record the beauty of a chicken casserole is that the mushroom soup keeps it moist for hours. If you had just once tried to make your own casserole, you would know that. And just because you changed the subject, don't think the subject is closed. I am firmly on team Carl..." but Hannah had the last word as she wrapped her arms around her mother, her embrace effectively silencing her.

"My personal life is not a team sport, Mom. It is my job to tell you to back off, and yet I love when you are close— how's that for a dichotomy?" Hannah leaned back to look in her face, only to see her mother frowning.

"That's nice, dear, but, as dichotomies go, yours is flawed. Both sides should be a capital "T" truth, and *Ladies' Home and Hearth* says that a Mother's Wisdom trumps childish ways, so you really should defer to my..."

"Mom...."

✪✪✪✪✪✪✪✪✪✪✪✪

Hera

Playing the Odds on Martha's Vineyard

Hera handed her phone to Zeus without looking at him. The information Hermes had sent her had filled her with a feeling of rage that, truth be told, was a relief from the paralyzing anxiety that had been mastering her since yesterday. Apep, Egyptian God of Darkness and Death; what an ass. Archer and Lee were his minions and had been manipulating them into this ridiculous "gift."

She'd met Apep at a party Hades had thrown a century or so ago. What she remembered most about him was his habit of using words that started with "s" so that he could show off his forked tongue. A more egotistical, vain idiot didn't exist in the Egyptian pantheon. Zeus. The most likely cause of a vendetta was almost always her husband. She walked to the railing to distance herself from her own idiot, and tried to find the cold center of her anger while staring at the seagulls, "It's been Apep all along. What did you do, Zeus? Sleep with his sister? Sleep with his dog? Come on, Zeus, you must have screwed something of his. Why else would that Egyptian idiot be at the bottom of this? It's revenge for something, and I can't think of anything else you know how to do..." She looked back at him, but he was frowning down at her phone and jabbing his big fat adulterous fingers at the screen.

Just looking at him caused her rage to slide up a notch, and her next words where in a high falsetto. "You had to say yes to Apollo because you couldn't resist the urge to be worshipped again. Played. You were played. And I have been feeding and housing a pair of slimy Egyptian demons in my beautiful home, oh, and paying them for the privilege." She turned on her heel, infuriated that he hadn't looked up from the phone once the entire time she was talking. She dug her nails into the railing, knowing that she should stop talking, that Zeus had always used silence to infuriate her and make her seem crazy, but the words seemed to come of their own volition, "I'm so glad that you've been doing something with your time while I work. I make money and you make irritating enemies by following your base instincts..."

"Shut up, woman. I wish I'd been having enough fun to incur the wrath of that demon-hiring snake, but if you hadn't noticed I've been stuck under your terrifyingly efficient thumb for the past decade or so, or had you forgotten Archer's accurate assessment of my demotion to your pet?" His smile was dark as he cavalierly tossed her phone across the deck and opened a beer. "Given your power mongering, it's much more likely something you did ticked him off, or hadn't that occurred to you...."

Plucking her phone up from the deck, she waggled it in his face. "Really? Me. You think this is my fault? What do you think I did to piss him off? Became too incredibly wealthy? Provided for our family too much? Because that doesn't seem to bother you as you drink and eat and grow more and more...." Hera mimicked a growing gut flowing in front of her, but she was interrupted mid-mime.

The Myth of Cassandra

"More and more bored with your harping. Does venting anger really make-up for a lack of orgasm like your little magazine says? For your sake, I hope so." Zeus had to duck to avoid the phone that was flying at his head, "And you thought I didn't read...."

"I'm so honored by your taking the time to read my magazine. It must be hard to fit in between the time it takes for the brownies to bake, and the sugar coma that renders you insensible. Bravo. So in all of your eating and reading, when did you have time to screw with Apep, because there is no way this is my fault." She regretted throwing her phone at him, it was a new phone and didn't deserve such bad treatment. It was just a phone. She tried to make it seem casual that she was walking by to pick it up, but he reached out and grabbed her wrist, halting her.

"Are you willing to put some of your hard earned money where your mouth is? Hermes seems to have an idea of using the girl to get Archer, or Sek, or whomever the hell he is, to reveal Apep's big plan. I say we go to Cambridge and indulge the Messenger and find out who is to blame for this pyramid-sized pain in the ass, you or me." He had the gall to rub his thumb up and down the inside of her wrist, a move that in the past, the ancient past, had always made her ache.

Wrenching her wrist away, she sneered at him, "A bet? You want to make a bet? I have money to wager. What do you have that I could possibly want?"

His smile grew wider, and he looked down to his lap, his wager more than apparent.

Hera rolled her eyes, and sank down into the vacant chair next to him, suddenly tired of her marriage. "Get over yourself, Zeus. Like I need that. I think there has to be demand for the supply to have any value..." The trouble Zeus's "wager" had caused her over the centuries was beyond belief. If only she could have found some way to rein him in. Why hadn't she pushed Hephaestus harder to make that male-chastity belt she'd designed? There had to be some benefit from having a blacksmith for a son, their only child, but no, he'd made some excuse about the malleability of certain alloys...

Zeus was still talking, "Please. I think I know you better than that. You are the Goddess of Hearth and Home, and you honor your marriage vows, so I'm fairly certain that you haven't been swimming outside of the marital pool, so to speak, which would mean that it has been quite a long time without.... If we find out that it's my fault Apep is looking to screw with us, then I'm offering a year of me and only you...a year of living faithfully as your husband, and I'm confident that there is plenty of value in that wager..."

"And if it's my fault?" She leaned forward just enough to look him in the eye.

"You pay me the equivalent of a year of your salary. One lump sum. Cash."

She debated arguing with him about the foolishness of getting all that money at once, or how unnecessary cash was with banking being primarily an electronic affair, but she simply smiled and reached out her right hand. "Deal." He may be the worst husband in the world, but he knew how to make things interesting. A year of fidelity had value indeed.

As Zeus shook her hand, sealing the bet, the both settled back to watch the ferries and wait for Hermes to call them. Hera's reverie was interrupted as the housecleaners stopped before climbing into their minivan to compliment her on her lovely home, and her very fair wages, and her excellent use of toothpaste in a pump. The gift. How long was she going to have to put up with the stupidity that came from the gift? She had to grind her teeth to keep from yelling at their vapid kindness. Zeus handed her a beer dripping with icy water from the cooler that one of the housecleaners had delivered to him, blushing furiously at Hera's questioning glance.

Zeus noticed his wife's glare and opened his own beer with a smirk. "What? She's just being kind.... So kind." He leered at the housecleaner's retreating form, which seemed to Hera to be swaying way more than was necessary.

A year of fidelity was valuable indeed. His cavalier attitude toward their marriage vows had always enraged her, but she bit back on her fury and focused on winning the bet. "As soon as Hermes is done with her,

The Myth of Cassandra

and we know whose fault this all is, we have to get rid of her. The gift girl. Who knows what she'll say next. But she can't talk if she doesn't have a head." At Zeus's nod, she popped the cap off, and took a long pull on the cold beer. It was settled. Beer, bet and beheading, in that order.

CHAPTER EIGHTEEN

Good Things Come in Threes

○○○

Hannah

Back-up plans

They had left her parents in the kitchen with some flimsy excuse while they had taken care of this final detail in the plan. As she walked back into the room she saw that Carl was sitting next to John on her childhood bed, both looking oversized and out of place, and she hoped this wouldn't be her last memory of them. Neither one of them looked comfortable. Carl was trying desperately not to knock the figurine off her nightstand while he crossed and re-crossed his legs, and John looked angry and restless, trapped by dust ruffles and pillow shams.

"So it's all there, if you need it." And she handed Carl back his phone. She'd recorded it alone in the bathroom, not sure if she was ready for Carl to hear the things she had to say on it. It was the last piece of the plan, the failsafe, the last resort, the in-the-event-of-tragedy-push-this-button. The "when I end up a shrub, use this to save yourselves." The metaphors just kept coming. Pushing back from the abyss of a self-pity sinkhole, Hannah tried to refocus her panicking thoughts and considered "her" bedroom.

In the years since she'd left for college, her mother had meticulously reshaped her childhood by inserting the objects of a happy and tasteful girl from the motherhood of her own dreams. Gone was the pile of dog-

The Myth of Cassandra

eared paperbacks detailing the mysteries solved by Trixie Belden, replaced by museum quality first editions of Nancy Drew. Hannah frowned. Gone also was her stuffed animals, replaced by a vintage Raggedy Ann. The bed itself was covered in a light blue quilt with an evening star, nine-block pattern. Her mother had made it; actually, they had started it together as a mother daughter project, but her mother had finished it. Hannah remembered that she'd wanted to add in some Kelley green squares that she'd cut up from her old scouting sash, and her mother had "intervened" so that the quilt would be "something Hannah would always love." In fairness to her mother, the quilt and the room were lovely— all understated quaintness and grace, but she felt detached from it— not just because it was like she was in the room of some other girl, but because it was in reality not her childhood.

At least, not directly. In a meta-way, the artifice of the room did reflect a fair amount of her real life experience, mastering the art of appearances. A skill she'd have to use to get everyone she cared about through this mess. The entire plan was dependent on a series of lies and half-truths. She could only hope that she'd made the right decisions about when and to whom she'd lied.

"Which we won't need, right?"

John's question broke into her reverie, "We won't need what?" Hannah mentally scrambled to place what he was talking about.

"The recording. We won't need it, right?" He was giving her that long stare that she had found made her stumble in her lies.

Turning to look into the trusting gaze of Carl, she discarded the truth and tried for believable, "It's a backup plan, in the unlikely case that something goes wrong. But nothing's going to go wrong. We've been over this a dozen times, and there's nothing to worry about. I'm just my father's daughter; planning is my thing. So humor me, and keep it safe."

"Okay. We'll keep it safe, and tomorrow morning we can delete it together." Carl's voice was confident, but John was silent, still staring at her. He at least didn't challenge her outright, but then he was in on one of the lies, so maybe that was all that his stare meant— their shared lie to keep Carl safe— though she'd had to lie to John about which danger she was protecting Carl from. Carl was also in on a lie, one she'd had Hermes tell him to keep John safe, so he didn't even know to suspect her of a possible double-cross.

Thinking about it made her head hurt, and she walked to her bedroom window, keeping up the stream of bravado, "For a day that started out discouraging, I'd say we've had some lucky breaks..." By her accounting they had gotten three unexpected breaks— three openings that gave her at least an even chance to see tomorrow.

John launched into a new argument about said breaks, but she tuned him out as she watched the empty sidewalk outside her house and went through it in her mind. The first break had come when they'd sat down to eat her mother's casserole. At least most of them had gotten some casserole. John had not been faring well with her mother. Elise had only served him a plate of iceberg lettuce, ignoring John's attempts to clarify his non-vegetarian status, while heaping steaming portions of chicken casserole on Carl's plate. Hannah had taken pity on John and passed him a roll under the table. Her father, a devotee of the SOT, was ignoring all of them; listening to "all the news of the world" on a small portable TV he'd been carrying constantly.

After that her mother had wasted no time on small talk and demanded to see what information Hannah and "that vegetarian boy" had gathered on the Vineyard. John, still apparently hoping to curry her favor, had leapt at the chance to run and fetch his laptop. They'd shown the photos John had taken of the gods on the porch. Carl had been scrolling through the pictures with Elise looking over his shoulder. Next to each photo from Martha's Vineyard John had found an image from a classical painting or ancient urn that identified each, along with a short description of each god that Hannah had jotted down. Elise took one look at the photo of Hera and had started shaking her head.

"That's not Hera. That woman is my hero, I'd know her anywhere..."

Her mother's voice had gotten all high and breathy, as if she'd been running, and turning to her kitchen bookcase, she'd pulled out the June issue of *Ladies' Home and Hearth* and flipped to the editorial page, and handed it to Hannah. There, under the heading of "Editor in Chief" was a headshot of Hera with the name "Heloise Montgomery." Hannah gave into an irresistible urge to laugh. Of course the Goddess of Hearth and Home would be at the head of the most deterministic women's magazine in the free world, a magazine that her mother had used for the last four years to try to shape and mold her life into an ideal that the goddess of her studies would approve of. Carl and John were both looking at her with concern, and it occurred to her that her mirth must sound somewhat maniacal, but it was cut short by her mother's next words.

"If Heloise Montgomery is Hera, then the answer of how to return the gift will surely be in one of my issues of *Ladies' Home and Hearth*..."

"Hannah? Have you heard a word I've said?" John had started pacing. "I feel like there are holes to this that you are glossing over. We could still make a run for it..."

John's voice brought her back to the present. She turned from the window with a reassuring smile. "Yes, of course I was listening, but we've been over this. I have my dad's phone and I programmed all your numbers in, so we'll be linked, if anything goes wrong, we can run then.... We should get ready, it'll only be a minute or two before..." Hearing a jaunty whistle in the hall, Hannah paused, giving John and Carl what she hoped was a look significant enough to forestall any ill-conceived responses, and turned to face the door as the second unexpected break sauntered into her bedroom.

"All right, girls, are we ready to transform? The golden idiot will be here soon and it's time for Line Boy to lead him astray with the help of Former Boyfriend. And I must say, FB, you will make a lovely decoy..." Smirking, Hermes rudely looked Carl up and down.

Flustered, Carl covered himself with his hands and a scowling John protested, "Are you kidding me, how can we trust this..."

"Okay, okay, easy..." Hannah tried for a confident tone. "We can trust that Hermes wants this plan to succeed as much as we do." She turned to Hermes, "Would you mind dialing it back? Your sense of humor is not helpful, given the circumstances...just play nice, okay, we aren't used to your shape shifting tricks."

"We're just changing our hair, right? Only the hair..." Carl narrowed his gaze on Hermes, keeping his arms crossed over his chest.

"Well, it would be more believable if you'd let me do a little tweaking...." Hermes made a suggestive cupping motion, "We need him to believe you are Hannah, and H is at least a B-cup, maybe even a C..."

All hell broke loose as Carl tried to lunge at Hermes while keeping his chest covered, and John started to renew his arguments about not trusting the Messenger God. Hermes was looking at her, his amusement clear. Rolling her eyes at him, Hannah raised her voice over the din, "Okay, okay, everyone stop! You," and she pointed at Hermes, "will give John back his long hair and turn Carl's hair pink. Period. You," and she pointed at John, "will keep your doubts to yourself, this is the plan, and you have to be a team player on this one. And you," Here she looked more kindly at Carl, and softened her tone, "you're going to have to shave your legs. I'm sorry, Carl. You can use my bathroom— it's right through there." And looking at the three, she nodded at them, as if that would force them into agreement, "I'll give you all a little privacy," and slipped out, closing the door behind her before they could start arguing again.

Hermes. She still wasn't sure, when it came down to it, which way he would break— was he good or bad luck? He'd shown up while they'd been looking for Hera's answer for returning a gift with the maximum of tact. Apparently *Ladies' Home and Hearth* had a thing against digital media files— so they were manually sorting through back issues when the doorbell had rung. Her dad, who was still deeply under the sway of the SOT, offered to answer the door, it was the kind thing to do after all. He'd returned with a rather swarthy looking Girl Scout in tow. Just as her mother was about to launch into a lecture on the impoliteness of door-to-door solicitation of cookie sales, Hannah had found herself staring at the girl, trying to place her.

The Myth of Cassandra

The Girl Scout, for her part, had held up her hand, silencing Elise, and had clarified in a husky voice, "I'm not here to sell cookies, honey. I'm here to work on my *save-a-mortal-from-certain-death* badge."

And as the meaning of "her" words had sunk in, Hannah found herself staring at the identical smirk of the busboy and public safety officer from her recent past. Before she could say a word, pandemonium broke out. John, having also recognized the smirk, had started taking vaguely martial arts like stances, telling Hermes to "bring it" in a loud voice. Carl, watching Hermes transform into his natural state, started chanting in some ancient-sounding language, again causing the air around him to shimmer. She really had to look into what Carl was doing. Elise seemed to have swallowed her tongue, choking out guttural noises and pointing at the now naked man in her kitchen while Tom had offered said naked man an apron to cover himself— the kitchen being a dangerous place for unprotected appendages. And as the chaos had risen in volume and the air around Carl had started to spark, Hannah found herself meeting the very direct gaze of Hermes, Messenger God.

"You've done a pretty good job so far, H, but you're going to need my help to end this...."

Coming back to the present, she leaned her head against the kitchen door and listened to the low murmurs of her parents coming from inside the kitchen. Their voices sounded tense. She knew that they were even less certain of this alliance with Hermes than Carl and John were. When she had managed to calm everyone down, Hermes had laid out his case for working together. Mutual interests. If they could get the real intent of the "gift" out of Adams, then Hera and Zeus would be pleased, with all of them. Mutual risk. Hermes and Hannah would be confronting Adams together. Mutual gains. Hermes insisted that he had negotiated a stay of execution for her out of this with Hera and Zeus— they would give her an audience without immediately smiting her. What she did with that time was up to her, if and only if, she could convince Archer Adams, publicist to the stars, to talk. To do that, they needed to distract Apollo— it was Hermes idea to have them use Carl as a Hannah decoy with John on the bike to lure Apollo away. In theory, that would work with the lies she'd told each of them to get them safely out of the way. Privately, Hermes had assured her that as soon as Apollo figured it out, he would leave John and Carl alone and come back here for Adams. She knew that Hermes had assured Carl and John that Adams was no threat and they were protecting Hannah by leading Apollo away. It was complicated— and no one had the same story because she had spent time lying to all of them to keep them safe, so it could work, right? Hermes gain in this plan involved not only money, but the chance to take Apollo down a peg. All of it rang with enough truth based on her studies of Hermes to persuade her that in this instance, they should trust him. At least until he got what he wanted. Hermes, her savior, sort of.

She heard the water running in the upstairs bathroom, and sank slowly to the floor, resting her head in her hands, taking the moment to remind herself, that no matter which way Hermes broke, she had a back up. Strangely enough, the final break had been through her father's trust, her mother's cooking and John's involuntary vegetarianism that they'd stumbled on the third, and to her, most important, unexpected break.

Elise, once she'd sent Tom to get Hermes a change of clothes, had pulled an apple pie out of the fridge and warmed it in the oven. The pie had smelled heavenly. Offering slices to Carl and Hermes, she'd skipped over John and Hannah, much to Tom's obvious dismay. "Elise! You're forgetting Hannah and John!" Ignoring Elise's too casual shrug, he'd forcibly intervened, taking the pie plate from her and offering a slice to them both, asking, "Would you like some pie?"

Though John had nodded enthusiastically, Hannah had been focused on an article from the December 2002 issue of LH & H, "What to do when your BOSS gives you DEODORANT for Christmas and other inappropriate gifts." Certain the answer to returning the gift to Hera was in the advice, she had mumbled absently, "No thanks, Dad, there's no time for pie." The effect of her words would have been funny if it weren't for the terrifying nature of Tom's enthrallment.

He immediately dumped what was left of the pie in the kitchen garbage, and then proceeded to snatch the remainder of the slices off of Carl

The Myth of Cassandra

and Hermes' plates, the entire time chanting, "There's no time for pie. So sorry, hate to be unkind, but there's no time for pie..." While Carl and Hermes had both quickly swallowed the bites that were in their mouths, and John had stared pathetically down at his empty plate, it was her mother's stoic acceptance of her father's SOT driven behavior that broke Hannah's spirit. Whatever hope that'd been growing since Hermes arrival was as lost as the pie in the trash. All she could think was that none of this would matter— not the plan to distract Apollo, not the trap for Adams, not even the audience with Hera, if the worldwide population was left like her father, mindlessly following the commandments of the SOT. Would her father always now feel like pie was a forbidden food?

John later claimed it was the clarity of his involuntary fast that had helped him put it all together, but regardless of the source, it was inspired.

"Hannah, I have an idea, something I've been thinking about, you know, the gift..." John skirted past the pie tossing Tom, who had turned to the freezer and had started piling frozen pies in the overflowing trash can, and leaned down, whispering in her ear, "Tell him something you lied about. Something he can't ignore..."

As the words had left his lips, the idea took hold of her, and she also had a moment of clarity. John and her mother had never been affected by the "gift"— which, if the idea was right, made perfect sense. She and her mother had engaged in mutual lying for years, and John, well, her first three hours with him on Monday had been one lie revealed after another— but Carl, he was the case study. He had been affected at the dinner when the "gift" first took effect, but not after he realized she'd lied about his grandmother's engagement ring.

Misconstruing her silence as lack of understanding, John had stood and taken the frozen pie out of Tom's hands. Tom frowned and tried to wrest it back.

"Can I get you something, John? Besides pie, of course, there's no time for pie."

"No thank you, Tom. I'm all set. But there is something I'd like to tell you and I really need you to listen, okay? Then I'll give you back the pie, I promise. Tom, your daughter, Hannah, she lies, on a daily basis, mostly lies of omission, but sometimes outright, good old fashioned lies."

Tom's smile hadn't faltered, as he kindly explained to John how his daughter would never lie, not to him. John had been nodding while Tom talked, and turned to Hannah, holding out the frozen pie to her, his smile encouraging, "Go on, Hannah, Something he can't ignore."

Taking the frozen pie, which had become some sort of talisman of the truth, she'd held it in front of her and started quietly,

"Daddy, I know you don't think I lie to you, but I do..." Tom was shaking his head and reaching for the pie, so she raised her voice, "Yes, Dad, I've been lying to you for years."

He'd tried to stop her confession, holding up his phone, urging her to watch all the news of the world and began an animated description of the news of Steve McKing, the reporter— did she know that he was on location in Sierra Leone reporting on a local restaurant's decision to start using yellow potatoes in their signature dish— they'd been using white potatoes. And the news station had to fly him home to Boston because he'd contracted a severe case of dysentery. Whether it was the "news" of Steve McKing's intestinal troubles, or the weirdly blank look in her father's gaze, something in her snapped.

"Stop it, Dad! Of course I lie. Sometimes I lie to protect your feelings, like telling you that I think your chili is delicious when it really tastes like glorified ketchup. Sometimes I lie for purely selfish reasons, like when I told you that I needed some pocket money. I didn't need the money. I would take the extra money you sent and hide it away in a private bank account. That deceitful practice has actually bankrolled other lies. I let you and Mom believe that I'd be moving home after graduation to conduct a job search, when really I've already signed my contract with the University for the Curator job. I've even looked at several different apartments to move into— though I haven't found the right one yet, and

The Myth of Cassandra

I'm going to pay the deposit in part with the money you've been sending me through the years because I lied to you."

Carl was staring, mouth open, clearly aghast at her admission. Hermes was smirking, of course. But it was her father's reaction that the rest of them waited for. Tom's response had been both a surprise and a gift. The gift was that now she had irrefutable proof of how to short circuit the SOT and end the gods' meddling. The surprise had been what had upset him.

"You really don't like my chili, Hannah?"

"No, Daddy, I'm sorry, but no one does. Ask Mom. We would've fed it to the dog if we had one, and even he wouldn't have eaten it. It's awful. I just never wanted to hurt your feelings..."

"Elise? You hate it too?" he turned to his wife.

"Oh Tom, of course not, that's just another one of your daughter's lies. I love your chili, honey..."

Tom's freedom from the SOT had cleared him up to ask an array of questions, and Elise filled him in on all that had happened since he'd been under the spell of the god's gift. With Elise distracted, John took advantage of the power vacuum and reclaimed a large, mostly intact piece of pie from the garbage, served himself some chicken casserole from the fridge, and commenced eating. Once Tom was up to speed and John was fed, they'd all worked together to finalize their plan.

That'd been over two hours ago, and time was getting short. As she slid back up the wall and considered walking through the door to join her parents in the kitchen, she reviewed her mental list of pros and cons. Pros: they had the advice from Hera's magazine, an alliance with Hermes, a potentially non-fatal audience with the gods, and a way, if the plan failed, to short-circuit the gift and save the world from the continuing saga of Steve McKing's dysentery. The Cons: she'd lied to John and had convinced him to lie to Carl, and had agreed with Hermes lying to them both to get them safely out of the way, but their safety depended on Hermes trustworthiness, not his strong suit; she'd lied to her parents by omission when she'd let them believe what Hermes had said about Adams being a publicist. She'd seen Adams on the deck of Hera's house, and he'd made her skin crawl. In every photograph John had taken, Adams eyes had glowed red. John had run an edit on the pictures, which had corrected it, but she knew that whatever he was, it wasn't simply a publicist. And the biggest con on the list was her. Despite everything that'd happened, and everything they hoped would happen, if she couldn't find the right words to convince the gods to take back their gift, they would kill her, and possibly her friends and family. The Hera she had come to know through LH &H did not seem like a goddess who liked to leave loose ends.

At that moment, Carl, John and Hermes came up from behind her in the hall, and Carl cupped her shoulders in his hands, "Are you okay?"

She looked at them. Carl now had bright pink hair and was wearing one of her least favorite dresses, a purple clingy thing. John looked exactly as he had in the line at the bookstore— long hair, t-shirt and jeans. It caused her a moment of disorientation, and she was tempted to answer truthfully to Carl's rote question. Of course she was not okay.

She felt the tension in her twist, and her lies all felt so cold; there were no Nereids coming to her defense, she didn't really trust Hermes, she was terrified to face the gods, and success felt nearly impossible. She wanted to confess that she needed them. That she wanted them to stay. But she caught sight of Hermes knowing look and plastered on what she hoped was a convincing smile. "I'm fine. We have a plan. And everything will work. I'm sure."

Carl seemed to buy it, echoing her words while nodding, "We have a plan." But John didn't answer. He only looked at Hannah, frowning.

She'd come to know that look. She'd never really been able to convince John of much. Except when she told him the truth. In the last three days, she'd found herself telling him far too much altogether. She considered, for a moment, telling him the truth now. Her gaze slid from his eyes to his hair. She slipped back into that night at the motel when she'd cut it off. There'd been something there, that night, as much as she'd denied it to her mother. Something electric and she had felt temptation like the ache in the back of her knees when she looked over a ledge. But the timing had been wrong, and she'd stepped back from it—

the ledge and the temptation. Now looking at his hair long again, she could imagine that it had never happened, and she ruthlessly reminded herself that this was her curse, and she wasn't going to let him get hurt again. Getting a grip, she purposefully misdirected him, "With the help of our Olympic friends, we'll be fine, right Hermes?"

She knew that John would think she was referring to the Nereids, and she knew that Carl would think she was referring to Hermes, but would also be thinking of the Nereids, as John and Hermes had both told him about them, swearing him to secrecy. Hermes, aware of her web of lies to them both, cut her a break. "That's right H, we won't be alone." It was enough. Carl nodded again and John's frown lightened and he even gave her a tentative smile.

Shooting Hermes a grateful grimace, she pushed into the kitchen followed by the boys. Her parents' audible shock at John and Carl's appearance gave way quickly to an anxious silence, as they all listened to the ring of the doorbell.

Hermes was the first to react. He became the stage manager, pushing them in various directions, "Time to take your places, people, I'll get them settled next door…"

Hera and Zeus had arrived. Pros and cons, truth and lies, it was all irrelevant now. They had a plan. All they could do now was play it out.

✹✹✹✹✹✹✹✹✹✹✹✹

Archer/Sek

Immortals on Public Transport

"Here, Archer, you need this Charlie Card ticket to go through the turnstile…"

Sek only vaguely registered that Mot was mumbling something to him about tickets, but he'd lost his patience for playing the human, "Archer Adams" and walked through the turnstile, melting the protesting ticket machine with a light touch.

Now he could make out Mot's words, as he squeaked, "Or you could do that."

Apollo, oblivious as always, missed it all, surely distracted by all the shiny surfaces in which he might see himself. Sek released a slow hiss of a sigh and reminded himself that it was almost over. He would complete his assignment and get her today. Soon. He just had to pretend to be Apollo's "best friend and publicist" for approximately one more hour. He'd better get a bonus for this job. Working with Olympians qualified for hazard pay if you counted the intense level of aggravation inherent in the work. The Greeks were like caricatures of their human counterparts; sure they had some impressive bells and whistles in the power department, but they had no self-control. They were the embodiment of human failings on steroids; but it was almost over.

He saw that Mot had found the subway map and joined him there. Mot flinched as he approached, and Sek smiled, "Um...it looks like there are several places where we could get off the silver line to get on the red line...the earliest would be South Station, but, um, we might want to avoid such a busy stop, if we ride out the silver line, we could switch to the commuter line...."

Sek frowned. If he didn't know better, he would think that Mot was trying to mislead him, but that was impossible. That would require both intelligence and subterfuge, two items Mot lacked. Sek ignored Mot's continued blather and traced the colored lines himself. Of course South Station was the right stop. Hermes. It was the only explanation for Mot's pathetic attempt to delay. That smirking idiot would pay, but first things first. Sek licked his lips, the moment before inflicting pain was always so rich, and Mot's pain was always so satisfying, but then Apollo threw his arm around his shoulders and tapped the glass over the subway map.

"Archer, my man, which smile do you think is the best one for rescuing a damned girl in distress?" And he used the map's reflective surface to alternate between a blinding head on smile, and a shyer, more "aw shucks" smile. "Which is your favorite, Lee?"

Mot/Lee paused, twisting the unused Charlie Card in his hands, "Um...do you mean a damsel in distress?"

The Myth of Cassandra

"No Lee, a damsel is a mother sheep— Hannah is not a four-legged woolly thing. The human expression is to 'rescue a damned girl in distress.' Which do you think is more heroic? This? This?" Apollo continued to mug in front of the map, alternating between looks of concern or pleasure.

Closing his eyes, Sek chose discretion, and postponed his retribution. First, finish the job. In his most affable human voice, he smiled at them both. "You'll have to make that momentous decision on the train, Apollo. We have to get to the girl before you can use your heroic expression. Lee told us that Hermes was after the girl, and Hermes is still at that address on Franklin Street, so that is where we can rescue the girl, right Lee?"

Mot/Lee's face blanched, confirming his suspicions about the traitorous demon. Sek watched the sweat pop out on Mot's wide, pasty forehead and roll down into his beady little eyes, all but writing the story of his betrayal. He smile grew more brittle as he waited out Mot's struggle to confess his sins now and face the pain, or to continue playing this game. Surprisingly, Mot chose the later.

"Uh huh, I mean, yep, I mean, yes sir. See, still there." And he held up his phone, the screen blurry from the sweat of his palm.

Sek weighed his options. He could torture Mot on the spot and get all the info he needed— but public torture could lead to tedious questions from the authorities. Whatever trap Hermes and Mot were setting, he had no concern that it would work. Hermes had no subtlety; Sek would simply spring the trap and take the cheese. The girl.

"Fantastic. That's the inbound train now. Let's get on." And Sek led the way onto the train, slapping Apollo on the shoulders and helping an elderly woman enter the train with her walker.

She tilted her face up to him. "What a nice young man. Thank you. You are so considerate. And so clean. However do you keep your clothes so white?" And the little grey haired lady peered at his suit through her glasses, leaning forward and rubbing his sleeve between her gnarled fingers.

Sek smiled benignly down at her. "Oh, that's easy. I marinate it in the screaming souls of innocents— it stays clean for years."

"Oh, that's... OH. Dear." She released his sleeve as if it burned her and spun with much more agility than one might have suspected from her earlier progress, "I can catch the next train... I have to recheck my route... Excuse me, pardon me." And she wound her way out of the car and off the platform without one look back.

He caught Mot's eye and winked. "Oh, I'm looking forward to meeting our girl. Humans are so fun."

Mot spent the rest of the ride whimpering and twitching, and Apollo droned on about his plans to destroy the longhaired hippy, breaking occasionally to ask his advice on heroic postures. He had learned months earlier the sounds he needed to make to approximate listening to the golden fool, and he focused all his thoughts on the girl. Despite whatever plan Hermes may have cooked up with Mot, his instincts told him this trip to Cambridge was bringing him closer to her. Leaning back against the plastic seat, he feigned concern at Apollo's choice of the heroic catch phrase, if only to keep the fool occupied. Noting his expression, Apollo frowned and insisted that he, Archer Adams, publicist to the stars, chose the best version of his heroic catch-phrase and launched into variations of emphasis, "I am your HERO, Apollo" "I AM your hero, Apollo," "I am YOUR hero, Apollo..." Sek let his focus slide past Apollo's face to the name of the station they were entering: Kendall/MIT. Two more stops.

By the time the train pulled into Harvard station, Apollo had chosen his means of punishment for the longhaired boy, burn to ash, and his heroic catch phrase, I am your hero, APOLLO. Stepping out into Harvard Square, Sek was done with being patient. Mot was pulling on his sleeve, babbling about stopping to use the bathroom at Au Bon Pain, or begging to wait a second while he checked out the homeless people and useless academics playing chess on the concrete chessboards.

Sek resisted the impulse to smack Mot in his face; he'd spent enough time in his Archer Adams persona to know that humans were averse to public displays of violence. The bleeding hearts around him

The Myth of Cassandra

might call the police, and he didn't want to waste time with the local authorities. He itched to dispose of both of his "companions." Mot would be easy to dispose of, but Apollo, though stupid, was powerful and could interfere if he ever figured out Sek's true goals— not that that was likely. All of the Olympians were pathetically easy to control. Zeus hated being emasculated. Boo hoo, girly-man. Hera hated being thought of as controlling. As if anyone would ever think she wasn't. Hermes imagined he was so clever, but his obvious jealousy of Apollo made him the perfect fall guy. When this was all over, and the Olympians were hiding in disgrace, it would be Hermes that they blamed. Sek smiled. It was the cherry on the sundae.

You wouldn't catch Egyptian gods falling prey to feeble conceits. Egyptian gods couldn't care less what anyone else thought of them; they did what they wanted. They were gods! Even Ra, for all his moralizing, was bad-assed. Apep, his master, was the god of all evil and darkness, a god to be proud of. He derived his power from being worshipped against, none of this pathetic desire to be liked that the Olympians were so prone to. When the boss had assigned him this job, he had to admit, he'd been disappointed— the Olympians were really below him. But then he'd seen the girl.

The girl. She was clearly not as weak as Hermes had reported. That pleased him. Once he disposed of Mot and Apollo, he would take her away to somewhere private. He'd spent the T ride here considering his options for a good torture spot, and had actually found one on a poster at the Harvard Station encouraging tourists to visit Boston's great historical monuments. Excellent. The only place more deserted than historical monuments were bookstores. Unless that bookstore had a coffee shop, and well, then there might be a few people lurking about.

"Archer, look, look, look! See here, a bookstore! It probably has a bathroom I can use, please, please can we stop. I'll just be a second." Mot's expression was desperate and he was actually crossing his legs and hopping from one foot to another. Apollo appeared to be in deep conversation with a homeless man on the corner, and he heard Apollo say, "Tell me which of my angles is more, you know, heroic...." The homeless man appeared to be sincerely considering the different angles of Apollo's profile. That would keep him busy for a few minutes. He'd dispose of Mot first.

"Apollo, Lee and I are going to pop into this bookstore. We'll be back in a second." And he smiled benignly down on Mot, whose desperation only got more exaggerated, as if he sensed the pain Sek was planning for him. What a waste of demon seed! It still grated that Apep had insisted that he, Sek, a level twenty-eight demon, had needed Mot, a mere fifteen, for this job.

Time was of the essence, so he'd have to contain Mot with as little drama as possible. He would trap Mot in the grain of the wooden bookcases, painful but discreet, and when he was done with the girl, he'd come back to retrieve him. He only needed a moment alone to get it done. That shouldn't be hard to get in a bookstore— it should be empty. Who the hell bought books anymore?

They entered the bookstore only to be accosted by the sales clerk asking them if they needed any help. Sek stared at the boy. His clothes smelled of Ramen noodles and marijuana, and he was wearing a sweater vest with cigarette holes burned into the side: college student. The boy's eyes were slightly bloodshot— he might actually be currently stoned. Excellent. For fun Sek let his eyes burn bright red, leaned in and answered in his true demon voice, "Yes, I need to eat your soul, could you open your mouth wider for me to reach it?"

The boy blinked slowly once, and then snapped his mouth closed. Sek watched his Adams apple bob visibly in his throat, and for fun, licked his lips, watching the boy's face whiten. Mot stepped between them, asking in his squeaky voice for the bathroom, and the boy looked down at him and answered, "Down the stairs and to the left, ma'am." But it sounded like "Dnh th strs n to th lft, mmm, " due to the fact that he had kept his mouth firmly shut the entire time. Sek laughed out loud and slapped the sales clerk on the shoulder and said in his Archer Adams voice, "Relax, I was just kidding..." and the boy smiled weakly. Mot hurried down the stairs, and Sek followed, looking back over his shoulder at

The Myth of Cassandra

the boy, frozen in place, and in a deep demon whisper finished him off, "Or was I?" The boy wet his pants on the spot. Ah, humans.

Downstairs would be the perfect place to trap Mot; it was bound to be private. He turned to the left at the bottom of the stairs, only to find himself at the end of a long line of college students, all clutching stacks of books. What the hell was going on here, and where had Mot disappeared?

He must have spoken these last two thoughts, because a ponytailed blonde girl in front of him looked over her shoulder and smiled back at him, "This is the book buy-back line. I am so excited to see the last of this!" And she held up a thick textbook with the title, *Introduction to Organic Chemistry* on the cover. She looked at his empty hands and spotless white suit, and frowned slightly, "Are you looking for that little woman who came through here a second ago looking for the bathroom? She went that way..." and she pointed with the hand holding a copy of Derrida's *The Post Card: From Socrates to Freud and Beyond*. She turned to face him more fully, shifting her books in front of her, cradled by both arms, drawing the eye to her impressive posture, "I'm sure she'll be back soon. Is she your mother? You don't look like you're from around here...are you a visiting lecturer?"

With the crowds of undergraduates getting rid of their books, Sek knew he wouldn't have time to find a new, empty location to trap Mot. But maybe that was unnecessary. All he really needed to do was prevent Mot from interfering with his plan for the gift girl. Maybe the eager blonde could help him. He smiled with just enough disdain to keep the blonde interested in helping him, but insecure enough not to ask too many questions. "No, I am a casting agent from MGM, and I am here in this absurdly grim place looking for the next "it" girl. And that woman is not my mother, but my assistant. My fired assistant. Which means I am looking for a new assistant. You wouldn't happen to be interested?"

She took the card he handed her, nodding. Sek leaned in closer to her and whispered in her ear, "I need you to keep my ex-assistant here for the next hour. I need to clean out her files before she knows that she's fired. One hour. Think of it as your first assignment, yes?" She nodded mutely at him, and he smiled, more warmly this time, "You'll do great, doll. Her name is Lee, and she is not to leave this bookstore for the next hour. Who knows, maybe I can get you a walk-on part in my next project."

Now she smiled broadly again, "Really? Me? Yes, I mean okay.... I did play the Caterpillar in my middle school's production of Alice in..."

"Yes. I can tell. Very talented. Now, run along and get to work... detaining Lee...." Sek resisted smacking her, and instead nodded encouragingly.

She nodded back and her books falling unheeded from her hands, wound her way through the crowds, calling out in a peppy voice, "Lee! Lee! I have some great news for you...."

Sek turned on his heels and headed up the stairs. One nerveless, annoying demon down, one vain, imbecilic god to go.

CHAPTER NINETEEN

The Absence of Sense

◐◐◐

Elise

What's a little Asian moss amongst friends

Elise looked at the monitor showing the couple waiting at the front door of the University House. They made for a formidable pair, but that made sense, given that they are the king and queen of the Olympian Gods. Sense. That was funny. Sense had taken a vacation about three days ago. She exhaled slowly and played over the plan in her mind.

Hermes had been all smooth reassurance, "That's right. John and Carl will lead Apollo, the dangerous one, away, and Hera and Zeus, both dangerous, will be safely contained in the sitting room of your neighbor's house, while they watch on closed circuit cameras as Adams reveals who he is working for, and his secret plans to Hannah in the garden. Then Hera and Zeus will be so grateful, boom, they take back the gift. Everyone is happy. And you and Tom can watch the whole thing from the control center in the house."

The truth about the "neighbor's house" had taken some time to explain to Hannah. She'd always suspected that Hannah had built up her own private fantasy about the whimsical house next door. The truth was unusual, but not surprising for Cambridge. The house belonged to Harvard University. She'd become the caretaker for it five years ago when she'd filed a complaint with the city that her neighbor's gardener had introduced an invasive Asian moss. The Cambridge city officials had contacted the University with Elise's complaint and the University had conducted a private investigation. They found that not only had the gardener introduced said moss, but he was also cultivating psychotropic mushrooms and selling them to under-graduates. While this was not technically illegal, the mushrooms were not on the DEA's list of controlled substances, some genius in the public relations department realized that growing and dealing hallucinogens in a residential neighborhood would be a hard story to spin. So they moved the gardener and his mushrooms to a greenhouse near the chemistry department and offered the job of caretaker of the house to the woman who had filed the complaint in the first place: Elise.

After eradicating the offensive moss, Elise had set herself to mastering the technology of the house. Built as part of a boondoggle of government spending in the 80s, the house was one massive sociology experiment; "What happens when private spaces are Public." A moot point now, but at the time it was considered cutting edge, and the University had not spared a dime. Not only were the gardens fully monitored by cameras, but the rooms in the house were also wired for video and sound.

With the "experiment" over, the University had repurposed the house as lodgings for their most important guests. Elise functioned as a sort of hostess; welcoming guests, handing out keys, giving tours and answering questions. She was very ethical about not using the surveillance equipment to spy on the guests, though she'd been sorely tempted when Daniel Day Lewis stayed at the house several years back. *Last of the Mohicans indeed.* But this week it was empty, as Elise had closed it, so that she and Tom could spend the weekend at Hannah's graduation.

They had been debating the safest place to both expose the publicist and give the gift back to the gods. They needed someplace where the publicist felt like he was alone with Hannah, so that he would drop his façade, and where Zeus and Hera would have a front row seat. Elise suggested the use of this house, and after Hannah got over her shock, she agreed that it was ideal.

But now that Hera and Zeus stood at the front door, she felt uneasiness growing in her bones. Hermes. Why had she trusted her baby's safety to a god who showed up naked in her kitchen? Surely *Ladies' Home and Hearth* would not approve. Tom tapped her on the shoulder and silently pointed to the couple on the monitor. Actively relaxing her clenched jaw, she tilted the microphone towards her mouth, and said in her most elegant voice, "Welcome, Zeus and Hera, we are honored with your presence. Please come in. My name is Elise Summers, and I am your hostess this evening. You will find a sitting room behind the door to your right. Inside we have hot and cold beverages as well as some light refreshments on the sideboard for your comfort. You will be able to view the unmasking of the publicist on the monitor above the fireplace. We expect him to arrive in the next few minutes, until then, please avail yourselves of our humble hospitality. I hope you find the accommodations to your approval, and if you have any questions or concerns, you need only speak up. I am at your disposal."

The deep frown that creased Zeus's brow at the commencement of Elise's speech was wiped clear as Hera opened the door to the sitting room and the smell of Elise's fresh brownies filled the room. Hera crossed the room and ran a gloved finger over the mantel. Finding it free of dust, she lifted her chin, zoning in directly on the camera that was monitoring the room, and pronounced, "Well, at least it's clean. We will wait here." And she turned to the sideboard to join her husband in filling her plate with Elise's offerings. Despite her earlier misgivings, Elise did a silent victory dance, thrilled by the approbation of her homemaking idol.

She turned off her mike and shared a look with Tom. It was such a relief to have him back from under the sway of the "gift." If she'd had to listen to him tell her one more time about the teachings of the SOT she might have had to dope slap him. She had missed him so much— he was always so steady— she couldn't have handled this without him. "Give them the call." He squeezed her hand and nodded, turning to the handset mounted on the wall.

For communication purposes they'd linked their phones. Hannah had to borrow her father's as her phone had been on the losing side of a confrontation with an SUV on Monday. With the phones linked and set to conference, they could all hear what was going on at all times. As Tom dialed, she replayed her last exchange with Hermes.

"She won't be in any danger from Adams?"

His smile was toothy and his tone soothing, "Of course not, Adams is just a publicist. He has no powers, except his ability to get a table at Sardo's. He just works for someone who wants to make trouble for the Olympians. Once we know his plans, then we, the gods, will take over. Hera will be so grateful she'll tell Apollo to take back the gift, and you will all be free to go about your human lives undisturbed by immortals and their problems. Don't worry."

Don't worry. She could hear Tom talking with Hermes, and she caught site of two figures heading down Franklin Street. The one who was clearly Apollo seemed to grow bigger and brighter with each step and as much as she disliked John, she felt a frisson of concern and hoped he could stay in front of him, if only to keep Carl safe. She angled the camera to catch a close up of Archer Adams and as his face and eyes came into focus she felt the sickening jolt of being right when you most dreaded you might be. Don't worry my ass.

Acting purely on instinct, she grabbed the phone out of Tom's hands, "Hannah Baby, get out of there! John, use those winged shoes, grab Hannah and Carl and get the hell out of there! Adams is evil. Like REAL EVIL with HORNS! I repeat, Hannah get out of there NOW! Hermes tricked us! Hannah! RUN!"

The sound of the phone going dead was deafening. Tom and Elise stared at each other, the moment stretching, filling the small chrome space in the control room.

"Dammit, Elise. He cut us off! That goddamned messenger is setting Hannah up, and he cut us off! We have to get her away from him!"

Elise was at the door of the control room, pulling on the handle, "It's locked. We can't get out!"

Tom was at the monitors, switching feeds, "What the hell are we going to do? That's our baby girl out there. And she's going to be in the garden alone with that thing! That evil, evil thing! We have to do something!"

Elise sat next to him at the control panel, pulling up all the available views on the bank of monitors. "We're going to have to sit tight and watch. The good news is that Hannah is smart enough to have suspected Hermes of a double cross, so she might be better prepared for this than we think. I hope. I also prepared a little myself. Those brownies Zeus is inhaling..."she pointed to the image on the monitor of Zeus double fisting the brownies into his mouth, "I laced them with some of the marijuana I found growing in the attic here, with the hope that it might make Zeus more relaxed...."

"What? You wanted to get the god of lightning stoned? Have you seen how many brownies he's already eaten? What if he freaks out? Did you think of that, Elise? He brought his lightning rod! His lightning rod, Elise!" Tom strode back and forth in the tiny room, shaking his head back and forth, "and since when have you known how to make pot brownies? What else do you do? Cook meth? Sell crack?"

Elise narrowed her eyes at her husband pacing in the cramped confines of the control room. On every other word he had thrown his hands up in the air, and she was fairly certain he had not inhaled during his entire speech. She spoke sharply, to get his attention, "Tom!" His pacing stopped abruptly and he faced her. In a softer tone, she continued, "I think you should sit down, honey. And breathe slowly, in and out. Count to three."

Tom followed his wife's suggestions with the compliance of the panicky in the face of someone with clear control. He nodded at her to continue. Her tone was pragmatic, "Unlike the last caretaker, I am not a drug dealer. He just left some plants behind when he moved, and I've been keeping them alive— you know how I feel about plants. Never having grown marijuana before, I researched it on the Internet. I learned a lot."

Tom's calm was visibly eroding with her explanation, so she spoke faster, intent on explaining herself, "I only get a small crop and most of that I give to the AIDS clinic for their patients. It helps with the nausea from the medications they have to take." Tom's face slid from incredulous to consternation, a good sign in Elise's experience, so she elaborated, "I had a good harvest, so there was enough for me to keep a little, just in case. *Ladies' Home and Hearth* says that a woman with a well stocked pantry can confront any calamity."

"I think they were referring to cans of tuna or jars of pasta sauce, Elise, not weed."

Tom sounded much better, sardonic, but not frantic. She continued, "Well, yes, you might be right, but I thought I should keep some, just in case. There are hundreds of sites online with recipes for making pot-brownies. Marijuana, from what I've read, is not a dangerous drug, really. In many cultures it has long been used..." Her voice died off at the severe look from her husband.

"Aside from the illegalities of possessing a controlled substance, why on earth did you decide to use it on our guests?"

"I'm trying to help Hannah. From what I inferred from reading Hannah's thesis...You know, that is one very long, dry, and meticulous tome she wrote. Our daughter is very enamored of lists and categorization. I think she gets that from you, Tom."

"The pot brownies, Elise?"

"Oh yes. So I read her thesis, and I think Zeus is the most unpredictable of the gods we are dealing with, and the most powerful. From what Hannah wrote, Zeus is at his most dangerous when he is angry. So, I thought it couldn't hurt to stack the deck. Besides, I thought that marijuana, a naturally occurring plant, would be safer to use than some of my stockpiled Ambien. The pot will most likely make him relaxed, and at the worst, he might fall asleep. He's a big guy, and it really shouldn't hit him for at least 20 minutes."

Tom nodded slowly, "Okay, okay.... Maybe pot brownies were a good idea. Time will tell. But what about now? What about Hannah?

The Myth of Cassandra

How can we help her? We can't protect her from Adams locked here in this room."

Elise, grateful for her husband's reasonableness, began scanning the monitors again. "Look, there she is in the street, rubbing that iron bird. Oh, Hannah." Elise took a long slow breath herself, and willed her worry to take a back seat. With her hair cut short, she looked so young. Elise was struck forcibly by the memory of Hannah as a child of nine. How many mornings had she watched Hannah rub that bird on her way to school? She'd been such an awkward child, all elbows and knees, so serious, so private.

Elise had watched from her kitchen as the child Hannah talked to the stone bird and had felt jealous. Jealous of a stone bird that her nine-year-old confided in. She had tried to talk to Hannah, to be her friend, but there was so much she needed to teach her. Elise had long ago accepted that her role as Hannah's mother was more important than her desire to be liked and confided in by Hannah. The roles had felt incompatible. Then.

As the now adult Hannah rubbed that same bird, Elise hoped that Hannah could handle what was coming, and wished she'd taken more advantage of her daughter's recent openness to ask her what she used to say to that damn bird. Elise felt the panic swirling around her knees again, and remembering a *Ladies' Home and Hearth* special series, "Top Five Psychological Crutches: How they can Help you, not just Hinder you," decided that "Projection" fit the bill nicely.

"Tom, I know how worried you are and it will be hard, but we'll have to be brave and watch as closely as we can. There might be some way we can help her." Tom, not a stranger to his wife's coping strategies, nodded in agreement.

Elise heard the sound of Hannah's footsteps on the crushed gravel as she approached the garden bench. She heard the footsteps. "Oh god, we're so stupid, Tom— there are speakers in the garden…" in a whisper Elise called out Hannah's name, and watched her face lift on the monitor, "Hannah, baby, I only have a few seconds to catch you alone— Hermes has cut off our phone— Adams is not, I repeat, NOT a human. We saw him on the camera as he approached the house. He has red eyes and horns on his forehead. He is something evil. Be careful honey. We are locked in here, but we can see and hear you. Be brave, honey. We believe in you." The last was said in a whisper so soft, Elise wasn't sure if she had said it out loud or had just thought it.

She watched Hannah listen and nod grimly. Finding the camera with her eyes, Hannah smiled briefly and gave them a thumbs-up. Elise felt the strangest sense of pride. Hannah was her daughter. Who cares if Jean Granger's daughter will be wearing Vera Wang and having a Summer Wedding to an Ivy League Investment Banker on the Vineyard, Jean's daughter would have dissolved into tears at being told that she had to face pure evil all by herself. She and Hannah were descended from a long line of women who looked power in the face and stood straight. Cassandra of Priam might have been cursed, leading to a life of insanity and pain, but no one bullied her, not even a god. Elise fervently hoped that in this case, Hannah had only inherited her ancestor's courage, and not her fate.

Then she heard three things happen in quick succession; the sound of a motorcycle engine roaring to life, the pounding of a door knocker echoing through the street, and a high pitch laugh so piercing that it seemed like every bird in a ten block radius lifted and flew away, their fear palpable. Through it all, Hannah had held herself perfectly still, determination etched in every line of her face.

●●●●●●●●●●●●

Adams/Sek

Making his way down Franklin Avenue

"Are you sure this is the house? Lee would know. Where could Lee have disappeared too? As my publicist, I trust you to see to my career interests, and you have never let me down before, but this is so unprofessional of Lee, and in some ways, you. Will you fire him? I think you should."

The Myth of Cassandra

Sek gritted his teeth. Apollo had been talking non-stop since they'd left the bookstore, one inane comment after another. The longer Apollo had babbled, the thinner Sek's control of his demon features got. He tried to ignore Apollo and concentrate. It wouldn't do to scare the girl unnecessarily at first. Taking a deep breath, he forced his human shape to reform, his horns receding, his eyes returning to their bright blue of Archer Adams. Excellent. Sek looked over his shoulder at Apollo, "Her house is the white one with the red door, on the right. Remember Apollo, after you save the girl from the communist, bring her to me, and I'll have her read from the script, okay?"

Apollo nodded, and followed him to the front door. Sek looked for a doorbell, but finding only a doorknocker shaped as a hand, he lifted it and brought it down on the corresponding metal ball. Then several things happened at once.

The door slid open silently to reveal an ancient Asian man dressed in an old-fashioned butler's uniform. A motorbike with two people, a man and a woman, one with long brown hair and the other with short pink hair respectively, pulled out of the driveway and into the street. Apollo let out a yell, "Stop! Unhand that Damned Girl in Distress!" The "girl" on the bike turned back and looked directly at Sek while the butler murmured, "That's not Hannah. Hannah wants to see you. But not Apollo. Stay."

The bike sped off and Apollo started running, yelling, "I, Apollo, god of Sun and Light, will save the innocent pink-haired chick!"

Sek found himself staring into the gap between the old man's front teeth. The butler nodded ambiguously, and disappeared into the house murmuring, "This way, please." Sek shrugged his shoulders and followed the old man. By sending a decoy of herself on the run, the girl had helped him get rid of one idiotic, powerful god. One easily scared human girl to go. Oh, and one annoying, smug, gap-toothed god as well.

"Excuse me, but where is the girl?" Sek moved quietly behind Hermes, who was clearly the ancient Asian butler.

Hermes, still in character, answered in a quavering voice, "Waiting for you in the garden."

With one viscous movement, Sek grabbed Hermes' neck, twisted him back into the front door which was opened into the hall, and without hesitation cursed him, locking him into the grain of wood, the door knocker changing into Hermes anguished face.

Sek smiled, "There, that's better. Oh, is it painful, Hermes? I wish I could be sorry, but, well...there you have it." And his smile cut the edges of his face, turning his mouth into the slit of a snake. His eyes burned red, "Poor Hermes. Did you underestimate me? What a surprise. And I'd hoped you'd be more of a challenge. I'll get to the girl in a minute." He leaned in closer, lifting the Hermes' head knocker up in the air, "I just want to thank you for getting rid of Apollo for me. That was really very considerate of you. One good turn deserves another. Except I don't think you'd classify this as a "good turn" for you!" And with that he slammed the knocker up and down on the door repeatedly. The knocker, though made of iron, seemed to change, pain transforming Hermes trademark smirk into anguish. The banging of the knocker was unnaturally loud and created a steady beat to underscore the sound of Sek's high pitched, maniacal laughter.

●●●●●●●●●●●●●●●●

Lee/Mot

The Internet to the rescue

The blonde undergraduate calling for Lee entered the women's bathroom at the back of the bookstore and sagged against the locked stall door. Bracing her arms against the sides of the stall, she listened intently to the sounds in the store outside of the room. She did not hear any screams of terror or sounds of mass hysteria, so Sek must have decided to leave without eating any souls. That was a relief.

Mot morphed out of the blonde undergraduate body back into his more recognizable Lee body, glad that he hadn't shared his improved ability to take human shape with Sek. His online course work had paid off. There was a lot of downtime when you worked primarily with computers. It was a choice for him between World of Warcraft or working on his demon level tests at the University of Phoenix. He had chosen to improve himself. The young blonde woman was his best shape yet. He had also mastered an elderly man of European descent and he was working on a young child, who, though androgynous, was cute.

Another skill he hadn't shared with Sek was his mind-reading abilities. His ability was fairly limited— so far Sek was the only one he could get a solid read on, and that was mostly because he was so predictably evil. It would have been easier to improve on this skill if he could have practiced it with Sek, but it didn't take a genius to figure out how Sek might feel about being read, so Mot had never let on. He knew that Sek thought he was a weak, low-level demon, and it had been hard not to brag about his elevation to a level 21 demon. But that close call just now in the bookstore line made him glad he'd kept his mouth shut.

He'd read Sek's mind as they'd entered the bookstore and knew that Sek was planning on cursing him. Sek's favorite curse involved merging his victim's body with the grain of large wooden objects— bookcases, wardrobes, doors. Aside from being extremely painful, it left you firmly stuck until someone could come and unlock you. He had to stay mobile if he was going to help his friend, Hermes. So he'd pretended to be a college student. It had all gone rather as planned. Now all he had to do was find Hermes and help him protect the girl until they could convince her to say what Sek wanted her to say, and in that way protect her from Sek's violence.

Yep. That was all he had to do. Leave the bathroom stall. Leave the bathroom stall to interfere with Sek's plans. Leave the bathroom stall to help Sek's enemy, Hermes, Greek god. The very gods they were tasked with bringing down. Except, well, he liked Hermes. And all Hermes wanted to do was help the girl to do what Sek wanted, right? But he was only just now seeing the problem with that. What would happen to Hermes when the girl read the script? He didn't know the exact plan, but he knew Apep was out for revenge, and revenge was not likely to be good for Hermes. Or Apollo. Pretty, pretty, Apollo. And then there was

Sek... Oh... this had all seemed so simple when it had just been him and Hermes talking it out over a fine slice of Blue Stilton.

A woman's voice called out, "Are you okay in there?" and she knocked on the stall door. "You seemed upset by that man in the line...."

Mot's face registered panic and he braced his short legs against the stall door to prevent entry by the overly-helpful woman on the other side. He squeaked out in a high falsetto, "I'm fine! I just need a little privacy, please."

After a short pause, he heard a murmured, "okay" and listened for the sound of her retreating step. He knew he needed to leave the bathroom stall soon, but first he needed to think this through. Oh, how he wished he had a bit of cheese: he always thought better with cheese.

CHAPTER TWENTY

A Very Special Blossom

❂❂❂

John

Back to Whitfield

Carl had a death grip around his chest, and the only thing he'd said the entire time since they'd left the house was right after he'd looked back at Adams. He'd shuddered, leaned into John's ear and urged, "Hermes lied. We have to lose this idiot, Apollo, fast. Hannah is going to need us; that thing Adams has horns. Lose Apollo, John. Fast."

Fast was definitely the operative word. John had never felt such speed in his life. He was grateful for the shield on the helmet he was wearing, afraid that at these speeds his face might just smear off his head. He aimed the bike down the centerline on the road and tried to trust his instincts for when to lean, hoping that his brain could keep up with the speed of the images his eyes were absorbing.

Hermes had instructed him to stay on the ground at all times. The winged shoes would take him up into the air if he thought about flying, and, according to Hermes, that would be signing his own death warrant. Hermes claimed that Apollo had winged horses at his beck and call and would overtake them in a matter of seconds in the sky. Hannah had confirmed this fact. Apparently the winged horses refused to run on the ground, so if he stayed earthbound, no magical horses for Apollo. On the ground, Hermes shoes should keep him and Carl ahead of Apollo's running until Apollo lost interest in the chase and in Hannah. Hermes insisted that Apollo was too vain to chase after a woman who was clearly running from him. But that wasn't happening as Hermes had said it would.

They'd been riding for five minutes and already they were at the Connecticut border. At this rate they should make it to Whitfield in another five. He felt the bike shimmy violently, and he quickly cleared his thoughts. That was close. Think about the road in front of you, John. The road in front of you. Hermes had explained that the winged shoes worked off of your thoughts. Think of a place, and they will take you there. They had almost jumped immediately to the University, and that would have ruined the back-up plan.

Because they needed it now. There had been two plans: the plan that Hermes had laid out and the plan that he and Carl had made in secret. While the first plan relied on Apollo giving up on the chase and losing interest in Hannah altogether, it was important for the success of the other plan not to lose Apollo. John felt warmth on the back of his legs and glancing in the mirror saw that it was coming from Apollo's golden glow. The knowledge made him feel dizzy.

He couldn't panic. If he allowed his thoughts to jump them to a different place, they would lose Apollo. And then Apollo might double back to Cambridge and Hannah. He had to keep Apollo close. Feeling like the mechanical rabbit at a greyhound race, John focused his thoughts on the road in front of him and sped on. Anything else could be disastrous.

Apollo had dropped back a bit in the last few minutes. From what John could tell in the rear view mirror, he appeared to be fixing his hair. The extra distance was useful, as he'd felt the need to slow the shoes as they entered the Centreville City limits. He'd taken the surface streets down to the river, hoping to catch a clear turn to head back up towards campus. It was a little nerve-wracking to contemplate turning at these speeds, but it was also nerve-wracking to consider slowing down. It didn't help that Carl was whispering a mantra of "faster, faster" in his ear while using his arms as an iron vise.

The Myth of Cassandra

Glancing at the mirror and judging Apollo to be a good distance down river, John took a chance and slowed to turn up High Street. All right! They had not spun out, though Apollo had gained some ground and looked to be directly behind him. But objects in the mirror were not as close as they appear? Right? Or was it the other way around? Are objects in the mirror closer than they appear? Why couldn't he remember? Why were his fingertips feeling numb? Maybe he was becoming oxygen deprived by Carl's death grip?

Trying to stay calm was nearly impossible as he could hear Apollo behind him. He caught the phrase, "I will rescue" and then, "tear limb from limb" and finally, "dance on his bloody remains." He tried to shut the words out of his head as he willed the fluttering shoes to take them up the street faster. It was all he could think. FASTER.

They were seconds from the frat house, but they would need a little time to jump off the bike and make it inside if this was going to work. Using the shoe's ability to read his thoughts he pictured the driveway of Deke and in an instant, they were there. In the next second, like a gear that catches, his mind met up with his muscles and he leapt off the bike, Carl still attached to him.

He could hear Apollo again, yelling, "I'm coming Hannah! I'm coming my damned girl in distress! Gotcha!" and he felt Carl's hands inexorably slipping away. He looked past Carl's white face to see Apollo in his golden glory pulling on the hem of Hannah's purple dress, reeling Carl in. Apollo smiled at him, and John felt momentarily charmed by the God of Sun. The emotion was fleeting.

"Long-haired Communist Boy, release The Hot Chick this second! I, Apollo, God of the Sun, have come to rescue her from your evil plans! Unhand her, sir!" All of this was said with the dramatic restraint of a Broadway star playing to the back row. Carl's eyes were closed and he seemed to be mumbling. John felt the sidewalk sliding under his feet as he clung to Carl's hands.

The shoes. John looked down at his shoes and thought, "Go far away fast!" Nothing happened but Apollo's laughter.

"You don't think that I, the God of the Sun, can be moved by Hermes' fancy little sandals, do you? Oh that's funny. Is that what Hermes told you? He lies. All the time. It's your own fault for listening to him."

Apollo started to detail how he would smash John into a thin layer of humanity to be scraped off the sidewalk and John started to think of all the things he would miss when he was dead: really good coffee, sex, books...his mom, Carl, Hannah...when he noticed that Carl's mumbling had become chanting. The air around Carl started to thicken, as if it was suddenly viscous. John felt all the hair on his body stand on end.

Carl, with his pink hair standing up as if electrified, calmly turned to face Apollo, whose face made a comical "oh" at his first look at "Hannah." Carl's voice seemed to come from deep within him, "I, Carl, Sorcerer of Clark Hall, call forth the Prismatic Storm!" And with that there was an explosion of bright blue light.

John had covered his eyes a little late, and now rubbed at his face frantically, trying to force his eyes to see again. He felt a hand on his shoulder, squeezing tight, and Carl's excited voice in his ear, "It worked! Check it out, John! It really worked! Look at him!"

John's vision was still filled with bright spots, but he strained to see what had happened to Apollo, "I can't see, Carl, did you kill him?"

"No, no, no...of course not. He's immortal, John. You do know what that word means, right? No, I used the Prismatic Storm because I thought that the blue light would be strong enough to stun a god. And it worked! He's totally knocked out! How cool is that?"

John's vision finally cleared enough for him to see Apollo, God of the Sun, lying prone on the sidewalk, his head cushioned on the lawn next to an empty keg. He looked asleep. John could hardly believe it, but he'd just witnessed Carl stun a god using a curse learned from afternoons playing Dungeons and Dragons in their freshman dorm room. Stunned himself, he turned to Carl, "What the hell, Carl? How did you do that?"

Carl smiled broadly, "I told you back in Cambridge, I've been practicing the spells I learned in D&D. Cool, huh? I'm not sure how long it'll last, though, so we might want to get him in the house. Our Apollo-trap is inside. Can you lift his head if I grab his ankles? He looks heavy, but I think we can drag him a little." And Carl grasped Apollo's ankles.

John did not relish getting close to the head of the god who only moments ago was detailing how he would kill him, but Carl had first dibs on the ankles, so he had to man up and grab Apollo's shoulders. He was heavy and it took several stops for breath to carry him into the house, but they managed to do it without rousing him. They dropped him on the beer-stained couch and stood back, "Carl, man, you saved my life!"

Carl gave John the quick, one-armed guy hug then turned to the crowd gathered in the room. It had been Carl's idea to lure Apollo to Whitfield as a back-up plan, "Hey guys. I want to thank you so much. Our friend here is having a really unpredictable trip— we aren't sure what he took, but he thinks he's Apollo the God of the Sun. Just play along. We need you to keep him here and distract him, so that he stays safe until he's feeling better. He gets really insecure when he's high, so maybe you could make him feel like he's a god?"

A short, broad white man with dread locks, Carl's frat brother whom John thought might be named Scully, slapped Carl on the back, "No problem, man, what are brothers for? When you called for help and gave me the 411 about your friend's weakness for the ladies, I called my sister. She's the coxswain for the varsity eight, and they'd just finished their afternoon row." He pointed to a very pretty petite brunette who smiled and waved at Carl and John, "She asked her team and they all agreed to help out." John stared at the tall, lean, beautiful women filling the room, and wondered if maybe they were Amazons, "We'll keep him here, right women?" The women were already surrounding Apollo, stroking his hair back from his face and admiring his build, and there was a general murmuring assent.

Scully leaned into Carl and John and whispered, "I have a special herbal drink that'll keep him very mellow, nice and safe until he's no longer high. Psychedelic trips are my specialty. I am going into practice after graduation, so if you wouldn't mind taking my card." He slipped a business card into John's hand. It was a rainbow colored card with simple black lettering:

"Have You or Your Friends Met Doctor I-Don't-Feel-So-Good? Get Help for a Gentle and Safe Re-Landing. Call Abraham Scullerson, Vibe Consultant 513-555-6161- bonded, insured and Red Cross certified. Specializing in bad trips and drunken hangovers. If your situation is life threatening, call 911 immediately."

John looked up from the card to see Carl fist bump Scully, "Thanks, man. You're the best." And then, as if the fist bump had knocked him back, Carl fell onto the couch and let out a slow breath. John watched him collapse like a balloon deflating, onto the cushions, "Oh no, man. I don't feel so good." John moved quickly to his side, just catching him as he slid to the floor. "I'm so tired; I just need a second to catch my breath. Just a second…"

He felt oddly calm at the sight of his best friend dropping like a stone— was there a point where panic has saturated your cells, making it unable to create a reaction in your body anymore? He moved Carl into a lying position on the floor and after checking that he was still breathing, he exchanged a look with Scully, who mouthed "911?" John nodded, and Scully disappeared out the front door.

"Easy there, Carl, easy. Can you still talk?" John slid his fingers down Carl's arm to the pulse in his wrist.

"Of course I can still …" Carl's answer was so faint that John had to lean in just to make it out. Something very bad was happening to Carl and John realized that there was a new level of fear that can happen even after you think that you are numb to it, the fear that something is irretrievably wrong. Not recoverable. He clenched his jaw to keep his teeth from chattering.

"Then you should rest, Carl, just conserve your energy. Here, let me help you." John had never seen anyone look so pale, so fast. He looked at Apollo who was still out of it on the couch surrounded by beautiful women and realized that if the paramedics came inside, they were likely to cart Apollo off, too. And that would put them all at risk. There was

The Myth of Cassandra

only one thing to do. He slipped his arms around Carl's now prone form and cradled him like a baby. Then he carried him outside to the lawn.

A beach chair was lying on its' side next to the empty keg. John hooked it with his foot, righting it, and carefully lowered Carl into it. Carl let out a slight "Oof" as John slipped and dropped him the last few inches into the chair.

John ran through the first aid checklist in his head. Carl was breathing. Check. Carl's pulse was regular and steady, which was a good sign. Carl was still conscious. Okay. John couldn't explain why—given all these very good signs—his hands were shaking badly. He shoved them in his pockets. Checklist. Think. "Carl, does it hurt anywhere? Don't try to talk, just nod..."

Carl looked up at him, blinked slowly, and talked anyway, "I feel so tired. It must've been the spell. In the game it takes a lot of magic points. Maybe I just need to replenish.... But Hannah...."

"Don't worry about Hannah; she's going to be fine. Remember the Nereids. Right now you need to see a doctor. Scully has already called 911 and the ambulance is on its way." Scully was standing in the middle of the road, ready to flag down the paramedics, but with his arms spread wide and dreadlocks floating in the wind, he looked as if he was summoning the ambulance with his vibe consultant powers. John felt relief as the faint sound of the sirens was now noticeable.

Carl grabbed John's sleeve, and John leaned in close to hear Carl's labored whisper. "You have to know something. Hermes must have lied, he told me Hera was going to hurt you, it was why I agreed to be a decoy, to get you safe, I told Hannah.... But what if he lied? He lied about Adams. We left her alone with him and that thing."

"But Hannah told me Hera was going to hurt you. I made up the story about the Cyclops, to get you safe, and she promised she wouldn't be alone. The Nereids..."

"You lied too? Oh crap. And Hannah knew about both lies?"

John nodded and forced his mind to sort through the facts. Hannah had told him to get Carl away, and Carl had told Hannah that Hermes had told him he needed to get John away, but also that Apollo was no threat, which would mean that if the threats to Carl and himself were lies, then Hannah had arranged to get them away, to keep them safe, which wouldn't be necessary, if the Nereids were really helping her, would it? Dammit.

"It's okay, Carl. Just rest. I can see the paramedics turning up the street. We'll take care of you, and then I'll go back to help Hannah..."

"No. You have to go now..." Energized by his anger, Carl gave John a shove that landed him on the ground with a thud. Carl seemed to have gotten a second wind. "Listen, I'm not going to die. I'm just drained. Scully's here and you'd be useless at the ER ..." The sirens from all the emergency vehicles interrupted Carl's words. "I am NOT going to die. Go help Hannah. GO." And he kicked John from his prone position in the lawn chair, "GO!"

John cradled his head in his hands, his voice cracking, "What if I can't help her? It was my fault Apollo caught us, and you had to use that spell, and now, what can I do to help her with a demon? What if it all ends badly? For everyone? What if?"

Carl did the one thing John least expected, and maybe the only thing that could break through his panic. He laughed. At first John thought he was wheezing or maybe choking, but it quickly became apparent that Carl was doubled over laughing his ass off.

John looked at Carl, limply prone in the battered lawn chair, laughing. "Really? I bare my pathetic soul, expose my fears, and you laugh at me?" But John's indignation only made Carl laugh more, and John found himself smiling, his pathetic soul ironically comforted by Carl's unusual reaction.

Carl took a shaky breath, "I am not laughing at you, really, but you looked so tragic. It just felt unreal, like we were on a 'very special Blossom,' so I laughed." He took another long shaky breath and smiled at John. "I'm sorry, John. But I'm lying here because I used a powerful spell from D&D to knock out a Greek God. It's hilarious." He leaned forward in his lawn chair to grasp John's shoulders, "This is no time for self-doubt, man. We are living in a freaking mythical world— where the rules are beyond what we thought they were. Based on my experience, we now know one; apparently, it takes a little toll on you if you cast a spell." Carl laughed again, and then sobered suddenly. "You need to get back to Cambridge, NOW! Forget the bike— just fly— you're wearing Hermes' winged shoes. Go help Hannah kick Adams' ass and then you can tell me all about it when you're done..."

John smiled and felt his stomach settle for the first time in the last twenty minutes, "Okay, okay, man, fair enough." He stood up in one fluid move. "I'll just pop back to Cambridge and help Hannah with her little demon problem. But no more magic from you until the doctor says you've regenerated. Remember, when your life points are low, you can be susceptible to troll rot." Now they were both laughing. John leaned over and grabbed Carl's arm, unconsciously channeling the ancient grasp of men going into battle. "I won't let you down."

He looked down at the shoes on his feet and watched the wings unfurl. He gave Carl one last thumbs-up. With Apollo out of the picture he could fly to Cambridge. He closed his eyes, pictured Hannah's parents' front door, and thought, "Fly me there, NOW!" He had the faintest impression of Carl's smiling face and a shocked paramedic falling back as he accidentally kicked him in the chest during lift off. John made a mental note to be more careful with his landing.

●●●●●●●●●●●●

Hera

Marital impetuosity

Hera sipped at her perfectly brewed tea and wondered what recipe that woman Elise had used for her baklava— it was exquisite. Flaky without being dry; sweet, but not too sugary. Hera set her teacup down and resisted the urge to get another piece. It would be unseemly to have more than one. Raising one eyebrow, she noted that Zeus had no such concerns and was working on his fourth brownie, washing it down with a large glass of cold milk. She really needed to find some way to channel her husband's interest in chocolate into a more sustainable choice. She'd lived for the last five hundred years following a strict code: live your life like your choices mattered. This simple idea had helped her avoid many of the pitfalls she'd watched Zeus, Apollo and other immortals fall into.

Hera straightened her hem and smoothed the linen napkin over her leg, studiously avoiding looking at the plate of baklava. She was not one to pass judgment on strangers, but it was her responsibility to provide constructive feedback for those in her familial sphere. Take Zeus and his unhealthy eating habits. Granted, as an immortal, he was immune to the more physical side effects of overeating: high blood pressure, heart attack, or stroke. But that did not mean he was unaffected by the psychological damage of gluttony: low self-esteem and depression. It was only recently, with his photography, that he seemed to be recovering himself. If he reached for one more brownie, she would have to say something. It would not be right to let him indulge.

She frowned. Indulgence was what had brought them here, to this point. Apollo. She'd let Apollo down. She'd watched him struggle with his role as an immortal in the last 50 years. At first, he'd seemed the least affected by the fall from Olympus. He'd moved from one long-term relationship to another, up and down the Grecian Isle. She'd learned the term for it researching an article for her magazine, serial monogamy. Apollo would cast his blue eyes on some winsome village girl, play his lyre, and they'd set up house for 20 or so years. She'd get old, and he'd move on. It was not a meaningful life, in her opinion, but he'd seemed incapable of reining in his romantic notions of love.

It was around the time that he lost out to Ringo Starr as drummer that he'd started on a downward spiral. He'd begun showing up with his hand out for "just a little pocket money, Aunt Hera," when she'd noticed that he no longer carried his lyre. She'd asked him about it and he had laughed and claimed that he'd pawned it to pay for a weeklong cruise for singles to the Bahamas. Zeus had joined in the laughter, making some crude comment about the number of "lays" Apollo's lyre had gotten him, and she had felt too uncomfortable to say what she thought— that without the sun or music, Apollo had nothing to do. No real purpose.

The Myth of Cassandra

All she could imagine was Zeus saying something cruder about the purpose of women, and so she had bit back her criticism of Apollo's choices.

What she realized now was that all of Apollo's bragging about conquests was just that, bragging. She'd watched how the women on the Vineyard had reacted to him. He had no game. It was Adams the women had flocked to on the rare occasion she'd agreed to go out with them. Apollo had chased after so many women in the past century that it was as if his aimlessness had left a scent clinging to his clothes, a scent women could smell as desperation. So despite his classical beauty, they turned away from him. Their rejection led to more self-doubt, until he was a perfect victim for that Adams creature's manipulations.

So, because she'd felt sorry for him, because she'd indulged him, because she'd refrained from passing judgment out of some weakness on her part, she was now waiting to see how big this problem might be. That thing, Adams, had played her as well. She could see that now. He had exploited her fear of appearing controlling, especially to Zeus, and now she had to put out not one, but two fires. She had to extinguish whatever plan that thing had, as well as *deal* with that unfortunate girl, who might not have deserved this mess, but was in it nonetheless.

Looking up at the screen she saw a scared, mousy girl who had been gifted with immense power. Despite Hermes' rather unflattering report, the girl had shown some moxie during this week. Hera was not impressed easily and was still waiting, but the girl had lasted longer than Hera would have imagined. The girl on the monitor flinched. She seemed to be listening to something that shook her deeply. And then Hera heard it too, a high-pitched, eerie laugh. Adams. The show was about to start, so Hera turned to get Zeus's attention. she was at a loss for what he could be doing. He was slumped in the leather armchair staring at his hand in wonder. She said his name sharply, and he looked up, startled.

"Zeus, come see the girl on the screen. It's starting." Hera stood up, napkin in hand, and gazed at the image on the monitor. She jumped and let out a short gasp as Zeus' arms encircled her from behind, his hands resting on her chest, cupping her breasts.

Zeus bent down to nibble on her neck, and she whacked at him, which only set his hands in motion. "What is wrong with you? Are you seriously wanting to, you know, are you trying to, you know, really..." She had intended to say all of this in the indignant tone commensurate with the inappropriateness of her husband's intentions. Unfortunately, she would later have to admit to herself, that it came up in the wondering tone commensurate with her excitement at her husband's intentions.

Did it really matter what that thing Adams wanted the girl to say? When she and Zeus were done....you know...well then, they would deal with this Cassandra mess. This really was too complicated a plan anyway. Trick the demon Adams into revealing his bigger plan, get the gift back from the girl and then kill them both. Ohh.... Zeus had found a wonderful use for the banquet table and she cringed as she thought of the tea stains she would have on her silk dress. The stains became moot, as she felt the dress give way to Zeus' demands. She stared with amazement into her husband's eyes, which seemed slightly glassy.

He smiled down at her and began to compliment her on many levels. Closing her eyes, Hera soaked it in. Sometimes the simplest answer is the best. They would simply skip to the last step and put an end to it. As soon as they were finished. Opening her eyes, she smiled mischievously at Zeus. "A few years back I hired a young woman to provide counsel for wives in an advice column on intimate issues. She had some very interesting suggestions for the usefulness of everyday objects I would love to try, if you're game?"

Zeus leaned back, arms wide, clearly up for anything. Yes, when she and Zeus were done, they would finish this story in the simplest of ways.

CHAPTER TWENTY-ONE

Irony in the Garden of Lies and Truth

❋❋❋

Hannah

Plan B

All the birds in the surrounding blocks took flight at once, filling the sky with a dark, flapping cloud. The tabby cat that'd been sleeping on the garden bench arched up and sped away. The nearby dogs stayed behind, but only because they couldn't leave, trapped by stockade fences or tied to back porches. Their howls joined the eerie laughter, harmonizing in some twisted minor key. In the garden Hannah felt frissons of fear slide up and down her arms. In her short acquaintance with Hermes, she'd heard him laugh often, and it had never made animals cower, so it must have been "Adams." She frowned and resisted the urge to follow the cat's escape path.

She thought back to when Hermes had showed up at her house disguised as a Girl Scout. Was that just a few hours ago? He'd spun a story about Adams truly being a publicist; wielding power only in the realm of media markets, the pawn of some evil god. Standing here, waiting to chat with said publicist as all forms of life fled from the sound of his maniacal laughter, she admitted to herself the pathetic truth that she'd wanted to believe Hermes, despite all the information she had to the contrary. The best lies are the ones we want to believe are true. It was all so Greek. Didn't most myths involve some arrogant idiot who gets hosed by the very thing they were most confident in: Achilles, Arachne,

Icarus... the list was a long one. Hannah Summers, serial liar, screwed by a lie. But she did not have to eat of the fruit of the poisoned tree, or be the victim of her own hubris. She was butchering her metaphors, getting stuck inside her head, but then again, she was in the first stages of panic. She wondered if *Ladies' Home and Hearth* had done a series on the stages of panic; stage one: engage in moot literary analysis with self; stage two: imagine magazine articles; stage three.... run? Maybe. She had approximately 90 seconds to decide if she should stick to the plan, despite the clear evidence that Hermes had played her.

The plan itself had been one they'd made together in her mother's laundry room, just hours ago. Hermes leaned back against the washer and watched as she folded and stacked her mother's dinner napkins. "Adams pushed for you to get the gift, even though I thought you were a bad idea." She scowled at him, but he ignored her. "At first I thought he wanted you because you'd be easy to intimidate. I might have implied that you've had no original thoughts, and were willing to roll over at the first sign of conflict." Hermes' expression was definitely mocking now. She'd been gritting her teeth to keep from interrupting, but the teeth gritting failed, "Hey!" And she threw a napkin in his face.

Smirking, he folded it neatly and added it to her pile. "We have to come up with an airtight reason as to why you defied that email he sent. The Hannah from my report would have called right away unless she'd flipped out." He scanned her face more thoughtfully. "I thought you didn't call because you were scared, but you hunted them down. What did happen, H?"

She'd heard her mother's voice in her head, "Use what you think he wants to hear. What does he think the reason is? Tell him that."

She gazed into Hermes' dark brown eyes, and like a flash of light, saw the answer. Looking down at her shoes, she softened her tone. "You were right, I was scared." She raised her gaze to explain, anxiously twisting the napkin. "It was Carl and John, they were the ones in charge. I was so overwhelmed, I wanted to call the number and just get this over with, but they talked me out of it. John tricked me into going to Martha's Vineyard. He's a reporter, and he couldn't let the story go." Looking

The Myth of Cassandra

straight into Hermes' eyes, earnestly, she went for broke, "If you hadn't come to my rescue, well, I'd probably be dead. I don't know what I would have done without your help."

Hermes wrapped his arm around her, rubbing her shoulder. "Well, you're right, Hannah. I have come to your rescue. I am going to help you come up with a much better lie, because there is no way Adams will believe that load of crap."

She shoved him, knocking over the neatly stacked napkins. "It was not crap! I had you. You were eating that up, weren't you?" But he was too busy laughing to answer. "Oh dammit, fine. It sucked. What did I do wrong?"

Catching his breath, he sat up on top of the dryer, knocking over even more clean linens. "That was almost worse than your attempt to cut in the bookstore line." At her gasp, he continued with his lecture. "Yes— I saw that. Secret swinger commune? Really? How can someone who is so naturally adept at deception be so bad at active lying? Think about it, H, imagine Adams is your Former Boyfriend and tell him what? You have to use the truth, at least part of it." Hermes leaned forward and really looked at her, no smirk in sight. "Adams has seen my report and knows how smart you are. There is no way that he'll believe that Former Boyfriend and Line Boy are in charge. He will have just seen you send them off to be bait for the golden buffoon. To him, it will look like you are clearly in charge here. If he senses that you are playing dumb, it'll be all over. You can't play the victim. You will have to sell him on the idea that you didn't call him for a good reason. One that he can believe. Because every good con begins with trust."

Trust. It was the very commodity she'd handed over to Hermes, and con or not, she was surprised at herself; she still trusted him. She knew that Hermes was selfish, and a liar, but she'd believed him when he said he would stay and protect her. Something about the way he called her H and tormented John and Carl revealed affection for them. So, would he have lied because he thought she couldn't handle the truth— lied out of some protective under-estimation of her? That he had simply kept a part of the plan to himself, because he was so arrogant as to believe that he

297

could manage it? But the sound of that eerie laughter made her think that she was not the only person experiencing a mythical level of Greek irony at least for the moment. Adams' laughter had to be at Hermes expense, so it was up to her for the moment. What could she use against some foreign demon until help arrived? What powers did she have?

What had her mother said as they'd been cleaning up from the vervain rope? She'd been whining about how she'd realized she'd wasted years lying to people, that she didn't know what about herself was real. And her mother had said that she hadn't spent years just lying, she'd spent years listening and learning what people need to hear. The last thing she'd heard her mother say before Adams' maniacal laughter had filled the air was that she believed in her. Her mother didn't tell her to run, or try to direct her from the sidelines. Hannah's frown cleared as she thought about the restraint her mother must have drawn on to resist giving advice. That had to have been hard for her. She felt herself smiling, and turned her thoughts to the creature heading her way.

She could hear his approaching footsteps now, and she made up her mind. Despite Hermes' lies, she'd follow through with the plan she and Hermes had come up with. She could hope that Hermes would come to help her, soon. In the meantime, she had to convince Adams to believe her. She perched on the edge of the bench and tried her best to look excited to see him.

She watched as the man in question stood at the entrance to the garden, hand on the iron sparrow. He was looking at her, smiling, no horns or glowing red eyes. But then she glanced at the bird in his hand and all she could see was molten iron streaming down on the pachysandra. Terror caused her mouth to go dry and her hands to sweat. She rubbed her palms on her thighs and hoped he hadn't seen her see him do that. The story she and Hermes had come up with as they restacked the napkins had hinged on the idea that she was not afraid of him, which seemed physically impossible at the moment.

She took a long slow breath, and smiled, "Archer Adams? Is it really you?" She needed him to come to her, so that they'd both be on screen, so she stayed where she was and extended her hand out to him. "I'm so glad you're here, I've wanted to speak to you alone, but we'll have to talk quickly, I don't know how long my friends can keep Apollo away. I need your help. But you might not like what I want to do..."

Archer seemed to slide toward her without effort, making only a whispery, slithery sound among the plants. He was looking at her intently, and as he took her hand in his, asked in a surprisingly normal sounding voice, "Now, why would I not like what you want to do, my dear Hannah?"

She stood still as he took her hand, and his grip was dry and tight. Hannah found it hard to breathe and fought her impulse to shake him off and hide her hands behind her back. She ignored his grip and met his pale blue eyes. "Because I want to destroy your clients, the Greek Gods. I have the power to, you know, with this "gift" they've given me, and I will do it, with or without you. But I'd rather do it with you. Before you try to convince me not to, let me tell you my reasons and why I'd like your help."

And with that opening move, the game was afoot. Forget Cassandra. She'd been the victim of Apollo's gift and subsequent curse. Hannah had her own present from Apollo, and she had no intention of being at the mercy of it. It was time she put it to use.

⁂

Hermes

How many blondes does it take to "unstick" a god?

Hermes had never suffered this particular form of curse before, and he was not a fan. The pain from Sek's knocking had subsided, and he was left with a profound sense of embarrassment. He had been caught by some lame Egyptian demon and pressed into the grain of this wooden door. He'd been so certain that his disguise had fooled Sek, that he had turned his back on a known enemy.

If Hera found out, he'd never live it down. Literally. There are some major drawbacks of immortality, and one of them is that there are some mistakes you never outlive. Letting Sek get the better of him was one such mistake. Dammit. He tried to feel his body immersed in the wood grain, but it was impossible. He was going nowhere unless someone came along and freed him. And who was left to do that?

He should've told Hannah the truth about Sek. He'd made a calculated decision that she would be too frightened to follow through with the plan if she knew what Archer Adams really was. So he'd lied to her. But he'd assumed that he'd be available to intervene when Sek went all demon on her. Which was inevitable. Sek's sick laughter as he'd banged his head-knocker told him all he needed to know about this particular demon; he didn't just use pain to motivate his victims, he liked to cause pain. Straining every part of himself he could find, he tried again to tear his body out of the door, but achieved nothing for all his effort.

In the next instant two things happened at once; a beautiful blonde woman ran up to the door just as Line Boy landed on the front stoop. Their collision knocked them both into the door, which hurt more than he'd imagined it might. He'd figured that it was only the knocker that felt pain, but no, the entire surface was very sensitive. It would definitely give him pause the next time he felt like slamming a door.

In the silence that followed the collision, all Hermes could surmise was that they had had the wind knocked out of them, too. It was Line Boy who got his voice back first. "I'm sorry for crashing into you, are you okay?"

She was staring down at her hands, and she raised them to his face, "You broke my nails! Look! They're all broken. Do you have any idea how hard it is to get long nails right? It was the bonus question on the final exam, and I scored all ten extra points for having beautifully shaped, long nails. You ruined them!" And she started to sob, tears streaming down her face.

Hermes could see John's face contort, watched him struggle with his basic decency and his impatience to get to Hannah. Decentness won out. "I'm sorry. Here, please stop crying. I'm really sorry; did I hurt you anywhere? Besides your nails?" The blonde woman looked up from her destroyed nails and stared at John while Line Boy kept talking. "I'm sorry I bumped into you, but I need to know, did you see a gap-toothed man, woman or child walk by? Or a man in a white suit? Or a woman with short brown hair? It's a matter of life or death."

She sniffed, apparently accepting his apology, "I think I'm okay, other than my beautiful...wait...." The blonde woman looked more closely at John, "I know you! You're the long-haired communist who has kidnapped the gift girl!" She pointed at him with one of her broken-nailed fingers. "I've caught you!" And before John could reply, she whispered some incantation, and John was frozen in place, unable to move. "Hermes will be so pleased I caught you! If only I could find him, he would know what to do with you..."

The look on Line Boy's face was priceless. Rarely had decentness been delivered such an instantaneous blow. Hermes laughed out loud from his knocker, and the blonde spun around at the sound coming from the twisted iron.

Being a door must not have affected his nose, because the odor of Limburger cheese finally found him, clearing up any lingering doubts he might have had about the identity of the blonde. Hermes called out, "Lee, you have found him, I mean me. I'm right here, trapped in the door. If you could get me out, then I'll take care of Line Boy here."

Surprised, the blonde leaned closer to the knocker, smiling. "Hermes! You recognized me! What do you think? Do you like?" And she spun slowly on the spot.

Despite the urgency of the situation, Hermes found himself taking the time to appreciate the transformation. "Well done, Lee. You've really mastered this shape. It's only because I know you so well that I recognized you."

"I don't think I would have recognized you! That knocker does not do you justice. Regardless, I am so glad to see you! The plan is all out of whack! Sek tried to curse me, so I had to hide and then I lost track of Sek and Apollo—I don't know where they are, I hoped they would be here. But I did catch the kidnapper though, look, I froze him. That's good right? But I don't know what to do next! Where is the girl? Where is Apollo? Where is Sek? What do I do?" The last sentence came out in a familiar whine, and despite the curvaceous shape, Lee looked very much like, well... like Lee.

Hermes needed to get the situation under control quickly, "I have answers to all of your questions, Lee, but first I need your help. Can you undo this curse? Sek got the jump on me and trapped me here. H is all alone with him, and none of us want that...." Hermes' little speech was as much for Line Boy's credit as it was for Lee. It was clear from the Line Boy's questions that he had thought Hermes had abandoned Hannah. Not that he cared what Line Boy thought.

The blonde woman morphed into his more traditional Lee shape, and if Line Boy's eyes weren't already frozen open, they would have gotten wider. Lee looked down at his hands, which still had broken nails, and shook his head, "He broke all ten nails— what a disaster! And me without a nail file." He ran his hands up and down his now much fuller hips, as if he were a potter considering his clay, "She's a useful shape, but it still takes a lot of concentration to keep it. And the estrogen rush makes me a little weepy. Oh well, let's get you out of that door...." And he placed both hands on the door and started singing. It sounded otherworldly to Hermes, an ancient rhythm. Lee's voice slowly got louder and deeper. As the song began to peak, Hermes felt a deep vibration inside the door. At the end of the song, Lee slammed both hands on the door, and Hermes fell out onto the stoop, landing on his hands and knees.

The sense of freedom was tremendous— he had limbs again. For the briefest moment he had the urge to take back his shoes from Line Boy and get the hell out of here, to the safety of his houseboat. He hadn't liked being trapped in that door at all. He looked at the other two on the stoop. Lee was looking at him with such trusting confidence, and the Line Boy was frozen in such anguish. Even with that he still considered running, but then he thought of H. H breaking into the Honors College; H setting the trap for him; H hunting down the gods, intent on getting rid of the gift. It wasn't every human who would work so hard to give up power....

The Myth of Cassandra

"I need you to listen to me, Lee. This boy you see in front of you is not a kidnapper. Adams, I mean Sek, told Apollo that to manipulate Apollo into being a "hero" and saving the girl. Think for yourself, Lee. You've been tracking their progress from the beginning, did it seem like she was a prisoner to you?"

Hermes watched Lee chew on his broken nails, clearly sorting through his memory of images of H and Line Boy. "But he made her say all that nonsense about healthcare for the universe, didn't he?"

"No, Lee, the girl never said those things. Remember Lee, that was all Adams, I mean Sek. Sek didn't like me poking at the script, so he distracted Apollo with the idea that Hannah needed to be rescued. This boy is Hannah's friend. He's been helping her. I call him Line Boy. But his name is John and he is working with me." Hermes looked meaningfully at John, hoping this last bit would spare him a fistfight with Line Boy once he was free.

"Are you sure, Hermes— because he is long-haired, and probably a communist. Look at his clothes— no capitalist would wear that jacket."

Hermes lost his patience. "I don't have time for pretending to consider your ideas, Lee. I am going to be brutally honest with you. There comes a time in a demon's existence when he has the choice to work for the somewhat-mostly-good or for the definitely evil. This is one of those times for you, Lee." Hermes complete lack of smirk held Lee's full attention. "Lee, I don't want to convince Hannah to read Adams' script. I want to expose Adams for the demon he is, Sek, and find out his plan. Hannah has agreed to help me do this if I help her convince the gods to take back her gift. We have a plan to trick Sek. Line Boy here and the Former Boyfriend helped out by luring Apollo away. My job was to keep Hannah safe from Adams, I mean Sek, while she gets him to reveal the script. But since he locked me into the door, she's been on her own with him. You need to make a choice, Lee." And here Hermes leaned in, lifting Lee's chin up so that they were looking eye to eye, "You can choose to work with me and help Hannah, or you can work against me and help Sek. But you need to choose now."

Lee stared at Hermes; neither one breathed. Hermes knew it had been a gamble to lay it all out there for Lee. At his heart, "Lee" was Mot, and he had worked for Apep, the God of Evil, his entire existence. To switch teams, to join him against Sek, would be an irrevocable choice for Lee, alienating him from everything he'd always known. Hermes also knew that if Lee did join him, he'd be responsible for Lee. Responsible for his livelihood, his needs, his happiness. He couldn't ask Lee to leave everything and not offer him an alternative life.

Lee was the first to exhale, to look away and Hermes felt his stomach turn. Only when he realized he was wrong about Lee had he realized how much he'd assumed he'd be right. Dammit. Now he'd have to curse Lee, and he really liked him, honestly regretted having to hurt him. Hermes opened his mouth to do it just as Lee turned to him with a small smile, hand extended, and said the one word that saved him from pain, "Partners?"

Hermes shook his hand and smiled back, swallowing the curse he had been about to unleash on Lee, grateful that Lee's powers didn't extend to mind reading.

"Actually, I can read minds, well, some minds, but it's a relatively new skill for me. I was on the fence about saying yes, but I liked how much you regretted having to hurt me. That was the nicest thing anyone has thought about me, ever." And he wrapped Hermes in a smothering hug.

Hermes patted Lee's back and thought loudly, "I do like you. Assistant."

Lee countered, out loud, "Assistant on a Partner Track?" And Hermes nodded, then turned to John and started to untie his flying sandals.

"So, Boss, should we unfreeze this human or is he safer as a statue until this is over?" Lee's head was tilted, admiring John's bone structure, "It'd be a shame if he got hurt. He's very good looking, isn't he? Did you say he was Hannah's boyfriend?"

"No. They're *just friends*." And he stroked John's cheek. "You are a pretty one, Line Boy. While it would be better for you if we left you as a lawn ornament until this was over, something tells me that you wouldn't like that. You, FB, and H are really very sweet together. Very Loyal. Speaking of FB, I wonder where he is. I hope Apollo didn't catch him. I guess the only way I'll know is if you release him. Set him free, Lee, he could be helpful."

And with that Lee waved his hand and John fell to the ground, his muscles twitching. Lee bent over to help him stand, but before they could exchange a single word, they were all silenced by a gut-wrenching scream coming from the garden. One single, anguished word rent the air.

"Nooooooo!"

CHAPTER TWENTY-TWO

The View from the Control Room

❂❂❂

Tom

Don't look away

"But then I started to think about it. It was watching everyone jump when I made the second speech that it hit me. Everybody listened to me. Me. Hannah Summers. I said something and people did it. Most people…" Here she smiled at him and looked up through her lashes, flirting with lord-knows-what-kind-of-evil, "Not everyone is under my influence; I don't seem to affect you that way." Not giving him a chance to comment, she turned her back on him and continued, "I've spent my life pretending that everyone else was right. That everyone else's needs were more important than mine. I spent my life listening. I'm so sick of it. Do you realize how many people think that if you are quiet you are shy? Maybe some people are. I was quiet because it wasn't worth it to try to convince someone else to listen. But now I talk and everyone listens." She looked towards the street, turning as if addressing the throngs. "It's ironic that Apollo decided to give this gift to me. I've spent the last four years studying, among other things, the myriad ways the Olympians screwed over humanity, played with us for their amusement. We were pawns in their personal battles. Cursed and raped and killed on their immature whims. They are going to find out that humans are not their toys." She looked back at Adams, her eyes clear, a small smile playing around her mouth. "I want revenge. And all I have to do is open my mouth and speak."

Adams tilted his head, appearing to be looking for the edges of her story. "If that were true, why haven't you done it already? It's not like you haven't had the opportunity."

She stared at her parents' house next door, brows drawn. "I needed to get home, and I wanted to make sure my parents were safe before I declared war on the Greek gods. They would've had no qualms about killing my mom and dad to get back at me. But my parents are safe now." That last part was said with extra emphasis, and Hannah looked directly into the camera that was concealed in the branches of the dogwood behind Adams. "And they will stay safe."

Smiling again at Adams, her words took on emphasis. "The Greek gods deserve to be the myths we all thought they were. Finding out I was a descendant of Cassandra's only made it better, more satisfying. What was Apollo thinking?" In a whiny falsetto, Hannah cranked up the crazy. "Oh, sorry I cursed you. Sorry that your family died, and you became insane all because you had the gall to reject me." She shook her head and continued, "There are some crimes for which there is no reparation. So, I can start with Apollo. I want your help, Archer, because, while I know their past, you know them now— you have inside information that could make my revenge swifter, sweeter. You may not know the Greek myths, but as a fellow human, you should want this revenge as much as I do. What do you say, will you help me? I really want you to, but if not, stay out of my way. Because I am not going to be their latest toy, and now that I know what it feels like to tell people what to do, I am not going to accommodate anyone. Not even you."

Tom tore himself away from the garden monitor, where Hannah was turning in a stellar performance as a power drunk, vengeful, mad woman, to see how Hera and Zeus were handling this performance, and he couldn't stop himself from yelling at the image he saw before him. Zeus and Hera were completely naked, writhing around on the buffet sideboard that had previously held an assortment of fruits and cheeses.

Now it had an assortment of body parts at full arousal and various household objects being put to bizarre use.

"What happened? Why are you yelling?" Elise was still staring at Hannah and Adams in the garden, clearly torn between looking and not looking.

"Don't look! Whatever you do, do not look!" If Tom could spare his wife the trauma of seeing her favorite serving platter being used for....

"OH MY GOD! Is that the Wedgwood? What is he doing with that vase? And why is she hitting him with that serving spoon? Are they fighting? Is that the gouda on her?"

"I told you not to look! Why did you look?" Both Tom and Elise were yelling at this point.

"They aren't fighting. Oh, no, it must have been the brownies, the pot, the furniture... my eyes! Why didn't you tell me not to look?" Elise covered her face and moaned. Tom's compassion for her prevented him from defending himself. He had told her not to look. It was not a pretty sight. Hera and Zeus were into some kinky stuff; aside from the vessels, tableware, and cheese, they appeared to have dismantled the ottoman, but to what purpose?

"What do we do, Tom? Do we stop them? Even if Hannah gets Adams to reveal his plan, they won't even notice. Hannah! Oh god, how could I look away...Tom, where is she?" Elise had spun back to the main console and started flipping through all the camera angles, desperately hitting buttons. "She's not in the garden, not on any of the monitors! He must have taken her somewhere! OH, how could I have looked away! NOOOOOooooooo!"

The last button she hit was the volume on the microphone in the garden. The flock of starlings who had returned when Adams had lifted Hannah in his arms and disappeared, were dislodged again, frightened by the anguish in that one lone word, and filled the sky, momentarily blocking the setting sun.

The Myth of Cassandra

●●●●●●●●●●●●

Hannah

The lesser of two evils

Hannah steeled her muscles against flinging herself out of Adams' arms. The physical revulsion was hard to contain. Her skin was crawling and she breathed through her mouth to keep from gagging. It wasn't that he smelled bad, or even looked bad— he felt bad. Evil. But staying in his arms...what was that expression, the lesser of two evils? Well, staying in his arms might not be the lesser evil, but it was definitely the lesser dead. Looking down she estimated that they were at least three hundred feet up. So she closed her eyes and tried to think of something good to keep from jumping. Kittens. Cute, cuddly kittens playing with string. Oh, that's not right. Now the imaginary kittens were strangling each other, while smiling evil feline smiles. What form of demon was she clinging to that even her imagination was affected by his touch?

Opening her eyes, she stared at the rooftops and cars below. Where was he taking her? None of them had imagined that Archer would leave the garden, let alone take her with him. She searched the ground below for landmarks, hoping she'd be able to send a message on her phone of where to find her. They were leaving Cambridge. She could see 93 below them, a traffic jam snarling southbound. Was that Route 1? The cars were weirdly still, as the drivers sat waving each other on, waiting to let the other go first. Why weren't they just merging?

And then she remembered the gift. That's right; she'd told people to be kind. Good grief, the last thing the drivers in Boston needed to be was kind. Driving in Boston was built on a strong foundation of self-interest. As a teen she remembered cringing as her mother cut across three lanes of traffic to make a left hand exit. She clearly recalled her mother's blasé attitude. "Don't make that face, Hannah, I have my blinker on. It's their job to be looking out for me." Hannah had to admit that when she did get her license, she found that no one had appreciated her adherence to the rules of the road, often seeing her turn signal as a sign of weakness and jumping across her in traffic.

This is good, she silently told herself. Keep thinking about anything but the fact that a demon is whisking you away to some lair because you convinced him that you are a maniac intent on destroying the Olympians. Despite her current circumstances, she felt satisfaction at having played Adams. She'd read an editorial in *Ladies' Home and Hearth* that suggested that sometimes the mutual hatred of a third party could really prop a marriage up. The writer had encouraged her readers to mirror their spouse's hatred for a politician or late night talk show host. At the time she'd read it, she had thought it was a shockingly Machiavellian sentiment for a column that usually focused on the best way to remove ketchup stains, but now she realized it was probably just some rationalization of Hera's. It couldn't have been easy to be married to Zeus.

Crap. That was another problem with this "change in location" that Adams had instigated. Without the end of the story, Hera and Zeus might think that little Revenge Speech she gave in the garden was reflective of her true feelings about them. That would be very, very bad. She needed a chance to tell them the truth. Before they crushed her to bits. If Adams didn't disembowel her first. Kittens. Think about the kittens.

The truth was that when she'd been studying the Greek gods in school she'd thought they were crazy, vain, and mercurial, but fabulous. The stories were just so good. Irony, fate, and character all mixed together with beautiful people and exotic locations. There was no striving for perfection in the relationships between the gods and the humans. They were both guilty of hubris, jealousy, and longing. If anything, the Olympians became more flawed the more enmeshed they were in human civilization. Now that she'd had first-hand knowledge of their craziness, she was less enamored, but she certainly didn't hate them. She needed to get back home and make them understand.

Home. She closed her eyes briefly and hoped that her mother had heard her when she told them to "stay safe." She didn't want her mom and dad to get any more mixed up in this than they already were. Despite her resentment of her mother's professed need to "improve" her, she felt like they had reached some new understanding. She wanted a chance to see what that would mean, and not have it snuffed out as collateral damage in a demon war. Shaking her head, trying to clear it of all these cascading thoughts, Hannah knew that to see that future she had to outwit Adams and make it right with Hera and Zeus.

Adams was slowing, and Hannah looked down, stunned. She could not believe where he was taking her. It was too random. Why were they here? What advantage did this give him? She had to try to tell someone. With her hand in her pocket she slid her fingers over the buttons of her father's cell phone. The conference call they'd linked with was broken, but she'd programmed the speed dial with each person's phone: her parents, Carl, John, and Hermes. She ran through the names and numbers in her head and texted the one person she needed.

It was an old phone, with no sliding keyboard, just letters on numbers. Closing her eyes to help her visualize which letters were on which numbers, she tapped quickly, wanting to send it before they landed: two twice, eight twice, six once, five twice, three twice, seven twice, four once, four twice, five three times, and again, five three times. Hoping that she had it right, she hit send, at the same time Adams whispered in her ear, "We're here, my vengeful darling."

●●●●●●●●●●●●

Lee

The Lady of the Garden

John, Hermes, and Lee all stared at each other as the flock of starlings filled the sky. John whispered, "Hannah," and all three made for the door at the same time. Lee's height left him the only one standing while the other two collided over his head and fell to the ground, landing on their butts.

Hermes and John struggled to stand up; both had recently been cursed and were not as agile as they usually were. Lee discretely offered them each a hand, and no one spoke as they rose. John glared at Hermes and pushed through the door, and they all ran through the house to the garden path that connected the back yards. The garden was completely empty, and the scream they had heard was now replaced by Elise's voice calling for Hermes.

Hermes and John both spoke at once:

Hermes: I'm here, Elise.

John: Where is Hannah?

But what Elise heard was, "I'm where is here HanElise." And all they heard in reply was a very irritated, "What?"

John and Hermes started to yell at each other. "Shut up!"

"You shut up! You lied to us and abandoned Hannah!"

"You don't know what you are talking about!"

"I know exactly what I am talking about! She wants to talk to me!"

"This isn't about you!"

"This isn't about you!"

And with a wave of his hand, Lee froze them both where they stood, mouths open in mid-retort. Into the silence he spoke to what he could only imagine was a mystical being, a spirit of the garden.

"Lady of the Garden, please tell me what happened? I'm an Assistant to Hermes, and I'm helping him, so you can trust me. Can you see me? Are you a Spirit Voice?"

There was a slight pause during which Lee felt distinctly observed. Oh, he hoped that he'd be found acceptable. In his experience, Spirit Voices could be very judgmental. He'd heard Spirit Voices tell him he was fat, smelly, and stupid. But when she spoke again, she sounded very nice, though worried.

"Did you kill them?"

Lee blinked, trying to think what she was talking about. "I'm sorry, who? Because it's possible that I may have inadvertently…"

"Hermes and John! Please tell me that what you just did, you can undo. You didn't turn them into stone or anything dreadful like that?"

The Myth of Cassandra

"Oh, them. No. No! I definitely didn't kill them. They're just momentarily frozen. They were arguing, well you heard them, and I just thought we were in a rush, and so ..."

"Oh, okay, good. Listen, Adams took Hannah. I rewound the tape. He said to her, 'I would love to work with you.' And then he picked her up and flew out of the garden. He took my little girl, please, you have to find her."

"Hmm...umm...I don't understand.... Why does he want to work with her? What does she want to do?" Lee's voice had risen in pitch and the last words out of his mouth dripped with anxiety.

"Easy now, easy little...guy? Easy." The Spirit Voice was very soothing, and Lee stopped and listened. "This is all Hermes' plan; you did say you are working with him, right? Maybe you should unfreeze him, and he can tell you about it. But quickly. Adams has Hannah, and we have no idea where she is." The Spirit Voice sounded so kind and so worried; Lee took a deep breath and decided to do what she suggested. He released Hermes from the freeze.

Hermes leapt across the distance between them and grabbed Lee by the shoulders, shaking him hard. "Don't ever do that to me again! EVER. If you ever freeze me..."

His threat was left hanging as Elise's voice cut into his rant, "Hermes, focus! You can discipline your... whatever it is... later. Did you hear what I told it? Adams believed Hannah, but then he took her away, and Zeus and Hera, oh god, they are otherwise occupied and saw none of it. Please find her! Tell me you can find her."

Hermes stopped shaking him, "Lee, can you track Sek? Follow his scent or find his thoughts?"

Lee shook his head. "I can't sense his thoughts unless I'm near him, which only means that he isn't here, which we already know."

"Hermes, please do something! You promised you'd protect her. Please..." The Spirit Voice now sounded very scared to Lee. He had to think, was there something he could do? What was that sound? It was like a low buzz, and it was coming from the frozen boy.

Hermes was pacing, muttering, "I can call in all my contacts, but that could take hours before we get a lead, and even then, if he can fly, who knows how long he'll stay in one place."

Lee backed away from John. "Um, Hermes, the boy here is buzzing. He isn't going to blow up, or something is he? Because if he is, we should probably take cover."

Hermes cocked his head and listened, then pounced on the boy, trying to reach into the frozen boy's pocket, but it was impossible. "Quick, Lee, free him! That's his phone— it could be Hannah!"

Lee passed his hand over John's face and John gasped for breath, hands on his knees. Recovering fast enough to knock Hermes away from his pockets, he ground out, "It's my phone. I'll answer it." And he pulled it out and flipped it open. Both Lee and Hermes were reading over his shoulder and Elise's voice rang out, echoing in the stone fountain.

"What does she say? Where is she?"

John grabbed Hermes with one hand, Lee with the other. "You have the shoes, take us there. You do know where it is, don't you?" Lee held on tight to the pretty boy's arm and half hoped that Hermes did not know where it was. Because where the girl was, there too was Sek.

In a flash they left the garden, and the birds circled still, unsettled by the plaintive voice calling, "Where? Where is she? Where?"

CHAPTER TWENTY-THREE

The Three Musketeers

❁❁❁

John

To the rescue

It took all of John's strength to hang on to both Hermes and the computer dude. He'd heard Hermes call him Lee. Well, Lee was definitely the lumpy little guy from Martha's Vineyard, but he was also capable of taking the shape of a beautiful blonde woman, and of freezing people into statues. Having been frozen twice in the last five minutes, John indulged in a quick mental note to be careful around him...or her... or it? Whatever it was, that thing, Lee, was way more dangerous than he smelled. And he smelled pretty bad.

As powerful as Lee was, John was glad he appeared to have joined forces with Hermes. Despite being a smarmy liar, Hermes did seem intent on rescuing Hannah now. Whether he believed that Hermes had actually been tricked by Adams, or had simply sold Hannah out and was caught in the process, was not important. Hermes and Lee both had stated their desire to protect Hannah from Adams, though they were calling him Sek. That was fine with him. The more weirdly powerful beings on the side of Hannah and against Adams/Sek, the better.

Bunker Hill. Why would Adams have brought her here? The thought was no sooner in his head than he was falling forward onto the ground, dirt filling his mouth, head just inches from hitting the bottom of the tall white obelisk. Spitting dirt out, he looked back over his shoulder at Hermes, who was standing next to Lee, smirking.

"Rough landing, Line Boy?"

John's retort died on his lips as the sound of Hannah's scream could be heard out the tiny slit window at the top. Eyes widening, John turned his back on Hermes and ran to the front of the monument, where he found the door shattered in a pile of wood slivers. Hermes joined him at the entrance and peered at the circular stairwell, granite blocks twisting upwards. "Well, it's too tight a space to fly, which Sek must have counted on. There's only one way up— the old fashioned way."

John frowned at him. "Can't you just blow a hole in the monument and grab Hannah?"

"Well, genius, I can blow a hole, but then the monument falls down, which might be hard for Hannah to survive if I happen to miss when I try to "grab" her. And then there is the chance that the hole blows right into her, but if you're feeling lucky…"

"No! It's just that Sek, Adam's name is really Sek, right? Sek must've known we'd have to come up the stairs, so it stands to reason that he might've booby trapped the stairs."

"Look at Line Boy, Lee, he's been thinking! You're right, Line Boy, Sek, demon minion of Apep, Egyptian God of Evil, probably has thought of slowing down any potential rescuers." Bowing low and pantomiming a formal introduction, he continued, "May I introduce you to his partner, Lee, otherwise known as Mot."

Lee interrupted, "Former partner."

Hermes dropped his farce and smiled at the aforementioned partner, "Yes. Lee has decided to go into partnership with me. Lee is an excellent assistant, providing he keeps his freezing spells off me." Hermes glared at Lee, and Lee whimpered.

John's impatience made him forget his decision to be cautious around the others, and he bit out, "The stairs?"

Hermes narrowed his eyes at John, but then looked speculatively at the first step and backed up. "It's a fair observation that Sek might have booby trapped the stairs."

Lee's eyes went wide. "What is a Booby Trap? None of us have boobies...at least not now."

"Booby traps, Lee, are just a silly human expression meaning a trap intended to catch idiots, not breasts. I suggest we take the stairs as slowly and quietly as we can, and let the idiot go first." Hermes stared at John.

There was a tense moment as John glared back, but the staring contest broke as Hannah's second scream echoed down the stair well. John moved instantly, taking the steps two at a time. He could hear Hermes behind him explaining to Lee, "Humans, they are so emotional. It makes them such fools."

He had to keep running, climbing. The air in the monument was dank, at odds with the heat of June. Of course, the chill John was feeling might be sweat-induced hypothermia. His hand was slipping on the railing, and he kept trying to wipe the stinging drops out of his eyes, but he was still wearing the leather jacket from the bike ride, and the sleeve just smeared it across his face. He could hear voices up ahead. Hannah's voice sounded normal, didn't it? Her second scream had filled him with a potent combination of anger and fear, and he was ashamed that he'd wasted time at the bottom in a pissing match with Hermes.

Trying to stretch his stride to take three stairs at a time had been a mistake, and he'd landed hard, the stone risers hitting him squarely in the shins. Swallowing back the pain, he'd gotten up and started back up two at a time. Hermes and Lee were somewhere behind him, their progress much more sedate. One more landing and he'd be able to see the top. He slowed down and crouched low as he turned to face the top landing. But instead of Hannah and Adams, all he saw were two pigeons, which took off through the narrow window slits at the sight of him.

Where was she? He could hear the faint sound of her voice, could even smell her hair, but there was no one here. How could she be gone? He stared at Hermes as he and Lee rounded the landing. "Where is she?"

Hermes tilted his head and spoke to him like a child. "How many steps have you come up, Line Boy?" John frowned and shook his head, and Hermes scolded him. "A smart man would have counted, don't you think? A man intent on helping his friend and knowing that there were traps, might have considered it important to count, don't you think?"

John grabbed Hermes with both hands and shook him. "Say what you mean, now! Or do you want to wait until the next scream to find her?" Hermes' look of icy anger caused John to let go and focus. "I don't know how many steps I ran up. I just ran until I reached the top— did you count? Come on man, this isn't 'lecture the idiot human' hour. Hannah needs us..."

Hermes smiled, "I like that, 'Lecture the Idiot Human Hour.' That could be a new talk radio show. But of course, you have a valid point. Hannah's in trouble and I can mock you at my leisure after she's safe. By my calculations you have climbed three hundred and twenty-five steps. Is that what you have, Lee?" Lee looked down at his fingers, wiggled them randomly, and nodded agreement. "Three hundred and twenty-five steps, Line Boy. What is wrong with that number?"

John stared at Hermes, feeling as if he was on some bizarre reality TV show, and the time had come for the quiz portion. He pulled back the mental photograph he'd taken of the plaque at the bottom of the stairs:

The National Park Service Welcomes You to the Bunker Hill Monument

IMPORTANT PLEASE READ

The monument has 294 steps. Persons with heart and respiratory conditions....

"Two hundred and ninety-four. There should only be two hundred and ninety-four stairs. How can I have climbed more stairs than there are?"

"What kind of trap did you expect Sek to set? A bear trap?" Hermes' voice dripped with derision and John had to swallow back a retort; he needed to focus on getting to Hannah, no matter how much he wanted to punch Hermes in the face.

"Okay, Hermes, explain in really simple terms how the hell we get to Hannah if this monument only has two hundred and ninety-four steps and I've climbed three hundred and twenty-five."

The Myth of Cassandra

Lee piped up. "It's an illusion. Sek likes to play with people's minds. I think you might have to go back to the bottom and climb up again, but this time stop when you reach the two hundred and ninety-fourth step."

"Wait, why didn't you stop me? What is wrong with you two? And why do I have to start again at the bottom, can't we just count backward?"

Holding out his fingers for each answer, Lee enumerated, "One: You started up first, so you'll have to be the one to break the illusion. Two: We didn't stop you because, well, you're a human, unlikely to believe what you don't see with your own eyes, so we thought it best to let you reach the fake top. And Three: you have to start at the bottom because I think it is probably likely that you will have to have touch each of the two hundred and ninety-four steps to break the illusion."

A third scream filled the monument, the sound cutting through his skin. Even Hermes flinched. John pleaded, "What's the fastest way down? Please..."

Hermes looked down the winding staircase. "I have an idea, but I am going to need your help, Lee." Lee looked eager to help, and nodded. Hermes stared at Lee, and before John's eyes, Lee flattened. Hermes waved a hand for John to climb on. "a Lee-sled should get us both to the bottom quickly. Sorry, Lee, it might be a little uncomfortable."

Thinking of Hannah being tortured by Sek did away with all of John's caution, and he sat in the front and grabbed onto Lee's shoulders, which had curved up like the front of a toboggan. Hermes got on with a shove from behind and they flew down the spiraling stairs. Hermes appeared to be creating cushions of air all around them, so their descent was silent. Silent but dizzying, as each bend swirled into the next. It was as if Hermes had turned the historical marker into an amusement park ride. As the sled turned the last corner, John flung himself off and started climbing the stairs, one at a time, as quickly as he could, counting under his breath.

Hannah

The Mry factor

Hannah was trying her hardest to keep her gaze focused on Adams, but she was struggling to make sense of her current situation. Adams was going on about the arrogance of the Greek gods, and their pathetic need for human worship, and how much he agreed with her that they should be destroyed. She was perched on a pile of silk pillows doing her best to look like she was hanging on his every word while at the same time trying to figure a way out of this mess. It had gotten very strange.

When they'd first arrived at the monument, Adams had blown up the heavy oak door padlocked with an iron brace like it was made of tissue paper, and then had bowed low and said, "Ladies first." That should have given her a hint of what was to come, but she was so focused on trying to figure out why he'd brought her here that she hadn't noticed the change in him.

She'd grown up in Cambridge and lived in New England her entire life and had never been to the Bunker Hill Monument. It was something of a lame duck site. The battle it was supposed to commemorate really happened on Breed's Hill, not Bunker. And it was the battle where the Revolutionary Commander had famously told his troops, who were outnumbered and under-prepared, "Don't shoot until you see the whites of their eyes..." This economy was necessary because of their shortage of ammunition and the notoriously unreliable muskets. Not exactly the history lesson teachers want to emphasize to elementary school kids; the patriots were all likely to die, but their commander told them to wait so they could kill as many of the British as they could on their way out. Definitely not trifold poster material.

As she'd climbed up the circling staircase she felt like she was heading further and further into a trap. There were no windows on the way up, no way out but back down. Only one stairway. Only one direction to go. Up. Adams was climbing behind her, stopping every few feet to murmur and stomp on the stairs, sending a vibration up through the soles of her shoes. Oh, no! What if he was setting traps for anyone following them? If John got her text and followed her here, he'd walk right into it! She had to distract Adams from setting more traps and get out of here before John arrived.

"Argh! Ouch! Ohhhh!" She screamed as loudly as she could and fell to her side, cradling her ankle, and crying like a baby.

"What happened, my mry?" Adams was at her side, kneeling, and reaching his hands out to Hannah's ankle, "Here, let me look."

"No!! I think it's broken, it hurts so much…" What had he called her? She sobbed again for good measure, "I think I might have broken it. Please, take me to the hospital, I need to see a doctor. Please," and she opened her eyes to plead with him. What she saw on his face floored her.

Adams had seemed upset. He looked back down the stairs, then down at her curled on the floor. "I wasn't able to finish what I was doing, but it should be enough to give us privacy. Here, I'll carry you to the top. When we get there I can take care of you, darling. In time you will grow to appreciate the poetic side of pain, but until then, I can make the pain stop."

Hannah was spared having to reply to this bizarre declaration, as he scooped her up and threw her over his shoulder, patting her bottom.

What the hell was he talking about and what was he doing touching her butt? She would have to try again. With her head hanging upside down, she screamed loud and long, then begged, "You don't understand! I need a doctor!"

But Adams only laughed. "You don't need a doctor, funny girl. You must have realized by now that I have powers beyond your imagination. I can fix you right up. And when we are finished with our work for Apep, I can help you harness the joy of pain. It's all in your attitude, my mry."

Hannah braced her hands along his back, stunned by this turn of events. What the hell was going on? Was this a trick on his part, trying to get her to reveal herself? "Um, Adams, I mean Archer, what is a mry?"

And she sucked in her breath, as he started rubbing her butt slowly, punctuating his speech with squeezes.

"I knew you were the girl for me. The moment Mot showed me your photo; I knew you were my mry, my beloved. I have been looking for you for centuries, and then, like the twisted arm of Ra, there you were, on Mot's computer screen. And I knew. I made certain those Greek fools gave the gift to you, my dear, so that you would come to me. You had to invite me; it is our way. So I sent you that email. I couldn't have been clearer. You were supposed to call me. But then you ran off with that ridiculous boy, and I knew that I would have to punish you for your disobedience. It made me sad to know that I might have to disfigure my beloved, but there you have it, the life of a demon is not easy."

Hannah swallowed convulsively, trying to absorb the twisted train of Adams' thoughts. He was on a roll, "And please call me Sek, darling. Archer Adams is my fake name. I have a very important job to do for Apep, my boss, and when it looked like you were refusing to play your part, I thought I was going to have to torture you to make you do it, and that also made me sad. No one likes to torment their one and only, unless it's all in good fun. A job is a job and I have a living to make. But then, in the garden, when you spoke so eloquently of your hatred of the Olympians, and your love of power, oh…how my heart soared! And then I knew, we were of one mind, and it only made me more certain of you, my other half."

She had to calculate quickly; if Adams was playing her, what would he gain? Could he be calling her bluff, trying to make her admit she'd been lying? But he could have done that without all of this "beloved" crap. She replayed her conversation with Hermes; he had said that Adams had insisted on her getting the gift, but Hermes had assumed that was because he thought Adams was looking for a gift girl he could easily manipulate. But if Adams had intended to torture whoever had the gift to use it to destroy the Greek gods, why would he need someone accommodating? Wouldn't it serve to reason that anyone could be accommodating when it came to torture? Maybe Adams had picked her for more personal reasons. Oh, god, he was still talking….

The Myth of Cassandra

"After we dispose of this job, we must get away. I want to take you to my favorite place in the world and show you its treasures, its hidden gems, its $10 black jack tables...Mohegan Sun! I know some people think Vegas is the end all and be all for demon vacations, but it's so obvious, and it's crawling with low level demons. Scum, really. There is something so private about Mohegan Sun! "

He had reached the top of the monument and slid her forward in his arms, nuzzling her neck. Hannah flung her head back and screamed directly in his face. Startled, Adams dropped her onto the hard concrete of the landing, and she felt the jolt on her coccyx, certain that she'd broken her recently molested bottom. The angry glare she shot at him was authentic, and she grabbed at her ankle for good measure. He claimed to love her and admire her love of power, maybe she could use that to her advantage. "You hurt me!" she accused. "How can you claim to be my beloved, and then toss me around like a sack of potatoes? Why would you treat me so? First you bang my broken ankle and then you drop me on the floor! Do you care so little for my comfort?" Hannah held her breath, waiting to see how he would respond.

It worked like a charm. "Oh, my darling, of course not. Here, sit here," and he waved his hand, filling the concrete landing with luxurious silk pillows, lifting her onto them. "Is that better, my vengeful dove?"

She raised one eyebrow imperiously. "Somewhat." Since then he'd been rambling on about how he wanted to shower her with gifts, but that first they must execute the plan. He explained that Apep was really the best of gods— so disdainful, so evil. Who could ask for a better master? And then he laid out in detail why Apep wanted revenge and what he, Sek, wanted her to say to destroy the Olympians. That sent him off on his favorite topic, how lame and pathetic the Olympians were.

He was so caught up in his recitation he did not hear what Hannah heard. Her heart kicked up a notch, whether from fear or relief she couldn't say. It was a man's voice, counting: 292, 293, 294. It wasn't just any man's voice. It was John's.

Hermes

Time is one-directional

Hermes pressed the heels of his hands over his eyes and tried to erase the sight in front of him. It had all happened so quickly. Over before it started. He replayed the events in his mind, wondering if he could have done something to change the outcome.

The Line Boy reached the 294th step and stood there, silently staring at the space in front of him. He reached his hands out and said her name and the air in front of him slid open and they were all on the landing together: Hannah, Sek, Line Boy, Lee, and himself.

He wasn't prepared for what was revealed. Hannah was sitting atop a pile of silk cushions, with Sek kneeling in front of her, one hand on his heart, the other clasping H's hand. As the illusion faded and Line Boy became visible, H moved without a look back. She leapt off the pillows and flung herself at Line Boy, who caught her with one arm, sliding her behind him as he turned to face Sek. She yelled and tried to push her way to the front, but Line Boy was surprisingly strong.

For an instant, he thought he saw a look of anguish on Sek's face as Hannah ran to Line Boy, as if the demon had lost everything. It was so fleeting. He must have imagined it.

Because the look he was certain he saw on Sek's face in the next moment was hatred, pure and brilliant. And without a word Sek flicked his hand, the one that had been over his heart, and Line Boy fell to the ground, unmoving. Hannah screamed for the fourth time that night, and Sek disappeared on the spot.

He had no explanation for why he hadn't stopped the demon, hadn't protected Line Boy. All he could think was that it happened so fast. He pressed his hands harder against his eyes until he saw bright spots, and

The Myth of Cassandra

yet when he looked again at the landing, the sight of H weeping over Line Boy had not changed. Ignoring Lee, who was pulling on his sleeve, he turned his back to give H a moment of privacy.

CHAPTER TWENTY-FOUR

A Search for Answers

Hannah

Attempts at CPR

"John, John, John." She repeated his name quietly, in counterpoint to her desperate attempt to find a pulse on his neck, but he was stiff all over, and so cold. She tried to start compressions on his chest, but she couldn't push down. Why couldn't she push down? "Do something, Hermes. Please, do something, anything, he's not moving, please … please, Hermes! Bring him back, please…can't you make a deal with Hades, get him back…I know you can do that…. Do it, just do it, please."

Hermes knelt next to her and gently pulled her arms way from John's chest. "I can't do that. Shh…easy…it doesn't work like that."

She twisted away from his touch. "Why didn't you protect him! You could have protected him! You just stood there and let him kill John! You could have stopped it! You let him die!" She shoved him back so hard he hit the wall, her anger amplifying her strength.

Hermes was rubbing his elbow, the concern on his face tinged with anger, "You're stronger than you look, H. I don't take kindly to being pushed around by a human, but you're grieving, so I'll cut you some slack." He walked a few steps away, and then faced her, enumerating his points on his fingers, "First of all, it's highly unlikely that Line…" but her icy look must have given him pause, "unlikely that John would go to

The Myth of Cassandra

Hades when he died. Only true worshippers of the Olympians travel to Hades when they die. So there is no bartering for his soul. And second, I wish I had stopped Sek. Not only stopped him from killing John, but stopped him from getting away. I'm no closer to learning his plan for destroying my gods." He reached out to touch Hannah's shoulder, but she shrugged him off. "I am sorry, H. He's gone. There's nothing we can do about it."

She would not let him go. She just needed to save him. Think. Running her hands across his shoulders, she couldn't seem to move his clothes. "We have to call 911, I want to try CPR, but I can't get his coat off, I don't understand. What did Sek do to him?"

Lee cleared his throat, "Um, knowing Sek, he probably used the Ka expulsion curse— it would smash the life force, the Ka, out of him. No one can live when their Ka is removed from their corporal body."

"I don't understand; would that make his clothes stick?" She felt the tears streaming down her face, tasted them on her lips. She could hear that her voice was shaking, that the anger that had given her strength was quickly being replaced with despair, and she lowered her head to John's chest. It was so cold.

From behind her she heard the little demon approach. "No, his clothes are sticking because in the moment before Sek cursed your friend, I cursed him, freezing him. That's why you can't move his clothes, and that is why you can't push down on his chest. He's frozen."

Lifting her head, she stared at him, and he smiled at her, cautiously. She reached out to him, desperation pushing at her from all sides, making her voice strident, angry. "I don't understand, did you kill him?"

Lee backed up quickly, "No, no..."

She leapt up, but before she could reach him, ask him what he meant, he took another step back away from her, and stepped into air. With a small, "Oh no," he fell down the stairs, head over heels. All two hundred and ninety-four of them. At least that's what it sounded like to her, as each impact was punctuated by an "oomph" or an "ouch." At the end of the fall, the silence was ominous.

"Great work, H. Now I have to go and get him— he's my assistant. I can't leave him for the police to find." Hermes turned to head down the stairs, but Hannah grabbed his arm.

"Wait! Did he mean "no" I didn't kill him? Could John still be in there? Frozen? Or was he just afraid of me?" She held her breath, wanting the answer to be the first, staring at Hermes like she could make it true.

He shook her hand off. "Really, H? The only person who can answer that question is at the bottom of these stairs, most likely unconscious. You might have thought of that before you pushed him."

She didn't bother to correct him. She might as well have pushed him. She touched John's face, terrified by how cold it was, and whispered, "What do we do now, Hermes?"

"Well, I will go get Lee. Then we need to go. I don't feel like explaining to the police what we are doing with a most likely dead Line Boy Popsicle and an unconscious demon in an historic landmark."

"Oh..." Only now did Hannah notice the increasingly loud sirens. She felt stupid from grief and she found herself baffled by Hermes' rapid-fire banter. "Go? Go where?"

"To Hera of course. She has some decent healing abilities. At least good enough to heal Lee, and then he can answer your questions about John. So we have to get them to Cambridge, preferably before the authorities show up. Not enough time for me to make two trips. So while I fetch the little guy, why don't you figure out how we can all make it out in one trip..."

Hannah stared at John on the floor, and struggled to think, the welter of emotions threatening to swamp her. If it was possible that he was still alive, then she needed to act like he was and solve the problem of getting them all out of here in one trip. She let her mind go blank and found herself thinking of a book from her childhood where Big Bird had to stack boxes to reach the sugar on the top shelf of Mr. Hooper's store, Big Bird's Big Blunder. Big Bird had mistakenly stacked the smallest boxes on the bottom, causing it to all tip over when he tried to climb up. Apparently the book was interested in teaching size differentiation, but

Hannah had always felt as if Big Bird had been set up by Mr. Hooper. Why hadn't he given Big Bird a stepladder? Who the hell climbs up boxes? Clearly an OSHA violation.

She rubbed her face with both hands. Focus. What was the question? Right. How to get out of here in one trip? She looked up from John's face and saw that Hermes was already back, standing next to her on the landing, the little demon all crumpled in his arms. "What if we stack up? Big to little. John is stiff, which makes him a great base. If I sit on John and hold Lee, can you carry us all?"

Hermes pursed his lips, "Not a bad idea, H. We might as well try. Stand back; I need a little room..."

"Room for wha..." But the explosion of the top of the Bunker Hill Memorial flying into the air and then crashing down answered her question. She stared at Hermes. "You could have killed someone..." and she ran to the exposed edge of the monument, hanging over it to see the tip of the monument wedged between two apartment buildings across the street. The sounds of the fire engines were now ear splitting and joined by the yells of the firemen as they stormed the monument at its base. She looked back to Hermes, who was holding out Lee to her.

"Come now, H. I am sure Charlestown's finest have this under control. We really have to fly." And he lowered Lee into her arms. Though he was not too heavy, he was weirdly slippery and smelled of bleu cheese. Hermes had picked John up and was holding him like a lunch tray. "All aboard the frozen Line Boy express."

Hermes seemed to be enjoying this too much, so she whispered an apology to John as she climbed up on his stomach. At least she hoped he was still there to hear it.

Hermes took to the sky, leaving behind a slew of rescue workers trying to make sense of what had caused a two-ton block of granite to fly into the sky.

✺✺✺✺✺✺✺✺✺✺✺✺

Apollo

Apollo denies himself...sort of

He was having the best day. He was lounging on one of those incredibly comfortable chaises that they have at Palm Springs, all teak and crisp linen. He was sipping on a delicious fruity drink with an umbrella that was being held to his lips by a beautiful woman. A tribe of Amazons was surrounding him, massaging him, while the one with the drink was whispering seductive nothings in his ear.

Ahh. Paradise. I could stay here forever. Except.... Except there was something I was supposed to be doing, wasn't there? Think, Apollo, think. It had something to do with Cassandra.

No, not Cassandra. The girl. What's her name? Hannah. That's right. I needed to save her from the communist. I'd been saving her, hadn't I? Hadn't I been telling the communist how I would crush him? Yes, I had. I'd been telling the longhaired motorcycle boy with Hermes' shoes exactly how I was going to destroy him, when there was a brilliant blue light. That was the last thing I can remember— a bright blue light.

Apollo's eyes snapped open and the sight that met him was a long way from Palm Springs. Instead of a teak and linen chaise, he appeared to be lying on a lumpy old couch that had been marinated in beer, pot, and yes, just a hint of vomit. He was swallowing some hideous green drink that tasted like shoe, and while the women who were tending him were extra tall and beautiful, he counted carefully, yep, two breasts per woman: definitely not Amazons. The only part of his dream that was surpassed by this reality was the tiny brunette beauty sitting at his side, smiling at him.

"How are you feeling? Do you still think you are Apollo?" Apollo winced and closed his eyes. There was no way a voice that loud and big came from such a small person. He considered how to answer her question. He must've fallen into a trap. The blue light he remembered must've been the result of a curse from an enemy. But who? Were these women his enemies?

The Myth of Cassandra

They could be one of those Gaia sects— they'd never let him live down his childhood mistake of killing that stinking dragon. How was he supposed to know that Python was Gaia's child? He didn't look a thing like her. But if they were Gaia's minions, why would the little one want to know if he was okay? And why would she want him to deny himself? There was only one way to find out.

"I am Apollo. And I feel like hell, just for the record. Who are you and what do you want? Are you working for Gaia?" Apollo tried to sit up. He didn't get far.

The little one barked out, 'All oars hold!" and the four women on either side of him pinned him down. It must have been the aftereffect of the curse that had been used on him, because he found himself completely trapped and unable to throw the women off. The little one picked up the cup with the disgusting green drink in it and held it to his lips, a concerned frown marring her adorable brow.

"Abe said that it might take some time for you to come down. Here, I know this smells awful, but it'll help you rest while you wind down, and you won't be plagued by those delusions and paranoia. It's for your own good." Apollo clamped down his lips and shook his head, but she smiled again, and held his nose until he opened his mouth to breath, and she poured it down his throat. He swallowed to keep from choking and felt the effects of the drink immediately. As he was drifting back into his Palm Springs dream, he felt her fingers lightly stroke his forehead and heard her whisper in his ear, "Just rest. Everything will look better when you wake up."

He had no idea how long he had been under, but as he felt himself resurfacing again, the images of luxury and comfort were replaced by the reality of dingy, beer-soaked lumpiness again. The only constant was the lovely face of the sprite, who appeared to be either his captor, or his nurse, he was still unsure of which. He feigned sleep while he listened to the women around him talk. They were saying something about the time at the split and complaining about someone named Carol catching a crab. Were they a strange band of fisherwomen? Wait... now they were talking about him...

"I hope he wakes up himself. He may not be Apollo, but he could pass for a god. He is fine. I wouldn't mind helping him get in touch with reality." Murmured laughter and agreement. "I called first dibs, Wendy, so get in line." More catcalls, followed by what must have been Wendy's complaint, "It isn't like he is a favorite spot on the couch, Nan, you can't just claim him." This was met with a third woman's exclamation, "I'd like to recline on him." Louder laughter. Apollo was starting to feel distinctly uncertain as to whether he should open his eyes or not. But then he heard the loud bell tones of his sprite as she took control of the Amazonian women. How did such a loud voice come from such a tiny person?

"Settle down, settle down. Wendy and Nan, hold off. Abe said that we were to keep him company, not defrock him. If he's feeling better, we can invite him to the Deke party tonight, and then you can both take a shot at him. For now, our goal is to help him come down from his trip and get him back on his feet. And if I am not wrong, I think our guest is awake, aren't you?" Apollo smiled slightly as she ran her fingers across his brow, repeating in a whisper, "Aren't you?"

This time he was ready to say anything to avoid that disgusting drink. "I am awake. And I feel so much better. If I could just get some water, I think I'll be able to get up and..." And Apollo's attempt to sit up was stalled by her small hand on his chest.

"Whoa. Slow down. Here let the girls help you sit up. You need to take it one step at a time…. Hey, what is your name?" The sprite was smiling at him while the other women were easing him forward on the couch.

"My name is….my name really is Apollo." Her cute brow wrinkled up, but before she could force-feed him that vile herbal concoction he clarified, "My mom was really into the Greek myths— she named all of us after the gods. I was the lucky one. My poor brother has had to go around named Hephaestus. It must have been why I thought I really was Apollo, when you know, I was high…." Archer had taught him that the best lies were those that were closest to the truth. He ended with a sheepish grin that had all the women sighing, all but the sprite. She still had a small furrow on her brow. On her perfect brow. She was delightful. He just wanted to pick her up and fly her to his home in the... Oh yeah, he no longer had a home in the sky. Well, he could take her camping... Yeah, that'd be nice. His sister Artemis always knew the best camping sites. He could impress the sprite with his knowledge of the constellations and his ability to make fire. He would pledge his undying love. He was jostled out of his camping daydream by the suspicion in her tone.

"I should probably call my brother, to check you out."

The Amazons looked ready to grab him again. But he had already figured out that they only acted when his sprite ordered them to. He ignored them and looked directly into her eyes. "You have made me better." The blush spreading over her cheeks gave him the confidence to act. He stood up and when no one stopped him, stretched his arms over his head, taking care to flex all of his muscles, to the appreciative murmurs of the Amazons. Kneeling at his sprite's feet, he pressed a kiss onto her wrist, "Thank you for taking care of me. I am in your debt. I have to go take care of a small detail, and then I was wondering if I might see you tonight, at a certain party..."

She smiled widely. "Yes. Definitely. Please come back. Here. Tonight."

She was so perfect, he had to resist the urge to scoop her up and take her with him, but he had learned that modern women were resistant to abduction. Whether she was an actual wood sprite or not, she was clearly modern. So he would court her at the party. "I'll find you here. Tonight."

She nodded, and just like that, he felt his energy come back in full force. Love. He was in love with her! He'd been in love before and knew that this was it. He stood up; clearly a foot taller than her, kissed the top of her head and headed off into the faint light of dusk to find Archer in Cambridge. He would just tell Archer that he needed to postpone his return to Olympus. It no longer seemed as important. He would just take the gift back from the girl. It was his gift after all. Or, he could let Hera take care of it all. Yes. That was better. He didn't have time to fix it himself. He had a party he didn't want to miss.

CHAPTER TWENTY-FIVE

Everybody Hurts, Sometimes

❂❂❂

Hera

Patience is not her strong suit

Hera fidgeted with the belt around her waist, and grimaced. It galled her that Adams had played her. She'd rationalized her inaction as discretion, and that was weak, wasn't it? He'd known just how to manipulate both her and Zeus so that they did what he wanted. She'd allowed that sniveling thing to shut her up using her own martial insecurities against her. Well, that was both a mistake she would not repeat and one someone else would have to pay for. It might as well be the girl. She was disposable.

On the other hand, the girl's mother claimed that the girl had a plan to gain information about Adams' plan, all to ingratiate herself with Hera and Zeus. At least the girl understood whom she was dealing with. Bribery was number eight on the list of ways to graciously return a gift. And she would be pleased to get the goods on Adams; it would decide her bet with Zeus, and while she did not relish another story of his salacious ways, a year of fidelity would certainly provide her with satisfaction, however temporary. If the girl could deliver, she might be magnanimous. The parents were another story. Blackmail was a one-way ticket to garden gnome status.

The Myth of Cassandra

She and Zeus had been mid-way through a rather complicated version of position 37 in the Kama Sutra when the woman's clipped tones had made them lose their balance and tumble off the ottoman.

"Excuse me, Zeus and Hera, if you could please cover yourselves, anything will do— the curtains, the tablecloth, you know, any of the fabrics that you haven't already destroyed in your relations. Just wrap them around yourselves so that you are decently attired. I have a small announcement to make, and I would appreciate your complete attention."

She'd lifted her head off the floor from where she'd landed and stared at the monitor over the fireplace, stunned by the words that had emitted from it. The monitor no longer showed a scene in the garden, but instead the disapproving face of what had to be the mother of the gift girl. She didn't really look like her daughter, her feature were more elegant, more classically beautiful. But she had the same determined aloofness that her daughter projected in the videos she had made as the SOT. Hera admired aloofness, but only in herself. She much preferred to be addressed by humans cowering with fear.

Nevertheless, she also preferred to be clothed when punishing said humans. Turning her back on the cameras mounted on the fireplace, she had rifled through the items that hadn't been destroyed in their tête-à-tête. She belted a cashmere throw around her body, found her shoes, and threw her suit jacket on over the whole ensemble. Zeus had made his way to the couch, a tablecloth draped in toga fashion around his powerful build. He'd found another brownie and was already halfway through it. Hmm...maybe she should say something to him about his eating habits...a "powerful" build could quickly become a "stocky" build and then it was just one tray of microwave brownies until one had no "build" at all. Yes, she would talk to him about making healthy food choices and now that she was really looking at him, he needed a haircut....

"Excuse me, Hera, if you could please join Zeus on the couch, I'd like to begin."

Hera jumped a little and frowned at the woman on the monitor. She did not like to be interrupted when she was silently improving her husband, and she was never reprimanded, especially by a human. The punishment she had envisioned for the woman's temerity progressed to a smiting. She would smite this woman. As soon as the woman finished whatever it was she wanted to say. "Yes, fine. What is your name again?" And she perched on the couch next to Zeus attempting to remove the brownie from his hand nonchalantly. The reaction was instantaneous.

"Get your hands off my brownie, woman!" He stood moved to the armchair and took a huge bite, glaring at her while he chewed.

"As I said before, my name is Elise Summers. I am Hannah's mother. You do know who Hannah is, yes? The girl you "gifted"? The girl who is currently risking her life to help you figure out what Archer Adams is up to? You do know that girl." The woman paused and seemed to collect herself, because she continued with much more control, "Well, I am her mother, and I invited you here, provided you with hospitality, of which you have definitely, ahem, availed yourselves, and now I have a proposition for you." The woman's voice had started out strained and anxious, but by the end she was becoming more confident, and Hera had found herself leaning forward, curious.

"I propose that you take back the gift. Completely. Immediately. And erase the effects of anything she has said in the last three days. And to help convince you to do the right thing, my husband and I have a short video we would be compelled to release over the Internet if you do not cooperate. Hit it, Tom."

And with that, the screen no longer showed a haughty blonde woman making demands of the gods, but instead it was filled with images of their lovemaking set to the tune of The Sound of Music theme. The hills were certainly alive… and what was he doing with that spatula? That could explain some of her more exotic aches. But Zeus's snickering brought her back to where she was, and she'd had enough.

"Stop it. Now." When the blonde woman was once again on the screen, she continued, "I think you and your husband should come here so that we can work out the details of this arrangement in person. I find video conferencing so impersonal…"

The Myth of Cassandra

"Good. I am so glad that you agree. We'll be there in just a minute." And then as she'd walked off camera they heard her say, "Tom, it worked! We did it!" and the screen went black.

Zeus had laughed out loud. "Are you really that embarrassed by a silly little video? You surprise me, Hera. The Hera I married would have pulverized a human for even thinking of something as impudent as blackmail. Do you remember that Mycenaean woman who demanded that you..."

"Don't be so dense. I didn't invite her to come here to agree to her demands. It is simply easier to turn humans into stone in person. Don't you think they would make a lovely addition to the garden?" Hera tightened her belt. "Besides, who sets a sex tape to Rodgers and Hammerstein? I should punish them for that alone," and she'd flexed her fingers, ready to mete out some Olympian justice.

Since then she'd been waiting. She hated being kept waiting. She turned sharply towards the monitor over the fireplace, as once again the thin-nosed blonde woman filled the screen.

"I'm so sorry, but we've been trying to disable the lock on our door. You see, Hermes locked us in."

Hera, done with excuses, raised her arm to curse them, wherever they were, when she was startled by the familiar sound of Hermes and Apollo bickering. Looking over her shoulder at the doorway, she could see Hermes carrying a stack of bodies and Apollo, who had wedged himself into the doorway with them, yelling at Hermes to give way. Zeus was pointing at the scene and giggling, providing no leadership whatsoever. The woman on the screen started yelling for Hannah, who appeared to be one of the bodies in Hermes arms, and that started Apollo yelling, "Where? Where is Hannah?" Hera rolled her eyes at the chaos, waved her hand, causing the room to be cast in impenetrable darkness. The silence was immediate.

"I'm going to turn the lights back on, but I want everyone to stay silent. I will ask the questions." As the lights came back on, she was sitting in the armchair, looking down at them, for all the world like she was holding court in Olympus, except that Zeus was lying on his back on the floor, engrossed in the shape of his hand. Okay, not quite Olympus, but it would have to do. She leveled a cool stare at Hermes and commanded, "I want to know what happened with Archer Adams, but be succinct. I have postponed my punishment of the couple in the control room for too long, and I would hate to lose the edge of my anger. Hermes, speak!"

CHAPTER TWENTY-SIX

The Gift

❀❀❀

Hannah

Setting priorities

Blinking rapidly to adjust to the sudden brightness after the equally sudden darkness, Hannah scanned the room from her perch up on top of John. Given Hera's alarming declaration of her intention to curse her parents, she tried to decipher what might have happened here. Food and dishes were splattered on the floor, the couch had been flipped over onto its back, and there appeared to be a curtain hanging from the light fixture in the center of the room. Also, Hera seemed to be wearing a blanket and Zeus was rolling on the floor wrapped in a tablecloth eating one brownie after another. Was that a hickey on Hera's neck? Eew. If Zeus and Hera had been doing what it looked like, what could her parents' participation have been? She consoled herself with the observation that whatever involvement they had, it must have been remote, because she could see both her parents on the monitor, still in the control room. So what could they have done to incur Hera's wrath?

She worked to order her emotions quickly. She now had two diametrically opposed dictates fighting in her brain: She had to get Hera to understand quickly what had happened with Sek so that she could ask her to heal Lee, who could help John. Hopefully. She had spent the ride here frantically making all kinds of lists in her head about the likelihood that John was still alive inside his frozen body. Every thought she'd had since Lee's ambiguous declaration was that they had to hurry, that there might still be time for John.

But now she was worried about her parents. She had to have enough time to figure out what her parents, most likely her mother, had done to tick off Hera, and then figure out something to mollify the Goddess of Hearth and Home. She needed things to move slowly, so she could protect them. Fast but slow. How do you go fast and slow at the same time?

She was interrupted in this frantic inner dialogue with herself by Hermes' quiet voice in her ear, "H, can you hop off the Line Boy Express here? I'd like to have my hands free when I make my case to Hera." And he looked pointedly at Hera, who seemed to have gotten even angrier in the last ten seconds.

"Sure." Hannah hopped off John, only now realizing that her butt had gone numb from sitting on him. She looked down at Lee, still unconscious in her arms, and could make out no less than eight raised bumps on his head, not including his horns. Lee. She needed to get Hera to save Lee, so Lee could save John, and then she would figure out how to save her parents from cursed poison ivy, or medieval boils, or whatever punishment Hera had in mind. That was the answer; fast then slow. She discreetly turned towards Hermes, who was leaning the frozen John up against the bookcases that lined the wall to the left of the door and whispered, "Hermes, we need to get Hera to heal Lee so he can unfreeze John, right away..."

Hermes' look was unreadable. She couldn't even tell if he'd heard her. He walked past her to the center of the room without a single indication that he'd help. What did she expect? Hera was clearly out for blood, and Hermes was nothing if not protective of his own. Hannah bit back her impatience and waited to hear what he'd say. Shifting Lee's weight in her arms, she watched Hermes launch into an excessively flattering description of the goddess, followed by a listing of each point in the adventure, and his own successes when confronted with adversity. He'd found out who Archer really was with his thorough investigation. He'd hunted down the gift girl using his amazing powers of deduction.

Aside from being nauseatingly self-serving, Hermes' story was completely not working. Hera's face had gotten, if possible, more severe.

He'd reached the part of the story where Sek had trapped him in the door (Hannah knew this because Sek had bragged about how easy it had been to trap Hermes on the flight to the monument)....

"Apollo had followed our decoy and I found myself detained..."

"I did not follow a decoy! I was heroically rescuing the gift girl from the communist!" Apollo had leapt to the front of the room and had literally shoved Hermes aside. "I can't stand by and let him lie to you, Aunt Hera. And why is he telling you that Archer is some demon named Sek? Archer wasn't the enemy. The enemy is the frozen communist over there," and with this he pointed at John, who was slowly slipping down the wall.

"Oh!" Hannah shoved Lee into Hermes' arms and got to John just in time to keep him from hitting the floor. "Umph." She levered him back against the bookcase, murmuring an apology as his head hit with a thud against a thick, leather bound book. Hannah's eyes widened at the title on the spine, Boswell's *Life of Johnson*. Wasn't that one of John's bathroom books? Could books take revenge? She angled his body towards Hera so he could watch what was happening, desperately hoping that he was still in there to witness it.

Satisfied he would stay put, she looked for herself. What she saw reminded her vaguely of watching the Three Stooges. Hermes pushed in front of Apollo, dropping Lee into Apollo's arms, apparently having decided that it would be best if he delivered the bad news himself, "Sek trapped me in the door, and he ran away to Bunker Hill with Hannah, but he escaped before I could find out what he was up to or destroy him. I had a plan to expose and catch him, but golden boy here ruined it all with his incredible stupidity..."

Apollo hip-checked Hermes, then tossed Lee in the general direction of Hermes, who caught him, barely. "Hold your own pet, Hermes. He's staining my sweater; it's a linen/silk blend, very hard to clean." Apollo smiled up at Hera, "Listen, Hera, we all know that Messenger Boy has been jealous of me for decades. He's lying, about everything. Archer was just a publicist, not a demon. What a story! As much as I would love to sit around and watch you deal out some Olympian justice on the humans and Messenger Boy here, I have to go, a new deal brewing, big stuff, big stuff, and I have to fan the flames, you know, stock the pond, gild the lily and such. I was only coming back to tell Archer that I want to put a hold on this whole "worship me" thing." He walked over to Hera and kissed her on the cheek. "You look fabulous, by the way, this color brown is really good on you. Have you been working out? Because you are glowing...."

Hera's voice was thin and it seemed to take her great effort to speak, "What, exactly, do you mean, "I'm out of this whole 'worship me' thing"? Explain yourself. And please refrain from the unnecessary compliments, as it just wastes my time."

Apollo, who'd been backing out of the room toward the door, stopped, shock clearly registering on his face. "What? I was just telling the truth, you look fabu..."

"Sit down, NOW," and she pointed at the couch, which flipped back upright, "and answer one simple, direct question, Apollo. What "new" plan are you pursuing now? What plan is so enticing that you'll abandon your father and me, who have spent considerable time and resources trying to make your most recent plan work? Please, I need to know."

Hannah was amazed by Apollo's reaction. He seemed to be impervious to sarcasm. Perhaps he was too dumb to really understand Hera's question, because he launched into the most ridiculous speech...

"You know, dear Hera, how much I appreciate your help, all of your help. But I know how much you want me to be independent, and now I have a plan to be that, to be independent with the help of my wood sprite, at least I think she's wood sprite. She looks like a wood sprite. I don't know her name, but she's the one. The most perfect woman. She is small and perfect and has an army of Amazons, or at least Amazon-like women, though they do have both breasts, so they aren't technically speaking, Amazons, but I am sure they are her servants. At least she has a clarion voice that keeps them all under her control. It's so thrilling to watch her order them around. She has invited me to come to her party

The Myth of Cassandra

tonight at Deke house, and I will go and be her king, and together we will rule the Amazon-like women. It's my destiny." He smiled his brightest wattage grin and batted his eyelashes at Hera.

But as the light from Apollo's spark started to fade, it was clear that Hera was not pleased. An idiot could tell that she was furious. Even Apollo figured it out.

Before Hera could speak, Apollo scrambled, "Well, it was terribly great of you to support me and Zeus, and to foot the bill and all, but as you can see Zeus, well, he's not really committed to the project. " Everyone looked at Zeus as he snored lightly, curled into the fetal position on the floor. From her vantage point, Hannah could see that he was sucking his thumb. Apollo continued, "And if Hermes has driven away Archer, the publicist to the stars, well, that leaves us without representation, and you can't do anything these days without representation. It just seems right to take it as a sign. If you want to blame someone, blame the gift girl. She never did what she was supposed to. She openly defied us. That's terrible. Really very insulting. And Hermes, of course. Since he picked her, I think you could say that they share the blame for this failure. Let me know if you need my help punishing them, you can reach me on my cell...." Apollo shook his head sadly and slowly started to inch out of the room.

"Apollo. Do not leave this room until I give you explicit permission to do so." Turning from the God of the Sun, Hera's gaze narrowed in on Hannah, who resisted the temptation to look away, "I will hear from the girl."

Hannah found the eyes of all on her. It was her moment. What was it her mother had told her, the years spent learning how to read what people wanted to hear was not a waste, but a skill with its uses? Besides, she knew the truth about why Sek had conned Apollo and what his plan for the "gift" had been. She could use that information to protect the people she cared about. She marshaled her thoughts and gave herself a quick mental pep talk: Summers, you know this goddess inside and out. Aside from four years of studying the classics, you've listened to your mother dissect every issue of *Ladies' Home and Hearth* for the last ten years. You can do this; pull yourself together and out-think this situation. People you care about are counting on you to do this right.

She bowed her head, hoping that her skill would be enough, and decided on her story.

She walked over to Hermes. "Can I have Lee, please."

He handed Lee over and whispered, "Good luck, H. You've got one shot, I hope you know what you're doing, I've grown accustomed to your...."

"Yeah, yeah. Don't worry, Hermes; I'm not going to throw you under the proverbial bus; just follow my lead." She smiled at him and knowing the gamble she was taking, turned her back on Hermes, and walked toward Hera, lifting Lee up in the air like a sacrificial offering. "Thank you, Hera. It's time you got the full truth. As much as all of us, Hermes, Apollo, my parents, my friends, and I have worked together to bring down Archer Adams, the demon Sek, and defend your honor, it was this magnificent creature, Lee, who succeeded. For you. It was his bravery that led to Sek's defeat. And Sek was defeated due to Lee's heroics, Sek fled, a broken demon. And his plans to destroy the Olympians were equally broken." Walking closer to Hera, Hannah cradled Lee and feigned adoration as she gazed on his face. "Lee, this...guy, he suffered greatly in the final battle. I am so distressed by his injuries that I find it difficult to speak. If you could but heal him, with your tremendous powers, then I would feel free to share the full story with you." Hannah tried to project subservience out of every pore in her body, looking down at the floor and holding her breath. Everything depended on whether Hera's curiosity about Sek's plan outweighed the affront to her ego at being given a condition to continue. It would either work, or Hannah could resign herself to becoming a shrubbery. She wondered if she would know if she had been turned into a bush, or if she would simply stop knowing....

The Myth of Cassandra

Elise

Inside the Control Room

With her finger carefully on the "mute" button, Elise shushed her husband, who was pacing behind her, his hands pulling his hair back from his head, muttering, "What is she doing? Why did she say we were all working with Apollo? Did they really defeat Adams? I mean Sek? I thought Hermes said they'd failed? Why is she trying to help that thing in her arms? Can't you see his horns, Elise? He's some kind of evil thing, isn't he? I mean, horns aren't usually a good sign. What is she doing?"

"Quiet, Tom. She has a plan; I can see it in her eyes. Shh.... Come on Hannah, sweetie..." Tom stopped talking and gripped her shoulders, while she panned the camera back to take in how the other occupants of the room were responding to Hannah's short speech. Hermes' face was carefully blank, Apollo looked like he was trying to solve a very complicated math problem, and Zeus was awake again, but ignoring them all and searching under the table for something, another brownie, perhaps? Elise frowned, wondering what the effect of eating a half-dozen pot brownies would have on a body his size. She had no idea what an overdose of marijuana looked like, but at the least, he was going to make himself sick just from the sugar intake... Focus, Elise. There was that MacCallister boy, frozen stiff in the corner. She was certain that somehow that inert demon was linked to Hannah's frozen friend. Otherwise Hannah would be angling to have Hera heal him first.

Hannah was looking down, almost curtseying, while lifting the demon up. It reminded Elise strongly of Hannah's dancing days, and she was incapable of not flashing back on Hannah at thirteen, dancing the male part in Swan Lake, lifting the prima ballerina up in the air. At the time, Elise had felt embarrassment, and she blushed now with the shame of it. All she could think at the time was how much she wished Hannah had been wearing a tutu, worried that other people might think her daughter was somehow manly. That had been the last recital Hannah had danced in. She tried to remember what reasons she'd used to dissuade Hannah from dancing, and she couldn't remember what they'd been. Now, as she looked at her daughter, all she could think was how strong she was. How brave. Breathe, Elise, breathe. This is not the time to cry. Her daughter might need her.

She angled the camera on Hera. The time since Hannah's request had stretched out until it was as thin as paper, and Hera's face was still, any calculations she might be making carefully guarded. With a brief nod, she finally spoke, "Bring him closer, I will need to touch him to heal him. What is his name again?" Though Hannah's face was carefully demure, Elise thought she could see the excitement in her daughter's eyes.

"Oh, Tom. It might work! Whatever she has planned, this was the first step...."

"Shhh...Elise. We don't want to miss a word."

Hermes had stepped forward to help Hannah bring the little demon to Hera in her chair. Hera laid her hands on the demon's head, murmuring words, almost singing, ending with the words, "Wake, Lee."

Hannah was looking anxiously down into Lee's face, and her look of relief as the little demon opened his eyes and grinned weakly at her brought tears stinging back into Elise's eyes. Good lord, you'd think that she cried at everything.

"I have healed your little demon, who was apparently so valiant in my defense, so now I want to hear your story, and I need not remind you of what hinges on it...." Hera's voice was cold and metallic, and Hannah looked at Hermes, a wordless request passing between them. As Hannah rose again and curtsied, Elise saw Hermes carrying Lee to the frozen boy in the corner, whispering in his ear. Elise knew that she could angle the microphone to pick up their conversation, but Hannah had started to speak, and all of her attention was fixed on her daughter, addressing Hera, the goddess of hearth and home, in all of her wrathful glory.

"First, I need to let Apollo know that Archer is no longer around, having been vanquished by Lee, and so he can stop pretending that he doesn't know that Archer Adams was really Sek, minion of Apep, Egyptian god of evil. Apollo played one of the most important roles in the entire plan, pretending to believe Archer was a publicist and that he was clueless about Archer's evil plan. Apollo was the only one with the acting talent to pull off such a critical deception; only a genius could be so believably gullible. But my admiration for Apollo takes me too far ahead in the story." Hannah's gushing stopped abruptly as she stared raptly at Apollo and then dramatically tearing her gaze from him, she took a slow deep breath, looked up at Hera and spoke, "I should start at the beginning."

Elise wasn't certain, but she thought she heard Hermes laugh out loud at the part about Apollo's talent, but it appeared that he had merely swallowed wrong, as she could see Lee banging on his back. The MacCallister boy was no longer frozen. He was slumped on the floor, shaking, and he looked a horrible green color. At least he seemed to be alive....

"The story, as I know it, began when I received that email from Archer, informing me that the Olympic Gods had gifted me to make reparations for Cassandra. I was immediately suspicious, for with the small knowledge I have from my studies of the Olympians, I could not fathom them ever making reparations. Reparations would imply that you had something to apologize for, some reason to make amends. That was clearly ridiculous. Gods do not make mistakes. So we, my friends Carl and John and I," at this point Hannah looked to John, her smile eliciting the first signs of life from the boy. She pivoted back to Hera, "We decided not to contact Archer Adams, but instead try to figure out what might be going on. By that time I had become aware of my gift and was witnessing the chaos it was creating, so I made a recording with my best attempts to bring balance back, but you no doubt have seen how that worked. It has been an unqualified disaster."

"Carl stayed behind to distract the media, while John and I traveled to your home on Martha's Vineyard to find out what might be truly going on. Hermes found us immediately; his skills at investigation made it impossible for us to evade him, and after determining that we were indeed on the side of right, he informed us of your brilliant plan. Hermes explained that you had decided to let Archer play out his scenario, letting him choose the gift girl, while Apollo had agreed to act as if he trusted Archer implicitly. Hermes' role was to appear incompetent at bringing us in, while we were to run, until finally, let Archer catch us, here in Cambridge. John and Carl were to act as decoys, supposedly leading Apollo away, and Hermes acted as if he was stupid enough to be caught in Archer's trap in the door, all so that I would be left alone with Archer. To convince him I was on his side, so that he would reveal the full plan."

"And it all would have worked. But I messed up. I found that when I needed to lie about how much I despised the Olympians, I could not do it convincingly. Archer saw through my lie and whisked me away to the Bunker Hill Memorial to torture me into playing my part to use the gift to destroy you all."

"But like any arrogant evil villain, he seemed compelled to tell me in detail his entire plan. He explained that his master, Apep, had been disgusted by a movie released many years ago, *The Adventures of the Young Sherlock Holmes*, where the Egyptian god of evil is mistakenly identified as Ra. Apparently that mistake happens often, people confusing Ra with Apep, and it was the straw that broke the evil god's back, so to speak. When he looked into it, it turned out that Apollo had been the consultant on the film, and Apep decided to take revenge. It seemed like overkill to me, I mean, the movie wasn't very popular, but it was a Spielberg movie, and there you have it. The Egyptian gods. You know how vain and petty those gods are."

Zeus perked up at this, "So...it wasn't my fault."

"Nor mine. So we both win." Hera's voice dripped with satisfaction. Hannah kept an impressively blank face at the roaring irony of the words coming out of the gods' mouths. Elise frowned, appalled that the gods had apparently wagered on this debacle. It took considerable self-control not to lift her finger off the mute button and lecture them on the evils of gambling. Hannah appeared to take it all in stride, and continued.

"Lee overheard Sek and Apep discussing the plan and was disgusted by both his master's intent, but also by his pathetic vanity. By that time Lee had gotten to know you all, and he was in awe of the depth of your wisdom and restraint, Hera. Compared to you, Apep seemed childish and mean, not at all a master to admire. He approached Hermes and secretly joined forces with us. At the crucial moment when I was about to be tortured by Sek, Lee, Hermes, and John arrived. They all fought bravely, but it was Lee who saved the day, thwarting Apep's plan. Sek did not escape, so much as ran away to hide from Apep's retribution."

Hannah walked forward and lowered into a deep curtsey. "I know that I was the weak link, and that all the others executed your plan brilliantly, but I ask for your compassion. I am merely a human, with all the frailties a human has. I have none of the wisdom, strength, or courage that you all are so gifted with. But I do have humility. I humbly ask for your forgiveness. I also humbly ask that you not punish my parents for whatever it was that they did to offend you. What they did, they did out of love for me. My mother is a devout reader of *Ladies' Home and Hearth*, and is one of your most ardent followers. Everything here is to please you, from the tasteful floral arrangements to the dusted picture frames; she was led by your guidance. Even the brownies came from her kitchen for your pleasure. I ask for your forgiveness for their rash act of protectiveness, whatever it was."

At that Hannah bowed her head and waited in silence. Zeus had drifted over to stand next to Hera while Hannah had been making her case, and he was now whispering in Hera's ear. Hera's impassive face began to redden, and she pushed against his shoulder, batting her lashes at him. She cleared her throat and gripped the arms of the chair, leaning forward ever so slightly.

"Hannah Summers, if I am to believe your recitation, you would claim that Apollo and Hermes, Lee and your friends, even your parents, are all blameless and have acted courageously and honorably to fulfill my brilliant plan, and that it is you alone who have failed me. Is that true?"

Elise found it impossible to protest, as Tom had a firm grip over her mouth, a pose that was mirrored by Hermes and John. Tom whispered, "Wait, look at Hannah, I know my girl, she isn't worried... Wait and see what happens."

Elise zoomed the camera in on Hannah's face and searched it for clues. She pulled Tom's hand down from her mouth and murmured, "I hope you're right."

Hera was continuing to speak. "Apollo, for your inventive display of intelligence, I thank you. You have my blessing to pursue your wood sprite. Hermes, for your diligence in working on my behalf, even to the extent of humiliating yourself by allowing Archer to trap you, you have earned a bonus; consider your houseboat bought and paid for. I will have my accountant take care of the details. Lee, for your courage, you are welcome to continue to work for me, with Hermes, and can consider yourself a minion of the Olympians, with all the protection that alliance provides."

Hera nodded at Hermes, "Bring the boy here, Hermes." John, still a little green, and too weak to walk, was carried to Hera in Hermes' arms, mouth discretely covered by Hermes' hand, his eyes moving wildly back and forth between Hermes, Hera, and Hannah. Hera laid her hands on John and spoke, "For your help to vanquish our enemy, I heal you..." She paused and looked at Hannah, who murmured his name. "I heal you, John MacCallister." John's color came back instantly, and he elbowed Hermes sharply in the chest, causing Hermes to release his mouth. Before he could say anything, Hera was asking, "Where is the other boy?"

John looked fleetingly at Hannah. "Carl's in the hospital in Centreville..."

Hannah's eyes widened, but Hera forestalled any conversation with her announcement, "I have healed him. And now you, Hannah Summers. Your parents, though stupid and ignorant, are forgiven, with the condition that your mother continues to make brownies for Zeus, in perpetuity."

Sitting back in her chair, Hera pointed at Hannah. "As for you, you failed, by your own admission. And so, I will have to punish you. I insist that Apollo take back your gift. You've proven that you are unworthy of such a gift. For the sake of the world, and my own patience, we will also rescind any of the effects of the gift. You will no longer be the SOT, but just plain Hannah. I will force you to go back to your life as it was prior to the gift."

"Despite your failure, I have been impressed with your honesty in relaying the events of the last three days, and for that, I will be making you an offer in the coming days. You will accept it."

Elise watched her daughter drop her head, nodding at the last, rather obscure condition Hera had made. Tom kissed her head, "Hannah did it. She did it. And all you have to do is make a few brownies...."

"Have you seen how many brownies he eats? The cocoa alone will cost a fortune, not to mention the time it will take." Elise started to list the downsides to the arrangement. It was the best defense she had against breaking down and sobbing.

●●●●●●●●●●●●

Lee/Mott

The love of a demon

He wasn't bothered by the lies she'd told. She'd gotten Hera to heal him, which might not have happened if she hadn't painted him as a hero, so her lies were actually pretty great. She even protected Hermes from the embarrassment of being caught by Sek.

She might have been telling the truth about Apep's reasons for attacking the Olympians. Apep and Sek had never told him the plan. The Egyptian gods, though not nearly as obsessed with humans as the Olympians, are vain. Apep more than most. And she was right about Apep's response to Sek's failure to destroy the Olympians. Sek would most certainly hide away, at least for a while.

No. None of that bothered him. What he didn't understand is why she didn't tell them the truth about what broke Sek. That Sek has bonded to her, claimed her as his one and only. And because she chose the boy over him, his heart was broken. Sek's final words had been, "My mry. Mine!" He'd been so surprised when he'd heard Sek's thoughts about Hannah that he almost didn't save the boy in time.

Hannah as Sek's beloved. That would complicate her life. Demons only get one beloved, and they can be really hard to find. The most recent incarnation of his own beloved had been a sea turtle. That had been a wet century ...

Sniffing, he found a tasty bit of bleu cheese under the couch and settled down to savor it while the others discussed traveling back to Centreville. He thought about talking to the girl. Warning her. He'd worked with Sek for a long time, and there was no way he would stay away from his beloved, not for long. And if Sek couldn't convince her to join him in this life, well, he was likely to end hers and wait for her spirit to return in another form. It might have helped her if she told Hera about it. There aren't many beings with enough power to protect her against such an attack, but maybe she didn't say anything about it because she's considering joining Sek?

Lee polished off the cheese and remained silent. Careful observation was often overlooked as a viable way to assert oneself. He'd read that somewhere and thought it was brilliant.

CHAPTER TWENTY-SEVEN

Back Up Plans

●●●

Hannah

Long talks in uncomfortable chairs

Hannah crawled into her bed, kicking off her shoes but not bothering to get undressed. She closed her eyes and scrolled through the events of the last few hours.

After making the appropriate goodbyes to Zeus and Hera, Hermes and Lee, she'd promised her dad to be careful and her mother that she'd call in the morning. Then she and John had left with Apollo, to ride his sun chariot back to Centreville. The flight had been breathtaking. If the view of the earth below weren't stunning enough, the sun horses themselves were mesmerizing. They were majestic and wild and glowed from within. She had wanted the ride to last forever, but it took only ten minutes to arrive at Carl's frat house. In retrospect, that was probably for the best, as John had not enjoyed the trip. He'd started shivering the minute they were air-born. It was ridiculous, but Hannah had felt too self-conscious to hug him to help him warm up, so she'd lent him her sweater. The sweater only made him look colder, somehow, like a really cold, young Mr. Rogers. Clearly there were side effects to being frozen. She only hoped they were short-lived.

After confirming the identity of the "wood sprite" as Naomi Scullerson, they said goodbye to Apollo, who had already forgotten about them, having been enveloped by the women's crew team to raucous cheers, and she and John had slipped out the front door. They'd ridden to the hospital on John's Vespa, which was parked in the Deke drive. They were both silent for the short drive, intent on getting to Carl. John had handed back her sweater before they went into the party, and the ride on the bike caused his shivering to return. This time Hannah had no qualms about wrapping herself around him; it was necessary to ride the bike safely. It seemed to help.

Carl claimed to be feeling fine, and the doctor couldn't find anything wrong with him, but his hair remained shockingly white. The doctor explained that this happened sometimes, and it might grow out or be permanent, only time would tell. Carl had forestalled Hannah's apologizing with a quick, uncompromising "No!" as she opened her mouth. She sighed, realizing this wasn't the time or the place for her long apology to Carl. It wasn't just Carl's "no" that stopped her, but his mother's presence in the bedside chair that kept her silent.

Helene was knitting a cap for Carl and she was none too pleased to see Hannah, though she fawned over John. She left around ten o'clock after being told by the nursing staff that visiting hours were over, while John and Hannah hid in the nurses' station and waited for the coast to be clear before coming back into Carl's room.

Helene at least proved that the gift had been retracted. She seemed to have no memory of her declaration of wanting to be a black jack dealer in Vegas. That wasn't all. The local interest story on the eleven o'clock news involved a citizens group that had filed a complaint against a homeless shelter. It turned out the shelter had handed out T-shirts with the logo "I'm with the SOT" to some of the men who had visited the shelter, and the spokeswoman for the citizens group was appalled that the shelter was promoting alcoholism. The group, Mothers Against Inappropriate T-Shirts, was insisting that the men be dressed, well, more appropriately. So much for the Speaker of Truth....

It wasn't until later that Hannah learned what had happened to put Carl in the hospital. When the three of them were alone, they shared their stories while eating packets of saltines from the hospital's guest kitchen. Carl seemed to have enjoyed his experience with casting a spell,

The Myth of Cassandra

but John said very little about being frozen. Hannah, though she'd talked about her time with Sek, didn't share everything, specifically Sek's declaration of being her soul mate.

She felt a slight twinge of guilt now, as she lay in her bed, but quashed it. There was no need to open up that particular twist. It would only make them worry. Besides, she didn't really believe it herself. Having had time to think about it, she'd decided it had been a ploy by Sek to get her to cooperate. He probably thought all women loved him, and would be thrilled to be told they were his one and only. Ridiculous. Fantastical, and not in the fantastic meaning of fantastical, but in the "impossible to believe" meaning. As a whole, they all agreed that their future lay in sticking to the everyday and ordinary world, unanimously ignoring the fantastical envelope that had opened for them all in the last three days.

The three of them talked for hours, on every subject but the last three days. Then they watched TV, Carl propped up in his bed while Hannah and John sprawled in the world's most uncomfortable armchairs. They all must have fallen asleep, because the next thing she knew John was shaking her shoulders, trying to wake her without waking Carl. They'd slipped out of the room, leaving Carl a note, and John had dropped her back here, at her dorm.

Hannah rolled onto her back and stretched out, her arms falling off the sides of the long twin bed. Her fingertips stilled tingled from the extraction of the gift. The extraction had been brutal. Apollo had held her head and as the heat inside her head rose, she felt a sharp pain, as if her skull was splitting, and got sick in the philodendron plant. Her mother had refrained from complaining about her choice of location for losing her lunch, though Hannah suspected she would hear about it later, under the guise of a *Ladies' Home and Hearth* article about inconvenient places to puke.

Despite this, she'd felt much better after vomiting, almost great, actually. Hermes had returned her hair to its original length and color. She could almost imagine that it was a normal Wednesday night— technically early Thursday morning— and that none of this had really happened.

She started with the muscles in her feet, tensing them, and then releasing. She worked her way up her body, a relaxation technique they had learned freshman year during Frosh Week. Frosh. She smiled at the ridiculous word, tensed her back, and released. She and John seemed to have slipped into a comfortable friendship, a camaraderie built over the events of the last few days, and while there'd been moments where it had felt fairly charged, they had navigated the treacherous seas of lust to land safely on the island of "just friends." It was a relief, really. He was a notorious womanizer, after all. Always better to be friends with those. She tensed her neck and released.

And she and Carl also seemed to have navigated the churning waters of breaking up onto the adjacent island of "mutual break-up and still friends." This island was considered mythical by some, but Hannah felt like she and Carl really had landed there. In part because they still cared a lot about each other, and in part because their break-up was unavoidable, with him going to Japan and her staying here in Centreville. They had always really just been friends, but now they were independent.

She felt like she was floating, her body asleep before her brain. She was aware of the first rays of sunlight crossing her closed eyes. The last thing she thought as her brain joined the rest of her in unconsciousness was that she'd done it. She'd faced the Greek gods and found the right words, she'd used what she'd known and had trusted her instincts, and everyone was safe and she was free.

✦✦✦✦✦✦✦✦✦✦✦✦

The Myth of Cassandra

Carl

Morning in the hospital

He had sent his mother and father off to speed up the discharge papers, though he was fairly certain that his mother's involvement was sure to have the inverse effect. She hadn't made friends among the staff during his short stay. Nevertheless, he needed a few minutes alone to decide his next step.

He looked down at the note that John and Hannah had left him early this morning and smiled. He was relieved that his best friend and his girl...his former girlfriend, were friends. It was good.

His former girlfriend. He let that thought roll about his mind. He didn't know if it was the wild adventure of the last few days, the casting of a fictional curse, or the miraculous healing spell, but he found he was not as hurt by the end of his relationship with Hannah as he had thought he would be. If he were honest, he was relieved. He had wanted to marry Hannah, but he could see now that they wanted really different things, and he felt an overwhelming sense of freedom.

He tied his shoes and stood up, opening the side table drawer to get his things. Slipping his keys into his pocket, he looked at his phone and remembered the recording Hannah had made. The back-up plan. It had turned out to be unnecessary, since Hannah had snowed the gods into doing exactly what she wanted, but the recording was still on his phone, and he sat back on the bed and hit play:

"I am the SOT. This is the last time that I will talk to you. I've said a lot of things about what you should do, but I haven't really told you about myself. I am not who you think I am. People think that I'm honest, easy going, accommodating, but the truth is that I have held myself away from people, convinced that it was more work to disagree with people than it was to simply let them think I agreed. It started out as a way to please my mom, but it became a way that I hid myself from everyone. The older I got, the more I kept to myself, and the more I intentionally lied to keep from having to deal with other people. I relied on other people to share their ideas, so I could learn. I listened to people who might've been friends tell me their problems, but carefully kept my own problems to myself. Even in my closest relationship, with my boyfriend, I kept myself stowed away carefully, giving out only what I thought he wanted to see, being the woman I thought he wanted me to be, and in the end I hurt him, because I had to finally be honest with him, to tell him that the woman he thought he was engaged to didn't exist, not really. So you see, I am a liar. I am trying to do a better job, but it's a hard habit to break. So I take it one relationship at a time.

"There is no Speaker of Truth. We, all of us, tell both truth and lies. It's the human work to sort through it– to find our own way. You shouldn't listen to me anymore. Think for yourself. Weigh the truth and honesty of your thoughts with the balances of kindness and compassion and choose for yourself what to believe, what to do, what to share with others. I am sorry if I led you astray, Goodbye."

Carl hit pause, the image indistinct, Hannah's face obscured by filters. He sat and stared out the window for what felt like hours, but was more likely minutes, until his reverie was interrupted as his mother and father reentered the room, discharge papers in hand.

"Come on honey, it's time to get you out of this excuse for a medical facility, and get you back home with us. Marching in graduations is overrated. Besides, your father and I are looking into a lawsuit against...."

"Mom, Dad, please sit. There are some things I need to tell you."

CHAPTER TWENTY-EIGHT

Hot Tubs and Mixed Drinks

❋❋❋

John

Still feeling cold; really, really, cold

He groaned as the water got increasingly cooler, a sure sign that he had drained the hot water heater again. It was his third marathon shower, and while he waited for the hot water heater to fill up, he had been drinking Irish coffee. The result was that he was very clean, slightly inebriated, and still chilled. Flipping the faucet off, he climbed out of the shower, drying quickly and pulling on his heaviest sweats, tube socks, and mittens. He cursed his vanity at not having a hair dryer; he'd considered it too girly an appliance, but now would give his left arm for one.

Instead he used his left arm to rub his hair dry while he contemplated his next best move for warming up. He Googled "hot tub rental" and found a company in nearby Stanton where he could rent one of those party hot tubs. That would be really warm. He wondered if Candy would let him set it up in the back yard. For that matter she might let him borrow her hair dryer.

Pulling one mitten off, he dialed her number. Holding it to his ear, he heard the distinctive click that meant her answering machine was picking up. John looked at the clock. 7am. Oh, maybe that was too early to call someone to borrow a hair dryer. John had a moment of crisis as he considered just hanging up or alternately making up a reason for calling that was more legitimate for an early morning call when Candy's voice filled his ear:

"Hey, this is Candy, and if you are a friend, I am out of town for a little bit. I will be back soon and I will call you, so leave me a message. If this is one of my tenants, please call my buddy, Joe. He's a licensed handyman and he'll help you. His number is 403-667-7777 and his business hours are 9-6. Thanks!"

John hung up the phone slowly. With Candy out of town, there really was no one to ask about a hot tub rental. He called Hot Tubs R US. Apparently hot tub rental companies worked early hours. A quick call confirmed that they would deliver to Centreville. The guy on the other end of the line said that he could have the tub delivered and setup by noon. Warmth. Deep warmth would be here by noon. John felt relief filter through his body. Relaxing back into the chair he idly pulled up his email. There were at least a hundred messages, and he began the soothing task of deleting and sorting his email. He got the reminder about the graduation robes and wondered what Hannah was doing right now. There was no way she'd had time to pick up a robe. Was it too early to call her?

He dialed without thinking, her number still in his speed dial, and got her voice mail. Her left her a long message about picking up graduation robes and asking her to call him if she wanted a ride to the hospital to see Carl. Ending the call, his phone informed him he had talked for two minutes and forty-three seconds. That wasn't too long, was it? That was completely a friend-length message. Feeling uncertain, he moved her number from speed-dial to his long and varied list of contacts. That would make her merely an acquaintance. Sure, he might see her socially, as friends, since they'd both be living in Centreville after graduation, but it wasn't like he'd be forced to see her every day. He would start to date other women. That would fix it all.

Starting now. Hot Tub Party. Here. Tonight. He posted it online for his friends, confident that women made up over 50% of that population. He could get started on his return to normal life. Carl would be out of the hospital, so they could make it a "Congratulations on Surviving Casting a Spell" party. Okay, not that, but, it would be a welcome back party, or at least a graduation party.

Heading toward the kitchen to brew another pot of coffee, he made the command decision that for this pot he would hold off on the whiskey. He needed to clear his head. He measured out the coffee and hit brew when he heard the distinctive high-pitched hum of the water heater. Excellent! He bolted for the bathroom, stripping his clothes off as he went, and jumped into a hot spray of water.

●●●●●●●●●●●●

Hannah

Mixed Drinks on Thursday Night

Hannah had volunteered to man the bar for the Hot Tub Graduation Welcome Back Carl party. She'd grown up in WASP central, her parents having hosted more than a few cocktail parties after all, and mixing drinks was second nature. They'd set up the bar outside of Candy's kitchen window, so that Hannah could pull the kitchen sprayer out for any running water needs. John had initially lobbied to use the hose, but that was before Hannah revealed that Candy had asked Hannah to apartment sit for the summer.

"So we'll be neighbors for the summer?"

"Well, yes and more— when Candy gets back she's renting me the apartment over yours. Great, huh?"

It must have been a trick of the party lights that they had strung up reflecting on his face, because he'd appeared slightly green at that news. But he'd smiled and said of course, that's fantastic news; they would see each other all the time. She wondered what bugged him about it, because he was clearly lying, but she wouldn't be asking him tonight. John was in charge of the hot tub, and was currently in it surrounded by the very beautiful women of the crew team that had helped with Apollo. All nine of them seemed to be enjoying themselves tremendously. Typical.

Carl was manning the tap and she could see him chatting with Caroline Collins, another senior who was heading to Japan in a week. They had internships with the same investment company. When she and John had made it to the hospital to see him, Carl was hugging his mom and his father was filming it. Carl had told his parents everything that had happened, everything. Hannah's estimation of Helene went way up, as it was clear that she and Roger believed every unbelievable word of it.

Turned out his mother was happy to have Carl go to Japan, as it would be several thousands of miles away from both Hannah and John and the mayhem they courted. Seemed she blamed them both for everything. Hannah didn't mind being used to Helene's disapproval, glad only that it made it easier for Carl to leave. But John was really bothered by it. Helene used to love him, and he'd grumbled about it the entire time they waited to get their robes.

"Can I get a gimlet?" Hannah shook herself out of her memories to tend bar. She'd been really busy at the start of the party, but traffic had tapered off in the last half hour. This party had maybe another thirty minutes left. There were parties all over campus tonight, and though she was certain John was not leaving the hot tub, she'd decided to close up soon and check them out. So this might be the last drink she mixed tonight.

The gimlet drinker was a woman from her classics classes, Gretchen Holder. Hannah hadn't ever really talked to Gretchen, but she'd listened to Gretchen for four years. She was brilliant and no one had a better knowledge of the arcane of early religions. She was looking at Hannah with a cool stare. It was a little daunting.

Hannah, committed to trying out her new lease on life, decided to make an effort. "Hey, Gretchen. One gimlet, coming up. Do you take it with vodka or gin?"

Gretchen blinked, clearly surprised by the conversational tone coming out of Hannah, but to her credit, she played along. "I don't know, I've never had a gimlet. It was the only mixed drink name I could think of. What do you recommend?" Gretchen seemed to wait, apparently not convinced that Hannah could offer an opinion, even on something as mundane as an alcohol choice.

Hannah sized up the general inexperience of her customer. "Well, if this is your first, I'd recommend vodka. It's a little smoother than gin. I'll make you one, and if you don't like it, I can mix you something else...." Hannah set to measuring the drink, mixing it in a shaker.

"Are you some sort of professional bartender, Summers?" Gretchen's reserve was slowly fading, and she took the drink from Hannah's outstretched hand.

"No, just the only child of professional social climbers." She smiled to take the sting out of her somewhat exaggerated description, and noticing Gretchen's look of confusion changed the subject, "So, what are your plans after graduation? Are you doing grad school?" Hannah waved back to Carl who'd just hollered that he was heading over to the party at the Center for the Arts.

"Isn't that your boyfriend leaving with that girl?" Gretchen sipped at the gimlet, leaning against the makeshift bar.

"Oh, we broke up. We're just friends. Good friends, but friends. What do you think of the drink?"

Gretchen looked down into an empty glass and laughed, "I think I liked it. I also think I should stick to beer. Much more straightforward, as alcoholic beverages go. Speaking of straightforward, this is the longest conversation we've had in the three years we've been in the classics department together. Are you on something, Hannah?"

Hannah shook her head. "Consider it a late New Year's Resolution; I am trying to be more honest. Not that I am honest all the time, I mean, because sometimes honesty is not called for, but I am trying to be more present, more willing to be myself. Oh this all sounds very Oprah, doesn't it?"

Gretchen grimaced, but her tone was easy-going, "A little, but that's okay. Graduation hits everyone differently. To answer your question from before, I am not doing grad school, at least not now. My dad has a bookstore in VT. Used and new. Sometimes we get our hands on something rare and unique. Anyway, he needs someone to help him get online, so I am going back to Montpelier to give him a hand. I hear you got the job here, that's cool; it's an amazing collection. But won't you feel a little, I don't know, stalled, staying here after graduating…"

Gretchen started to help Hannah break down the bar, loading bottles into boxes and going around the side of the house to the kitchen door. Hannah talked over her shoulder as she led the way. "I guess it's all this new resolution and all, but I feel like I am just starting here, in a way. And I am really looking forward to being on my own. My own apartment, my own job. The job isn't complicated, but the University is really committed to acquisitions, and they have deep pockets, which should be fun." She walked back outside to collect up the glasses, Gretchen still helping, "Besides, I have new friends close by. My friend Candy is the owner of this house— I'm housesitting for her now, but she has an attic apartment that's all mine when she gets back. And John lives here.…"

"Hmmm…John MacCallister? He's yummy. Are you and he…"

"Just friends. Candy is charging so little for the apartment; I'll have enough money left over to travel. Have you ever been to Greece? I've always wanted to go…"

"I know, me too. Walk the grounds they walked on. See the ruins they left behind. I've never been. Hey, what is that necklace you are wearing? Isn't that a Gorgon? Wow, it looks real, Hannah, like authentic.…" Gretchen brought the medallion up to her face for closer inspection, but her eyes crossed as she stared at it, "Where did you get it?"

Hannah laughed and pulled it firmly out of Gretchen's hands, "It's a gag gift from my parents. They're hilarious people. They like to make jokes about my Classics Degree, you know, they think it isn't very practical. I think they bought it on eBay from some woman in Albuquerque who makes them out of clay. If you like I can introduce you to the yummy Mr. MacCallister."

Gretchen was effectively diverted from the medallion, and within minutes had joined the crew team in the hot tub with John. Promising to stay in touch, Hannah headed back to her dorm room for the night, betting she'd have a quieter sleep there than at Candy's place tonight. Slid-

The Myth of Cassandra

ing the medallion back against her skin, she relaxed. Gretchen was one of a handful of people who, when not drunk, might actually recognize what Hannah was wearing. She'd have to be more careful to keep it hidden in the future.

✺✺✺✺✺✺✺✺✺✺✺✺

Professor Tetley

More than cribbage and tea

I have to admit that when Tobias claimed that my quiet but intelligent advisee, Hannah Summers, was the one, I was skeptical. I mean, tea leaves aside, she just didn't strike me as strong enough to take on the job. Maybe I didn't want to burden her with the job. I have grown extremely fond of her. She is like a daughter to me. Ahem, honesty compels me to correct that; she is more like a great, great, granddaughter to me. Either way, being the one does not precipitate the smoothest of futures, and I was ambivalent about Tobias' prediction, to say the least.

So I protested, and Tobias agreed to a trial period where we would test her. She had not done particularly well on the tests. Time and again Tobias would leave clues out for her about his true identity, and not once did she indicate that she had seen them, let alone recognize what they meant. Although I now suspect it was her inclination not to comment on clues, whether she noticed them or not. At the time Tobias had grudgingly agreed with me that she was not suitable for the job. We had arranged for her to take on the job of curator with me overseeing, while Tobias set out on a quest to find the one. But then it happened. The gift. The SOT was clearly the handiwork of the Olympians. Then we knew, without a doubt that she was the one, and I owed Tobias an apology, and a year's supply of tea. Wagers are my Achilles' heel.

I was not sure how it would end, but she must have held her own, because not four days later, poof, the gift was gone and she was still alive. I felt certain that she would check her email, she is very fastidious, and so I sent her the message. Tobias came over around seven that morning for hot cross buns and tea, and we both sat around chatting about university gossip pretending we weren't just waiting. Waiting for her to come.

We were not disappointed. She arrived by seven-thirty with coffee in hand, explaining that she knew I was a confirmed tea drinker, and she hadn't wanted to put me out. Fastidious and considerate. She is really very sweet. I offered her a bun and she devoured it at a somewhat shocking pace, such that I decided to whip her up an omelet before we got down to business. She ate that at a more conventional rate, but did not turn down my offer of bangers and mash.

After eating, we took the time to explain to her who we really were and Tobias showed her his true form. I explained that I had met Tobias as a young classics student and immediately recognized the signs of his true nature. Since then we have worked together to rein in the Olympians whenever they have gone too far in their meddling with humans. We work for the Immortal Council. It has been a very successful partnership for many, many years. But I have been slowing down, and the Council likes having a human monitor, so Tobias has been on the lookout for the one to replace me. When he met Hannah, he thought she might be it, so he had arranged for her to take over his own job at the university, so we could ease her into the work. Telling her all this took so little time, that she had barely finished her breakfast. We watched as she slowly lowered her utensils at the end of our recitation.

She handled it very well, all things considered. Then she told us her story, really quite an adventure and her telling of it was the epitome of entertainment. I suspect, though, that she left out some details, but it is no matter, she will tell us when she needs us to know. Tobias then explained that along with caring for and increasing the university's rare book and classics collection, he would like her to take his place in working with me to rein in the Olympians when need be. She asked a lot of questions and in the end told us she would consider it and give us her answer on Sunday after graduation. She then invited us to a brunch at her friend's house. I do hope she will be serving those brilliant little quiches.

The Myth of Cassandra

I will admit to being surprised by her reaction. I suppose I had assumed that she would agree, she was always so agreeable. She agreed to all my editing suggestions on her thesis, she agreed to the courses I suggested, she even agreed to take honey in her tea instead of sugar. But I see now that her experience has wrought some changes in her, and it is a good thing for her to wait to answer us. Tobias convinced her to take the Amulet of Gorgon regardless, emphasizing that it would protect her from the enchantments of other mythological and mystical creatures.

Originally there were three Gorgon amulets, one for each sister, Medusa, Stheno, and Euryale. Medusa's perished with her. But the other two survived. I have no idea where Tobias came upon this one. The Gorgon were vicious creatures, females with long nasty teeth, but they were also very ancient protective deities, and wearing the amulet of Euryale would be powerful protection for Hannah. She tried to laugh him off, saying that she no longer needed any protection, that she was finished with the gods, but then he asked her if she had ever lost time, or slept too much, or found someone in her thoughts. That gave her pause and Tobias explained that if she wore this amulet, those things would not happen. Hannah agreed to wear the amulet, if only to ease our worry for her.

So now we wait. Until Sunday.

EPILOGUE

Food is Essential to a Well-Planned Party

❖❖❖

Hannah

Sunday

She pulled the second tray of mini quiches out of the oven and felt the satisfaction of hosting a successful party. Graduation had gone off without a hitch and now Candy's house was filled with friends and family. As she loaded a tray with the quiches she moved through the crowd to place them at Prof. Tetley's elbow.

Friends and family. It was a funny combination. John was here with his mother, as was Carl and his parents. John had filled in his mother about their adventure, and all three mothers had encamped in a corner of the dining room, whispering intently. Lord knows what they were talking about. They looked like a coven of witches conferring around a cauldron drinking a potion. It was just that, in this case, the potion was Bloody Marys.

Her father was giving Mr. Blean retirement advice, and Mr. Blean was congenially listening to him while making "save me" eyes at Prof. Tetley, who was ignoring him completely. Prof. Tetley was holding court with Gretchen and her father, who had stopped by briefly before meeting up with Gretchen's housemates for lunch at Turlington's. Miller and Eloise had just arrived and were hanging out on the porch with John,

The Myth of Cassandra

Carl, and Carl's dad, Roger. Hannah and John had run into the Copy Center Duo at the University Bookstore while getting graduation robes and had learned that they were both staying on campus for the summer. In keeping with her new goal to live life a little more externally, Hannah had invited them to brunch. She was surprised and pleased that they'd come. Eloise was encamped in the porch swing with a bowl of grapes while Miller was entertaining the crowd with a story. Hannah could see his hands flying and hear the rise and fall of his voice from the kitchen, certain that the story involved his efforts to self-diagnose his latest illness using various Internet medical sites.

She had just decided to mix another batch of Bloody Marys when she caught sight of her mother mouthing, "We need more," and pointing to her glass. Hannah channeled her inner serene hostess and smiled at her mother, resisting the urge to mouth back, "I know." She had to give her mother some credit. She'd been very understanding when Hannah had informed her of her plans to work at Whitfield. She had refrained from giving a single piece of *Ladies' Home and Hearth* inspired advice.

This new and improved Elise, while very pleasant, was a little bizarre. Hannah felt certain that her true mother would reassert herself once the stress of the last week wore off. At least she hoped so. She found herself looking forward to their first real argument. It was no fun asserting yourself if everyone around you was too accommodating. The irony of that thought was not lost on her, and she indulged in some self-mocking laughter and started assembling the Bloody Marys.

She'd decided that she would take on the work with Prof. Tetley of reigning in the Olympians. She wasn't sure what it would entail, or how an aging academic and well...Mr. Blean... had asserted any influence over the gods, or how she exactly fit into the picture, but she wanted to do it. After her first-hand experience at how fast and loose the gods played with humanity, someone needed to enforce some boundaries. Telling Prof. Tetley and Mr. Blean about her decision was the first thing she'd done when they arrived. They'd seemed genuinely pleased and had promised to sit down with her next week to outline what she could expect. She hadn't told John and Carl about it, yet. She wasn't sure she would....

"Hannah, there is someone here to see you. Our cheese loving "friend" in all her blonde glory. She said that she has something she has to give to you personally." John walked across the kitchen to pick up the tray of glasses and celery Hannah had laid out, and with Hannah carrying the pitcher, they headed toward the mothers in the dining room. "I thought they would leave you alone now...."

"I'm sure it's nothing, don't worry, John." His look seemed to challenge that idea, but he remained silent. They deposited the drinks on the table in front of the mothers, who didn't pause in their conversation, and continued toward the front porch, where she could see Carl's dad, Roger, fawning over Lee, in all his rumpled wonder. That was weird. She frowned at John, certain he had told her "she" was here. "Lee! I wasn't expecting you! Do you think it's wise to look so...so..." demonic, was what she was thinking.

She stared at John, who filled in, "...so beautiful! It's a crime." Hannah stared as Roger and Miller concurred heartily and Lee simpered.

What was happening? Hannah pinched her own arm. Ouch. No, she was not asleep. Why was no one commenting on the fact that a short, somewhat clammy demon was on her front porch, horns and all? And it wasn't like they were ignoring him, her...Miller was clearly checking out Lee's butt and she was not imagining Roger flirting with him. That was when she remembered the amulet. While Miller inquired about Lee's plans for the night, Hannah slid her hand through her hair, discreetly slipping the amulet off her neck and gasped out loud.

"Are you okay, Hannah? Are you choking?" Carl had crossed the porch in record time and looked ready to execute the Heimlich if Hannah couldn't answer.

Hannah nodded and quickly answered, "No, I'm fine. See I can talk, so I can breathe." Hannah had taken the life saving course with Carl last year, and he'd been eager to use the Heimlich ever since; a little too eager. Hannah had taken to confirming she could breathe after coughing, sneezing, or yawning. "Everything's fine. I must have swallowed a mos-

The Myth of Cassandra

quito or something." Hannah reached out and firmly grasped the arm of the beautiful blonde woman chatting with Roger. "Lee, can you join me in the kitchen? I have some lovely cheeses."

Lee waved goodbye to Roger, and eagerly followed Hannah through the house into the kitchen. "If you have any Gorgonzola that would be great, but if not, I suppose some cheddar could do."

"Forget the cheese, Lee. Why are you here?" Hannah slipped the amulet back over her neck and watched as before her eyes the beautiful blonde woman morphed into the homely demon. Damn. If Lee could take different forms, could Sek shift like this? Feeling weak in the knees, Hannah lowered herself onto one of the stools at the kitchen counter and watched Lee dig in his pockets, grousing about the lack of civility among humans.

"Just a bite to eat, that's not asking too much. Ah! Here it is!" He produced a cream colored envelope and placed it in Hannah's unsteady hands. "Would it be okay if I hung out for a bit? I noticed you had some of those little quiches."

"Sure, fine... Hey Lee, stay away from Roger, okay? He's married."

"All the good ones are. Fine, I'll stay away from him. He's not my type, anyway." And Lee, the blonde bombshell version, left the kitchen. Hannah could see him cozying up to Prof. Tetley and the tray of quiches. After their conversation the other day, she felt confident Prof. Tetley could hold his own with a shape-shifting demon.

Turning her attention to the envelope in hand, she could see that it was made out of high quality paper, thick and smooth. She sat for a moment just holding it, feeling its weight in her hands. Her name was written across the front in a strong, elegant script and she realized that it must be Hera's writing. Touching the amulet around her neck once more, for luck and reassurance, she slid her finger under the flap of the envelope to reveal its contents. A single sheet of paper was inside. In contrast to the envelope, the paper inside was incredibly thin, translucent. The message was brief:

For your cleverness, I am awarding you the high honor of working for me. I will be in touch. Hera

Hannah read it through twice and watched, bewildered as the paper in her hands faded away to air. She looked up to see both Prof. Tetley and Mr. Blean watching her intently. She raised her eyebrows and waggled them, while mouthing, "Hera." They both nodded and she knew that the three of them would figure out the meaning of this latest turn together. If there was one thing she had learned from her adventure with the gods, it was how to compartmentalize her thoughts. She would not dwell on what this new task might entail. For now, she had guests to join and a beautiful Sunday afternoon to enjoy.

The Myth of Cassandra

Acknowledgements

I live my life in conversation with other people. So when I think about it, *anyone* who has been patient enough to listen to me ramble on about this project deserves to be mentioned. But that is daunting to list, so I will have to defer to a general yet heartfelt acknowledgement; to *all* my friends and family, you have my profound gratitude.

There are particular people who went above and beyond in bringing Hannah's story to the page. And so, taking a page from my character's book, here are my thanks, in list form.

People I Need to Thank Who Helped Make this Book Possible

1. The readers, whose enthusiasm and encouragement helped me to have the courage to persevere; Jen, Melanie, Katie, Susan, Amy, Tricia, Barbara, Diane, Carol & Ellen.

2. The artists who created the cover: Amy Flannery, whose beautiful portrait of Hannah in clay mosaic brought to the eye a story I had heard in my head, and Ricky Puorro, whose cover design brought her art to the reader.

3. The editors, whose questions and insights helped me to define and vastly improve the story; Tia McCarthy, Sue West, Clare Fedolfi, and Barbara Clere Klain. Four of the smartest women I know.

4. My writing partner, Rebecca Farmer. Whether at your dining room table or our corporate headquarters, you are the finest sounding board, critical mind, and friend.

5. My beautiful family. Lily and Ethan who, even amidst the stress and challenges of living, fill my days with laughter and Steve, the love of my life.

Finally, I want to thank my mom. When she found me as a child reading on the couch at 2 am because I *had* to finish the book, she gave me a blanket and made sure I had enough light.

Coming Soon
the second book in the series...

REVEALING HANNAH
The Myth of Arachne

Hannah is feeling pretty great about the world just about now. Her job might appear to be a dusty exercise in tending antique texts, but it has secret parameters that would blow the mind of the average student at Whitfield. Her apartment, in the attic of Candy's house, is small but affordable. And she has saved enough money to go on her very first trip out of the country, with her new friend, Gretchen. She and Gretchen spent the summer working on their grad school applications, commiserating about their unconventional childhoods, and plotting a week long trip to the Grecian Isles. Sure, the cruise line was in chapter eleven and had advised them to *bring their own drinking water*, and yes, their airline was literally called "Fly By Night Air" with an address *adjacent* to Bradley Airport, but she was certain it would be epic. She just had to make it through her to do list, meet Gretchen at midnight *near* the airport, and it was all sun, sand and ancient ruins.

Except that her neighbor, John MacCallister, who has spent the last three months avoiding her even though she had thought they were friends, shows up just as she is closing the library with the news that Hermes and Lee are waiting for her back at the house. *Hera is calling in her favor.*

Despite all her careful planning Hannah will not make it to Greece, but she will be going on a trip. The adventure that awaits her involves cursed amulets, kidnapped gods, murderous spiders and choices that challenge her idea of who she is and what she is capable of.

About the Author

Laura Fedolfi grew up in Chichester, NH, where she shared a bedroom with her patient sister, Barbara, who she inadvertently tortured by claiming that she *only had one more page to read*, and would *turn the light out soon*. **It was never true.**

She went to Wesleyan University where she studied Philosophy and English. She had excellent professors, to whom she is grateful. Wesleyan was also where, with her friends, she descended a manhole in the wee hours of the morning and ran through the hidden tunnels under campus, played football at night in the snow, and in general, had fun. It was there she met the love of her life, who she married soon after.

She has lived on both coasts, finally landing in Chelmsford, Massachusetts, renowned for its ginger ale and friendly population. She and her husband have raised two children, several dogs and a cat with the help of excellent friends and amazing family.

REVEALING HANNAH *The Myth of Cassandra* is the first book in a series following the adventures of Hannah Summers based on Greek Myths. The second book, REVEALING HANNAH *The Myth of Arachne* will be available in 2016.

Visit www.revealinghannah.com and check out Prof. Tetley's blog, learn more about Hannah and her Olympian compatriots, and find all the hidden images in the mosaic...

Made in the USA
Lexington, KY
15 March 2017